THE DEBBA

a novel

AVNER MANDELMAN

Other Press
New York

Copyright © 2010 Avner Mandelman

Production Editor: Yvonne E. Cárdenas

Text Designer: Simon M. Sullivan

This book was set in 11.75pt Dante by
Alpha Design & Composition of Pittsfield, NH.

10 9 8 7 6 5 4 3 2 1

LIBRARY OF CONGRESS CATALOGING-IN-PUBLICATION DATA
Mandelman, Avner.
  The Debba / by Avner Mandelman.
       p. cm.
  ISBN 978-1-59051-370-5 (acid-free paper)—
  ISBN 978-1-59051-375-0 (e-book)   1. Israel—Fiction.
  2. Dramatists—Fiction.   3. Theater—Israel—Fiction.
  4. Fathers and sons—Fiction.   5. Jews—Israel—Fiction.
       I. Title.
  PR9199.3.M34814D33   2010
  813'.54—dc22   2009041120

To my parents—and to A.

THE DEBBA

Prologue

MEN IN MY FAMILY always left their place of birth. When my father was seventeen years old he bought passage on a boat to Yaffo. It was a two-way ticket. The British, who ruled Palestine then, would never have let him enter without it. He did not have an immigration certificate.

I am told he was a quiet, slim youth, strangely intense, and fierce when aroused. My grandfather once had to buy off the head of police after my father had beaten up the son of a rich barrel merchant. The young goy taunted my father and called him a dirty Jew. The taunter was big and fat, and smoked cigarettes. My father, who was half the goy's size, almost killed him with a stick he had grabbed from a lame old charwoman. It took three policemen to tear my father off his victim.

Aunt Rina, who was eight then, claims no one could pry the stick from my father's hand. Finally the chief of police broke my father's thumb with a hammer. They put my father in jail, where he stayed for four days. He was fifteen at the time.

Aunt Rina, who now lives in Toronto, was hopelessly in love with him then. Half the town beauties were. Even now, at the age of sixty-seven, when she speaks of him her eyes light up and her husband, Yitzchak, looks aside or busies himself with a book.

When I asked my father why his thumb was crooked, he said it had bent when he sucked on it, as a baby. My father had beautiful hands and the crooked thumb was glaringly notice-able. Only when I was old enough to talk to my uncle Morde-chai as an equal did I learn the true story.

It had cost my grandfather two thousand zloty, a fortune, to get my father out of jail. When my father finally came home he was sick for a month. Wild stories circulated. He had been beaten up. Two of his front teeth were missing. Some said he was raped by the guards, who had been bribed by the rich mer-chant. These were old Cossacks who remained from the days of the Russian occupation. They were short and thickset and their sexual appetites were legendary.

My father kept to his bed for two weeks. He did not notice anybody. All the time he was in bed he was sharpening a long knife he had made.

My grandfather was in the leather trade, and there were many knives around the house: small knives for trimming fine leather used in ladies' slippers, flat knives for splitting raw leather, and sharp, long blades for cutting through tough hide. My father made a new knife from a saw blade and sharpened it endlessly—no one could make him stop. My grandmother cried and begged him, but he paid her no heed. When she brought him chicken broth, he would sit up in bed, hide the knife under his thigh, and eat. Then he would pull it from under the covers and start all over again.

My grandfather was a tall, husky Jew. He had a thick black beard and testy blue eyes. His one passion was the cards. The only one who could beat him at a card game was my father. When my father lay in bed recuperating, they played cards every night, and talked. My father would not surrender his knife. Each morning, when the shiksa maid peeked through the keyhole, she saw him spitting on the black whetstone, and soon the *srik-srak, srik-srak* sound recommenced.

It was autumn and just before the High Holidays. The atmosphere in town grew tense; there was talk of a pogrom. The Cossacks at the town jail muttered among themselves. All the Jews were nervous.

On the eve of Yom Kippur the rabbi, Reb Itzelle Tuvim, came to the house. Aunt Rina says his face radiated light. To hear her tell it, he was walking on an inch of air. He came in, washed his hands at my grandfather's porcelain basin, and ate a piece of challah. Then he went into my father's room and closed the door behind him.

This was just before the Large Supper, the last meal before the fast, and the yard was teeming with beggars and the needy. The day before, my grandfather had sold a hundred pairs of felt boots to the hetman of the Cossacks, and in celebration my grandmother cooked *tshulent* for all the town's poor Jews, to fortify them for Kol Nidre, the Yom Kippur eve prayer that annuls all vows.

But the Kol Nidre was delayed. Reb Itzelle remained closeted with my father for three hours. Finally the door to my father's room opened and Reb Itzelle emerged. He was pale, says Aunt Rina, and his hand trembled. In his right hand he held the knife, its blade pointing upward, like a *lullav* in Succoth. Wordlessly he laid it down on the cabinet, on which it remained, untouched, all during the Day of Atonement. Then he went to the synagogue and chanted the Kol Nidre. Two and a half years later my father left for Palestine, taking with him all his wooden lasts, his shoe templates, and a few favorite knives. His phylacteries he left behind.

He landed in Yaffo, after an eleven-day sea voyage, on the eve of Purim, 1922. He almost didn't make it. During the landing the rowboat taking him ashore capsized near the Rock of

Andromeda and he and two other passengers—another Polish boy (one Paltiel Rubinsky) and an elderly Briton—nearly drowned. The Arab boatman jumped into the churning waves and rescued all three.

I still have a torn copy of the Yaffo biweekly *Fillastin*, carrying a faded photograph of the event. It shows two men: the hero, chief boatman to Messrs. Thos. Cook & Son, a broad-shouldered young swain in a striped bathing suit with slightly effeminate lips, squinting shyly into the camera, and on his left a portly Briton, lank hair hiding his eyes and nose, clasping his rescuer's reluctant wrist. To the right, a boat's bow intrudes into the picture; a faint line at its edge may be an oar. Of the two young Jews there is no sign. This was a mere ten months after the May Day riots in Yaffo, at which twenty-one Jews (among whom were two full-fledged poets) were slaughtered. Showing disembarking Jews on the front page could have sparked fresh riots.

The Arab hero can be seen clearly in the photograph, though his name is smudged by a yellow stain; but the Briton is clearly identified. He is Sir Geoffrey Mewlness, publisher of the London *Grand*, on pilgrimage to the Holy Land for his health. The article notes that upon his return to London, Sir Geoffrey thanked the directors of Thos. Cook & Son in person for his rescue, and sent a hundred gold sovereigns to the Yaffo boatman in gratitude, and a gold watch to each of his boatmates, in memory of the miracle that had befallen them in the land of the Bible. Both watches were expertly inscribed with the Hebrew prayer of thanks, HaGommel, in Rashi script.

Paltiel Rubinsky (who later changed his name to Rubin) right away gave his watch to a Yemenite actress. My father, after hanging on to his for three years, at last sold it in 1925 for fifty gold pounds to his landlord, a Mr. Efraim Glantz, with whom he and Paltiel Rubin had taken rooms in Tel Aviv the day after their arrival. With this money my father opened his cobblery and shoe store on Herzl Street, taking in Paltiel Rubin as a salesman, and in that same store he worked on and off throughout the Events of 1936–39, before finally closing it in 1946, as he began rising in the ranks of the Haganah, the budding Jewish resistance, and later, in the Israeli Army. But a day after Ben-Gurion signed the Armistice agreement in 1949, my father left the army and went straight back to that same store, where, taking neither helpers (Paltiel was dead then) nor vacations, he kept cobbling heels and selling sandals, until the day of his murder.

PART I
Jahilliyeh
(The Age of Ignorance)

1

IT WAS IN TORONTO in 1977, seven years after I had last seen him, that I learned of my father's murder. When the phone rang I half expected to hear Aunt Rina's voice, inviting me to the Passover seder. Instead I heard the line crackle and a faint voice said, "Starkman? David Starkman?"

In an instant I knew. *"Ken?"* I croaked in Hebrew—yes.

"This is Ya'akov Gelber. I am an attorney in Tel Aviv—"

"My father," I said.

"I am afraid so."

Perspiration broke out on my chin as Mr. Gelber said without preliminaries that my father had died. "You of course have my most profound sympathies," he said in Hebrew, "but there are some . . . urgent matters to discuss, or else I would not call you on the holiday."

It was only April but the Toronto weather was freakishly hot and my cheap one-room apartment on Spadina Avenue was baking in the heat. My sole white shirt, which I had put on for an evening out with Jenny, was soaking with sweat, as Jenny kept massaging my neck, the back of my head, the veins at my temples. I again had a migraine after last night's black dreams. It often hit me when evening fell, and so we rarely went out. I had hoped tonight would be better, but it wasn't. Why Jenny was willing to put up with it I didn't know. As her fingers kept battling the pain, I dabbed at my face with a dish towel and tried to concentrate on Mr. Gelber's voice, which was explaining in my ear how someone had broken into my father's shoe store the previous night while he was taking inventory, and following the robbery (an unsuccessful attempt, really, since nothing of value was taken), my father was stabbed in the heart with one of his own knives—the one used for cutting soles. "It was probably an Arab robber," Mr. Gelber said, his voice neutral, "because the body was also mutilated. He never had a chance to use the telephone—you of course knew he had a telephone in his store."

"No." I didn't.

Mr. Gelber began to explain at length how my mother, three years ago—a mere month before her death—had made my father install a telephone in the store. "Six months it took her to get to the right people, to speed up installation—six months! Here he was, Isser Starkman, the hero of the Castel, the slayer of Abu Jalood, alone in the store—without a telephone, and his heart not strong—and nobody cares! Can you imagine? Finally Gershonovitz himself intervened. Gershonovitz! It's a shame, a bloody shame, that she had to go to this big shot for such a thing. Two hours she had to wait in his office! Two hours! Abase herself before that scum, may she rest in peace! And she and your father not even living together anymore." Mr. Gelber paused. "But I am sure you know all that."

I didn't. "Inventory," I repeated. A tickling started in my nose and the room rotated in a semicircle around me.

Jenny whispered fiercely that I should lie down and rest, not talk on the phone, but I waved her away and tried to concentrate on Mr. Gelber's voice, which, calmer now, was speaking with legalistic precision about the funeral, the Kaddish prayer, the reading of the will, and some obscure points regarding national insurance and a pension from Germany for loss of schooling. "And there are a few other matters that we have to discuss. Really small, minor matters."

"What matters?"

"*Tz.*" Mr. Gelber clicked his tongue. "Not over an open phone line."

This was a military expression I hadn't heard for more than ten years. "Mutilated how?" The tickling in my nose had descended into my throat and I found it difficult to pronounce the Hebrew words.

"Mutilated, *nu*," Mr. Gelber snapped. "Like what the Arabs did in thirty-six, in forty-eight, *nu*. What they did to Rubin, and to all the others."

"To Paltiel? What they did to Paltiel Rubin? In Yaffo?"

"Yes, yes!" Mr. Gelber shouted. "Yes."

He went on, about my uncle Mordechai, or perhaps the police, but the line burst into a fury of crackles and hisses like a tank radio when a jet swoops low overhead and I couldn't make out a word. I dabbed at my chin, at my throat. The towel was soaking wet.

"So you will come to the funeral?" Mr. Gelber asked. "It must be before Saturday, you understand."

I said I understood and that I of course would come to the funeral. "Tonight. I will leave tonight."

"Call me the moment you land."

I wrote down Mr. Gelber's home phone, repeating his words in halting Hebrew.

Mr. Gelber sensed my unease with the language and switched to English. "The will, it must be filed before the end of the week. This is most important."

Yes, I said numbly in English. I understood. I'd leave tonight.

He spoke further about arrangements for paying the burial society (my uncle Mordechai, the other surviving relative, had said he would pay the two thousand shekels for the burial and I could pay him half later), where we would sit shivah (probably at my uncle Mordechai's home in Tveriah), and a few other matters that by now have completely escaped my memory. All I remember is rummaging in my pocket for a handkerchief to wipe my face, my cheeks, my eyes. My migraine had coalesced into an almost surreal pain, midway between my skull and nose.

Jenny's hands stopped mid-movement. "Leave for where?"

I hung up. "My father is dead," I said. Then I sat down and loosened my tie. We were supposed to go to a film festival after supper, before my migraine hit. "I have to go to Israel, to the funeral."

"Oh, I'm so—" Jenny began, then her face lost all color. "Don't—don't let them grab you for the army," she stammered. "Tell them you no longer live there—"

"I'm leaving tonight," I repeated, "if I can get a seat. It's a thirteen-hour flight."

There was a long pause.

I said, "I have to." I massaged my temples, shutting my eyes tight.

Jenny said in a quavering voice. "You want to—make love first, before you go? To relieve the migraine?" It often did, though I didn't like what it made me feel afterward, toward Jenny; the dangerous gratitude.

I went into the bathroom and washed my face. When I came out I called Aunt Rina. She wasn't really my aunt, only a cousin of my father; Yitzchak Kramer, her husband, was another cousin, once removed. I called them uncle and aunt because in Canada they were the only family I had.

I told Aunt Rina that my father had just died.

"Who killed him?" she said straight off. "The Arab?" Then she began to sob. Behind her I could hear Uncle Yitzchak muttering.

"He was stabbed by a burglar," I said. "Right in the store. He was working late."

"He was too young," said Aunt Rina, "for a Starkman. Only seventy-one. His friend, this Paltiel, he could have been what, now? Sixty-eight? Oh, God in heaven! Isser!"

Aunt Rina's crying turned into a choking sound.

"What Arab?" I asked.

Uncle Yitzchak's voice came on the phone. "It's a terrible thing, what just happened, I heard on the other line. I am telling you! Terrible! Did they catch him?"

"I don't know. It was a burglary." I wiped my eyes. I didn't feel anything inside, but oily tears kept streaming down my cheeks.

Behind me Jenny had begun to massage my back with her soft, warm hands.

Uncle Yitzchak said, "You going for the funeral?"

"Yes, maybe tonight."

He said, "You need money? You got money for the ticket?"

"Yes, I think so." I would have to borrow it from Jenny, who had just gotten her paycheck the week before.

There was silence on the line. Then Uncle Yitzchak said in a low voice, "You leave her behind, you hear? The shiksa. Don't you cause your father more grief."

What grief? My father was dead.

"Listen to me," said Uncle Yitzchak. "Listen—"

"No. It's okay. I am going alone."

Uncle Yitzchak said, "Don't be mad at me, Duvidl, but sometimes you gotta say something, so—"

"Sure," I said. Jenny had meanwhile begun to massage my shoulder blades. I tried to squirm away, but my body seemed to have developed self-will, as it always had, near her.

Aunt Rina came on the line, her voice breaking. "Give everybody our regards. And tell your uncle Mordechai we are sorry to hear the terrible news. You want to come here maybe for supper before you go?" I had forgotten this was the night of the second seder. Aunt Rina didn't say whether I could bring Jenny. The last time I had brought her along it had not been a success.

"No," I said. "Thank you. I'm flying tonight. I'll eat on the plane. I'll call you when I return."

After I hung up I saw that Jenny had begun to peel off her skirt. "Come," she whispered, "one last time before you go . . . so you remember . . ."

"Don't worry," I snapped. "I'll be back in a week."

I had met Jenny Sowa at a reading at the Harbourfront Authors Festival. She was a thin blonde with dark luminous eyes who had just won the Governor General's prize for a book describing in percussive rhymes the travails of runaway girls in a massage parlor on Yonge Street where she had conducted clandestine research. I had come to hear an old Hebrew poet passing through Toronto read his work in English translation. But that reading was canceled (the man had passed away the night before), and so I stayed to hear whoever was next. It was Jenny. The hall filled with overly-made-up young girls who cheered every stanza, but there were also some sullen men in tight pants, probably the parlor owners. Two marched up to the podium and began to berate her, snarling in her face. One raised his hand as if to slap her and it was then I heard her voice, clear and vibrant as in the reading, saying that they'd better be careful, because her boyfriend was watching.

"A whore like you—boyfriend?" one man snarled. "Where?"

To my astonishment she pointed to me. I had no idea why she chose me; or perhaps I had begun to rise already.

I stood up fully, half in surprise, half not. "Yes," I said.

And that's how we met.

She was a Polish Canadian shiksa and my aunt Rina was aghast when she heard from a friend about us living together.

"Once or twice, *nu*," she said, rolling her fingers in anguish. "But to live together? Like husband and wife?"

"So?" I said.

"Your grandfather would roll in his grave." She wept. "And a Polack, too!"

What did being Polish have to do with it? "Let him roll! I love her."

I was amazed to hear myself, speaking of love, just like that.

"You know what the Polacks did to your grandfather?" Uncle Yitzchak asked. "How they helped Hitler? I can give you books, so you can see for yourself. With pictures."

"She was born here," I shouted. "Right here in Canada. In Ottawa."

"A Polack is a Polack," Uncle Yitzchak said. "Let me tell you—"

But I didn't let him finish. I told him she was talented, and good, that she loved me, and I loved her, too—most of which was true. I also said that if they wanted to see me again, I didn't want to hear one word—not a single word—against the woman I loved.

What else could I say? That love was the last thing I wanted? That in the place I had run away from, love had to be paid for with killings?

I said a few other things I've forgotten by now. Somehow we reconciled; then we had tea, with almond cookies. They rarely mentioned her again.

Jenny was in the literary activism business. She appeared on cable TV on the community channel, debating Canadian Unity. She led a didactic-poetry workshop at the George Brown Community College. Every now and then she published a book of rhythmic poems that she then read out loud at the University, or at the Harbourfront Festival, before a crowd of fans who seemed to know her from her days of research.

I don't know why I went to these things. I myself never wrote anything. That is, every now and then I scribbled something very late at night, but in the morning I tore it into tiny pieces and flushed it down the toilet: detailed nightmares of takedowns I had done—in some the dead now evaded me; in others they didn't. I had plenty of these dreams after I left Israel, almost every night. I didn't want to write them down, but when my defenses were weak, I couldn't resist. After a while it turned into a real problem, because I often had to scribble for more than two hours to get the thing completely out, so I was always late for work and couldn't keep a job. Finally Uncle Yitzchak took me in, in his small bakery on College Street. I helped unload the sacks of flour, load the un-baked loaves into the roaring oven, then pull the steaming bread out and range it on the floury shelves. I didn't mind the heat. This was the best part: afterward I slept like a corpse myself and hardly dreamed at all. But Uncle Yitzchak couldn't pay me much, so after seven years in Canada I still had no money. I was really lucky I found Jenny. She had a job; she loved me. She tolerated my migraines, she even helped me fight my compulsion.

The first time she found my scribblings she flew into a cry-ing fit. "This is garbage! Pure garbage! Dead Arabs and killings and nightmares and shit!"

"I know," I said weakly. "That's why I . . ."

But before I finished she had begun to tear the pages up. "Don't waste your health on this crap. Take it from me. I am in the business. I know."

I knew that, too; but I couldn't help it. It just kept coming out. Sometimes I wrote ten, twelve pages at night, and then I hid them, in my half-sleep. You would think that in such a tiny apartment there would be no more hiding places; but in the morning, my head splitting, I sometimes wasted a whole hour trying to find that one last page.

Why I did it I don't know. It was one of those crazy compulsions, like biting on your nails, or scraping the paint off the wall and eating it. But Jenny was really good about it. Together we hunted—on all fours, sometimes. When we found the last rogue page under the entrance mat, inside the lamp shade, wherever, she would take my head between her hands and tell me not to worry. One day I'd forget all about the horrible place I had come from. "I can't wait," she told me.

I couldn't either; but now, this.

While Jenny took her turn in the bathroom I called El Al, put my name on the standby list (all flights were full), dressed (my frayed jeans for the plane and a sweater, in case it got cold: after seven years in Canada I still had not gotten used to the cold weather), threw some underwear and my shaving kit into my old army backpack, and left Jenny crying at the door, her hair framed by milky light.

I was in luck: a seat was available. I boarded the plane, sank into a place by the window, and promptly fell asleep.

I have no recollection of the first part of the flight, except for a thick residue of black dreams—the kind I used to have every night until Jenny's ministrations kept them half at bay; but now they were back in force. I woke up ten hours later, gasping for air, and dimly saw a trio of black-coated Jews praying at the bulkhead, swaying with their eyes closed; then I fell back into a profound slumber. But as my eyes began to close I suddenly had the strangest sensation—I could smell my father's sweat as if he were sitting beside me, the sour smell of a cobbler, mixed with acetone glue and dyed calf leather. I turned violently in my seat and buried my face in the cushion, and the sensation passed; then, just before I slid back into a black sleep, for no reason at all I remembered I had forgotten to ask Mr. Gelber if the robber had already been caught.

2

I HAD TALKED TO my father only once since I left Israel—that was when my brother Avraham was killed in that stupid retribution operation.

My father telephoned and in a tight, matter-of-fact voice told me what had happened to his other son. I asked (or I think I did) when the funeral would take place.

"There won't be a funeral," my father said. "They didn't find the body. May the Holy Name avenge his blood."

My father's voice was faint, I remember; but it could have been the bad connection. I think he called me from the phone in Zussman's kiosk, next door to his store.

"You all right?" my father asked, after I had mumbled my clumsy condolences. I remember hearing in the background the rumble of buses passing in front of the store, in Herzl Street. It was probably noon in Tel Aviv when he called.

"Yes," I said then. "I'm all right."

There was a pause.

"No shiksas?" my father said, half joking, half entreating.

"No, no," I lied. "Only bad Jewish girls."

"Ah, good, good," said my father. He then said I should call Aunt Rina and tell her, too. He didn't mention Uncle Yitzchak. Thirty-five years before, Uncle Yitzchak had been late in sending money to Poland (he claimed he did not have any at the time), and as a result—or perhaps not—Hinda Malka, my father's younger sister, had died in the Moloch's maw. He still had not forgotten.

"All right," I said. "I will."

My father said, "And, listen, about this thing with the passport—"

I then hung up, or perhaps the line went dead; at any rate I didn't hear what my father wanted to say; and this was the last time I spoke to him.

I knew very well what he wanted to say about the passport.

Two months before, four years after arriving in Canada (sponsored by Uncle Yitzchak, against the violent objections of my father and my mother's painful silence), I had become a Canadian citizen. A day after I falsely swore allegiance to the foreign monarch, I went to the Israeli Embassy on Bloor Street and asked to give up my Israeli citizenship.

The consul, a Mr. Iddo Ronen, was not amused. "David Starkman? The son of Isser?"

I didn't answer. What was there to say?

"*The* Isser Starkman? From forty-eight?"

"Yes. So what?"

For a moment I thought he was about to launch into a long and tedious speech—the kind Uncle Yitzchak used to give me. About how countless generations of my ancestors gave up their lives to maintain the flame, which I, the wretch, was so callously throwing away. About my disregard for values. My egotism.

Instead he pulled out two more forms and asked me to write why I wanted to give up my citizenship. "Then we'll send it to Jerusalem, and we'll see. You married?"

"Yes," I lied.

"Your wife Israeli, too?"

"No."

"I see. Well, have her fill out a form, too."

I said, "If it's not approved soon, I'm going to the United Nations Human Rights Commission." I then said a few more things, some premeditated, some not.

It was then that Mr. Ronen issued his speech. But I was well adapted by now. I listened to it all the way through. At the end I said, "You finished?"

"Yes," Mr. Ronen said. "I will see that this goes through. We don't want your kind anyway, *nemosha*."

I hadn't heard this word since my days in the army. It is Hebrew for a louse; the Bible used the word to refer to cowards who shirked their military duty.

One of the clerks in the Foreign Ministry in Jerusalem must have notified my father, because two weeks later I received a letter from him—five pages torn from an old school copybook of mine, written densely in his crabbed hand. I could smell on the envelope the acetone cement he used to glue rubber soles with, and his sweat.

I tore the letter to tiny pieces and didn't reply. A month later I received a small official form from the Israeli Embassy, notifying me that my request to have my Israeli citizenship revoked had been approved.

About three weeks later my brother Avraham was killed. It was really stupid. No one had told him to go. The operation was not even approved by the higher-ups at the Unit. Afterward he received a Chief of Staff Citation—posthumously of course. Or rather it was assumed to be posthumous, since no one could find his body. This was a common thing, at the Anonymous Recon. If you didn't come back from a deep penetration, it was likely no one would ever know what had happened to you.

Anyway, there was no funeral, and this was the last time I had spoken to my father; and now he, too, was dead.

3

I SLEPT THROUGH MUCH of the flight and missed the meals. Once I awoke in a cold sweat—I had dreamed I was being briefed prior to crossing the border for a takedown. This was a dream I used to have every night after I left Israel. It only stopped after I had given up my Israeli citizenship, but now, inexplicably, the dream returned. In it I saw the sergeant major who had taught us silent killing—he was standing on the doorstep of my parents' apartment on Ibn Gvirol Street, his eyes shining malevolently. In his hand he held a silenced Anschutz, or perhaps a Feinwerkbau single-shot. Behind him cowered a long line of dark subhuman creatures, stuttering and blubbering. These are the ones we must exterminate, said the sergeant major, if we are to cleanse the land. With one hand he handed me a black-bound military Bible, with the other the rifle.

"Sign here," he said, pointing to the Bible's cover, which for some reason carried the photograph of Moshe Dayan, the chief of staff.

I took pen in hand and looked at the picture, and before my eyes it changed into the picture of my father. He was standing tall and severe in his desert fatigues and heavy shoes, beside a slim elfin figure of a young man, the hair of both blowing in the wind.

I knew the other one. This was Paltiel Rubin, the "wrestler poet," whose books stood on a shelf in my apartment.

Or was he Rubin? This man appeared healthy, his throat without a mark. According to the early biographies (my father never spoke about it), Paltiel Rubin had had his throat slit by Arabs in a Yaffo alley, twenty-nine years ago. His private parts were then sliced off and stuffed in his mouth. This was a very common thing, in the events of '48.

The slim image wavered and my dream suddenly turned upside down. An animal figure, perhaps a hyena, perhaps a man, screeched into my face. With supreme effort I fended it off, but the screeching continued. I felt a hand on my shoulder, then on my chest.

It was the flight attendant. "We are landing," she said, her hand lingering. With the other she handed me a wet towel. "Are you all right?" Above her head the beeping continued. We were to put on our seat belts.

"Yes, yes," I snarled, shrugging her hand away. The plane banked; through the window, just underneath the wing, I could see the white surf of the Tel Aviv beach shining in the dark, and the ghostly buildings beyond, dotting the dark land. It was exactly as I had last seen it, seven years before.

All of a sudden a horrible hunger gnawed at me. It was as if a huge gap had opened in my belly, a deep gaping hole. It was more than twelve hours since I had last eaten.

I begged the stewardess to bring me something to eat. A piece of bread, anything.

"There's no bread on the plane," she said stiffly, eyeing a bearded Jew two seats to my left. "This is a kosher flight." She handed me two pieces of matza.

The bearded man glanced up; when the stewardess had left, he handed me a hard-boiled egg. As I thanked him awkwardly he handed me another egg and a chicken leg.

"I always bring my own," he said, exposing bad teeth in a one-sided grin.

I mumbled my thanks. I hadn't eaten kosher chicken in a long time.

I was still sucking on the bone when, half an hour later, I descended the stairs into the night and onto the bus that took the passengers to the terminal of Ben Gurion Airport.

I was prepared. In a flash the nocturnal smells converged on me like starved furies. Orange blossoms; the salty smell of the sea; the dust; the hot tarmac. I steeled myself and walked on. The hot wind ruffled my hair.

A sleepy policewoman slouched inside the passport control booth. She flipped through my Canadian passport, her eyes pausing over the section noting I had been born in Tel Aviv. I had made the mistake of speaking to her in Hebrew.

"And your Israeli passport?" she said, curling her fingers quickly back and forth, impatiently.

"I don't have one. I gave up my citizenship."

"You have proof?"

I pulled out of my knapsack a folded sheet of paper. She glanced at it and threw it on the counter.

"Okay," she said, eyeing me with contempt and envy.

Outside, the sky shone with millions of stars. The skinny eucalyptus trees swayed in a slight breeze. I was happy to see how little nostalgia they awoke in me.

An ancient Mercedes cab, its four doors dented, took me to Ibn Gvirol Street. The driver, a muscular man with a close-cropped head, assiduously avoided looking at me. I paid him (to my surprise he did not count the money) and got off at the corner of Eliyahu Street. Darkness enveloped everything, thick and fragrant like breath. The green glow of the streetlamps seeped through the *tzaftzafa* trees; white bedsheets, flapping slowly like ghosts, hung on clotheslines. A gray cat slunk into a yard. Nothing seemed to have changed since I left. I climbed the stairs of house number 142-Aleph.

Ehud Reznik opened the door and looked at me as if I were a ghost.

"David! I thought you are in Canada!"

"Yes," I said, unloading my backpack. "Can I stay here tonight? My father died yesterday and I came for the funeral."

Ehud stepped aside. "Sure, sure. You can sleep on the sofa in the living room. You want to eat something?"

The living room table was piled with dirty plates and innumerable dirty glasses. I had done my homework on this table.

"We just finished," Ehud said, "but we left the dishes for tomorrow."

From the bedroom came a mumbled query.

"It's all right," said Ehud, embarrassed. "It's a . . . it's David."

The mattress squeaked and the bedroom door was flung open.

"Go back to sleep, Ruthy," Ehud said. "You can talk to him in the morning. It's one o'clock already."

Ruthy made no sound; no sound at all.

I sat down on the sofa, under framed photos of HaBimah theater actors, all autographed. On the walls hung more pictures, some new, and also an old one, with my mother playing Queen Esther in an old Purim play. An old photo of Paltiel Rubin hung in the corner. It was generally accepted that he was Ruthy's father. He was married to her mother, the dramatic actress Riva Yellin, briefly in 1947—very briefly, for one week.

"I didn't know you two are married," I said.

Ruthy said, "So you came back?" She wore large men's pajamas, blue with white stripes, the buttons undone. Her stiff unbrushed red hair obscured her face. I was amazed to see how dead my heart was. This was good. It was all over long ago.

I said, "Maybe I can go to a hotel . . ."

"Don't be a donkey," said Ruthy. "You stay right here."

I nodded. "Maybe I can have something to eat? Anything?"

Ruthy disappeared in the kitchen. Her voice called out, "I am making you some yogurt with cheese, with a matza. You want some vegetables, too?"

Ehud helped me open the sofa—it became a bed after a mighty tug at its front edge, and together we spread a pale blue bedsheet on the mattress.

"A heart attack?" Ehud asked. "He was what, seventy-five?" He hopped around the sofa on his short right leg, tucking the bedsheet in.

"Seventy-one," I said. "A burglar killed him, with a knife."

Ehud stopped in mid-motion. "The fucking Arab. Did they catch him?"

"What Arab? Arab, Arab! They all are saying Arab. There are Jewish burglars, too."

"You know who I mean."

Ruthy returned with a tray. I ate, looking neither at my food nor at her. Ehud looked at us both. He said to me, "We're getting married next month, in Kfar Saba."

"Mazel tov," I said through the yogurt.

"You are invited, too," Ruthy said, "if you can stay." She paused. "Are you married?"

"Almost," I said, and ate a spoonful of my yogurt. "Thank you, really, I am sorry I didn't call, but I didn't want to go to a hotel and—"

"Don't talk nonsense," Ehud said. "It's your apartment, now. We're just the tenants."

It occurred to me that this was true. After my mother's death my father had rented out the apartment on Ibn Gvirol. For himself he rented a loft on Lillienblum Street from Mr. Glantz, from whom he used to take rooms long ago, before he met my mother.

I knew Ehud Reznik had rented the Ibn Gvirol apartment. I didn't know he was living there with Ruthy.

Ruthy said abruptly, "Good night. You know where everything is."

Ehud said, "You need a lift tomorrow someplace, maybe?
We can talk later, if you want."

"No thanks," I said. "I've got to see the lawyer, his office is
on Balfour Street. But I can take bus number five."

Both looked at me as I wolfed down the carrot, the tomato,
the cucumber. Israeli vegetables taste heavenly, unlike any others in the world. It's something in the soil. Maybe it's all this
blood.

"How's the chocolate business?" I asked Ehud. His father
owned a chocolate factory in Ramat Gan, where Ehud, since
he had left theater productions, now worked.

Ehud reddened. "Good, good."

I didn't ask Ruthy how the theater business was. I had read
someplace—I think in a copy of *Ma'ariv* I had once bought in
Toronto—that she played small roles in a new theater group
called Lo Harbeh—Nothing Much. At her age, twenty-nine,
her mother had already played the role of Leah'le, in *The
Dybbuk*.

Ehud said, "Really, about your father, I—"

"Yes, yes," I said, waving my hand. Yogurt sprayed on the
sofa and I cleaned it with my palm.

Both looked at me silently as I ate.

4

PRESENTLY THEY TURNED IN and closed the bedroom door
behind them. For a long time I watched the closed door and
listened to the sounds coming from within. Once or twice I
heard Ehud's voice, protesting weakly. "No, no. Not now."

"Yes, now," Ruthy's voice said. "Now!" Then there were
some more sounds.

Finally I slid into the old darkness.

Next day I was awakened by the clashes of garbage cans and
the screams of children, as the nightmarish black slowly transformed into a room full of gray light. Ruthy and Ehud had left
me a crumpled note. They would return that evening, they
wrote, he from the factory, she from some drama class. If I
needed anything I should take it. Here was a spare key, and a
hundred-shekel note, "for chewing gum," Ehud wrote.

I opened the fridge and poked a while inside. Cheese left-
overs, and Eshel (the Israeli yogurt), and tomatoes and cucum-
bers in plastic bags, and bottles of Maccabee beer—strictly not
kosher for Passover.

I peeled a cucumber and ate it while I shaved, glancing at
a *HaAretz* newspaper I had propped up on the washing machine. The religious parties were again threatening to leave
the coalition; one more Labor minister had been convicted of
bribery; six soldiers had died in an ambush near the Lebanon
border—

I threw the newspaper on a pile of wet towels. Nothing will ever change here; the young die so that the old can continue to bicker. I should call the lawyer right now, sign whatever I had to sign, and leave this damn place as soon as I could before the evil reclaimed me.

I rinsed my face and telephoned Mr. Gelber.

He picked up on the first ring. Y . . . yes, he stammered, he was expecting my call, yes, and I should come right away . . . He lived just around the corner, on Yahalal Street—yes, yes, just where Itzik Vasserman the violinist used to live. Third floor—

A line of taxicabs stood in front of Sharf's kiosk. A wiry young man in Atta jeans and a gray T-shirt stared at me narrow-eyed from a boulevard bench, pigeons strutting all around him. Three muscular yeshiva boys loitered at the entrance to the apartment house on Yahalal Street, in the ground floor of which a synagogue had apparently been installed. I pushed through them and climbed the narrow stairs. Mr. Ya'akov Gelber, his pudgy face drawn, opened his door dressed in short khaki pants and a loose stained undershirt, a knit skullcap on his head. "Good . . . morning, Mr. Starkman," he stammered, and made a jerky little bow, holding on to the skullcap, "and my . . . my most sincere condolences," he blinked moistly. "Coffee? Tea?"

"Coffee," I said. "Thank you."

His wife and two children were seated on the living room floor, playing dominoes; they didn't look up. A stocky man sat on the sofa, splitting sunflower seeds with his teeth. He threw me a sharp look, then stared pointedly up at the wall, where the ubiquitous photos of grandparents who had gone with Hitler were hanging, framed under glass.

"My . . . my cousin," Mr. Gelber stammered, "visiting from Haifa . . ."

He ushered me into his study by way of the kitchen. It was a tiny room overflowing with paper, overlooking the garbage-can shed in the yard. Children's pencil drawings were tacked to the wall. Mr. Gelber sank into a swivel chair and motioned to me to sit opposite him, handing me a glass of hot Nescafé. "Yes, yes . . . a tragedy," he stammered. "A vigorous man . . . but these things—yes, more and more . . ." He stopped, handing me the bowl of sugar. Its lid rattled.

"Yes," I said, not knowing what I was confirming. Some coffee had spilled on my jeans and I tried to rub it out. I felt an irrational urge to flee and pressed my palms down on my thighs to stay seated. There was an awkward silence. Mr. Gelber breathed shallowly and moistly, as if fearing to intrude upon my presumed grief, and with a visible effort asked about the length of my flight, the exact hour of my arrival, and how long I planned to stay. He seemed strangely cheered to hear I was returning to Toronto the day after the funeral, and from under a pile of papers he pulled a plain white envelope, extracting from it a sheaf of typed sheets clasped by a metal clip.

Mr. Gelber said, "He typed it himself and wrote on the back flap that it was to be opened only in case of his death." He stared at me with bulging eyes. "Did he talk to you about it?"

"We were not in touch," I said.

Mr. Gelber said, "The police found the will in the store—my name and phone number were inside—so they called me and I drove right over and we opened it together." His voice turned plaintive. "He composed it all himself, but it was cosigned by two witnesses, so it's legal—"

"I didn't know he could type," I said.

"Well, he could do many things," Mr. Gelber muttered crossly. "But it's very simple, really, except for one or two small things."

I waited, again forcing myself to sit still.

Mr. Gelber scanned the first page. "He owned the store, you know, and also the apartment, but the mortgages ate up more than half the value. What he borrowed the money for, I have no idea. Did he send you money to Canada?" He fixed me with an accusatory stare.

"No."

Mr. Gelber raised a disbelieving eyebrow. I scowled and he dropped his eyes; then without preamble he launched into a recitation of bank accounts: one at Discount Bank, where the store's cash receipts and rent from the apartment were deposited, with all month-end balances regularly given to charity. A foreign-currency account at Bank Le'umi, where deutsche mark compensation payments from Germany were deposited—also given out to charity ("How he had enough to live on," Mr. Gelber muttered, "I don't know"); and another account in Mizrachi Bank, for royalties on the literary works of Paltiel Rubin—

"Paltiel Rubin?" I said. "The wrestler poet?"

"Yes," said Mr. Gelber, evading my eyes. "Your father, may he rest in peace, was his literary executor. They used to be friends, many years ago, you know."

"Yes, I know." Everyone knew that. But executor?

Mr. Gelber blew his nose into his hand and wiped it absently on the seat of his pants. "There was also some cash in the store's register. It's in the hands of the police, but when they finish their investigation—" He twisted his mouth to show what he thought of the police's investigatory skills, or maybe of the chance to ever see this money again. "Some Moroccan inspector, Amzaleg, that's the one I talked to."

I felt feverish. "Do they need me for anything?"

"I don't know . . . but you can call them . . ." It was clear that, aside from the store's cash they now kept, Mr. Gelber was not interested in the police. He scanned the page in his hand. "*Nu* . . . to make a long story short, the estate, net of the mortgages, is worth a hundred and eighty-three thousand shekels, give or take." He blinked upward, his lips puckered as if looking at a distant calculator. "Something like sixty-five thousand Canadian dollars, what?"

I nodded, numbly. The room rotated.

Mr. Gelber said self-deprecatingly, "Minus my eight percent, of course, which you'll find is the standard fee, from the days of the British Mandate—from the days of the Turks, even—"

From the living room came a telephone ring, which immediately stopped, as if someone had picked up the receiver. Mr. Gelber threw a look at the study's door, then wrenched his eyes back to me. "I—I am going over all this quickly . . . Later you can read the summary for yourself—"

"It's all right," I said. "I trust you."

He squinted at me, as if checking whether I had spoken in jest. I hadn't.

There was a brief silence. Mr. Gelber spoke haltingly. "There are some . . . a few more details . . ." He probed with shaky fingers inside the white envelope. I glimpsed my father's scrawl on the flap and my nose tingled.

I forced my eyes away.

"It's only two people, really," Mr. Gelber said. "It's you, and your uncle in—" He consulted the sheet before him. "Tveriah . . ."

"Uncle Mordechai," I said. "Mordechai Starkman."

"Yes . . . Mordechai Starkman, from Tveriah . . . It's all to be divided ninety-ten between you two . . . ninety percent to you, ten to him, except for . . . for a few things that go only to you . . . There are the royalties on some old literary properties . . ." Mr. Gelber paused, then went on with an effort, "The royalties on seventeen poems of Paltiel Rubin, and half the royalties on the poem *Golyatt*, belonged to your father."

I sat up. "*Golyatt*?"

"Yes, and also a half interest in a few old plays, and full interest in a play called"—he made a show of squinting closely at
the page—"*The Debba*. It has only been produced once." His
eyes assiduously avoided mine. "In Haifa, 1946."

"My father wrote half of *Golyatt*?"

"No, no . . . It doesn't say that." Mr. Gelber wiped his bald
pate with a pudgy palm. "It only says he has a half interest . . ."
He gave me a wan smile. "What do I know? He may have
helped the destitute poet in an hour of need, in exchange for
a share—"

"*Golyatt*?" I repeated, quoting from memory the poem all
schoolchildren learn by heart at the age of ten, "'Thou art
my enemy, O friend of mine, my rival and my fate, thy giant
shadow on my bride looms . . .'"

"Yes, this one," Mr. Gelber said in a small voice. "Now about
the funeral . . ."

"And which poems?" I asked. "Not the sonnets?"

"I—I am afraid I am not much of a . . ." He looked down
at the page, "Here it says, 'Seventeen poems, first printed in
the newspaper *Davar* between 1932 and 1935, then collected by
the publishing house of Shomron in a special edition to com-
memorate—'"

"The sonnets," I said. "*Golyatt*, and the sonnets."

"I am afraid the income does not amount to much, no more
than two thousand shekels per year, and this is mainly from
royalties on the syllabus used by the Ministry of Education,
and they don't pay more than—"

"It's all right," I said. "I understand." I understood nothing.
A feeling of black oppression enveloped me, and the same
strong urge to flee.

There was the patter of feet. The study's door opened a
crack, and Mrs. Gelber, a small homely woman with a gray
mustache over a brown lip, poked her head in. "I am sorry,

Ya'akov," she whispered, "but he asked me to remind you that you should be going soon to your *meeting*." Her eyes fixed upon the white envelope on the desktop.

Mr. Gelber hissed back, "Tell him . . . we—we are almost finished . . ."

His wife flicked her gaze at me with something akin to fear before scuttling out. Perhaps she had learned what I used to do in the army.

My legs shook as I began to rise. "If there's anything else—"

Mr. Gelber said nervously. "Um, yes, we'll talk tomorrow in my office, but you should know there was this one little thing . . ."

"Yes? What thing?"

He seemed oddly ill at ease. "There is a request in the will— a legal stipulation, strictly speaking—that the play be staged within forty-five days of passing, before the estate is settled fully . . . that is—"

"Staged by whom?"

"By . . . by the senior beneficiary, it says."

My throat seized. Here he was, my father, still trying to make me do his bidding, even from beyond the grave . . . I began to snarl that I was not going to stage any play, but Mr. Gelber clutched at my wrist and spoke over my words. "Listen, if you try to do this, it could run to a hundred and fifty thousand shekels— what am I saying? Two hundred thousand. Minimum."

"Well, I don't—"

But again he did not let me speak. "There are four actors, one of whom is a woman, which since last year's legislation unfortunately must be paid the same . . . and the animal, which can be a drama student in a fur suit . . . but even if you use synthetic fur, it'd still cost . . . and the scenery, and the accompaniment for the songs . . . and to pay for the director, and the municipal license . . . and the hall for the rehearsals, and

the advertising—you know how much it'd cost?" He let go my
arm, wiped his face, and flicked a wide-eyed look at the door.
"I am telling you, it could eat up the estate . . . what am I saying? Even more . . ."

"What animal?" I said.

"The Debba, the spotted hyena . . . I looked at the play after
we opened the will." He gave me a quivering smile, indicating
the envelope with a palm.

I said, "Well, I'm not doing any damn play. After the shivah
I am gone."

Mr. Gelber's cheeks acquired a ruddy color. "You are not?"

"No. Tell the judge to give the money to some bereaved
parents."

I don't know why I said this. I hadn't seen any bereaved parents since I left. "Is there anything else?"

Mr. Gelber stared up at me with almost physical relief.
"Well, I suppose it's really all the same, since staging this play
would cost as much as . . ." He rubbed his hands. "All right, I
suppose you can just sign that you give up your claim to the
estate . . . Your uncle Mordechai already said he doesn't care
one way or another . . ."

"Yeah. For sure."

I hadn't spoken to my father (except for that brief telephone
conversation) for seven years. Uncle Mordechai hadn't spoken
to him for thirty.

I said, "So the estate will go to the state's treasury?"

"Probably." Mr. Gelber laid a densely typed legal sheet atop
the envelope on his desk and thrust a plastic ballpoint pen at
me. "Here. You sign here, and here, and here . . ." He gave me
a forced wink. "Between us, I don't think it could be staged
now anyway. Not today . . ." As he directed my fingers to the
dotted line to consign my father's bequest to oblivion, the pen
felt hot and slippery in my hand.

A whisper came through the door. "You finished, Ya'akov? He's *waiting*."

"Yes, yes!" Mr. Gelber hissed, his eyes on the hovering pen. "Tell him I am coming, Chedva." He turned to me. "*Nu?* Sign, sign!"

I began to write my name in Hebrew but my fingers had turned into gelignite putty. In panic and rage I pressed hard and the plastic shaft snapped in my hands, and as it did, a smaller envelope slipped out of the large one. Mr. Gelber made a swift grab at it but it evaded his grasp and fluttered to the floor. It was the kind used for sending New Year's greeting cards, but this one's flap was sealed shut. On the front was written in my father's crabbed scrawl:

To my son, my eldest, my beloved; David.

I stared at the script for a long while, my eyes blind with wet heat. Didn't my father ever let up? Through the wetness I saw Mr. Gelber bending over to pick up the envelope. I snatched it out of his grasp and inserted it back inside the larger envelope. For the first time, his desperation for my signature penetrated through my haze. Why was he so eager that I relinquish my father's estate? Without thinking, I tucked the envelope under my arm and shakily rose to my feet.

Mr. Gelber gaped at me, his cheeks taut. "So you sign or not?"

I stumbled through the kitchen to the front door, the envelope radiating heat into my armpit. Mr. Gelber's wife and children were nowhere to be seen, but his cousin was waiting outside in the hallway, leaning on the wall. He stared at the envelope under my arm and began to lean forward as Mr. Gelber barged out after me, waving a pen.

I called over my shoulder, "I'll see you tomorrow in your office, after the funeral," then skipped down the stairs. Mr. Gelber cried forlornly after me, "Don't be a donkey! I am telling you, it doesn't have a chance . . . not today . . ."

I thrust roughly through the trio of yeshiva boys still loiter-
ing at the entrance, shook off the hand of one who asked me
why I was pushing, and dashed out. A gray Toyota was waiting
at the curb with its engine running, the windows curtained.
I crossed Yahalal Street at a trot. Sweat poured off me as if I
had been lugging heavy flour sacks. I looked over my shoulder. Mr. Gelber's cousin had pushed through the knot of the
muscular boys and was now opening the Toyota's side door. A
moment later Mr. Gelber joined him, and the car disappeared
down Ben-Gurion Boulevard in a cloud of fumes. To my surprise, two of the yeshiva boys mounted Vespas and followed;
the third went back inside. As I jogged, rusty seven-year-old
instincts creaked back to life. Was Mr. Gelber's "cousin" keeping an eye on me? Were the yeshiva boys? I shook my head to
clear it. One day here and I was seeing pursuers everywhere,
as if I was again in enemy territory. Tomorrow, right after the
funeral, I'd go to Gelber's office and hand him back the envelope, sign whatever the hell he wanted, and return to Canada,
to Jenny, to the peaceful cold.

Back at the apartment I called Canada to tell Jenny I would
be back in two days, but she was not home. I left a message on
her answering machine with Ehud's phone number and raided
the fridge for a beer, then for another. I felt enormous fatigue,
as if I were swimming in glue.

Golyatt, and the sonnets, and the damn play. Why did my
father ask this of me? And why did Mr. Gelber seem so eager
that I not do it?

I prowled the apartment, poking my head into cupboards,
looking at the old chairs, at my parents' double bed with the
foam mattress, where Ehud and Ruthy now slept. My father
had rented out the apartment with all the furniture—even
my mother's old Singer sewing machine was still standing on
the kitchen balcony, covered by an army blanket of blue felt.

Under it, in an old shoe box, were my old black army-issued Nomex coveralls, with their myriad pockets, the legging torn, and the special night-vision goggles, the left lens cracked. In another shoe box was an assortment of odd-looking instruments under a thick layer of dust. I stared at them for a long while. These, too, I had left behind.

I kicked off my shoes, lay down on the couch, and awoke five hours later, at four in the afternoon. I tried calling Jenny one more time. In Canada it would be nine in the morning. She was out.

I gobbled three Eshels and a large cucumber, all the while pacing around the coffee table. Faint smells of almond blossoms came through the window, and salty sea air. It was as if a second pair of nostrils that had shut down when I left Israel had now reopened. I took lungfuls of air, my stomach sizzling. From time to time I picked up the small envelope and stared at my father's handwriting, before sliding it back into the large one. More than once I nearly slit the small envelope open with a kitchen knife, but each time I recoiled. I was not about to stay here and do my father's bidding once again. It dawned on me I'd also better leave the apartment soon, before Ruthy came back. The last thing I wanted was to talk to her alone. I could always call Uncle Mordechai from a pay phone, or from a hotel. Yet I lingered, staring at the small envelope.

After a while I picked up the phone and called Uncle Mordechai in Tveriah.

5

THE PHONE RANG FOR a long time before Uncle Mordechai picked it up. He was probably reading his *Davar* newspaper on the couch on the terrace overlooking Lake Kinneret.

"Who is this?" he asked. Fifteen years he had had the telephone and had still not learned how to answer it.

"It's me, David."

"Oh, David. Greetings! So you came from the diaspora for your father finally?"

"No," I said. "I came from Canada for the funeral."

"And how long are you going to honor us with your presence? A day? A week?"

"I don't know yet." For some reason I added, "I owe you a thousand shekels, for the burial society."

"You owe, you don't owe," Uncle Mordechai said. "You want to pay, pay; you don't want to pay, don't pay. Do what you want."

"I'll pay you after the funeral." Why was I talking about money?

"You want to pay, pay."

There was an awkward pause. "Mordechai . . ." I blurted, "did they catch him? The burglar?"

The line hummed. "How do I know? Ask the police."

I heard steps on the stairs, and the rattle of a key in the door.

"I—I will . . ." My voice seemed stuck. "But why would anyone—"

"I don't know anything. What do you want? I am in Tveriah."

I went on, obstinately. "Everyone is saying it's an Arab. Because of what he—you know." I pulled my handkerchief out and wiped my face.

"Who says? People have long tongues. There are Jewish burglars, too."

"Yes, I know. But—"

"The funeral is tomorrow? In Nachalat Yitzchak?" The line cleared up all of a sudden. "Ten o'clock?"

"Yes. Ya'akov Gelber, the lawyer, said that it must take place before Saturday. I don't know why."

Behind me the door opened. I sensed Ruthy coming into the room. Perhaps it was her smell. I don't know. Ever since we were children we could always sense each other's presence. But that was long ago.

"Of course before Saturday," my uncle shouted. "You heathen. You cannot keep a body unburied over the Shabbat. You forgot everything in Canada. What do they feed you there, *injill*?" Uncle Mordechai gave a sharp chuckle, a sort of bark.

Injill is a wild Galilean weed. The Arabs believe that the Debba, the spotted hyena that lures away children to teach them the language of the beasts, feeds them *injill* first, so they will forget their own.

"Every day," I said. "We put it in the hummus."

"Ha! Hummus in Canada? Maybe hummus ice cream, too?"

"Yes. With *s'choog*." S'choog was the Yemenite red pepper sauce that bit your tongue as if it had teeth. The Yemenites believed it toughened the male member.

Uncle Mordechai's voice now had the bantering tone I knew. "What do you need *s'choog* in Canada for? For the shiksas?"

Ruthy said behind me, "I came early. Hi, David."

"Yes," I said into the phone. "All hundreds of them."

After a pause my uncle said, "Listen, Duvid, about your father, I mean, listen— Anyway, I'll see you in Nachalat Yitzchak tomorrow, with Margalit. Afterward you can come with us."

"The shivah will be in Tveriah?"

"Where else? You want it in Café Cassit maybe?" His tone softened. "Listen. After the funeral we'll go back to Tveriah. You want a *buri* or a *musht*?" Fried in olive oil, *buris* and *mushts* were Uncle Mordechai's specialty—the Kinneret fish most suitable for frying.

"I—I don't think I'll come to the shivah. After the funeral I'm going back to Canada."

There was a long humming silence. "You do what you want."

I heard sounds of running water from the kitchen, and the opening and closing of the fridge.

"And, anyway, I am not going to do what he asked me, in the will—"

I waited for my uncle to ask what that was, but as the silence dragged on I told him about the stipulation. "Do you have any idea why—"

My uncle's shout seemed to resonate all the way from the Galilee. "Don't you understand Hebrew? I told you twice already I know nothing about this dreck. You don't want to sit shivah for him? Fine. But don't you mix me up in this. You hear?"

Before I had a chance to ask my uncle what he meant, he had already hung up. I knew he would make straight to the bottle of Stock 777, the common cognac he drank every day after supper, ever since his son Arnon was killed.

What was my uncle so afraid of now?

The image of Mr. Gelber running after me with a pen in hand came to mind, then that of his cousin, and the yeshiva boys . . .

What did everyone seem so afraid of?

I sat on the sofa, breathing shallowly, then got up and went to the kitchen.

Ruthy was sitting at the table. She was reading some gossip weekly with color photographs. Jenny read only poetry magazines.

"How was drama class?" I said after a while. My voice was rough to my ears, as if I had swallowed sand.

Ruthy made a face and swung her head from side to side, keeping her eyes on the page. "Blah. Nobody knew their lines so the instructor screamed for half an hour." She went on reading, not turning the page. The corners of her mouth trembled slightly.

I sat down opposite her. "It's in Nachalat Yitzchak cemetery tomorrow." My voice still came out all rough and I coughed several times, to clear it. "I didn't know they buried civilians there."

Ruthy did not look up. "Your brother is there; I mean, his tombstone." Her hair had been pulled back with a rubber band and I could see she had become thinner since I had last seen her, and also tanner. As for aging, I couldn't say. She looked to me exactly as if we had parted yesterday.

"But he was in the army," I said. Her smell, a warm lemony musk, reached me from across the table; I felt my eyes begin to sting.

"So was your father," Ruthy said, "once. He was what, in forty-eight? A major? Colonel?" Her face still reminded me of an apricot, soft and rounded and downy.

I said I didn't know. It was true. I never bothered to learn what he did then. All I knew was that he had killed Abu Jalood, the notorious leader of the Jaloodi terrorist gang, the one whom the Arabs claimed could turn himself into a Debba.

There was a brief silence as we both contemplated the coffee-stained table. I blinked several times, squeezing the corners of my eyes.

Ruthy leaned over the table and turned the radio on. Rau-
cous music spilled into the air. "It's the new Peace Station. I
worked there for a month."

The Peace Station, a pirate radio station transmitting from
a boat anchored fifteen miles off the coast of Ashqelon, was financed by a leftist restaurateur; half the peaceniks in the country did a stint on it for no pay.

"Great," I said. "Do they also broadcast songs of 'Um
Kulsum?"

Ruthy flared up. "She is a great singer! So what if she is an
Egyptian? She sings better than half—"

"All right. All right. Don't get all hot."

There was a short brittle silence.

Ruthy said in a dull monotone, "You know how long I
waited? You know how long?"

"I didn't tell you to wait."

"Seven years. Nobody can wait seven years."

"I asked you to come with me, you said no."

"I can't leave here, I told you. You know I can't leave."

The night before I left she had tried to explain to me why
she could not come with me. It was not because she loved this
place or anything, she said; it was just that when she thought
of leaving, she immediately got sick. I pretended I did not understand and at last she stopped trying to make me see it.

A burst of wailing came from the yard. Probably some cats
fighting over scraps.

"Anyway," I said, "it's all over now."

"Yes," said Ruthy. A slow flush was creeping up her neck to
her chin and cheeks.

We looked bleakly at each other.

I got to my feet; my legs were shaking. "I really should call
the police."

"The phone is in the living room."

"I know," I said. "I used to live here."

"Well, now you don't. Okay?"

I went to the living room and called the police station on HaYarkon Street, where I had once reported my bicycle stolen.

"Call Investigations, on Dizzengoff," said the policeman on the line. "I don't know what burglary you mean, there are so many; but they would know. Happy Passover."

Ruthy said behind me, "And tell them to catch him quickly so you can run away again!"

I turned my back to her and dialed.

6

"OH YES," SAID INSPECTOR Amnon Amzaleg in the Dizzen-goff station. "The one where they cut—"

"Yes," I said tightly. "I'm his son. Can I come talk to some-body who is responsible for the investigation?"

There was a short pause.

"Sure, *ya habibi*," Amzaleg said. "Come, come."

I turned around and said to Ruthy, "I'm going to the police. I'll be back in an hour, to get my things. I think I should go to a hotel, so—"

"Don't be a donkey." Her face was still flushed. "You stay right here in Ibn Gvirol. Don't be afraid. Nobody will eat you. You want a lift?"

"I can take the bus."

"You'll only bump your head." She got up, too. "Come, I'll take you. Which one, the one on Dizzengoff?"

"Yes. Just behind the kindergarten of Miss Chassia—"

"I know where it is."

Rattling the car keys on the handrail, she ran down the stairs two at a time, as we used to do when we were children, while I trailed slowly behind her, watching the blur of her legs.

"So you're almost married?" Ruthy asked as we sat in her beat-up Volkswagen, rolling down Arlozorov Street.

"Yes," I said. I didn't want to talk about Canada.

"You'll send us an invitation?"

"If you want."

"So long as you're happy." She turned on the car radio and fumbled with the dial. Her red hair brushed my shoulder as she leaned to look at the numbers on the dial.

We were now stuck behind a large truck unloading boxes into a restaurant. Since I had left, the street had become trendy, and every second building now housed a restaurant, or a pub.

"They tore almost everything down," Ruthy said. "They're putting pubs everywhere. How much beer can you drink?"

"Lots."

"No, really. Look at this!" She pointed toward a busy pub, where tables and chairs had spilled onto the sidewalk. "Just four years ago half their friends died on Yom Kippur, and look at them now, drinking."

"So what do you want them to do? Stay home and light candles?"

For a while both of us were silent.

Suddenly Ruthy asked, "You love your girlfriend? What's her name?"

"Very much."

"What's her name?" she asked again.

"Doesn't matter." I didn't want to talk about Jenny, or Canada, or anything else. I wanted to get to the police station. Maybe I should have taken the bus.

"If you don't want to tell, don't tell," Ruthy said.

I watched the darkening street and said nothing.

After a while Ruthy said in a low voice, "So who do you think killed him?"

"It was a burglar."

"So why did they cut . . . you know—"

"Maybe they wanted to make it look like Arabs." I felt dizzy just talking about it.

Ruthy persisted. "But maybe it *was* Arabs? Like—you know, in forty-eight?"

"It was a burglar!" I snapped. "A Jewish burglar!"

We drove the rest of the way in silence.

"It's here," Ruthy said. "I'm sorry about the brake. Did you hurt your head? I can wait for you in the car." She had parked behind a black patrol car, its doors scratched with the words "Avraham Molcho screws his sister."

I got out. The police station, a crumbly building overgrown with dead ivy, stood where it always had, between Rachmanov's hardware store and Berman's kiosk. Two of the front steps had been broken and someone had patched them up with old construction lumber, some long nails still sticking out, others bent with hammer blows.

"You can come in, too," I said.

"If you want. Just let me lock the car. There are lots of thieves here."

7

"AMZALEG?" SAID THE POLICEMAN behind the desk. He squinted at me in the dim light. "What do you want with him?"

"I came to talk to him about a burglary. The one on Herzl Street? In the HaYarkon station they said—"

"They sent you to us?" The policeman eyed me with suspicion. "Which burglary?"

Ruthy said, "Listen to what he's telling you. The one on Herzl Street, he said."

"Tell your wife to be quiet," the policeman said, not even looking at Ruthy. "You filled out the forms already?"

"What forms?"

Ruthy said, "No, it's from two days ago, in the shoe store on Herzl." She turned to me. "What number is it?"

I said, "Sit over there, Ruthy, wait until I'm finished."

There was a ruckus behind us. A gangly policeman entered, his arm around the shoulders of a hiccuping fat beggar with disheveled hair who threw off a strong stench of urine. "Amzaleg is in?"

From somewhere within rose a cacophony of shouts, and over and above them, soaring effortlessly, a thin tenor voice began to sing:

My life is full of loss and fear,
I stretch my hand but no one's there—

It was the song of Military Prison Number 4, where I had once spent thirty-five days for disobeying an order. The more serious charges had been dropped after my father had intervened with someone in the Defense Ministry, perhaps Gershonovitz.

"Amzaleg, Amzaleg," growled the policeman, "all the world wants Amzaleg." The phone rang.

"Investigations Branch, *shalom*," he said into the large black receiver.

Ruthy said to me, "Maybe I'll wait in the car."

"Whatever you want," I said.

The lanky policeman had deposited his charge on a bench, under a torn poster carrying the words "Be Wary!" over a picture of a large woman's handbag with a finger of dynamite sticking halfway out.

"See? What did I tell you!" the policeman said triumphantly, pointing the receiver at me. "Also for him." He tilted his head back and shouted, "Amnon! Aam-non! *Ta'al Hon!*" This was the paratrooper's war cry, calling on friends to come up and storm the hill. For some reason it is always made in Arabic, perhaps a remnant from the War of Independence, when Jews began to behave like Arabs.

From within a dark corridor waddled a burly man, his face puffy with lack of sleep. "Fuck your mother. What? What?"

I stepped up to him. "I talked to you over the phone, before? About the burglary on Herzl Street?"

He eyed me for a brief second, like a light-tower beam sweeping the terrain. "Come inside." He turned on his heels and walked into the corridor at the back.

The burly policeman kept on walking. Ruthy and I followed. The stench of urine intensified. Narrow nooks opened right and left; I heard moans and wails, and footsteps.

Inside Amzaleg's office I sat on the only chair. Ruthy remained standing by the door. I said, "I am his son. I just came from Canada."

The room was small and unlit, the walls painted some khaki

color. The metal desk was cluttered with piles of paper, and files, and on its corner stood a photograph of a teenaged boy and an older girl—his children presumably. Framed citations hung behind the desk. It was too dark to see what they were for.

Ruthy said, "The policeman you have outside, he should learn how to speak."

Amzaleg eyed her with tired eyes. "Yeah." He burrowed into a mound of file folders on the desk. His thick fingers were yellow with nicotine.

I said, "When did—"

"Wait, wait." He flipped a few pages.

I waited. Ruthy said, "No, really, he should—"

"Just a moment, ma'am," said the man behind the desk.

The tenor voice outside began to sing again, sweetly.

"The man from Lillienblum found him," Amzaleg said suddenly in a raspy voice. "Glantz, the landlord. Where he rented the room. The deceased was supposed to come to the seder at eight, and when he still didn't come by ten—they had already finished singing—this Glantz went to the store and peeked through the glass, and he saw him."

My stomach gurgled and I laced my hands over it. "Can I go to the store?"

I had no idea why I asked this. What could I see there?

But Amzaleg did not seem surprised. Perhaps all relatives wanted to see where their kin had died. It was the same with bereaved parents, in the army. "Next week maybe, *ya habibi*." Amzaleg kept his eyes on the file. "We are still looking for clues there." And without any transition he said, "I used to know him, in the army."

Ruthy said, "Who do you think did it?"

Amzaleg said to me, "In forty-eight, in the final Castel battle—I was almost there with him, but a week before, he had sent me to the Yonah camp, for a course." Amzaleg raised his eyes. They were bloodshot. "I am sorry about your brother."

What was he sorry for now? My brother had died three years ago.

After a while Amzaleg said, "I don't know. It looks like an Arab job to me. Did he have anything to do with Arabs?"

"I live in Canada. What do I know?" I began to sound like Uncle Mordechai.

Ruthy said, "I think he had an Arab partner once." She turned to me, "No? Forty years ago, something."

I said, "That's in the prehistory."

Amzaleg stared at me. He said, "He bought leather from some people in Yaffo, but they are all old, maybe seventy, seventy-five."

Ruthy said, "Maybe they have sons, no?"

Amzaleg did not move his eyes. "Ma'am, don't teach me my profession." He flipped through the folder. A few glossy photographs spilled out and he grabbed at them quickly and inserted them back into a flap at the back.

Ruthy turned around. "I'll wait for you in the car."

I heard her quick steps echoing down the corridor.

Amzaleg said to me, "Your girlfriend has a big mouth."

"She's not my girlfriend."

Amzaleg closed the file; his beefy hand remained on it. "We'll tell you when we find something, really." His eyes left mine and traveled up and down the wall, like Gelber's cousin. "Did he write to you . . . anything?"

"We didn't correspond."

"No, no," Amzaleg said, his eyes flicking at my face. "I mean in the letter—I saw it when we went through the will. It was sealed and addressed to—to you." His eyes glinted. "Did you open it?"

I shook my head. "I saw the lawyer only this morning, I arrived last night."

"Ahh." Amzaleg's eyes resumed climbing the wall. "Well, let me know when you read it, if there's anything."

There was an awkward pause.

"So you are going to stage it?" the policeman asked casually. "The play?"

I shook my head and said I'd be leaving right after the funeral. "I can't stay here too long," I added, not specifying why. Let him think what he wanted.

There was another silence.

"We are doing the best we can," Amzaleg said.

"Yes." I knew I should ask him about the murder, but it was as if a fist had closed around my throat, and kept my teeth clenched.

Amzaleg scrutinized my face, then lowered his eyes to his nicotine-stained fingers. "You just leave this thing to us."

"Yes, sure."

But with the new budget, Amzaleg went on, his eyes on his swarthy hands, they only had five people who could work, one was on sick leave, two were doing reserve service in Dimona near the nuclear reactor—

I said, "Just tell me when you catch him."

He looked up sharply, then his gaze slid up the wall. "Don't worry. We'll tell you."

The policeman at the desk outside was drinking from a Tempo bottle, his head thrown back. The other policeman, the lanky one, was gone. On the bench, his tattered clothes exceedingly dirty, sat the fat beggar, still burping, his disheveled gray beard spread over his bulging stomach. I now saw it was Ittamar Gabisohn, the music teacher at my grade school who had lost his mind after his son was killed in the 1967 war (or maybe it was this on top of his experience in Auschwitz), and who afterward lived under an overturned rowboat by the Yarkon's bank. Every anniversary of his son's death he would run up

and down Ibn Gvirol Street all night and make farting noises
through his fist. Only after my father would go down and talk
to him in Polish would he subside.

As I passed he hissed, "Armageddon. He has arrived."

I left.

In the Volkswagen Ruthy was listening to the Peace Station.

"Beasts!" she said vehemently as I folded my legs into the
seat.

I said, "They'll let me know when they catch him."

"Sure! Even flies they can't catch." She twiddled with the
radio. A series of sharp beeps came on. The news. The religious parties were threatening to leave the coalition; two more
soldiers had been killed in the Jordan valley . . . Ruthy abruptly
turned the radio off. "David, I am really sorry about . . . you
know." She looked at me; I looked at the window. She said,
"Mother cried so much when I told her. I never knew they
were friends or anything."

"What do I know?"

"I always thought she hated him."

"Yes. Can you drop me here somewhere? I must look for a
restaurant, or a café. Maybe near the old pizzeria?"

"I have to meet Ehud in Café Cassit, you want to come—no,
I forgot, you are in mourning. You can't go to a café." She eyed
me with reproach. "And you shouldn't shave, until the shivah
is over."

I shouldn't cause my father any more grief. She and Uncle
Yitzchak. "I don't give a shit about all this. Do they still have
hummus at Cassit?"

"Yes. But Chetzkel died. It's his son now, so it tastes like gefilte fish."

"They all died."

"Not me," Ruthy said. "I am alive."

8

ON THE WAY TO Cassit I told Ruthy about the will, and my father's last request.

"I didn't know he wrote plays," she said.

"I don't know if it's his. Maybe it's—Paltiel's." I had wanted to say "your father's," but reconsidered.

There was a pause.

Ruthy said, "And after you do it, you'll go back and get married? In Canada?"

"I'm going back in two days. I'm not doing any play!"

"No, really. I can postpone the wedding if you want—so Ehud can help you—"

"I told you I am not going to do any play. I can't stay here too long."

I didn't want to mention the black dreams; let her think what she wanted.

But Ruthy was off on one of her enthusiasms. "I can ask Ehud. He stopped producing shows because he says no one goes to good theater anymore, just to skit shows and crap, but he's always helping theater people, like your . . . your father used to. You know . . ."

I knew. My father had always been putting up penniless comedians for the night, giving actors shoes for free, "lending" starving dramatists rent money. I never knew how he could afford to do this.

Not that my mother had been much better.

"Don't do me any favors," I said. "You go ahead and get married, and good health to you both."

We were driving now in the midst of a thick double column of automobiles, the sidewalks on both sides a veritable zoo: soldiers in aleph uniforms; overly-made-up young women; gawking American Jews trailing cameras; ancient party hacks; smoke-trailing *Dan* buses; neon lights. Dizzengoff.

Ruthy said, "So you'll give it all up? Is it a lot of money, the estate?"

"Sixty-five thousand Canadian dollars." A bulb of wrath rose in me, about the will, and about my father's posthumous request, this transparent ruse to keep me here. "Next week I am gone!"

Honks rose around us. We had almost plowed into a red Volvo. Behind us, a gray Toyota had almost plowed into us. Ruthy swerved, sharply. "Everybody today has a car!" she said, her nose pink. "You know how much it costs?"

"I don't care." We sat in vibrant silence as she slowly inched her VW ahead, looking for a parking spot. Ruthy said in a low voice, "So you won't do what he asked you?"

"I've done enough for him already."

Ruthy said, "Can I read the play at least?"

"No."

We drove some more in silence. At last Ruthy said, "Here is a spot."

As I got out of the car, the entire street, the people, the lights, everything wavered as if I were seeing it all through a heat wave; as if I were once again in the Sinai in '67 and the people were a ghostly caravan treading up Um Marjam hill, a long procession of all those I had killed, Arabs at the front, Jews at the back.

"Careful of the sewage." Ruthy grabbed my elbow as I swayed.

"I'm all right," I snarled and pulled my arm away.

9

I WAS DRAFTED INTO the army in 1965, right after high school, and immediately volunteered for the paratroopers. The first furlough I got from boot camp, I hitchhiked home to Tel Aviv and proudly showed my father my red beret. "See?"

He nodded without expression. "How's it going?"

I said it was great: I couldn't wait to finish boot camp and go catch some fedayeen.

Those days, Arab infiltrators sneaked in daily from the Gaza refugee camps, to shoot at kibbutzniks, blow up irrigation pumps, and ambush buses.

"Don't worry," my father said. "You'll have a chance."

I asked him for any tips he may have. Any advice, from his '48 days. Anything.

"There are no tips. You just do what you have to do."

I pressed him further, but he would not elaborate. "You just do what's necessary."

What did that mean?

"You'll see."

Following the five-month boot camp, I was posted to Nitzana in the Negev for border duty. Ehud was posted nearby, in another encampment. Our squads laid ambushes for infiltrators in wadis and gulches, following information we received from the Intelligence Recon guys. From time to time we caught a few infiltrators. Those who were not killed in the first fireburst we delivered to the Intels for a brief interrogation, then finished them off. After a while it got to be just like work.

One morning when I was returning from an all-night ambush (we caught no one that night), a handwritten note was waiting for me at the operations tent, to go to the commander's tent immediately.

"What for?" I asked No'a, the operations secretary.

"Don't know. Someone came in, and he's interviewing guys."

"For what?"

I had declined offers before, to go to flight course, and to the naval commandos. I preferred the desert, the open spaces.

"Don't know."

I went to the commander's tent. To my surprise I found Ehud Reznik standing before it, too, dressed in his formal aleph uniform.

"What gives?" I asked him.

But Ehud didn't know either. Then someone inside called my name, and I entered.

Inside, seated on a field bed, was a small, sunburned man with a shiny bald pate and huge hands, dressed in rankless khakis. Without any preliminaries he said that his name was Colonel Shafrir (no first name), and that he needed a few volunteers who would do anything necessary, for their country. "Anything," he stressed.

I asked him straight off if my father had pulled strings to get me a cushy job, because if he had, I was not interested.

"Your father had nothing to do with it, and it sure ain't cushy."

I asked what kind of a job it was.

"Can't tell you. Only if you accept."

"But is it combat or staff?"

"Oh, combat, don't worry."

I asked where I would be posted, in what base camp. "Because if it's close to home, I don't want it either."

"Don't be a donkey. Most of the time you'll be far away. Very far."

He then proceeded to ask me a few questions to which I could not see the point—the languages I spoke (French, Arabic, Hebrew, some English), if I played chess (I did) or any musical instruments (the violin), whether I had ever played soccer seriously (I hadn't) or was a member of the Boy Scouts, Young Maccabees, or any other youth movement (I wasn't).

"I think you'll do," he said at last.

"But what is this job?"

"Can't tell you yet."

I asked a few more questions, to which I received no answers.

"The only thing I can promise you," he said, "is that you'll be asked to do the hardest thing and get next to no help doing it."

And this was meant to convince me? "What thing?"

"You'll see."

"And what did you mean by 'anything'?" I asked him again later, as I was signing the several forms he handed me. (I didn't read even one.)

"You'll see."

Later I learned that Ehud had signed up also.

And that's how it began.

10

As we were entering Cassit, Ruthy said, "Mother likes him. He's good. He never asks me where I go, or how much it costs."

"How much what costs?"

"Anything. And he helped me find—you know, get these roles, with Lo Harbeh, and others."

I wanted to ask her how much it had cost Ehud, but reconsidered. What did I care? He could spend his money any way he wanted. Jenny spent her money on me; Ehud could spend his on Ruthy. I had my shiksa. He could have his.

In Café Cassit, Ehud was eating hummus, his right leg extended. When he saw us he said, "Do they have any clues, the police? Who did it?"

"What do I know?" I said.

"I mean, fingerprints, footprints, whatever."

"You mean paw prints," Ruthy said.

Ehud flushed. "I mean, how he got in, how many they were—seventy-one or not seventy-one, your father was a wrestler once—"

"'Ana 'aref," I said in Arabic. I am ignorant.

All Unit graduates spoke in half-Arabicized Hebrew. Six months we learned Arabic, in total immersion, as well as Arabic customs, proverbs, and Islam, to be able to act like Arabs and pass for them so as to kill them more easily. It became so ingrained that even back home it was hard to chuck off.

The hour now was still early, but Café Cassit was already teeming. Old journalists, aspiring actresses, writers drinking their mud coffees in the waning half light, old actors strutting their practiced young walks, young soldiers on furlough. The early theatergoers, too, had already taken their seats at the front tables, to catch a glimpse of actors as they made their way to the Cameri Theater. A tall Moroccan in a blue T-shirt sat at the corner, writing in a notebook.

Two waiters came in, for the night shift. Leibele Shiffler, at seventy-two the oldest waiter at Cassit, peered into my face. "Is that you? David?" Since I had last seen him, seven years ago, his hair had turned completely white.

"No," I said. "It's not."

Ruthy said, "He came to his father's funeral, from Canada."

Leibele shifted his weight from foot to foot. "I . . . I am really sorry for . . . for you. He was a . . . a good man."

"Yes," I snapped. "A real tzaddik." A virtuous holy man.

I gave Leibele my order and he shuffled away.

More people kept coming, calling out to one another and waving their hands.

Ruthy said, "They will never catch him, these Moroccans in the police. Last year someone stole my car radio. You think they even bothered to look? It was probably their friends in the HaTiqva quarter that did it anyway."

"So what do you want me to do?"

"Go and ask questions, you know, look around the store, like they taught you in the army—"

I swiped some hummus off Ehud's plate, saying nothing.

"You learned tracking also," Ruthy went on obstinately, "besides the other things."

Yeah. The other things. "Well I am not investigating anything and I'm not doing any play."

"What play?" said Ehud.

I swiped more hummus off his plate and told him briefly about the will, Mr. Gelber, my father's request, and the forty-five-day deadline. I didn't mention *Golyatt* and the sonnets.

"But he wants to fly back to Canada tomorrow," Ruthy said, "to his girlfriend. So he won't do what his father asked."

The policeman was right. She had a big mouth.

"Oh," Ehud said, "I almost forgot. Your girlfriend just called. Jenny." He removed his glasses and rubbed them on a napkin. "She said you should call her."

The roar of the street intensified. The tall Moroccan ambled to the back toward the wall-phone, stepping around someone seated on the floor slurping leftover gefilte fish from a plate. I saw it was Ittamar, the beggar from the police station.

"All right," I said. "Anything else she said?"

"No. Only that you should call when you're finished with the will and things." Once more he looked at me, then at Ruthy, blinking slowly, insistently.

Ruthy said to me, "That's her name? Jenny?"

"Yes. She's Polish." I didn't know why I was telling her this. What did she care where Jenny came from? "It's English for Zhenia."

There was another short silence.

Presently a thin waiter came by and squeezed my shoulder, furtively. Then Chetzkel's son, a bald strapping fellow who said something about his father and mine. How, once, together with Paltiel Rubin, they had sneaked an Arab or maybe a Ye-menite into a Purim party of the old Tel Aviv *bohema*, for a lark.

From the other end of the café a high-pitched voice began to lament the rise of Menachem Begin in the polls, and of his right-wing coalition, the Likkud. Other voices rose, vehe-mently, in opposition.

"Listen to them," Ruthy said. "Talk, talk, is all they do."

I said nothing. It was no longer any business of mine.

After a while Ehud said, "What play is this, *The Debba*? I never heard of it."

My order had arrived: lamb ribs steaming under tahini sauce, a plate of *foule* with roasted eggplant, and a large bowl of lentil soup. I dug in.

I said, "The lawyer said it was staged once, in 1946, in Haifa."

More people came in, smoking and laughing.

"Anyway, I am not going to stage any play."

Leibele had also brought me a Maccabee beer bottle, without my asking, and I now drank it down. The lights across the street had begun to oscillate in little fuzzy circles.

"No, really," Ruthy said. "I mean, your father wanted you to do it. How can you say no?"

"So what if he wanted?"

I gobbled my lentil soup and sopped the green muck at the bottom with a pita. My stomach felt as if a huge beast had lodged itself between my heart and my groin. I kept eating. It was so good to eat, to plug the hole that felt as if it could never be filled.

"Really," Ruthy said. "Maybe it's a good play? Did you read it already?"

"No."

"Ehud can help, too. He doesn't do theater anymore but he knows everybody—"

"I don't need him to do me any more fucking favors," I said.

When Ehud and I joined Unit 508, it had twenty-two active members and fourteen reservists. Officially the unit did not exist, and so it was referred to as Sayeret Almonit—the Anonymous Recon, and its members, as Almonim—the Anonymous Ones. Our job was to do the necessary dreck, "so the rest of the Jews can live cleanly."

Doing dreck meant killing key individuals in Arab countries in times of non-war so that war, when it came, would be shorter and less costly for us. In my father's day, these cross-border killings were done by talented Haganah amateurs called the Mista'aravim—literally, those who act like Arabs; but after the State was born, everything became formalized and even dreck had to be taught in special courses. The one I took lasted six months and was held in the Sayeret's base near Jerusalem. There were three other trainees besides me: Ehud, like me an ex-paratrooper and a Tel Avivi boy; Yerov'am (Yaro) Ben-Shlomo, a kibbutznik and ex–infantry man; and Tzafi Margolis, an ex–naval commando from Natanya. On our first day, Colonel Shafrir gathered the four of us in the base's canteen, and gave us a short speech. "Everyone in the army, including yourselves, no matter where you served, is taught how to kill in groups. Each of you has had experience in this. But here you'll be taught how to kill alone, without help. Anyone who thinks he can't do it better step forward now, before it's too late."

None of us did. What did he think, that he'd scare us? Killing was killing, whether together with others or alone.

Wasn't it?

The course had three parts. The first two months, in between lessons in Arab dialects and Arab proverbs, we drove twice a week to the morgue at Tel Aviv's Hadassah Hospital, where the chief pathologist, Dr. Pinchas Munger, taught us about the human body and how it could be killed. (We called him "Dr. Mengele," which pissed him off greatly—he, too, had been to Auschwitz, where he was a bunkmate of Ehud's father.) The rest of the time we practiced using small arms, sharpshooting, hand-to-hand combat, and silent killing under the tutelage of a wiry Yemenite sergeant major who had once been a ritual slaughterer. (We practiced on dogs—their eyes are the closest to human eyes.) Toward the end we also got

a week's instruction in nerve agents and toxins, by a section
head from the chemical warfare center in Ness-Tziona. Today
this is a major part of every takedown course. But back in 1966
we were the first ones to get it.

The following two months, having dispensed with the raw
technicalities of dreck, we studied what Colonel Shafrir called
self-support skills: more sessions with the judo and karate nuts
from the Wingate Institute; lots of practice with two Tel Aviv
pickpockets and an active burglar from Yaffo (the latter lessons
we had together with a dozen Mossad trainees); fieldcraft,
both urban (mainly tailing) and rural (mainly tracking); and
finally, to our great surprise, we received acting lessons from
Re'uven Kagan, the HaBimah director and famed disciple of
Stanislavsky who taught us how to "get into a role" so as to
dispense with the need for disguises.

And of course there were the obligatory weekly Bible lessons, taught by Colonel Shafrir himself. "So you never forget
what you do all the dreck for." He thumped on the black-
bound volume. "God's own *Mein Kampf!*"

We laughed uneasily, dutifully.

We all hated the Bible lessons. But none of us shirked them.

The last two months were live exercises. Some we did in
teams, but most we did alone. We burglarized police stations
across the border (I did Qalqilia, Ehud did Amman) to retrieve
an item (mine was a razor blade) placed there the day before
by Colonel Shafrir; we simulated takedowns of government
clerks in Damascus and Cairo with Shafrir taking confirming
pictures alongside; and finally, in the last week, each of us had
to take down a live enemy target (for which the PM had to
issue a special "black" permit), with confirmation done a day
later by an Intel patrol.

We were all a bit apprehensive about this part, like pilots before their first solo flight. But after all the practice we'd had, it was almost a letdown. (Mine was a major in the Jordanian police in East Jerusalem, a nobody, whom I did with a pencil-knife in a café's washroom not three streets away from the Wailing Wall. He was short and thin and hardly struggled at all—it was easy. But I had probably eaten something bad at the café, because I later threw up for half an hour.)

My father must have been informed of my progress, because the morning after my final test, when I arrived home to sleep, he pulled a bottle of Stock 777 out of the cupboard and poured me a glass; then he poured himself one, too.

"*Lechayim*," he said as he tossed back the cognac. To life.

I echoed him sheepishly, and drank up.

I waited for him to say something else, perhaps to congratu-late me; but he just poured himself another glass of cognac, none for me.

"Go," he said at last, "go see Ruthy. You need to."

When I returned to the barracks in the morning, I saw Ehud sitting cross-legged on his bed, his face white, reading a book in English—a collection of plays.

His cheeks were etched with deep scratches, one cheek nearly raw.

I asked him stupidly how it had gone.

Ehud grunted and turned the page with shaking fingers.

"What you reading?" I asked, more stupidly.

"Antidote to Shafrir's fucking *Mein Kampf*," Ehud snarled. "Now can you leave me alone?"

The following week we graduated. It was a short ceremony, and an odd one. Unlike any other army graduation, no parents or girlfriends were allowed. We gathered, the four of us, in the canteen at the Sayeret's base, wearing long khaki pants and white shirts. Colonel Shafrir opened a 777 bottle, then brought out a photo album and showed us faded pictures of members of his family who had gone with Hitler. "You also have such albums?"

We nodded uncomfortably, avoiding looking at one another. What the hell was that about? Of course we had. Everyone did.

Shafrir thumped on the album with both hands. "From now on, let the goyim have such albums! No more for us!" He pinned our ranks on. "Now go do clean dreck!"

We laughed hysterically. Then we all got quite drunk.

It was about midnight when Ruthy, Ehud, and I left Café Cassit.

I had wanted to leave earlier, but the ceaseless stream of old actors, ancient pre-State fighters, and strangers kept passing by the table, shaking me by the shoulder and squeezing my hand surreptitiously, before scurrying away.

I hazily remember Leibele recounting to me in a trembling whisper how he had served my father a cup of Turkish coffee twenty-nine years ago, the morning after my father had slain Abu Jalood. "Black," Leibele mumbled into my ear, as if revealing a first-rate secret. "With *hel*." Cardamom seeds.

I tried to concentrate on my food, but he kept muttering into my ear. "His hand, steady, like that." He demonstrated discreetly, extending coffee-stained fingers.

Someone, a nondescript ancient with a leathery neck, whispered into my other ear, "His friend, the poet, they got in forty-eight. Now him."

Someone else said something about the police.

"Police, shmolice. *He'll* take care of it now. Like Isser taught him." The ancient slid a knobby forefinger across his goiter and patted my shoulder delicately, like a woman.

My stomach heaved.

"Nobody knows if it's an Arab," Ehud said.

"*'Esma mini,*" the ancient said in Arabic. Listen to me. "He came back, and no mistake."

"They remember," Leibele said to me. "They never forget."

We drove home in silence. The light switch at the bottom of the staircase didn't work, and so we climbed the steps in the darkness, silent still.

"Look, the door's open," Ruthy said. "You forgot—"

A black shadow burst out of the apartment and hurtled toward the stairs.

I received a fleeting impression of dark pupilless eyes, and a tight mouth under a bristling sparse mustache; a rancid smell came in my nose: old sweat and pungent spices; an almost animal smell. Then a huge hairy paw came from somewhere and crashed into my ear, and I found myself on the topmost stair, legs spread wide. With my arms flailing helplessly, I began to roll.

Ruthy screamed.

"Dada!"

I saw Ehud kick with the edge of his left foot over my head, twice.

The shadow stumbled, half racing, half tumbling down the stairs, clasping something under its armpit. Without thinking I clutched its arm and tried to drag it down. It kept going, immensely strong.

A white envelope fell out, fluttering, into the stairwell. I snatched at it. The smaller envelope slipped out and glided all the way down, like a white square butterfly.

At that moment Ehud sprawled over me, legs akimbo, and we both rolled down, from stair to stair. I grabbed at the rail and felt it scraping at my wrist as it evaded my grasp.

"Dada! Uddy!"

Ehud held on to my belt, like a paratrooper whose own parachute had failed to open. Desperately I tried to hook my thumb on the railing and reach for the large envelope with the other four fingers.

Thirty feet below, the shadow paused. Its eyes flashed briefly as it looked up, staring right at me. Just then my thumb caught one of the spindles and was nearly wrenched out.

When I looked down again the shadow was gone.

Ruthy screamed, "Did you see? A fucking burglar!"

Hissing and cursing, she disentangled us. "How's your leg, Uddy?"

"I'm okay," Ehud said, grim-faced with shame at his infirmity.

Doors began to open. Mr. Tzukerman, wearing red pajamas and carrying a black shoe by its tip, stared wildly at us, his pink mouth working. "Nazis!" he shouted. "Murderers!"

Mr. Farbel looked up from the first floor. "Anybody need help?"

"No," I said.

"What did he take?" Ruthy said.

"Nothing," I said, clasping the large envelope to my body.

But a moment later, when I went down to look, the little envelope with my father's letter to me was gone.

Back at the apartment I sat at the kitchen table and gulped down some tepid tea that Ruthy had made with hot water straight from the tap.

"Call the police!" Ruthy hissed at me. "What're you waiting for?"

When I didn't get up, she marched to the phone and dialed.

I heard Amzaleg's voice rasping tinnily.

"No," Ruthy said, "they took nothing, but—"

Amzaleg's voice squawked further.

Ruthy snapped, "What do you mean, what do I want? Maybe it's connected to the murder?"

The receiver squawked.

"Connected how?" Ruthy hollered. "*Connected how?* Maybe they don't want him to do this play? He has only six weeks—"

Squawk.

Ruthy cursed Amzaleg in Arabic and hung up. "Lazy Moroccan beasts. He said if they didn't take anything else to call him in the morning. They probably open only at ten." She sat beside me. "Why do you think the burglar wanted it, this play?"

I shook my head. The jet lag, and now this odd burglary, somehow combined to reproduce in me the same queer black sensation I used to get before a takedown, when the past merged into the future and both dimmed into nothingness until only the present remained, hard and monstrous and clear.

Ehud muttered, "Maybe he grabbed the first thing he saw, when we came—"

"From under the sofa?" Ruthy said.

There was a long silence.

Ruthy said, "You think it's the same one that—that killed him?"

"'*Ana 'aref,*" I said in Arabic. What do I know?

Ruthy whispered, "Maybe, like my mother said, it did come back, you know, like the stories from forty-eight—"

"Shit in yogurt!"

"Leave him alone," Ehud said to Ruthy, then turned to me. "Put it someplace safe. Tomorrow I'll make you photocopies."

Toward the end of May '67, two weeks before the Six-Day War started, Ehud and I crossed over into the Sinai for a couple of dreck jobs: I to take down the operations officer of the Bir Gafgafa airfield, and Ehud the chief of radar maintenance on Um Marjam hill, five miles to the north. We had gone together, dressed as Bedouins, via the Gaza Strip, then hitchhiked south on an Egyptian fuel truck, paying the driver with hashish. But because we walked the last few dozen kilometers across sand dunes, we were late by two days, and on the morning of June 5, within five kilometers of our target, we heard the roar of planes and saw Mirage jets with Stars of David on their wings streaking overhead and diving onto the radar station on the hilltop.

Ehud kicked at the sand. "These fuckers! They couldn't hold off until we finished?"

As if anyone in the Israeli Air Force even knew we existed.

Now there was nothing to do but wait; finally, a day and a half later, we saw the advance jeeps of the Armor Recon with their back-mounted recoilless guns driving down the Bir Gaf-gafa road. Ehud and I slid down the sand dune, in our Bedouin galabiehs, our palms raised with the fingers spread in the traditional gesture of Birkat Cohanim, the Blessing of the Priests, singing HaTiqva at the top of our voices, to make sure we wouldn't be shot.

In the first jeep, to our surprise, we saw Mooky Zussman and Yonathan Avramson, also Alliance High School boys. They didn't ask any silly questions about our Bedouin clothes, just fed us combat rations and gave us a lift to Um Marjam hill, where the Egyptian radars had just been toasted and where, until the airfield became operational again, the Sinai sector command would be stationed.

It was a windswept gravelly hill with one shallow incline and one steep shoulder, on whose peak a Hawk anti-aircraft missile battery was already operating. A platoon of Golani infantry reservists was to arrive any day for sentinel duty, but for now the Armor Recon unit was it. And to fend off boredom, while waiting for our ride north on a Hercules, Ehud and I joined them.

By that time, the Egyptian army was broken—thirty thousand Egyptian soldiers perished in the sand, and the remainder, mainly poor *fellaheen* who had been drafted against their will, threw off their shoes and tried to give themselves up, begging for water. But our sentinels, by direct order of the Hawk-base commander, chased them away: stragglers still carried arms and were considered treacherous.

On the third day, a few hours before Ehud and I were to drive down to the airfield to fly north, seven haggard skeletons appeared in the morning mist at the foot of the hill, and for several hours their thin voices wafted up, their pleas for water interrupted only for prayers, which they called out in a Masri accent, just like that of the muezzin at Hassan Ali mosque in Cairo, where I had once holed up after a dreck job. The beseeching voices wafted at us in the canteen, in the latrine, in the tent—just about everywhere. Once, Mooky Zussman shot long Uzi bursts from the cliff's edge over the stragglers' heads to chase them away, but their thirst was stronger than their fear and none left. Finally, unable to stand the unending pleas, I overruled both Ehud and Mooky and called down to the stragglers in Masri to come up to the water tanker.

I was helping a thin Egyptian boy-soldier hold my mess tin to what had remained of his mouth when the last skeleton in the line pulled from under his rags a Carl Gustav, and, cussing in high-pitched Arabic, shot Mooky Zussman in the stomach from a distance of five feet. The stuttering CaG swung on in a wide arc. More soldiers fell. When the barrel began to swing in my direction I nearly welcomed it, tensing my stomach to receive the bullet, but just then a sweaty khaki lump bounded off my hip into the line of fire—Ehud Reznik—and, spitting and hissing, caught the bullet in his right thigh. At that exact moment the top of the shooting skeleton's head blossomed. From where he sat slumped in a pool of pinkish water, Mooky Zussman had shot him once, under the chin, just before he died. And as the other skeletons fell to their knees, raising their hands in wailing supplication, Ehud slowly hobbled from one to the next, and with precision emptied one Uzi magazine after another into their upturned faces. The camp commander, his face lathered, came running out of his tent, heard what happened, and punched me in the mouth. I didn't even try to resist.

Two hours later Ehud and I were finally driven in a jeep to the airfield below—I accompanied by a military policeman, Ehud lying silent on a litter among the dead soldiers and sacks of mail in the back. From Bir Gafgafa we were flown in a dusty Hercules north: Ehud to Tel HaShomer Hospital; the eleven dead to the Sdeh Dov morgue; and I to military HQ in Tel Aviv, to stand trial.

My trial for disobeying a direct order and endangering the troops was held the next day, presided over by the Hawk camp commander himself. (He insisted that I had been under his jurisdiction when I committed my crime.) The prosecutor, an old reserve major who had once served under my father, apologized to me twice during his summary speech, saying he was only doing his duty. The young defense counsel spoke confusedly of the Bible, and the Prophets, and other such shit in yogurt. I did not bother to listen. The presiding colonel then informed me that I had to serve thirty-five days in Kele' 'Arba',

Military Prison Number 4, where I was to report that same evening on my own, after doing my duty to the fallen's kin. ("You tell them, not me.") Then, as he was signing the jail papers, he added, "And you are lucky your father is who he was, or I would stick you in for five years."

When I left the courtroom, the prosecutor offered me a lift, but I refused. Instead, I walked in the noon heat all the way to Mooky Zussman's home, a dusty two-room apartment on the third floor of an ancient building near the old Tel Aviv harbor. Mooky's father, thin and yellow in overlarge striped pajamas, offered me a cup of Nescafé with Tnuva milk, and tried to pat my hand shakily with his palm, while his wife wept in the toilet, helping Mooky's little brother, Oded, take down his pants.

Yonathan's parents were luckily abroad (they had emigrated to British Columbia), so it was the Israeli consul in Vancouver who gave them the news.

The other nine had come from one kibbutz in the Galilee. A jobnik colonel took it upon himself to let their parents know, so I wouldn't be late for jail.

Upon my release from Military Prison Number 4, I hitch-hiked back to base and had a long talk with Colonel Shafrir, at his request. That is, he talked and I listened, standing at immobile attention in his small heat-choked office while outside the window some rowdy bluebirds cackled in the sycamore tree. I forget what he said, exactly. Nobody could fault me, he said. This was the difference between us and them, he said. He was sure my father was proud of me, he said. (My father never said a word about the entire affair. My mother said nothing either but cried for an entire day, hugging me at length and shaking her head whenever I asked her why she cried.) "Your father was once like that, too," Shafrir said. "And I, too, was like this," he went on, "before I learned my lesson. You have now learned yours. We must do some things the Prophets would not approve of, if we want to keep these sons of whores away from Dizzengoff. You hear? So don't you ever fuck up again! For your own good, Dada, and for ours! All of us! We know them, not from today! You hear?"

He hit at my shoulder with a balled fist, hard.

"Yes sir," I said, staring straight ahead.

"Fuck this *yessir* shit! Get out of here before I get mad! Get out! Dismissed!"

He saluted me and I saluted back, slowly.

Ehud, with his bum leg, could not return to the Unit, and until the end of his service was posted to a staff job in army HQ in Tel Aviv. I went back to doing dreck, and over the next three and half years, until my release, didn't fuck up once—even though my nightmares became steadily worse. At first I tried to ignore them, but finally in 1970, after a routine dreck job in Cairo, I didn't cross back, just lay low in Heliopolis for two weeks, drinking coffee and playing backgammon with street idlers in the City of the Dead. Finally, a week before my five-year service was over, I returned to base, refused to sign for an additional period, hitchhiked back to Tel Aviv, and applied for a visa for Canada. (My father objected terribly; my mother said not a word.) Uncle Yitzchak cosigned it, and the visa arrived quickly.

A week later, I left.

There's a photograph of Ehud and me on Um Marjam hill at night, against the full moon, our hair blowing in the wind. He stands with his legs spread wide. I tower over him by a

head, my hand grabbing onto his shoulder, as if he's planted
in the soil and I must hold on to him so as not to be blown
away. Behind us is a shadow—the Thompson tent where
the Armor Recon guys are sleeping, unseen but still alive. A
darker shadow at its side may be a jackal, or perhaps a wild
dog, one of those the Egyptians had left behind. And high
above it all, round and jagged, floats the moon, like a peep-
hole in the sky out of which some invisible jailer is watching
over the birthplace of the evil scribblings that begat all the
blood.

Some time later during the night I awoke from a black dream,
my hair on end.

It was a dream I had never had before: I was standing in the
moonlit yard of Har Nevo school and my father was calling to
me from within a shallow hole in the ground, his tongue loll-
ing through his blood-filled mouth, as he struggled to make his
voice heard. I tried to get down on my knees to hear him, but
my Nomex coveralls were so tight, it was as if my body had
turned to wood. And when at long last I managed to kneel on
the gravel, my father had vanished and I inexplicably saw before me the black snout of some beast leering at me, its mouth
dripping blood and froth.

I awoke with a snarl. For a terrifying moment I imagined
that the black beast had touched its snout to my face before
retreating to watch me from afar.

I stared wildly about me.

Ruthy, in a white T-shirt and panties, was sitting on the edge
of the sofa bed, her freckled arms hugging her chest, her nose
a silver dot in the moonlight.

She said, "Did you read it already? I can't sleep."

For a moment I did not know what she was talking about.
"The play," she said.

I hissed at her to go back to bed, before Ehud woke up.

She said with derision, "Don't worry. One time, he's gone the whole night."

"Well, *I* have to sleep. The funeral—"

"So you'll sleep on the plane. Come on. Don't be a louse."

As we sat down at the kitchen table, Ruthy said in a tight little voice, "You want water with raspberry juice, something?"

"No," I said.

With the tips of her fingernails she extracted from the envelope several yellowing pages written densely, and held one up before my eyes.

"Is it . . . his handwriting?"

I extended my hand to take the page from her, but she held back. *"Is it his?"*

"Yes," I said. "It's my father's writing."

Maybe she had expected to see Paltiel Rubin's scrawl, but the handwriting was unmistakably my father's: the same angular aleph, the curling lammed, the down-thrusting gimmel. The pages had probably been torn from a copybook similar to the ones I later used in Har Nevo school—similar to the one in which I am writing now.

A bulky shape in blue-white pajamas appeared in the kitchen door. Ehud.

He looked at Ruthy, rubbing his eyes, then at me. "What you guys doing?"

"Reading the play," Ruthy said. "Come, Uddy, sit here. Move a little, Dada. Let him see, too."

Ehud sat slowly down. "How you feeling?"

"Okay."

I kept my head low and aligned the pages with my fingertips; I felt a slight tingle, as if I had just touched a live electrical wire, or toggled a pencil-knife's safety off.

I turned the first page.

The Debba, it said. No name of author, no date.

Without further ado we began to read.

It was a play in four acts, taking place in the thirties or for-
ties, but written in flowery, turn-of-the-century prose. The first
act presents Yissachar HaShomer, the Sentinel. Yissachar is a
farmer by day and a sentinel by night, when he must guard
the fields against the marauding animals of Eretz Yisrael, who
consider the land theirs.

The play begins with Yissachar plowing his field, Bible in
hand, against the backdrop of Mount Gilbo'a.

When Yissachar's horse dies in harness, he sings to it a song
of mourning ("O friend and companion, on whose back I rode
in my ancestors' fields, who plowed with me the bosom of my
motherland").

Behind a rock lurks the Debba, an enigmatic Arab hyena
that can walk like a man. The Debba has been charmed out of
its lair by Yissachar's song, and by his voice.

When Yissachar has finished singing, the Debba uncurls and
turns into a giant of a man, offering to pull Yissachar's plow in
place of the horse.

"You have charmed me, O son of man," says the stranger in
the striped blue-black *abbaya*, "against my will you have turned
me from all I know; against my will I shall help you cut the furrows of my cradle, this land."

While he pulls at the plow he tells Yissachar stories of the
birds and the beasts, and Yissachar tells him of his ancestors,
and of his new wife, Sarah. They then sing a song of friendship
and the Debba reveals to Yissachar the secret of his lair.

"Come to me, son of man," he sings to him, "tonight, so I
can teach you how to speak with all the beasts, sing with the
birds."

Once again, the two sing a song of friendship, and Yissachar promises to visit the Debba, whose secret dwelling he now knows.

When the sun sets, the Debba prepares to slink off into its lair, just as Yissachar's beautiful young bride enters, carrying a basket with food for her husband at his plow.

She laments with him the death of the horse ("O gentle beast that carried me to my wedding canopy, that helped my groom sow bread in the earth's womb") and ends with a prayer to God to open her own womb, for she is barren.

"Don't turn the pages so fast," said Ruthy.

While Yissachar eats his pita and olives, looking at the mountains painted on the backdrop, there is a brief encounter between the Debba and Sarah.

She asks, "Why have you this shiny pelt that asks to be caressed?"

And he replies, "O beautiful daughter of man, whose skin is thin yet hard as steel, whose eyes are soft as morning light yet burning as the sun who gives it, why ask you that which no Beast can forbear?"

He then curls into his animal form and runs off, while Sarah slowly backs off, to stand by Yissachar.

The curtain falls.

"Wait," said Ruthy. "I am going to take a pee. Don't turn the pages."

Ehud and I reread the last page, not looking at each other, until she returned.

In the second act, two other farmer-settlers, arriving for a day's work in the field, discuss with Yissachar the predations of wild animals, who slaughter the chickens and eat the crops. After dividing the night watch among them, they debate what to do about the Beasts.

"Let us cleanse the land of putrid beastly stench," says 'Ittay, brandishing a scythe. "Let sons of man make pure these gentle hills—"

Ruthy made an inarticulate sound deep in her throat.

"—the cradle of our ancestors, of all impure and foreign breed."

The other farmer, Yochanan, assents. "Only in toil," he thunders, "shall man's son conquer, only in sweat shall he mark his claim; only those who sowed the land have gained the right to reap."

But Yissachar is doubtful. It is clear he is torn between his love for his people, and his sympathy for the Beasts whose land he cannot help but usurp. "Why do you press me thus to kill?" he asks 'Ittay. "For is the sin not great enough, to chase those whom the land hath borne? To cleanse the lairs of gentle folk, whose only crime was happenstance, to be here born while we meanwhile were gone?"

"So wilt thou leave thy land to beast, to fowl, to insect, and to thorns?" asks 'Ittay. "Lovest thou thy people more, pray tell, or lovest thou something else still more?"

The three then sing a complicated song in which prayers from the Siddur and whole sentences from the Pentateuch are interweaved.

"Look! Look at this," Ruthy yelped in delight. "This line here. Where it takes the Avinu Malkeinu prayer and turns it around and connects it with the Kaddish, and then here, look—"

"Yes, yes," Ehud said, infected by her mood. "And also here, where—"

"Quiet," I hissed. "Let me read." My stomach had begun to growl. I turned the page.

The two friends grapple with Yissachar and shout into his face, "Tell now, tell now, soft-hearted louse, whom you love most, for know we must, ere night, when you stand guard on home and field."

Yissachar breaks free and runs to and fro, in torment, waving his Bible. "The Beasts I love," he sings, "for they are blameless, but God's command hath put my heart in chains; and now upon me love has no more power, since God has called me to do battle, in His name."

At last, as his wife Sarah steals across the backdrop dressed in black, Yissachar cries out, "O listen, friends and kin and folk, and know ye that I loved thee best. I loved the truth, and justice, yea; but thee, my folk, and God, cursed God, I loved still more, more still."

Ruthy's breath came out in a whoosh. "What language! It sounds just like Paltiel Rubin, in *Golyatt*, when the holy sheikh—" she stopped and looked at me sidelong, chewing her lower lip.

"No," I said in a tight voice. "It's different."

Ehud rubbed his nose, saying nothing.

We read on.

With Sarah still gliding at the back, the three sons of man plan their attack on the lair of the Beasts, whose whereabouts Yissachar (after a speech filled with anguish) has now revealed. At dawn, they whisper together, they shall cleanse the land. Yissachar then launches into a declamatory song, ending with, "My soul forgone, son of man am I no more, but truly brother to the beast, whom slay tonight I must."

As Yissachar sharpens a sword, the light dims; and as the moon rises over Mount Gilbo'a, Sarah is seen waiting by the rock. The Debba suddenly looms before her, and for a long moment he and Sarah stand close together, looking into each other's eyes without touching, without speaking, in the light of the moon.

Sarah speaks first. "Who art thou, man or beast, that hath into my eyes so plunged, and of my soul so rudely taken?" She tries to step back, but cannot.

The Debba then speaks in a voice full of thunder and anguish. "Nay, 'tis thou," it says, "who has my heart envelop'd, in web of silk, and whispers, and deceit. You know that I forever hence must love thee, thee daughter of man, thee shameless, thee Lilith."

"Hey!" said Ehud. "That's the Abu Jalood tall tale—"

"Quiet," I said, my eyes on the scribbled sheet. "Let me read now."

I couldn't lift my eyes from the page. The lines throbbed, the words pulsated, the entire page sang.

We went on reading.

The second act ends with Sarah and the Debba falling slowly into each other's arms, and as the moon disappears over Mount Gilbo'a they sink behind the rock, wrapped in the Debba's Arab cloak.

"*Yechrebetto!*" said Ruthy in awe, lapsing into the common Arab curse. May his house fall down! "Now I see why they had the bedlam in Haifa."

I said nothing. My head throbbed. My jaws ached from clenching. I could see the scene before me, in Haifa of thirty years ago, enfolding on the stage; then the furor of the crowd, the boiling wrath—

"Come on!" Ruthy raked my arm with her nails. "I want to read!"

Ehud rubbed his temples and said nothing.

I turned the page.

The third act begins with a whispered dramatic dialogue among the three friends, who are crawling toward the Debba's lair at dawn, led by Yissachar, his sword drawn.

"To cleanse we must, for kin and folk, the bosom of this ancient land," hisses Yissachar. "And if we beasts thereby become, so be it, yea—"

"Amen," "Amen," his two friends whisper in return.

As they approach the beast's lair ("a mound upstage") the lights dim further, and a spotlight frames Sarah, who is standing at the rock, singing in pain.

"Two secrets in my heart do dwell," she sings, "and choose I must, for in my choice lies death, for one or other, in my hand their fate. Shall I reveal unto the beast the secret of my man, and doom the one that God hath given me to wed, and with him, yea, my folk? Or shall I stay forever still and slay my love, the earthen-born, and doom my heart to hell?"

Ruthy got up and drank some water straight from the tap. "You want something?" she asked.

"No," I said.

"Me neither," said Ehud.

We read on.

The light framing Sarah dims now, and the spotlight illuminates Yissachar and his two friends, who are now almost upon the

Debba's lair. "My heart lies still, still lies the heart," Yissachar sings, "for beast I am forevermore. Forsooth when morning comes I shall to beast and fowl speak as kin, for soul of man have I no more."

Once more the light changes, and Sarah is lit. Her belly is shown to bulge—she is pregnant.

"Already?" said Ruthy. "It takes longer than that."

"It's a play," I said.

Sarah then sings at length, thanking God and cursing him at the same time, for opening her womb and for sending her the Debba. It is a song in the style of a Piyut, a Sephardic laudatory prayer, in the complex meter of two Shva'im and a stressed syllable. Her song weaves into that of Yissachar and his two friends, and as the light begins to rise, signifying the dawn, Sarah's song culminates in a shout of anguish and anger that mingles with that of the attackers, who now rush the Debba's lair.

The light explodes into whiteness, the Debba rises, his blue-black *abbaya* spread wide; then the light turns to black. A long scream is heard, and the curtain falls.

At that moment the phone rang.

"Screw it," Ruthy said, and went to get it.

After a moment she came back. "For you," she said curtly.

For a frantic moment I thought that Jenny had called; but it was only Yitzchak Kramer, my father's cousin in Canada. His voice was hardly audible; he, too, could barely hear me over the fuzzy echo on the line. I managed to say I was all right.

Yes, I had told all the family (who were all? There were now only Uncle Mordechai, Margalit, and me) how sorry they were in Canada. No, they hadn't caught him yet.

And no, I said. I was coming back right after the funeral.

I spoke briefly with Aunt Rina (yes, I said, I was dressing warmly), then hung up and bounded back to the kitchen.

The curtain rises on the fourth act, where we see Yissachar in torment. He has betrayed his friend the Debba, he sings, for the sake of his people, and now his heart is dead.

Yissachar's two friends, standing at his side, respond as one: "There is no place for love nor friends if you desire to aid thy folk; and truth, and honor, yea, must too be slain, so future sons and daughters of man shall live amidst their homeland free."

As Yissachar sheathes his sword Sarah approaches, and in a flat voice tells him that she bears a child, not to him, but to her truest love, which he, her man, had just slain and with whose death her own heart had also died.

Yissachar emits a long cry, draws his sword and flings it to the ground, then flings his Bible after it. He and Sarah sing back and forth two different songs—he about his double shame, she about her lost love. The songs weave into each other, while the two friends, leaning on their spades, sing an accompanying refrain about the homeland now pure and free.

Yissachar's song rises by an octave. He lifts his hands in the traditional gesture of Birkat Cohanim, the Blessing of the Priests, and vows to raise the child as his own. "I shall raise him as my seed," he sings, "and teach him all the ways of man, and beast; and yet no man nor beast shall he become, but changeling: at his will shall he become whatever that his heart desires, and so perchance, shall he one day join men and beasts as one."

The curtain falls.

I assembled the yellowing pages with unsteady hands and inserted them into the envelope. At the back were half a dozen lined sheets speckled with staffs and musical notes. After glancing at them I inserted these, too, in the envelope and got to my feet.

None of us looked at each other. There was a long silence.

"I want her role, Sarah," Ruthy said in a low voice. "I don't care about anything else."

Ehud drew in a long breath, and let it out slowly.

"I am not doing any play," I said.

Ruthy hissed, "So in six weeks this will go to the State with the money and everything—"

"So it will go."

"—and then it'll never be produced . . ."

"So it won't."

Ehud looked at her, then at me.

"Good night," I said harshly, and went to bed.

For a long while I tried to postpone sleep as I desperately filled my mind with images of Toronto, and Jenny, and the snowy cold; but soon the black dreams reclaimed me and I plunged once more into the darkness where I extinguished life so that my forefathers' ancient fictions could live on.

But for the first time ever, as I tossed and wept, I glimpsed a white dot in the blackness, like glowing milk. The darkness seemed to part before it, as singing voices emanated from its milky incandescence, and for a brief, magical moment I felt my despair lift. Breathlessly I tried to approach the whiteness, to query it, but then the singing faded and I plunged back into the horror-filled black.

Jenny called at three-thirty in the morning.

Her soft voice wept in my ear. "When're you coming back?"

At first I didn't know who she was. *"Mah? Mah?"* I kept shouting in Hebrew into the receiver. What? What?

I had again dreamed of the fearful beast; only this time it had the flowing locks and mocking eyes of Paltiel Rubin, not my father.

"David! It's me, Zhenia!"

The beast retreated, laughing shrilly.

Jenny began to recite a new poem she had written specially for me, the night I had left; a soft cascade of iambic hexameters about forgiveness, and love. I interrupted her in a panic and in one long rush told her about the will and my father's request, and the deadline. The apartment break-in I left out; somehow it seemed too fantastic to mention. "No way!" I shouted hoarsely. "No way I'm going to stay and do this—this goddamn play."

There was a long silence.

Jenny said in a choked voice, "How long do you have if—if you want to—"

"Six weeks—but—" I rasped, "there is no way in hell—"

"But your father, he asked you to do that? For him?"

Jenny's father used to beat her, even rape her (that's what she said), in that little village near Ottawa where she was born. That's why she ran away from home at fifteen, like those other girls on Yonge Street. Yet when he was diagnosed with cancer six years later, she went to stay with him in the hospital for nearly a month, until his last moment. I couldn't understand it.

"I don't know if it's for him," I said. "Maybe it's for his friend." It was too complicated to explain over the phone.

Behind my back I could hear someone moving around in the bathroom, opening the water tap and closing it, then the medicine cabinet.

"Well, if it's for your father," Jenny whispered, "then it's something else, if it's for him—it's not like you are waking up at night with nightmares, and writing shit and—and—" She began to weep.

I felt a piercing panic, like I had every other time she cried over me, or for me.

"I . . . I'll call you after the funeral," I said, and hung up.

Ruthy emerged from the toilet, and without looking at me went back into the bedroom.

11

My father's funeral started half an hour late. People kept streaming in through the stone gateposts, in great silent clumps. Oldsters who could barely stand, and ancient theater actors, and here and there a closed-faced Labor Party hack. Men of Genesis, the founders. No one looked at me as they passed, as if they all shared some uneasy secret. But among them, here and there, I saw younger men, negligent and immobile, never staring at me directly, yet keeping me in their sight wherever I moved. As they turned their close-cropped heads, I could see the skin-colored Motorola earphone-plugs. Each man kept one hand free and one hand in his pocket, probably with the thumb on the radio clicker. There must have been at least eight of them, all in clicker contact.

I gawped at them. Were they here because of me? Or did they expect something to happen? I had made up my mind to go and ask when I felt a hand clap me on the back. "So, Duvid," said my uncle Mordechai. "You can't deign to go unshaven for a week? Even for your father?" He seemed shrunken, smaller than his wife, Margalit, at his side, whose long braid, I saw, had turned white; probably after '73, after their son's death. "It is not important," she whispered. "Only what's in the heart."

"Heart, shmeart," muttered my uncle. "In the shivah you don't shave."

More old people kept coming. Ehud said at my side, "I never knew he had so many friends."

"Fine friends," Uncle Mordechai said. "So where were they when he was alive?"

I glanced at him askance. Look who was talking: the man who had not talked to his brother for close to thirty years.

Not that I had much right to criticize.

I pointed out the surveillance teams to Ehud. "You have any idea why—"

"Well, what do you think, with your passport and everything."

I felt my face go red. A trained lone killer who had disobeyed orders and shown fatal pity, had been punished for it, and emigrated, and here he was back and not even a citizen anymore, and so not subject to any orders . . . What were they supposed to do? I would have had me followed also . . .

But why so many?

Then I felt the pain in my wrenched thumb, and recalled that someone did try to steal the play. I turned to Ehud and started to ask him if he thought there was a connection, but Uncle Mordechai shushed me as a rustle went through the crowd. Three girl soldiers in starched khaki had laid a circular wreath of white roses at the graveside. Pinned to the stems was a silk ribbon of white and blue, crossed with the tiny golden swords. A Gibbor Yisrael decoration. Hero of the People of Israel: the highest honor the Jewish state can accord its warriors. Less than two dozen have been accorded, three posthumously.

I stared at it. Ehud stared, too.

"Yeah," said Uncle Mordechai. "I knew this."

"We all knew," said Margalit.

I hadn't. Nor, apparently, had Ehud.

More people kept coming. I recognized Riva Yellin, Ruthy's mother, in her signature black Arab galabieh, and Re'uven Kagan, the theater director who had taught the Stanislavsky Method in my takedown course; then three emaciated old actors who had gained fame in my father's Purim plays; then a crowd of HaBimah actors; then five old Cameri directors; and Professor Gershon Tzifroni, the failed poet who, so they say, had written a biography of Paltiel Rubin that had to be withdrawn because of its scurrilous inaccuracies, and who now taught at Tel Aviv University. One by one they all nodded at me, their eyes furtive.

Ehud said, "It's like a reunion, almost."

A reunion of what?

The crowd grew thicker by the minute. The average age seemed about seventy, but sprinkled among them were the young tailers who kept eyeing me, oblivious to anyone else. I saw they all wore their shirts loose over their pants, regulation form, for easy draw of a gun holstered at the small of the back.

Uncle Mordechai said through the corner of his mouth, "Amnon Amzaleg tells me a *ganef* tried to steal your underwear last night. What'd you keep in it? Your money?"

"No," I said. "He tried to steal the play."

Uncle Mordechai's cheek twitched. "Did he—get it?"

"No. But the letter to me he got."

Margalit smiled at me tenderly and said I must know what was in the letter anyway. I didn't respond.

Uncle Mordechai muttered under his breath. Two jeeps had stopped on the chalk-marked gravel, and a knot of sunburned old men alighted. Several nodded at Uncle Mordechai, who didn't nod back. "Sons of whores, all of them," he said.

"Shush," said Margalit.

A whisper ruffled the dense crowd, like soft wind over reeds. The military Rabbi pulled the prayer shawl over his head.

Ehud said. "You have a prayer book?"

I shook my head. My nose, my throat, my eyes were heating up.

"Here." Uncle Mordechai put a frayed volume into my hand.

"'*El male' rachamim*—" God full of pity. The military rabbi began to chant.

Two dense lines of men, holding on to the handles of a large litter with a white bundle on it, shuffled forward step by small step. The farthest man on the left, I saw to my surprise, was Leibele, the waiter from Café Cassit; and at the front, side by side, shuffled Inspector Amnon Amzaleg, and Shim'on Gershonovitz himself, the director general of the Interior Ministry, his immense body and flat face unmistakable.

"Hi, I'm here," Ruthy said breathlessly into the back of my neck.

Uncle Mordechai pointed my finger at a line of prayer in the Siddur.

"—*HaGibborim, ve-HaNehedarim*—" The heroes, and the magnificent, sang the rabbi.

Slowly, the twelve pallbearers laid the litter on the ground, clumsily trampling the wreaths. All around them, from within the dense throng, the tailers kept staring to my right and to my left, never directly at me.

Overhead a flock of pigeons flew by, swooping over the crowd in a semicircle like an absurd honor guard, their wings clacking. For a brief moment all eyes followed them. Then the wind picked up and the birds were gone. Behind me the flag gave a series of sharp cracks, like a slow-firing machine gun. Two tailers snapped their hands toward the small of their backs, then retrieved them sheepishly. A few oldsters saluted in the old style, their elbows out. Their images wavered. My eyes seemed filmed over and my throat on fire. I coughed at length.

"Enough!" rasped Uncle Mordechai. "It's the Kaddish, now."

I felt the pages being turned. Other hands guided mine down the page.

"Here," said Inspector Amzaleg. "Start here. '*Yidgadel ve-Yitkadesh*—'"

I mumbled the ancient words. Through a haze I saw the litter with its bundle being lowered into the pit, so much like the one I had seen last night, in my nightmare.

To my eldest, my beloved . . .

"Here are your sunglasses," Ruthy whispered. "I brought them."

My father used to sing the Chad Gadya at the Passover Seder, his voice warm and strong and vibrant. I tried to recall it but could not. For some reason it filled me with panic. I put my old Ray-Bans on and wiped my cheeks underneath.

The soldiers stepped forward and hoisted their Galil rifles. There was a moment of awkward silence. Then the sound rolled.

"Fire!"

There was another loud crack. My father died nearly thirty years after his most memorable act; the army still remembered him, but his son could not.

I tried once more to resurrect my father's voice, but all around me was a rushing, deepening dark; I swayed and felt hands grab me, and then suddenly his voice came, hot-white and clear and soaring, raging at the death of men and beasts by the order of an evil book . . .

More hands held me. I shook them off and stood up straight, listening; and as the words I had read last night sang in me, like Jenny's hexameters, I felt my heart broaden and deepen, as the chanting words congealed into something else, akin to operational resolve.

"—Blessed be the True Judge," the military rabbi chanted.

One by one the theater people came by to shake my hand, looking away from me; then the merchants. None of the old party hacks did; they had all melted away after the Kaddish. Gershonovitz was nowhere to be seen either. Ruthy and Ehud also had left. Of the tailers only three remained, lean-

ing on the stone cemetery wall, indolently smoking, staring
into space.

How can I say no?

Leibele shook my hand at length, "You watch yourself, now,
David . . ."

Uncle Mordechai clucked his tongue at him but Leibele
held on to my hand, stared into my eyes, nodded, then shuffled
away. Through the corner of my eye I saw the tailers tense up.
One stubbed his cigarette and inserted his hand in his pocket,
and I saw his fingers move as he clicked away. I turned to see
what had caused it. From behind the grave site three old Arabs
in white *abbayas* shuffled forward. I recognized Mansour, the
sandal wholesaler, and Seddiqi, my father's ex-partner, who
now sold leather. Stooped and dried up and ancient, he was
leaning on a pair of aluminum canes. His *'akkal* had a green
filament in it, indicating he was a sharif, a direct descendant of
the Prophet Muhammad.

The third I did not recognize. Probably the winter-boot man.

"Any help thou needst," Mansour droned in flowery Arabic.
"Mine house is thy house, mine food thy food, mine water thy
water—"

"*Na'am, na'am,*" I muttered. Yes, yes.

My stomach heaved. I hadn't spoken to an Arab in seven
years.

The three tailers stared at the Arabs, then at me directly,
their eyes hard. Another tailer appeared in the cemetery's gate;
probably the team leader.

Seddiqi touched four fingers to his narrow forehead, mumbling something about noble souls going to sit in the bosom
of Allah forever. Between his thumb and forefinger I saw the
brown crescent tattoo, signifying he had been to Mecca, a
hajj.

The third Arab stood to the side, saying nothing, blinking.

I couldn't wait for them to leave. Arabs at my father's funeral. I couldn't blame the tailers, really.

Presently Uncle Mordechai took Margalit by the hand and walked to his jeep, with me following.

"I used to know him, Seddiqi, when he was still your father's partner," Uncle Mordechai said as we were driving to Mr. Gelber's office, now tailed by a white Toyota, "before he had to sell his share to your father, in thirty-six."

In 1936 the Arabs of Palestine, incensed at Jewish immigration, revolted, slaughtering Jews and British alike. Most ties between Arabs and Jews were then cut. The rebellion ended in 1939, after the British hanged a few Arab leaders and exiled others.

My uncle squinted into the windshield. "Seddiqi's father used to own a brickyard, the cinema in the Adjemi neighborhood— his brother published a poetry magazine—"

I clicked my tongue to show I didn't care about these ancient Arab histories—I wanted to ask about my father's army past—but my uncle paid no attention. "His brother died in forty-eight, near Jerusalem." He massaged his unshaven jaw. "But the Arabs are quiet now," he added, apropos of an unstated memory. "They are getting old."

"We are all getting old," Margalit said, "Only the young ones here can't grow old."

We drove the rest of the way in silence, but as we turned into Rothschild Boulevard my uncle growled, "But everyone came today, the bastards."

"Sure," said Margalit. "They all remember. How can they forget?"

I didn't have to ask what it was.

12

T WENTY-NINE YEARS AGO MY father had performed one feat
that everyone remembered.

It was during the War of Independence, in the attack on the
Castel, the obdurate Arab village that guarded the entrance
to Jerusalem, that my father's commando unit had finally cornered Abu Jalood, the mysterious gang leader who the tall
tales insisted could change at will into a Debba.

The Castel battle, as most battles are, was confused and
uncertain. My father's unit was cut off several times; other
times it seemed it was they who had cut off the village de-
fenders, the members of seven Arab gangs who had arrived
the week before, at Abu Jalood's behest. For the first time in
memory traditional enmity was set aside in the service of a
common cause.

The fight remained bitter to the end. Half my father's
friends died that night. Nachman Shein, who had written the
operetta *The Penny and the Moon*, was shot in the leg and a
month later died of blood poisoning in Jerusalem's Hadassah
Hospital. Tzvi Zilbershatz, who had played the Moneylender
in the operetta, fell on the steps of the mosque. Two character
actors were mortally wounded.

An hour before dawn, my father and Nachman Shein were
alone. The other men from their unit were stuck on the other
side of the mountain, where most of the burned Armed Per-
sonnel Carriers lie to this day. There was no moon, but several

houses were burning and by the light of the flickering fires they could see Abu Jalood's renowned blue *abbaya* flapping in the window, as the cornered enemy rushed hither and yon, oblivious to the bullets.

Several times my father and Shein tried to storm the house, but obstinate fire forced them back into their hiding place behind a clump of rocks. And all the while, as Shein wrote later in *Davar*, Abu Jalood was cursing them from within the *mukhtar's* house, hollering in a high-pitched, spirited voice.

Finally my father could bear the curses no longer. He rushed the house, broke the door with the butt of his Sten, and disappeared inside.

There ensued a terrific fight, with oaths, and shouts, and cries, and inhuman growls, and yelps of pain, and at long last, after what seemed like an hour, my father emerged, white as a fresh wedding bedsheet, holding up the famous blue *abbaya*, the long Turkish rifle, and, in his other hand, the long mustache he had just cut off the face of Abu Jalood.

About the same time the others, who had finished cleansing the other end of the village, joined forces with my father and Shein. As they entered the *mukhtar's* house, they found a mound of earth, with a crude wooden crescent on top. The house today is a restricted military zone: too many Arab agitators used to come and hold demonstrations there.

"I have just buried a noble enemy," my father said to his comrades. (This is corroborated by many.)

It has been frequently noted that my father himself had never given a single interview about the battle, though everyone else who had been there was most voluble about it.

"What happened, happened," he said.

Perhaps it was my father's refusal to elaborate, or maybe the legends already were circulating, but a great many Arabs refused to believe that the Jews had slain their hero in the Castel. Abu Jalood, many insisted, had not been killed but rather secretly captured. Others hinted that, breathing his last, their hero swiftly turned into a Debba and faded into the darkness whence he had come—and from where he would one day return to avenge his own blood, and that of his people.

I remember how, as children in Tel Aviv, we used to go poking sticks in dark attics and in sewage pipes, "looking for the Debba." There even flowered in the 1950s a pitiful little underground of Arab teenagers who went by the name of 'Ibnat-el-Jalood, who were caught planting crude nail bombs in the Egged bus station in Tzfatt. I can't remember what happened to them; probably got ten years.

The conquest of the Castel was later seen by many as the turning point in the battle for Jerusalem, and two military historians at Tel Aviv University even went so far as to claim that the death of Abu Jalood was the major turning point in the War of Independence itself. Without Abu Jalood to hold them together, the Arab gangs fell back into their old squabbling, fighting with one another for prestige, instead of fighting the attacking Jews. So that when Menachem Begin's forces launched an attack on Yaffo on the eve of the British departure, in 1948, the city fell like a ripe pomegranate into their hands.

After his memorable feat, my father could have had his pick of military postings. Some said he could have joined the general staff in some capacity or other. Others even mentioned politics. Yet not a year after, when the UN-sponsored cease-fire was signed, my father inexplicably returned to Tel Aviv, reopened his shoe store, and went back to selling shoes, winter boots, and—later, in the times of the Tzena', the Scarcity—even cobbling shoes himself.

I hazily remember how once Shim'on Gershonovitz him-self implored my father to accept some sort of position in the party, or perhaps in the Interior Ministry itself. I was young then and did not fully understand.

I was sitting in my father's store, my bare feet before me, waiting for him to glue a torn strap in my sandal, when Ger-shonovitz suddenly entered. He had left his official Lark out-side, two of its wheels on the curb.

He sat down beside me, his already fat behind taking up nearly the entire width of the seat.

"So, young man," he boomed at me, "you came to learn the trade?"

My father raised his head and gave the fat man a brief look, then returned to his hammering on the strap, which a moment before he had smeared with glue.

"No," I said, feeling foolish. "I came to fix—"

"What do you want, Shimmel?" my father asked. His voice was even, the kind he used when I had broken something and he came into my room for a reckoning.

Without any preliminaries Gershonovitz said something about the party now finalizing its list for the Knesset, and that certain committee members had mused about the dearth of old *chevermanim*—literally, brave boys—in the ranks, so he de-cided, why not—

"I told you a thousand times," my father said, "the answer is no."

I had gotten up to go outside, feeling in a confused way that perhaps this was something my father wanted to dis-cuss alone with Gershonovitz. But my father held up his hammer. "No, David, you stay right there. He will be leav-ing soon."

The neck of the fat man visibly darkened. "It's not as if you will do us any favors," he said. "But think of the State, and the things you could—" He stopped. "It's a waste," he said at last, speaking softly. "Such a waste. And for what?"

"That's enough," my father said. Then, to my surprise, he said, "If you want, I can give you sandals, size forty-eight. That's your size, no?"

Gershonovitz got up. "All right, Srulik," he said. "Do what you want. I told them, but they said go try one more—"

"Only twenty-three lirot," my father said. "For you, twenty-two."

Gershonovitz sat back on the bench, beside me. My father sat on the inclined bench where the customers put their feet up to be measured, and, his own legs widespread, fitted the big, bulbous feet with a pair of brown biblical sandals.

As the fat man was leaving, he paused at the door and pointed his thumb at me. "And he and his brother? Also no?"

I didn't know what he was talking about, but felt vaguely afraid.

My father did not raise his head. "When they grow up, yes."

I recall I felt a slight shiver.

"Ahh," said the fat man. "Good."

After he had left, I asked my father, "What did he—"

"Doesn't matter," my father said. "If you want, you can put your sandals on now."

Then he said he had just received two tickets for *Tfilla Zakka*—Honest Prayer—a new play put on by the newest young genius in HaBimah, and that I could go with my brother, if I wanted.

Theater people were always leaving tickets for my father. He used to give them big discounts. For some, he fixed their shoes for free.

13

Uncle Mordechai parked in front of Mr. Gelber's office. The Toyota parked right behind us. We ignored it and went in.

It didn't take me long to tell Mr. Gelber of my decision.

"You will?" he squealed, "But yesterday—"

"So yesterday I said no. Today I say yes. It's for the money, what do you think."

"Shit in yogurt, for the money," Uncle Mordechai muttered.

I remained silent. What could I do? Tell him about my black dreams?

Mr. Gelber spread his arms wide. "But I told you! I told you it'll cost everything he left you! Maybe more! Why waste good money . . ."

I said that if I do it cheap, maybe the play would even make money.

It sounded feeble in my own ears.

Margalit said tenderly, "But Isser wanted him to do it, so he would remember."

"No, it's for the money," I said obstinately, and turned to my uncle. "For your share, too."

Uncle Mordechai bristled. "Don't do me any favors. What will I do with the money, start buying *Ha'Olam HaZeh* magazine?"

This was the magazine of the Israeli *bohema*; it dug up political scandal and often featured bare breasts on the back page.

Margalit blushed. Mr. Gelber also seemed offended. At last he gave an angry snort, mopped his face, and in a tight legalistic voice said that all right, if I had decided to follow the stipulation, it was his duty to inform me I now had until May 15 at midnight to fulfill the request, as per probate regulations of 1953, paragraph aleph . . .

I tried to focus on his words, but street noises made it difficult for me to concentrate, also the flying dust. Legal briefs were piled everywhere, and folded newspapers, the weekend issue of *Ma'ariv* on top.

RABIN TO RESIGN! proclaimed the headline. "Elections slated for May 16!"

At the bottom of the page was the black-bordered death notice for Israel (Isser) Starkman (G.I.), may the Holy Name avenge his blood.

I swiped at the dust in my eyes as Mr. Gelber finished his little oration. "All right, fine. I have no idea where you'll get actors or a hall, but if that's what you want to do, who am I to say no?"

"Don't worry," I snapped. "I'll get people and whatever else is needed. If the estate would advance—I think you said a hundred thousand shekels? I'd need actors, and a director, and someone with production experience—"

Uncle Mordechai yelped, *"Hundred thousand shekels?!"*

"Oh, at least," Mr. Gelber trilled. "What am I saying? Two hundred! With inflation today—"

"But if the judge gave an order—"

"Menuchin?" Gelber chuckled.

"Don't look at me," Uncle Mordechai said. "I have only a pension. Go ask Kramer in Canada."

There was a short silence. I said, "Don't worry, I'll get the money." I turned to Uncle Mordechai. "And I'll also need you to tell me something, about what happened then—"

"Like when?" he asked warily.

"In forty-eight, and before—I'll need to know the background—"

"No, no," Uncle Mordechai said in Arabic. "*Illi fat matt.*" The past is dead.

"For the play," I said desperately. "Only for the play."

Uncle Mordechai stood up and slapped his thighs. "You do what you want. But me, keep me out of it. You hear? Now: you want to come to Tveriah for the shivah, or you want to go back to your friends in the *bohema?*"

"I want a fried *musht,*" I said at last.

Perhaps in Tveriah, in the shivah, my uncle would be more forthcoming.

As we all got up, the phone on Mr. Gelber's desk rang. He picked it up and listened for a while. "No," he said, his forehead turning red. "No."

Mr. Gelber put down the receiver. "Wrong number," he said heavily.

The Toyota was still at the curb, one man smoking in the backseat. The driver was reading a newspaper. They could not have been more noticeable if they had hoisted a large sign over their heads.

My uncle pretended not to see. "So now we go home."

On the way we stopped by the apartment. Neither Ruthy nor Ehud was in. As I was picking up my knapsack the phone rang. For a heart-stopping moment I thought it was Jenny. But it was Mr. Gelber.

"Oh, it's so lucky that I caught you! Listen, listen!" He chortled, and in one long desperate whoosh said that he had just gotten off the phone with Judge Menuchin and the judge had agreed that if I just read the play for him in chambers, the court might be persuaded to consider this a performance and deem the stipulation fulfilled and thereby cause the funds to be freed. "So you could then depart as speedily as—"

I hung up, went out, and hopped down the stairs.

If I'd had any doubts before, I had none now. Everything revolved around my father's play, and someone did not want me to stage it.

Uncle Mordechai took the Haifa road north. The Toyota maintained a constant distance of a hundred yards behind us. Ten kilometers out, near the Mossad HQ in Glilot, I said, "They've been following me from the moment I landed. And I think Ehud's phone is tapped."

"Well, sure," my uncle muttered. "Someone like you leaves, then comes back without a passport, of course they'll follow you."

This was also what Ehud had said, but I no longer believed it. "So it's nothing to do with the play?"

Uncle Mordechai threw me a covert look. "From this I know nothing."

Margalit stared out the window and we drove on in silence, the Toyota following, insultingly close.

I expected us to be tailed all the way to Tveriah, but just before Hadera my uncle muttered an old army curse, turned abruptly into a dirt road between orange groves, and drove at high speed through *injill*-overgrown side roads between Yemenite villages, before emerging out of an avocado grove into the Afula road. He drove expertly and fast, watching the rearview mirror, every now and then slowing down, letting cars pass us by. But the Toyota had disappeared and no other one took its place, and so we drove free and escortless all the way to Tveriah.

I kept quiet, marshaling my resolve and my questions.

PART II

Al Infitar

(The Cleaving)

14

EVADING THE TAILERS WAS of course pointless—everyone knew where the shivah would be held—so when my uncle at last drove down the dark hilly street where his house stood, another Toyota, a gray one, was parked across the road, its roof sprouting double antennas. I could see the glow of a cigarette inside.

My uncle said nothing, just parked and then prowled around the house, listening, and—much to my unease—sniffing the night air like a wolf, head thrown back and nose up, nostrils open wide, swaying his head from side to side; at last, without speaking, he motioned for us to enter.

Once inside he made straight for the kitchen cupboard and broke out a new bottle of 777. Margalit brought three glasses and we drank, sitting at the window overlooking the blue-black Kinneret. I wanted to ask my uncle about my father's early days, but the moment did not seem right. Little blue lights bobbed in the middle distance—fishing boats going out for the nightly catch. The smell of the water was in my nostrils, and I could hear jackal howls coming all the way from the Golan Heights.

Next morning I woke with a sandy tongue and my head buzzing with remnants of blackness; but some white snatches of soaring chants were there, too, lacing the dark.

I looked outside the window. The Toyota was still there.

Uncle Mordechai was standing in the kitchen by the Primus stove, frying fish. "Yes, for breakfast, for breakfast. It won't kill you." He sprinkled pepper from the bottom of his fist.

I pointed to the window. "So it's nothing to do with the play?"

My uncle threw me a black brow-knit glare. Obviously the moment was still not right. I waited, then said lamely, "You think anyone else from the funeral will come to the shivah?"

Uncle Mordechai said nothing.

"Maybe we should invite the tailers in, to say Kaddish with us."

"Over my dead body," said my uncle.

But two people did come.

First, as I was digging into my fish, a black patrol car came to a halt in the yard, and soon Inspector Amzaleg entered, not even bothering to knock. "One for me, too?"

"I bought five *mushts*," my uncle said.

"He loved them so much, the bastard," Amzaleg said.

For a moment I thought Uncle Mordechai would start crying, but he only sneezed.

Amzaleg kicked his shoes off. "Bring the fish here."

As he burrowed in, I said, "These tails outside, they help you investigate?"

Amzaleg gave a curt head shake and dug into the crisp *musht* without looking up. "You want to be an idiot hero with this play, go ahead. But do yourself a big favor and leave the police job to us."

I asked him if he was warning me officially.

"Yes, I am," he snapped, pointing the fork at me.

"Shut up and eat your fish," Uncle Mordechai said.

When breakfast was over, we sat on the cool tiled floor to play poker. We were well into the game when I asked my uncle, as casually as I could, what he could tell me about the play and my father's doings before '48.

"That's not for now," he growled into his cards.

"So when?"

"When the Angel of Death comes for me, maybe."

"But Mordechai—" I began, but he cut me off.

"Ask Shimmel. Maybe he can tell you something."

I felt a slight shock. "You think he'll come?"

"No," my uncle said. "He would be ashamed."

"He should be," Margalit said.

But that afternoon the fat man walked in—like Amzaleg, he did not knock. Through the open door I could see his gray Lark parked behind my uncle's jeep. It, too, had a dipole antenna.

I shook his hand foolishly, torn between my sudden urge to flee and my desire to query him.

"So, young man," he boomed at me, "we are orphans now?"

A tickling had begun inside my nose.

Gershonovitz turned to my uncle. "So the emigrant is back?"

My uncle put down the newspaper and stood up. "So you deigned to come, finally."

Gershonovitz stabbed a thick thumb in my direction. "Hiding in a whale," he said to my uncle, "like his father."

Amnon Amzaleg came in, rubbing his eyes, then Margalit, her mouth clamped shut.

She said, "*Shalom*, Shim'on. So you came."

Gershonovitz deposited his bulk on the smallest chair. "Sure I came, a moral duty, *nu*." With much groaning he bent down and removed his shoes—rubber-soled French Palladiums, Unit shoes. "And where're the others? Gone?"

"What others? Nobody came," my uncle said belligerently. "Nobody except the policeman, and the fuckers outside. They're yours?"

Gershonovitz inclined his head, acknowledging ownership. There was a moment of hard silence. Then he blew out his lips. "Sit down, sit down," he said to me, as if he were the host, not Uncle Mordechai.

I sat on the chair's edge. I was taller than him by a head at least, but his bulk, his Mongolian face, the flat eyes, filled me with dread; my questions stuck in my throat.

Uncle Mordechai snapped, "I didn't know you still remember the way here."

"I remember, I remember." Gershonovitz declined my uncle's gruff offer of cognac, and drank down three glasses of water with raspberry juice—one after the other, crunching the ice cubes in his teeth—then turned to the policeman. "So, Amnon, you caught him already, this animal?"

Amzaleg said tersely, "We are talking to a few Arabs."

"Talking?"

"Yes, talking. It's early. If we get something, then maybe I'll tell you."

Uncle Mordechai said, "If you want, I can ask around the villages. Some still have connections with . . . the old guys."

Amzaleg said, "But we don't know yet if it's because of— what happened then."

My nose tingled again and I swiped at my eyes. Everyone stopped talking. I tried to speak but could not. Gershonovitz grasped my elbow and gave me a thump on the back, and all of a sudden the tickling in my nose became unbearable.

He put his arm over my shoulder. "Some cognac, *ya* Mordoch."

My uncle poured.

"He could drink cognac, this *mamzer*, a bottle, two, like nothing," Gershonovitz said. "Like nothing." To my surprise I saw him wipe his eyes.

"This *mamzer*," said Amzaleg, "was a good guy."

"The best," said my uncle.

We all drank. I waited for something further, but apparently the eulogy was over. After a while I found my voice and asked

Gershonovitz if he knew that someone had tried to steal the play. When he inclined his head I said, "One of yours?"

He shook his massive head with the same economy.

I said, "So maybe it's the same one who killed him, who tried to steal it?"

Gershonovitz spoke without looking at me. "Don't be a fool. Take the money and go back to your shiksa; don't be a bigger idiot than he was."

I half rose from my seat, my fingers curled tight. The fat man looked at me calmly.

"Sit down," Uncle Mordechai said to me, then turned to Gershonovitz. "Finish your cognac and get out."

"Yes," said Margalit.

The camaraderie of a moment ago seemed to have vanished in an instant.

Amzaleg rolled his glass between his palms, staring at the drink.

As Gershonovitz was lacing his boots I said into his back, "Why are your guys following me?"

I didn't expect him to answer, but to my surprise he did. "It's for your own protection, Dada."

Protection? Against whom, or what?

"Shimmel—" I began hotly, but Uncle Mordechai interrupted me and addressed the fat man. "I think I told you to go."

Without fanfare Gershonovitz left, his Lark roaring up the hill past the parked Toyota, its curtained windows like invisible eyes behind dark shades.

After the fat man left everyone dispersed. All at once the feeling of being constantly watched filled me with anger and I felt an urgent need to get away from all eyes. I picked up a towel, softly climbed out the back window, and slid down the hill.

I don't think the men in the Toyota saw me go.

15

I SWAM FOR HALF an hour, hoping the clean water would wash away my turmoil. What did Gershonovitz mean when he said that the tailers were there for my own protection? Whom—or what—did he think I needed protection from? My father's killer? The play's burglar? The Debba? As I swam out, I filled my lungs and emptied my mind, and suddenly all I could think about was how Ruthy and I had once swum here at night, long ago, she and I naked side by side, alternately kissing and flipping on our backs to watch the stars, only to join again in near desperation, like one animal with two beating hearts . . .

The pain of that memory was so sharp that I plunged my head into the water and, eyes open, dived deep, to the sandy bottom. Silver-gray *buris* swam not two feet away from me, flickering in the milky moonlight, then a school of red *mushts*. I extended my hand to touch them but they flitted by and were gone, like memories.

I swam farther out and looked back at the shore, the pain a distant throb now. The Lux lanterns hanging in front of the Lido beach club swung in the breeze and I could smell their petrol smoke in the wind. It used to be a British officers' club before '48, then became a local nightspot, where my father and mother went dancing during their honeymoon.

Did they both swim here, too, as Ruthy and I had?

My heart thrummed as I desperately tried to conjure up images of Jenny and Toronto, but could not. The land seemed to have seeped into me anew, enmeshing me yet again.

I swam in wide circles, looking first at the Lido, then at the far shore, where a yellow glow was probably the armor camp at the foot of the Golan. Ghostly vapors floated over the water, like smoke rising from a battlefield. The jackals had fallen silent. Everywhere was a vague, large imminence, as if an answer would soon be given to a vast question that had not yet been asked.

At last I swam ashore.

When I got out of the water it was dark and the jackals were still silent. Warm wind, like invisible fingers, mussed my damp hair. I could hear my sandals slapping on the gravelly earth as I ran lightly up the hill. The moon floated above the hedges, yellow and oily and luminous.

A piece of cactus detached itself and stood in my path.

"Who is it?" I called, my neck hair bristling.

"*Wallad el Mawt!*" the shadow whispered in Arabic. Son of death. It was the '48 Arab pejorative for the Jews. Cowards, good for death and nothing else.

The hair on my forearms crawled. *"Man hadda?"* I called out in colloquial Arabic. Who is it?

The figure advanced upon me, its *abbaya* flapping like big black wings.

For a brief second I stood frozen, then all at once old training took over and my legs and arms moved in well-practiced patterns long forgotten. Yelling hoarse battle obscenities I kicked at the figure before me, clawed at his throat, poked at his eyes with stiff fingers. But my legs kicked at air, my fingers grabbed at nothing. And when I searched behind the cactus hedge, there was no one there, only the bristling palms scraping against the wall, and the soft whistling of the wind.

16

WHEN I CAME BACK, the house was dark, and so were the windows of the Toyota in front. Uncle Mordechai emerged from the toilet, trailing newspaper. "How was the Kinneret?"

"G-good."

Uncle Mordechai peered into my face. "What happened?"

"N-nothing."

He grabbed my hand and held it up. *"Nothing?!"*

My palm was vibrating as if air jets were blowing through the fingertips. "I . . . don't know, I . . . it was—someone." Haltingly I told him about the figure I had just seen. "I don't know, maybe . . . maybe he wasn't there, and I just thought he was—"

A shadow darkened the terrace door. Amnon Amzaleg, in gray military underwear, stood rubbing his gray scalp.

Uncle Mordechai did not take his eyes off me. "The donkey just saw *him* again. Near the old sheikh's grave—"

Amzaleg wheeled around and, one hand at the small of his back, hopped over on the terrace wall and was gone. In a moment I heard his raspy voice outside, then the slam of a car door, and feet running down the hill. Then there was nothing.

Uncle Mordechai bent over and tugged at the drawer under the fridge, and pulled out an ancient long-barreled Parabellum. "Here, take this." He tried to foist it into my hand. "No, take, take, it's good for thirty paces, maybe forty." The gun must have been fifty years old.

I pushed his hand away. Seven years I had managed to live without weapons; I was not about to start carrying one again. We were both silent.

Uncle Mordechai said, "Me, I don't believe in the tall tales."

"No, no. Who does?"

Uncle Mordechai and I stared at each other for a moment. Then, just as he had left, Amzaleg was back, soaring silently over the terrace wall. "Nothing. Them neither." In his right hand he held a scuffed Beretta, its safety off. "You want?" he said, when he saw me looking.

I shook my head. Two days here, and again everyone was offering me guns.

As I went to bed I heard Amzaleg and Uncle Mordechai conferring in low voices in the kitchen. Once there was a knock on the door. My uncle went to open it and I heard a low murmur—it was one of the yeshiva boys—though I couldn't catch the words.

"No," my uncle's voice rasped. "You stay out. What do you want?"

The murmur continued.

"Well, I have a tool also," my uncle snapped, using the old '48 slang for a gun. "And he can take care of himself, too. Now get out!"

The door slammed.

Next morning, my head still fuzzy, I sought out Amzaleg to talk about the phantasm. But he had gone to Tel Aviv to meet his daughter, who now lived with her remarried mother in an Arab village near Haifa. Uncle Mordechai came back from some medical checkup in Afula and closed himself off with the newspaper. Margalit did not want to talk about last night either.

By noon I'd had enough of the silence, and the foggy memory of the night before, and decided to return to Tel Aviv. I called Ehud to let him know I'd be moving to a hotel. I did not want to stay near Ruthy; I needed a clear head to do the play.

But it was Ruthy who answered. "No. He's in the factory, I don't know. How is Tveriah?"

"Hot. I burned my back." All thoughts of the night apparition evaporated the moment I heard her voice. "Is . . . is it hot in Tel Aviv?"

"Very. When are you coming back?"

"In two days," I lied. "Maybe three."

Perhaps I could sneak in when she was not home, to pick up my shaving kit.

I could hear her shallow breathing.

I said, "I . . . I told the lawyer that I'll do the play . . ."

Ruthy said nothing. I could hear the Peace Station yammering in the background.

"Anyway," I said, "at least I'll stay for the wedding."

Ruthy said, "Can I read it again?" Then she added, "Come back quickly."

"Maybe," I said. "If you behave."

There was another silence.

Uncle Mordechai shouted at me from the kitchen, "Duvid! You finished with the phone? It's two shekels every minute!"

"No," Ruthy said. "Come back soon."

"Maybe," I snapped, and hung up.

17

AN HOUR LATER I took the bus back to Tel Aviv. All through the trip I buried myself in the play, reading and rereading its soaring lines until they filled me completely, leaving no room for anything but the hard resolve of the graveside.

When the bus arrived in Tel Aviv three hours later, I already knew the entire play by heart. It was amazing how easy it was to memorize.

Fortunately Ruthy was not at home. I quickly gathered my things, but before leaving called Jenny in Canada one more time, silently begging her to pick up. The phone rang for a long time without an answer. I hung up, got myself a beer, and sipped it slowly, my knapsack on my shoulder. My legs seemed to have turned to wood. After a while I heard a key at the door and Ruthy entered. Before she could speak I snapped that I'd decided to move out, maybe to a hostel on HaYarkon Street, something cheap.

To my surprise she didn't object, just offered to make me an omelet before I left. "In the hotel you'll have nothing," she said.

My heart drummed as I found myself nodding, then drank my beer through a constricted throat while she busied herself at the stove.

We sat at the table in the hot kitchen, eating egg in a pita— strictly not kosher for Passover—not looking at each other.

"You didn't come to your mother's funeral," Ruthy said.

"No," I said.

"Because you—didn't want to come back?"

"No, no." What else could I say? That I had learned of my mother's death only after her funeral? That until last week I hadn't even known my father had left her?

I tried not to look at Ruthy. "We didn't exchange letters. Maybe a New Year's card once a year."

I had learned from Margalit that my father had not been to my mother's funeral either. They were living separately by then, and she had told the registrar in Assuta Hospital, where she had gone for her cancer operation, that she was a widow.

Ruthy said, "She's not buried in Nachalat Yitzchak cemetery."

"No. In the Trumpeldor Street cemetery, near her parents."

Grandpa Yoel and Grandma Leah had been killed in a terrorist attack on a bus near Natanya. A month later my brother Avraham embarked on his unauthorized retribution operation on the Palestine Liberation Front headquarters in Damascus.

"I should go see her grave, too," I said. "Put a stone on it, something." At the thought of my mother, and her unanswered letters, my heart seized, but I tamped the pain down.

"She knew Polish and Russian and Hebrew and Yiddish—I can hardly speak English."

I said, "She had learned some Arabic, too, when she worked in Yaffo, in sewing."

I could not see why we were talking about my mother all of a sudden.

"I can't even speak French, four years I took it, in Alliance, because of Mother." She nibbled on a tomato. "You want a radio? The news is on, soon."

"No. What do I care what happens here?"

I knew I should go but my legs were still wooden, as if I were again battling a phantasm.

Ruthy hugged her knees and looked at me as I mopped the plate. "You still hungry?"

"N-no, I'm finished."

"So come," she said. "Time's a-wasting."

Like a sleepwalker, I followed her into my parents' bedroom.

"Ehud is away till tonight," she said, unbuttoning her shirt. "He went to talk to the bank again, something about the factory's line of credit, I don't know."

I sat down on the bed, my teeth clamped so they wouldn't chatter. The world had contracted into a blue cube and I was in it, fish swimming in my head.

"David," Ruthy said. "David, David."

She had taken off her shorts and panties and now sat beside me. With the knuckle of one forefinger she knocked on the front of my pants. *"Debba, debba, tze' hachootza,"* she chortled into my ear. Hyena, hyena, come out.

My heart in turmoil, I lay back and let her pull off my pants and the underwear, her nails drawing lines across my hips. She crouched above me on all fours.

"Oy yoy." She touched my shoulder with a finger. "You really burned it."

"What happened to your hand?" I croaked. She had a long, ugly scratch on her left forearm. I touched her skin.

"I had an accident today, in Sheinkin Street. An ass in a Toyota. Now it'll take forever with my insurance because he ran off and didn't want to give me his."

"And this?" There was a scar on her left breast, an old one. I didn't remember it.

"Someone, I don't know." Her small freckled breasts swayed with her breathing. "You can't tell them no, if they're going to die tomorrow."

"Who?"

"Anyone. Soldiers, what do I know? It's only a little thing. It makes them happy." Then, without warning, she plunged her teeth into my shoulder. "What do you care? You ran away to the diaspora for two thousand years. What did you want me to do, stay deserted and fallow forever and ever?"

"I don't care." There was moment of wild confusion as we wrestled, our teeth knocking against each other; and then I was upon her, and inside her, making animal noises.

Ruthy let out a sharp scream, the one I knew. I shoved my forearm into her mouth, giving my arm a half twist. Her voice came out muffled. "Is it better than with your Polish shiksa?"

I had wanted to say no, then yes, then, What does it matter, because why should a man have only one woman, only one country, only one people? But just then I plunged into the familiar abyss, the unknown, forgotten land, and I and the tan animal under me writhed together, and then it was over.

"The police will soon come," she said with satisfaction. "Screaming like this."

I rolled over and curled up. My spine felt hollow.

Ruthy jumped off the bed. "I'm first."

I could not talk. The enormity of what I had just done to Ehud, and to Jenny, began to sink in.

She called out from the bathroom, "So you have what, forty-two days, to do it?"

"Forty-one," I croaked. For one frightening moment her voice sounded just like my mother's.

Ruthy said, "So you'll come to the wedding?" She appeared in the doorway, toweling between her legs.

"Maybe," I whispered. "I don't know."

"Three hundred people," she said. "Can you imagine?"

18

WHEN MY FATHER MET my mother for the first time he was thirty-three years old. He had never been married. She was twenty-two, with shoulder-length brown hair and long legs.

My father's shoe store stood on Herzl Street, the main street in Tel Aviv in those days. He had opened it thirteen years before, with Paltiel Rubin as salesman. Herzl Street was already paved, but other streets were mainly sand, and cacti grew hither and yon. Many cacti. Their fruit was purple and good to eat, if you were mindful of the tiny thorns.

Camels wandered in from the sand dunes south of Yaffo and ate the thick, prickly leaves, oblivious to the thorns. They lay in the warm sand all afternoon and when the sun set meandered back south. It was a strange sight for the European Jews to have camels on their doorsteps.

For a long time I had no idea what my father did during the sixteen years between his arrival in Palestine and the time he met my mother. Hazy tales of theater ventures reached my ears. Some said my father had gotten the literary bug from Paltiel, whom he had met on the boat to Yaffo; others said it was the other way around. An usher in HaBimah told me my father had once written a play in which Riva Yellin was to have played the key role. It was a drama in four acts. The usher hinted at some tragic liaison between my father and the great actress, or some tragedy in her life in which he had played a part.

Riva Yellin was the queen of the Hebrew stage. When she passed in Dizzengoff Street all fell silent and stared.

She and my father?

Yet, in the shoe store overlooking Rothschild Boulevard, all the actors of HaBimah congregated between rehearsals. Everyone in Tel Aviv went to the theater in those days, doctors and artisans alike. And in the store there was always someone present from the theater: an actor, a director, a stagehand. Many bought shoes on credit; some repaid their debts with tickets.

My mother, Sonya Bukovsky, was at that time working as a seamstress in Yaffo, for some rich Arabs. Her parents were not wealthy and she had to take whatever work she could get. The month before, at the order of her father, she had stopped seeing some unworthy fellow—a Yemenite, or perhaps a Moroccan Jew—and in consolation Grandpa Yoel offered to buy her whatever she wanted, with half her weekly pay. She went to my father's store to buy high-heeled shoes—her first. She had beautiful long legs, slender and creamy white. My father took a long time fitting her. She was exceedingly choosy.

In the mirror frame stuck a theater program and a pair of tickets. Just the previous day Re'uven Kagan, the famed director, had left two gallery tickets for *The Dybbuk* in exchange for a pair of black biblical sandals. A renowned critic had lauded the performance highly. The review—autographed by Kagan himself—was pinned to the wall, above the tickets. The program was autographed, too.

When my father wrapped up the box of shoes, he stuck one ticket into the wrapping paper. My mother said he blushed furiously, but held her eye. She smiled and he smiled back. He had two gold teeth, which my mother found charming. After the show they went to Café Cassit to take coffee with the actors. They were married seven months later in Va'ad HaQhilla, the old community center on Allenby Street.

Tel Aviv, I am told, was then a dreamy, fragrant place. Orange groves came up to the very edge of town. In the afternoon tall Arabs emerged from the neighboring village of Sumeil, dragging tiny donkeys laden with huge boxes of fruits and vegetables. The yellow mimosa blossoms filled the air with musky perfume. Cool sea breezes blew. Every evening the bohemians and Haganah fighters on furlough argued late into the night at Café Cassit about theater, poetry, and the future of the Jews. Many took an evening stroll with their wives or friends, and ended at the sand dunes of Machlool, to look at the sunset.

In my mind's eye I can see them, as in an old, sepia-brown postcard, looking over the sea, trying to peer into the Jews' future.

Did they ever think it would produce men like me?

19

I DID NOT MOVE out of my parents' apartment. It would be far easier, I told myself repeatedly, to do the play while living in Ibn Gvirol, closer to the bohemian cafés. It was only because of the play that I stayed put, I told myself, not because of Ruthy. And indeed, this may have even been partly true, because my discovery that the play alleviated my black dreams was like a slow-burning white fire, nearly as strong as my dark attraction to Ruthy, and so for the first time since I escaped Israel, I felt there was hope for peace inside me. Every night before I went to sleep, I read and reread a few scenes, humming the songs so that they would sing to me while I slept, then stashed the pages under my pillow, from where they radiated heat, similar to hers.

But whereas the nights were now easier, the days were harder.

Ever since our afternoon in bed, Ruthy had begun to treat me with hostile formality, as if I had done her some sort of wrong, or injury. Ehud, too, she treated coldly; maybe to even things out.

Two days after I had returned from Tveriah the phone rang at eight in the morning.

"It's for you," Ruthy said stiffly.

I took it without looking at her. At first I thought it would be again one of the crazy adherents of Rabbi Kahane, the messianic madman from Brooklyn, warning me not to stage my father's play or they "would do to me what was done to him." They had been calling at all hours, their thin voices hysterical. I was ready to slam the receiver down, but it was Amzaleg. "You wanted to come see the store."

"Yes," I said, thrown off balance. "Now?"

"Yes. I'll meet you there in—" Before he could finish, the line went dead.

I hung up. "I'm going to the store to meet the policeman."

Ehud said, "Maybe the police found some clues?"

Ruthy said, "Or maybe they found nothing, and they want to investigate David." She laughed at her own joke.

Ehud looked at her, pained. Ruthy's hostility toward me was taking its toll on him. The night before, he had asked me in a low voice to be nice to Ruthy. "I know that you went out for a long time and everything, and maybe you had a fight, what do I know, but that's—that's in the prehistory, I—please be nice to her—" He looked at me beseechingly. Then, for no apparent reason, he started to tell me how astounded he was when Ruthy called him right after I had left for Canada and asked him to take her to a play he was then producing. "Of course I said yes," he whispered, his face flaming. "All these years I—"

But I did not let him finish. "I'm not saying anything to her. What do you want from my life?"

I felt like the worst kind of rascal. Like the stories they used to tell about how Paltiel Rubin stayed at the homes of his infatuated admirers and screwed their wives, then borrowed money from the cuckolds for his drinking and debauch.

"No, really," Ehud said.

Finally, my face flaming, I promised him to be nice to Ruthy. Maybe even take her to Café Cassit, when he, Ehud, was busy.

I couldn't look him in the eye.

But Ruthy was right. Amzaleg did want to ask me questions. When I reached the store, I saw him sitting in his scratched black patrol car, parked on the sidewalk.

"Come inside," he said. "It's hot." He opened the store's door with a key, the one I knew, tied with a brown leather strap, and I followed him in.

The store's floor was littered with elections posters that someone had slid under the door. "Time for a Change!" said one. Begin smiled at me toothily.

Amzaleg kicked at it sideways. "We didn't clean anything, just the—the body."

I sat down on the black wooden bench where I had sat innumerable times, watching my father seated at his low stool hammering on shoe heels and gluing soles.

Amzaleg sat on the table where my father's cash register used to stand. Above him hung a picture of my father, age twenty-five, lean and wiry and dangerous in a tight black wrestling leotard, one set of knuckles on the floor, the other on his lean hip.

I stared at it, bracing myself for a speech telling me to forget about the play and leave, but instead he looked at me with puffy eyes and said, "Maybe you could help me?"

I was taken off guard. Help? I thought he wanted me to keep out of it.

"Help how?" I said, not offering, just to know.

"Tell me about your father and your mother, and, you know, the family."

From outside came the cries of a truck driver, cursing, and honks.

I said, "I thought you knew him."

"Nobody knew him."

I said, "I—I don't know very much about him either—" It dawned on me that this was true.

"Just anything, how he was then, and later. What you remember about him, and your mother, and your family—" Amzaleg looked at me intensely.

I said lamely, "But—I haven't been here for seven years—ask his friends from the army, and from afterward—"

"Who? There's nobody to ask. No one knows anything about what he did the last twenty-nine years." He looked at me, his eyebrows joined. "So what do you want me to do?"

I said, "Maybe Uncle Mordechai—"

"Thirty years Mordoch didn't speak to him. What would he know? He only saw him maybe once, twice, in a bar mitzvah, or a wedding."

I said, "But—why didn't Mordechai speak to him?"

Somehow no one ever discussed this in our family. It was just one of those things; my father and his brother were not on talking terms.

Amzaleg said, "I don't know why. So I am asking you, any-thing you can tell me—" He looked at me, not pleading, just waiting.

I swallowed hard. "But—I want you to tell me something first."

Amzaleg did not appear surprised. "What?"

"Why did he leave the army?"

Amzaleg got down from the table. "I don't know. People talked."

I waited, my heart beating hard. "Like what, 'talked'? Who?" I had wanted to say, "Because he said 'noble enemy,' in the Cas-tel?" but refrained.

There was a timid knock on the door.

Amzaleg said, "Evil tongues, what do I know? Jews like to talk, behind the back. They said he didn't kill him, maybe. That he let him go, Abu Jalood."

The room spun. I sat slowly down on the bench. "In forty-eight?"

"Yes. Complete shits, some people are." He seemed genu-inely angry.

"Why?" I asked stupidly.

The knock on the door was repeated. Amzaleg opened it. It was Zussman, from the Tnuva kiosk near my father's store. "*Ahalan*, Amnon," he said. "Your car is blocking the way, the truck driver told my wife he is going to charge for the time he is—"

"All right, all right." He muttered an army curse and turned to me. "I'll be right back."

When he returned he said, "A good man, this Zussman, but his wife eats him alive."

"You also know him from the army?"

"Yes." Amzaleg didn't elaborate. "Some people—" He shook his head.

There was a pause.

I said, "But why? Why would he let the—him go?"

"I don't know why! Your father used to wrestle with Arabs, before the Wrestling Association kicked them all out. He had lots of business with Arabs. Some people said he didn't have the guts to use a knife up close. Or that he took money from Abu Jalood to let him go. If you ask me, people were jealous. At age forty-one, still commanding the unit he founded—" Again, he shook his head.

"So that's why they—" I swallowed. "Why they kicked him out of the army?"

Amzaleg leaned over and looked into my eyes. His were bloodshot. "They didn't kick him out. He could have been chief of staff one day. Moshe Dayan did much worse, a few times, and nobody said boo. Ask Gershonovitz." Amzaleg closed his eyes for a moment. "But he left. He just left."

"Maybe he was tired." I could understand that. When I had finished my five years of service I was so tired I wanted nothing but sleep. For two whole months I tried, often drinking a

bottle of Stock 777 every night to ward off the black nightmares, uselessly, until my visa to Canada arrived.

"Maybe," Amzaleg said cryptically. He looked around him.
"You want something from here?"

I got up and wandered around. My father was only six days
dead but already the store was dusty and smelly, as if no one
had ever worked there. I said over my shoulder, "So you are
getting close? Do you think you'll catch him?"

"Don't worry, we'll catch him." And then he sat down on
the bench, as if he'd just made a decision. "All right. To you I
can talk." And while I kicked through the scraps of leather, old
shoes, rusty knives, discarded lasts, empty glue cans, the three
decades of debris of a Tel Aviv cobbler, he talked at length
about some lab tests, and conversations over Turkish coffee
with Arab informants in Yaffo. "I am sure it's Arabs. Gershonovitz says it's probably someone crazy from here, maybe on
drugs, who got it into his head that he is . . . you know, this
Debba . . . But me—" He gave his head a quick shake. "It's a
new terrorist organization, I told him—"

I listened, stupefied, as he told in bewildering detail of some
burglary in the Atta store adjacent to my father's, the month
before ("So he wouldn't have opened the door to someone he
didn't know—no, no!"), and how none of the other merchants
nearby had seen anyone come or leave. "So it wasn't a cus-
tomer. Not on the Shabbat."

I listened numbly as Amzaleg kept spewing out details about
who went home at what hour, who could have seen the shoe
store's door from his own store or kiosk, and who couldn't.
The angles of view, the blind spots. He pulled out a creased
notebook and showed me a page of dashed lines scribbled in
blue ballpoint ink, the kind we used to draw before a sniper
job. "It's some young Arab *shabbab*." Amzaleg stabbed his fin-

ger at the page, as if it contained proof. "The old ones, two of them, gave me their word that it's not PLO. I don't know. I believe them."

"Word of an Arab," I said.

"Yes," the policeman said evenly. "Word of an Arab." After a little while he added, "Not everybody, but if I know them, then maybe." He leaned back and looked up at me.

"You talked to his old partner, what's his name, from Yaffo? Abdallah?"

"Yes. Him I believe."

A few more wrestling photographs hung over the old Rotter machine at the back, where my father used to sew soles. There was a small photograph of him alone; a larger one of my father with Paltiel, side by side; Paltiel and my father amid a dozen bright-eyed swains with flowing forelocks and thick mustaches, all in black leotards, arms folded. The Yaffo Wrestling Club, probably, from before 1936, before the club had split into a Jewish club and an Arab one. Before the First Events, when the real killing started, when everything fell apart. When history began.

Amzaleg said suddenly, "Next week, I'll have some time, we could go to his room, that he rented, on Lillienblum. This old man he rented the place from, he says he knows nothing. Maybe to you he'll talk, I don't know."

"Glantz," I said. "That's where he used to live before also, when he landed in Palestine. With Paltiel."

"See? I didn't know this." Amzaleg gave one more kick to the heap of leather scraps.

I took down two dusty albums from the shelf above my father's stool, with old theater programs. "Can I take these? Maybe also a few knives." I picked up three knives, in their leather sheathes, thinking of the play.

"Take whatever you want."

On the way out he locked up, then pulled yellow police tape out of his pocket and stuck it on the door.

Across the street two new men now loitered—younger ones, in jeans and faded tie-dyed T-shirts: fake beatniks.

I pointed to them with my chin. "These yours?"

He spit on the pavement, noisily, and to my surprise stuck his own middle finger at my tailers in the obscene Arab gesture of *zayin*; and before I could say anything, he got into his patrol car and drove away.

As I turned to go I felt a tug at my sleeve. Zussman, from the Tnuva kiosk, his sparse hair plastered wetly to his skull. He handed me a tall glass. "Raspberry *gazoz*," he said loudly, both his voice and hand shaking, "for the heat." Then, looking furtively behind him, he pulled a few crumpled bills out of his pocket and shoved them into mine. "For the play," he whispered. "Don't let them stop it!" He seized my hand and held on to it, as Leibele, the waiter from Cassit, had at the funeral.

I stared at him over the glass's rim, then asked in a low voice whether he had a minute to talk.

"Not now," he whispered, glancing over his shoulder. "Maybe next week."

His balding wife glared at me from behind the soda fountain. "Out of here, murderer *nemosha*."

I couldn't blame her, really. What I couldn't understand was how her husband was willing to talk to me, let alone help.

20

EXCEPT FOR A FEW people, no one wanted anything to do with me: the old as if they knew something I didn't, the young as if they had been warned by the old. Every day I called old friends and high school classmates, asking for a loan to help produce the play. All claimed empty pockets. The occasional envelope did appear in Ehud's mailbox with a few bills inside, but none carried a name, and these paltry gifts were far outnumbered by letters cursing me, my father, and the play, all unsigned, each nastier than the last.

I tried to disregard the poison letters—as I had disregarded the speech by the Israeli consul in Toronto—yet they weighed on me. So even though Ruthy was hostile, it was a relief to see her and Ehud in the late afternoons, as she returned from one more fitting at the seamstress, and he returned from the chocolate factory. Then the three of us would go to Café Cassit to eat, and simply yak. My constant followers—usually two, but often only one—would sit three or four tables away and stare at me, as if marking me for everyone else to see. I didn't point them out to Ruthy, and to Ehud of course I didn't need to.

Much later in the evening, I would go alone around Tel Aviv, from one bohemian café to another, trying to interest actors in doing the play, handing out photocopies of the main speeches and the songs. Occasionally some younger actor ignored the frowning hints of his elders and the grim stares of the constant tailers and read a few pages over his mud coffee; but when I said actors would have to work for "points," all demurred.

"No one wants to do it," I said to Ehud later at night, "without money up front. I thought actors took chances if they thought it was good."

"I would do this for free," Ruthy said.

I told her not to do me any favors. "You go ahead and get married."

Ehud said nothing.

Despite the rejections, or perhaps because of them, and because the play seemed to be my only hope against the blackness, my wish to stage it only grew. More than once I considered asking Ehud for help. But after all he had done for me, after saving my life at such a cost to himself, I now repaid him by screwing his future wife under his own roof; the last thing I needed was one more favor from him.

So I took the bus to Herzl Street, and went one by one into stores whose owners had known my father for thirty years, beseeching them, reminding them of my father's deeds. But like my old friends and classmates, no one had anything to give. It was tax time; after Passover it was always slow; how they wished they could help me. If they had any money to give, they would. Even for this play. Even for this.

It was strange how a play that, strictly speaking, had never been fully performed, still generated so much fear, even in those who had once been my father's friends, and mine.

Later at night, I called Jenny from the living room phone. She picked up on the first ring, cried with joy and began to recite another poem she had written for me. I closed my eyes and, when she finished, asked her whether I could borrow some money for my father's play.

There was a short silence. Then she said in a small voice, "Are you sleeping with her?"

"Who?" I said.

"Swear!" Jenny said. "Swear!"

For a brief moment I could not speak; then I rasped, my voice tight with panic. "She's the fiancée of my best friend. They're getting married in three weeks! In three weeks!"

There was a long pause.

"I—I'll try," Jenny whispered at last. "I can borrow maybe two thousand on my credit card, because the plane ticket already—"

"Whatever you can send, send." I gave her Ehud's address, and before she could say anything else or quote to me any more love poems, I said I'd call tomorrow and hung up.

But two thousand wasn't enough, and it was now clear what I had to do. That evening Ehud and I sat in the kitchen while Ruthy sat by, pretending to read *Ha'Olam HaZeh*. For an hour Ehud kept telling me all that had befallen him since I had left. His early ventures with small theater groups; how he no longer did this, "because no one cares anymore about good theater." How he and Ruthy came to live together; how he now focused on work at his father's chocolate factory, resisting the lure of the stage.

Finally, I interrupted him and asked roughly if he could lend me some money, maybe also help with the production. "I only have five weeks," I said. "I must do it by the fifteenth or lose it but no one wants to talk to me. Maybe if you produce it, not me—" I stopped.

"But we have the wedding in three weeks—"

"You can postpone it," Ruthy said without raising her head from her cinema magazine. "We're screwing already, no?"

There was a long brittle silence.

"All right," Ehud whispered at last, his face pale, "if you want." He looked at me.

I forced myself to look at him, nodded jerkily, then explained that Mr. Gelber had said it would cost 150,000 shekels. "But in five weeks, you'll get it all back—"

"Nah, it's eighty thousand maximum." Ehud explained how one calculated the actual costs: number of actors, props, play length, complexity of material, lighting—

"Ehud—" I said, but could not continue, so much love I suddenly felt for him; like the love I had once felt for my father.

"Nah. Leave it. I'll hang the ads in Cassit and Kapulski Café tomorrow, for the auditions. Then we'll go get us a director, and start on Sunday."

I could see I was in good hands now.

21

YET NONE OF THE directors Ehud called was willing, even those who were out of work and needed the pay. Everyone had different reasons; but it became clear that whatever fear was infecting the merchants and the actors was also causing directors to shy away.

Whether it was the play's peacenik message or something else, we didn't have a clue.

Then Ruthy learned from her mother that Re'uven Kagan had directed the play's ill-fated 1946 performance. So the next morning the three of us drove to see him. We climbed the four floors to his rooftop apartment on HaYarkon Street, not two hundred meters from the beach.

Kagan let us in without a word. Empty arak bottles were piled up in a wooden crate by the door, and a half-empty Stock 777 bottle stood on the floor beside the uncurtained window. There was very little furniture; it was an old rooftop laundry nook converted into a pauper's living quarters. The three of us avoided staring at the mess, as, one after the other, we implored him to direct the play for us.

Kagan kept saying no. He was done with serious theater; no one cared anymore. The public only wanted slapstick and dreck comedies. Good plays he was not even going to touch. "Especially this one. Last time, even with Paltiel and Isser and all the other Jewish wrestlers from the club—no, no." He lifted the arak bottle to his mouth and drank.

Finally Ruthy rose to her feet. "We're wasting our time, let's go find someone else—there must be some theater directors with balls . . ."

"Just a minute." I turned to Kagan. "Why didn't they finish the show in Haifa?"

"The Events," he said in a distant rasp. "Also, there was . . . this rumor—"

"What rumor?"

"Oh, nothing." Kagan flushed. "That this—that the Debba would appear after the show—the real Debba, the Mahdi—this *fakakte* Arab savior—"

Ruthy said to Kagan with exaggerated disdain, "So that's why you say no? What are you, a superstitious Bedouin?"

Kagan's flush deepened, "I am not saying this was the reason for the bedlam . . . They probably rioted because of—of what happens in the play . . . Also, the week before, this was April forty-six, a bus with nurses from Rambam Hospital was ambushed. And this kind of play, shown right after such a massacre—" He stopped.

We were all silent, digesting this. Finally Ruthy asked, "Who played the parts?"

"They did," Kagan said. "Isser, Paltiel, Nachman. Who did you think?"

Ruthy said, "And her? Sarah? Who played her—my mother?"

Kagan laughed bitterly. "Riva? No, no. *She* played it. Sonya."

The little hairs on my neck rose. It was the first I had heard of my mother's involvement in the play.

I felt the familiar hole in my stomach. "And the Debba? Who played it?"

Kagan said to me, "Why do you need all this *cholera*? Go back to Canada, see movies, sit in a café, eat ice cream, enjoy life. Don't dig up all this past dreck."

He and Gershonovitz, and Gelber.

Ruthy said, "I didn't know Sonya could sing."

Kagan said into the wall, "Many other things you don't know, sweetie."

Ruthy said tightly, "I know about—about Mother, and, and him, Paltiel."

It was commonly known that, as a favor, Paltiel Rubin had married Riva in a sham ceremony, after she had told him she was pregnant. A week later Paltiel and Riva were divorced by the full rabbinical court of Tel Aviv. The rabbis were not pleased. Five months later Paltiel was dead.

"Yes, yes." Kagan waved his hand, as if this wasn't what he had meant. "*She* could sing, Sonya, she could dance, she could *act*—" He shook his head in marvel and sorrow.

Ehud put his arm around Ruthy's shoulders.

"Kagan—" I said desperately. "Please . . ."

Suddenly his nostrils flared and his bloodshot eyes moistened. "His friend, this Yemenite actor, what's his name. Ovadiah. He played the Debba." Then Kagan shouted in Yiddish, "*Nareshkeit!*" Foolishness. "I told him, Isser, why do you need this? You already wrote this crazy play? All right! It's written! You want to stage it? Fine! It's your money. Waste it. But why in Haifa? There are no better places in all of Palestine?—but he insisted. Why? I don't know why. Maybe he wanted some bedlam, for the advertising—maybe it was he who had started the rumor. I don't know. Don't ask me. Ask Tzadok."

I said, "Ovadiah Tzadok? The Yemenite actor?"

"Yeah. Him."

Ruthy said, "He's still alive? He had acted once with my mother in forty-two—"

"I don't know." He turned away.

"Kagan—" My voice seemed stuck.

"No," he said, looking at me fully for the first time. "I don't want to go back into the shit." His voice was pleading.

I said thickly, "I don't want to, either, but *he* asked me to do it, in the will . . ."

"Well, he didn't ask me."

"So I am asking you," I said in a strangled voice. "For his sake . . ."

I don't know how I could ask anything in my father's name, after the way I had rejected both him and all he stood for.

Kagan's face turned pale. He looked at each one of us, one by one. No one spoke. Finally he stood up, pinching his nostrils as if trying to hold back anger, or tears. "All right. I'll help you." His eyes twitched with moisture. "All right! But you do the research about the background, not me. You dig into this past dreck, not me. That's the condition!"

He looked into my eyes like Leibele had done, in the cemetery; as if trying to convey a meaning, or a message.

I managed to speak. "All right."

When we came down we saw that someone had broken the window of Ehud's Volvo. I stammered that I was sorry and would understand if he wanted to pull out, but he cut me off.

"You just do exactly what Kagan asked you," he said.

He didn't say "your father asked you," and I loved him for that.

As we drove away, Ruthy was quiet in the backseat. But Ehud leaned over and pulled out an old Unit knife from the glove compartment, its serrated blade blue-black and dull with use. I said I didn't want it, but he said he wasn't offering. "You get your own." He put it in his pocket.

I said I didn't need a knife.

"Yes, you do," Ruthy said. "Or they'll do to you what they did to him." She paused, "Or *it* will."

"You be quiet," Ehud snapped.

She obeyed, with unexpected shock; he had never spoken to her like this before.

"Did you hear this?" she said to me. "One might think we were married already."

22

THE NEWS THAT *THE Debba* was about to be staged again raised waves of alarm in various circles, and the vandalism of Ehud's Volvo was just the beginning.

A day after an article about the play had appeared in *Ha'Olam HaZeh* magazine, the daily newspaper *Ma'ariv* ran an editorial fulminating at the "unseemly wallowing in guilt, so typical of Labor circles, which brought us to the brink at Yom Kippur in '73." *Davar* ran an editorial in reply (". . . it has never been the policy of the Labor Party . . .") and the phone began to ring right after breakfast, the callers no longer just youthful Kahane disciples. "In this fateful hour," one caller intoned in flowery Old Hebrew style, "in these wind-tossed days, when the people's ship of state has nearly sundered—"

"Eat shit," I said, and hung up.

There were half a dozen more calls, mostly from old men, some incoherent in their rage; but the last one was different. A voice of a young man asked diffidently if he could speak to "the son of Isser from the Castel."

My stomach lurched as I said it was I.

"D-don't give up!" the young voice stammered. "D-don't let anyone stop you! I r-read the play and . . . and . . . it's your duty to do this for—" I interrupted him and asked angrily how he had gotten a copy. "There—there are lots of copies now," he stuttered. "I—please don't give up—" There was some muttering in the background and the line went dead.

"Well, send us money," I said into the dead receiver.

A little before noon, Yaro Ben-Shlomo, from the Unit, called. "I read someplace you are staying."

Just like that. Seven years I haven't talked to him, and no hello, no nothing. Typical kibbutznik.

I said it was only for a few weeks, until I finished. "Then I go back."

There was a short silence. "Anyway, so you be careful—"

"Of what?"

"I don't know— anyway, if you need anything, you know—"

Like what? Was he, too, going to offer me a gun, or a knife? "I don't need anything, but if you can lend us some money—"

But he had already hung up.

There was one more phone call. Abdallah Seddiqi, my father's Arab ex-partner. In the background I could hear a donkey bray. He probably was calling from his basement store in Yaffo. More condolences, but in Hebrew this time.

"Yes, yes." I interrupted his flowery speech. "My heart aches too at the loss—"

"Anytime you want, any help you need. Or if you need leather—"

What would I need leather for?

When Abdallah finally hung up I called Mr. Glantz, my father's landlord, and said I'd like to come talk to him, ask him a few questions.

If no one else would talk, maybe my father's old landlord would.

He said, "So when do you want to come? Come today, so long as I am still alive."

There was a buzzing sound on the line, and a faint murmur, and then the line went silent.

"I'm coming," I said to the dead receiver.

It took me a long time to lace my sandals with fingers gone numb.

23

"WILL YOU HAVE SOME tea?" said Mr. Glantz.

He was at least eighty years old, but as spry and agile as a monkey, drawn from the same mysterious stock of men of Genesis that seemed to age without losing their timeless vitality: like Gershonovitz, Amzaleg, or even my uncle Mordechai.

"Yes," I said. "Thank you."

"Me nothing," Amzaleg said.

To my surprise he had been waiting for me when I approached house number 71 on Lillienblum Street, seated in his scratched patrol car, reading *Ha'Olam HaZeh*.

The ubiquitous Toyota was parked across the road, its driver and Amzaleg studiously ignoring each other.

I didn't ask whether he had been listening in on my phone calls or whether he had been ordered to meet me by those who did. Besides, I was surprised at how glad I was to see him. Why that was, I couldn't tell.

It was cool in Glantz's kitchen. The heat engulfing Tel Aviv had somehow not yet penetrated this ancient enclave of crumbling houses where a few members of the second wave of immigrants still lived. As Mr. Glantz fussed around in his kitchen, Amzaleg and I sat on two wobbly chairs, saying nothing. At last he sat down at the table.

"Drink, drink." He pushed a tea glass toward me.

He himself drank his tea from a shallow bowl, blowing into it as he drank. Over the rim he said to Amzaleg. "So? Twice in one week? What else you want to know?" He turned toward me. "So many questions he asked me already, he should know me better now than my wife, may she rest in peace." He sipped noisily at his bowl of tea. "Better than his own wife, maybe." He gave a cackle. "And you?" he said to me.

Amzaleg's face turned dark ocher.

I said I wanted to take some of the things that my father had left. "Maybe also ask you a few questions—"

Mr. Glantz pointed a belligerent thumb at Amzaleg. "I told the police already everything, that I went to look for Isser in the middle of the seder, when he hadn't—"

"No. I—I wanted to ask you about the time he lived here before, with Paltiel."

Mr. Glantz's eyes narrowed. "Why?"

I explained about the play, what my father and now Kagan had asked of me. "So I'm trying to learn about the prehistory, to make the show look good—" I paused, searching for words. "The atmosphere."

"Of this, I know nothing." Mr. Glantz threw a swift glance at Amzaleg, who now kept silent.

I said, "But did he write it here, this play?"

"*Ich veis?*" he said in Yiddish. What do I know? "He was writing all the time."

"When? Now? Or then?"

"Oh, then, and also now, all the time."

I stole a glance at Amzaleg, but his dark face remained impassive, as if now he, like my tailers, were a mere spectator at an enfolding show.

"At this table," Mr. Glantz went on, "and in his room, all the time he was writing. Poems, letters, stories."

I said, "Did Paltiel write his poems here?"

Mr. Glantz shrugged. "What do I know? He wrote here, there, everywhere."

There was another pause, a longer one.

Amzaleg asked, "Before he got married, he also lived here, the deceased?"

"Yes, yes," Mr. Glantz said. "He and Paltiel, seventeen years. Straight off the boat they came, with the horse-drawn cart that used to run between Yaffo and Tel Aviv. Also Nachman Shein, later, after the Zirahtron Theater threw him out because of the Purim party, when he brought the Arab in. So I put a mattress on the floor."

"What Arab?"

"Someone they found and dressed up like an old *Arabusha*, and he came and read everyone his fortune. Maybe he was the *feigele* of Shein, or Paltiel, I don't know."

Amzaleg and I waited, not looking at each other.

Mr. Glantz said, "The first time they came, your father and Paltiel, both of them were still wet from the sea, dripping on the stairs—they had both fallen into the sea, coming off the boat," he cackled. "Lucky for them, this *Arabush* boatman knew how to swim."

"Yes." I had heard this story before. "So how long did he live here, my father?"

"I told you, seventeen—"

"Not then. Now."

"Now? Three years almost, from just before she died." Mr. Glantz darted at me a quick opaque look. "May she rest in peace."

"He came here before she died, or after?"

"Before, three weeks before."

Amzaleg shifted in his seat.

It didn't make sense. My parents had always seemed such a pair of lovebirds. My father bringing my mother cyclamens (whose smell she loved) and asters for no reason; she massaging his sore shoulders after work, and mending his socks. Yet he had left her just before she was about to go into surgery, with my brother only a month dead. It didn't make sense.

Mr. Glantz shrugged. "So maybe they had a fight. *Ich veis?*" Fought over what? "You sure?" I said. "Before, not after she—"

"Yes, yes, before! Like I told you. In May seventy-four, right after Independence Day. He called and asked if he could take the room again. So I didn't ask questions." Mr. Glantz looked at me directly. "Sure I said yes. Seventeen years, it counts for something." He got up. "Come. I'll show you his room."

We straggled in, but there was nothing much to look at. A wooden table with one chair by the window; a narrow military bed stretched taut with a blue army blanket, and under the bed, two scuffed leather slippers, neatly aligned. On the wall, the photograph of my grandfather and grandmother from Poland who had gone with Hitler; and, to the side, one more photo: my father with Paltiel Rubin, both in desert fatigues, their hair blowing in the wind.

No photograph of my mother, or of me or my brother. As if anything that occurred after '48 had never happened.

I blew my nose into my handkerchief.

I looked around me, trying to discern in this bare cell an answer to the mystery of my father's death, and of his life. But there was nothing. A few books were piled helter-skelter on a low plywood shelf by the window: mainly poems by Nachman Shein, Paltiel Rubin, and Michah Cohen-Kadosh. On the table were *The History of the Jews*, by Professor Chayim HaM'eiri-Roggell, all five volumes of it; an old Cassuto Bible; a Siddur; and, to my great surprise, my own three blue copybooks of poetry and stories, which I had written during the service, against regulations. A ballpoint pen lay on the top copybook, a clot of ink on its tip.

I felt my nose heating up inside.

Amzaleg said, "Did Paltiel also live here? In this room?"

"Yes, yes, here. They used to write at this table, together."

"Together?" I said. This was news to me.

"Yes, sure, together. They were friends, once."

I thought Mr. Glantz would launch into a story about the rocky friendship of my father and Paltiel, how they fought the Arabs in '48, and each other, and made bedlam in the Tel Aviv *bohema*, but he seemed to have lost interest. "Look around. Maybe you want to take something now, or later, I don't care."

I leafed through the copybooks, my cheeks burning. Some pages had been corrected, for grammar and punctuation; but here and there were small sharp check marks of approval. I felt my eyes sting.

"Did anyone come to visit him?" I asked. "After my mother died."

"Sometimes." Mr. Glantz went on about the Yaffo suppliers who arrived once a week for their checks, then stayed for coffee, and actors who came. The friend who had come every Friday to help translate Paltiel's poetry books into Arabic; and more actors, who came probably to ask for handouts. "Why they didn't come to the funeral—"

"*Cholera*," Amzaleg said. "All of them."

"Yes," I said.

Mr. Glantz went on, "And once or twice on Saturday he came with me to the synagogue—you know the synagogue? On Bugrashov?"

"Yes. That's where I had my bar mitzvah." Then, for no reason at all, I asked, "Did any women come to visit?" I felt my face redden.

There was a pause.

"Yes," Mr. Glantz said at last. "Sometimes, once a week, also after Sonya died."

I looked at him, waiting.

"Riva," Mr. Glantz said. "Riva Yellin."

He went into a fit of coughing and I waited until it passed.

Later, going together down the stairs, neither of us speaking, Amzaleg suddenly said to me over his shoulder, "She has an alibi."

"She is old," I said into his back.

"Everyone is old."

We emerged into the street. For a moment we stood in the intense yellow sunshine, breathing slowly through our mouths, blinking in the glare, ignoring the tailer who leaned on the fence opposite. Then, making an odd squeak with his lips, Amzaleg thumped his fist on my shoulder as if to encourage me before a tough mission, got into his car, and roared off without offering me a lift.

I stared after him for a long while. Was he really only after my father's killer? Or was there something else?

24

THE AUDITIONS TOOK PLACE Sunday morning, four and a half weeks before the deadline, in an empty warehouse at the back of the Reznik chocolate factory in Ramat Gan. They did not go peacefully. Outside on the sidewalk, two small crowds congregated, face to face. On one side were perhaps twenty youths wearing knitted skullcaps and oversized orange T-shirts sporting a picture of a raised fist, and the word *"Kach!"*—Thus!—who kept clapping and chanting, "In blood and fire Judea has fallen, in blood and fire Judea shall rise!" They were disciples of Meir Kahane, the mad rabbi from Brooklyn who wanted to expel all Arabs from the land of Israel.

Across from them was another, smaller crowd—high school students, both boys and girls in standard uniforms of dark blue pants and pale blue shirts like those Ehud, Ruthy, and I used to wear to Alliance High School, and a few Tel Aviv bohemians in their own standard uniforms of jeans and Peace Now T-shirts, like Ruthy's. Every now and then the high school crowd tried to drown out the screaming of the orange shirts with soppy kibbutz songs, but this only served to inflame their opponents. The result was an ongoing cacophony. At last we had the chairs moved to a large storage room, windowless and stuffy, but quiet, and there the audition finally began, an hour late.

Only young actors had come to try out, most clutching copies of the play—how they had gotten them no one knew. But a few arrived without knowing what they would be auditioning for, and two of these, after scanning the first act, got up wordlessly and left. A third, a curly-haired girl with a Star of David medallion on her neck, gave a short ranting speech similar to the one I had gotten from the Israeli consul in Canada. The remaining actors just stared ahead, waiting for her to finish and leave, which she finally did. Immediately afterward, Kagan stood up and asked for quiet. His face was flushed, his bloodshot eyes distant as he spoke. The play for which they were auditioning, he announced in his trained HaBimah voice, was a rediscovered masterpiece written by Isser Starkman, hero of the Castel, recently murdered by evil hands whom justice would one day surely reach.

The room was silent as Kagan went on to say that the play had been staged only once before, in the days of Genesis, but that performance had been interrupted by other malign hands. And, as all could now see, Kagan continued, similar hands were still trying to stop the play from being performed. Here his voice strengthened dramatically. "Anyone who auditions today must be ready, if chosen, to sacrifice for the play, since the same hands that cut short Isser Starkman's life would no doubt try to stop his song also." Kagan scanned the small crowd, his eyes flashing theatrically. "So any soft-hearted louse among you who cannot take it better leave now, for know we must, ere we start on this sacred task!"

No one got up, no one spoke, no one moved; the crowd seemed transfixed.

"It is an important play," Kagan went on, "a key play in pre-Genesis Hebrew literature, conceived in suffering and born in blood. And the son of the slain author and brother to a fallen soldier will help direct it, as his father asked him before he died."

Chairs creaked when, as if pulled by a string, everyone turned
in their seats and looked at me. There was a low hum as all
mumbled gutturally together, like the crowd repeating the Kaddish at my father's funeral. Blood rushed to my face and I felt
my eyes sting. There was a strange softness in my belly.

Ehud punched at my shoulder with his fist, not hard, and
left the fist there.

Then the moment passed.

"*Yallah,*" I said to Kagan. "*Siftah.*" Opening move.

Kagan began matter-of-factly, distributing copies of the play
to those who did not have them, allowing fifteen minutes of
reading. He then let the auditioning actors read whatever part
they wanted. To my surprise, he made Ruthy audition like
everyone else. I thought Ehud had assigned her Sarah's role
in advance, as the price for postponing their wedding. But she
waited in line as three other Sarahs walked up front and sang
their chosen parts. When her turn came, she stood up in her
seat, silent and fulminating. She began softly, staring at Kagan,
Ehud, and me in turn, and after a while her voice strengthened
as she sang of her plight. And all at once her voice acquired
massive volume as it soared, hitting the highest notes with violent precision. She remained standing for a moment, then sat
down. No one spoke; two other actresses who had sung before
for the role got up and left.

By afternoon Kagan announced his choices without expla-
nation. To no one's surprise, Ruthy got Sarah's role. Other
choices seemed no surprise either.

"Thank you all for coming," Kagan said. "Be careful when
you leave. I suggest you exit in twos and threes. Those who did
not get chosen, please leave your names and addresses with
me, in case of need. For the chosen, take your copies home and

memorize your lines. Reflect on the play at length—tomorrow would be a good day to do so. Then have a good sleep—first rehearsal is Friday morning, nine sharp."

Next day was Memorial Day, the day before Independence Day. It was also the start of a heat wave that lasted all the way to our performance. Early in the morning, before the heat started, while Ehud and Ruthy were still sleeping, Amzaleg rang the doorbell as I was rereading the play for the hundredth time. When I opened the door he asked without preamble if I wanted to go play poker.

"Now?"

"First we go for Yizkor." The memorial prayer for the dead. "You want to come?" He squeaked his lips at me.

"All right," I said.

It was clear that neither the Yizkor nor poker was the real purpose of his visit.

We drove by the Moroccan synagogue at the HaTiqva quarter so Amzaleg could pick up his prayer shawl. The synagogue was a decrepit structure shaded by old eucalyptus trees. Through the open door I could see the cantor, a young man about my age but already balding, swaying before the holy arc, trilling the notes. I looked away.

Presently Amzaleg returned carrying a velvet bag. "For my son, also for two of my brothers," he said, staring ahead. "He was killed in the Golan Heights in seventy-three, they in Jerusalem in sixty-seven. May the Holy Name avenge their blood." He ground the gears, then gunned the engine.

Avenge upon whom? Or what?

Nachalat Yitzchak cemetery was more crowded than it had been two weeks before. Thousands of people had come, and it seemed that everyone was weeping. There was something nearly monstrous in so much grief all at once. Women of various ages were lying prostrate on graves, hugging tombstones. Men stood in small and large clumps, talking in low voices. A few stood beside graves, idly flicking pebbles onto them.

"Here." Amzaleg lassoed my shoulders with a blue-and-white Moroccan prayer shawl. "Was my son's. You want?"

"Okay," I said at last.

I sat down on a narrow bench, fingering the shawl. Amzaleg had gone to stand before twin headstones fashioned from crude basalt. He held his small brown Siddur, mumbling intently, then moved over to a third grave. A young woman with a nose like Amzaleg's was weeping silently over it, her brown cheeks bright with tears. As Amzaleg came near her she rose, wiped her eyes, and walked out of the cemetery.

I averted my eyes. Amzaleg's family was no business of mine.

For a while I watched the mourners, trying unsuccessfully to deaden my heart, and finally walked over to my father's fresh grave, and put a pebble on it, too. Words I had nearly forgotten rose in me, and through gritted teeth I said them. How many friends have I said these words for? How many enemies?

An antidote to God's *Mein Kampf*, Ehud had said.

A low siren sounded, slowly gaining strength as it rose in volume and in pitch. It rose and climbed until it reached a sort of hum that resonated with everything—the transparent air, the thin dusty sycamores, the black-clad women, the throng of soldiers in aleph uniforms. Then it died down. Bursts of weeping came from all sides.

"He's coming," said Amzaleg. "Peres."

Shim'on Peres, Labor's new leader following Rabin's resignation, walked by, stooped and gray. Behind him walked four tall gorillas in suits, one nearly as tall as me. All nodded at Amzaleg, their eyes flicking over me.

When the prayer ended Amzaleg drove me back to the Ha-Tiqva quarter. No car followed us as far as I could see.

"Now we play poker," Amzaleg growled savagely, "in their memory."

Amzaleg's apartment in the HaTiqva quarter was the smallest I had ever seen—three cubicles of rooms, a shoe box of a kitchen, and a tiny low-ceilinged toilet. I had thought Amzaleg and I would eat and play cards and talk, but to my angry surprise, when we arrived I saw Shim'on Gershonovitz sitting in the kitchen, splitting peanut shells in his thick fingers.

"What's he doing here?" I snapped. "Is it poker, or official business?"

I thought Amzaleg himself had wanted to talk to me, not this man who was responsible for my tailers, and probably also responsible for putting the fear into everyone about my father's play.

Amzaleg's face darkened. "Sit down."

I sat slowly, tamping down my anger with difficulty.

The kitchen was so tight no one could move without poking a knee or an elbow into someone else. A black frying pan stood on the gas range, emitting a strong smell of fried onions. There were no curtains nor a woman's touch anywhere; it was evidently a single man's dwelling. But on the high shelf, besides several photos of a boy and a girl, some together with a younger Amzaleg, others alone—probably his son and daughter (there was a diagonal black patch on one of the boy's photos)—I saw a line of poetry books in Hebrew, Arabic, and French, with paper tabs sticking out. Farahidi's book of sixteen Arab meters; Nuwas's love poems; Mallarmé's sonnets; Bialik and Tchernichovsky; Alterman; and also Paltiel Rubin's first edition of *Flowers of Blood*.

I raised my eyebrows, trying to catch Amzaleg's eye, but he evaded mine. He tugged at the fridge's door and pulled out a large bottle of Tempo and, from the back, a pack of well-thumbed cards. "My ex used to say, it's either them or me."

"Them," said Gershonovitz.

Amzaleg swigged at length and passed the bottle to Gershonovitz, then cut the cards. "*Siftach*," he rumbled.

The fat man drank and passed me the bottle (I curtly declined), as his eyes flashed with false bonhomie. "The Toronto embassy *katsa* tells me your shiksa has big tits."

Rage blossomed in me. "You had me followed in Toronto, too!"

"Only now and then, to make sure."

"Sure of what? That I didn't kill anyone?" But I really shouldn't have been surprised—an ex Anon, no longer a citizen, and with the speech I gave to the consul . . . "And here? Tailing me day and night like an *Arabush* . . ."

"It's for your own protection, Dada, we told you." He slapped two cards. "Raise you ten."

"Protection!" I pushed a ten-shekel bill. "Against whom? More burglars? Amzaleg still didn't catch the—first, then the one who tried to steal the play, then this *Arabush* in Tveriah—" I made a farting sound with my lips.

Amzaleg growled and picked a card, and Gershonovitz picked another equably.

I said, "Or maybe you think it's a Debba that did all this?" I repeated the sound.

"Well, you can laugh," Gershonovitz said. "But how did the . . . killer get into the store? With the door locked?"

I slapped down my cards. "So maybe my father opened the door himself, when someone he knew knocked, or someone asked for money?" I collected the bills.

Amzaleg dealt fresh cards and kept darkly silent.

"Yeah, maybe," Gershonovitz said. "But how could the killer lock the door after . . . what he did? There was only one key, and it was in Isser's pocket."

It was true. My father never made a duplicate key to the store's door. I had never asked why. All at once the image of my father sitting at his workbench, cutting a thick leather sole, a long knife in his hand, came to me, and I felt my eyes sting. Silently Amzaleg handed me the Tempo bottle. I took a swig and gagged. It was pure arak. Amzaleg retrieved the bottle and said in a low voice, "Well, we found he did have a visitor in the store that night."

I breathed shallowly. "Who?"

Amzaleg said, "Someone. We don't know who. Zussman came back later to get something from the kiosk, and he heard someone talking with him—"

Gershonovitz interrupted angrily, "This baldie, his wife, she sent him to the kiosk to bring more Tempo bottles in the middle of the seder . . . Can you imagine? We're lucky he married her only later, or in forty-eight he would have done nothing. She would have kept him home in the kitchen all through the war."

Did he mean Zussman worked for him in forty-eight? It seemed needless to ask.

Amzaleg said, "Well, Sonya didn't keep *him* from doing things."

Gershonovitz said, "Yeah, but she was doing things, too."

There was a silence, as if they expected me to ask a question. I asked it. "Did my mother work for you, too, before the Events?" My heart was thumping hard. It was now clear that this was why they had brought me here, to tell me this.

"No, no." Gershonovitz picked a card and pushed a bill forward. "She just—helped. She was only sixteen, not a full member; she was—doing other things for us—"

"For the Shay?" The Haganah's intelligence service.

More cards exchanged places; money piled up; I did not understand how I could continue to play.

"Yes, even though she was young, in thirty-three," Gershonovitz said. "Very young, when she began working in Yaffo, in . . . sewing."

There was a long pause. Amzaleg said into it, "But we don't think that this is connected to what happened then, in the pre-history."

"The murder, or the play?" My sarcasm didn't quite come off.

"Both," Gershonovitz said.

I waited, head ringing with unasked questions.

Gershonovitz said, "She was working in Yaffo, in sewing, with all the rich Arabs, they liked Jewish work—dresses, lace—and while she worked she kept her ears open, then she told us."

"Told you what?" My head had cleared suddenly and the words sang in my ears, each clear as a high gong.

"She spoke Arabic," Gershonovitz said. "She just picked it up."

"Better than me," Amzaleg said. "And I was born in Casablanca."

The cards were lying now in the middle of the table, forgotten.

"She told us things," Gershonovitz said softly. "The bomb in the Gordon beach, the attack on the Shapira quarter . . . so many things she found out for us . . . I didn't ask how . . ." He passed a beefy hand over his face. "But I don't know if she ever found out who he really was. Nobody knew; and Isser never said anything after he . . . finished him, in the Castel."

"Abu Jalood," I said.

For some reason the little hairs rose on the back of my neck.

"Yes," Gershonovitz said. "We were sure he was someone from Haifa, a lawyer or something, someone who knew how to organize, how to negotiate, give and take, keep people together, like Ben-Gurion was for us. A gift from history."

Amzaleg said, "Or maybe from East Jerusalem, from one of the old families. The Nashashibis, or the Erawats. I met some of them. Smart, almost like us."

"A cousin of the Grand Mufti," said Gershonovitz, "is what I heard. Or a Nablus *sa'eed*." A lord.

I said, "And she knew who Abu Jalood was, my mother?"

Gershonovitz said, "Maybe she heard something, in thirty-six, and she only told Isser, so he could catch him."

"In forty-eight," I said. "In the Castel."

It was not a question. I was merely repeating, to show I understood.

"Yes," Amzaleg said, heavily. "*Hada hoo.*" That's it.

There was a long silence. I broke it and spoke directly to Gershonovitz. "And you think he came back, the Debba?" I almost said "it," but caught myself.

"Don't be a donkey," Gershonovitz said. "It was a burglar who made it look as-if, a Jewish *ganef*, not their damn Mahdi."

I opened my mouth but Gershonovitz held up his hand.

"We'll catch the beast, don't worry," he said softly. "You just stop this foolishness with the play and go back to Canada to your shiksa." He gathered the cards and stuck them back into their box. Each of us picked up his own money pile. The poker game was over, but it suddenly felt as if another, bigger game had just begun.

As we congregated in the tiny hall, putting on shoes and sandals, Gershonovitz said to me with the same soft earnestness, "Leave this for us, Duvid, it'd be better for you. Listen to me!"

I laced my sandals, saying nothing. This, for the first time, sounded like a real threat.

25

THE FIRST FULL REHEARSAL took place two days later, Friday morning, right after Independence Day—it was just one long reading. Kagan sat in the midst of the small warehouse in Ehud's chocolate factory, while the chosen actors read their parts in a subdued fashion, milling about. Kagan paid attention only to the timing, which he measured with a large stopwatch and wrote down laboriously after every speech.

The two crowds outside—the Kach demonstrators and the opposing high school students—were smaller, perhaps because of the previous night's Independence Day celebrations, which had lasted till the early morning, with rowdy wild-eyed crowds roaming the streets, chortling and banging on one another's heads with plastic hammers. Ruthy and Ehud and I had also gone out, screaming along with the multitudes, singing soppy prehistorical songs at the top of our voices, until we were caught in a huge hora circle in Kings of Israel Square where, arms on shoulders of strangers and on one another's, we twirled and swirled for what seemed like hours, even Ehud stumbling-dancing on his game leg, hanging on to Ruthy, and to me.

I do not recall how we arrived home, nor how we all fell together on the sofa where, early next morning, the three of us woke up, silent and embarrassed, curled up with one another, reeking with drink and heat and smoke.

Perhaps every actor had been out the night before, because no one was fit for reading that morning. Furthermore, the

heat wave engulfing Tel Aviv had intensified during the night
and it was hard to breathe in the small rehearsal room. Yet
the screams of the Kach crowd were even more fervent than
before, and the responding chants of the high school students,
despite their smaller number, were stronger as well. When
toward noon the cacophony penetrated even the inner warehouse, I left and strode to the parked police cruiser nearby.
I rapped on its window; it rolled downward to reveal Amzaleg's swarthy face. At his side sat the skinny policeman from
the Dizzengoff station, poking a thumbnail between his front
teeth. I unleashed a tirade at Amzaleg, demanding that he get
rid of the noisemakers.

"And do what to them?" Amzaleg asked in a voice just as
loud as mine. "They have a demonstration permit."

"But they don't let us rehearse. They're making enough
noise to raise the dead, they're shouting—"

"So they are shouting! Nowadays anyone can say any damn
thing he wants . . ." He paused, as if baiting me to speak
further.

I turned on my heels. Slamming on the car's side, I hurried
back, toward the soaring, singing words.

26

AFTER THE MORNING REHEARSAL I made my way to the *Davar* newspaper's morgue, trailed by my twin shadows.

It was a dusty room on the second floor of a large industrial building on Balfour Street, not far from Gelber's office. They kept copies of all newspapers, including their competitors; perhaps out of a sense of noblesse oblige.

At first the bespectacled librarian refused to let me in. Suddenly she relented. "Starkman? Oh, yes, you are his son. He loaned me some money for rent, in forty-two."

Mr. Gelber was right: it was a wonder my father had not died in the poorhouse.

For the next three hours I browsed through old newspapers, decades-old literary supplements, long essays by forgotten theater critics about my father, Paltiel, and their small theater troupe. About the early Purim plays, the skits, the evenings of declamatory poetry. I photocopied *Davar*'s own poisonous editorial following the interrupted 1946 performance, castigating all involved in it. I also found a *Hatzofe* article mocking the "primitive rumor" that the real Debba would appear at the end of the Haifa performance, to avenge himself upon the Jews and liberate his people. "A pity the show was interrupted," mocked the long-ago writer, "or the Arabs would've seen they had no savior and then leave. Or perhaps," he added as an impish postscript, "our brave boys would have caught this animal Mahdi and made an example of him, for the same ends?"

I asked for Paltiel Rubin's annotated earlier works, where the Debba's legend was first mentioned, and how it tied to the traditional belief in the Mahdi's second coming and the Muslim legend of the End of Days.

The librarian removed a key from a drawer, unlocked a dusty glass-paneled cupboard, and handed me two small volumes bound in red leather—the rare first edition of *Flowers of Blood*. I copied by hand a few of the early poems which mentioned "the evil Debba," steeling my heart against their singing cadences, so much like my father's play . . .

Was this why Kagan had sent me to research the past? Did he really think the Debba's legend would help me understand the play and make clear why my father had asked me to stage it?

My father could not possibly have known that the play would serve as an antidote to his son's black dreams. Or did he really think that a mere piece of theater could serve as an antidote to the larger darkness here?

27

A FEW DAYS AFTER my visit to the *Davar* newspaper morgue, the paper published an article by Professor Tzifroni from Tel Aviv University, the Rubin biographer, who snidely alluded to the stylistic similiarity of the play to Paltiel's poems. The article did not say outright that my father stole Paltiel's play, but it came close. I was enraged, because even though I knew that my father—despite my grievances against him—had been most honest, it was still possible he had handed me Paltiel's play in all innocence—after all, there was no author's name on the front cover—thus causing himself posthumous grief.

At first I wanted to write to the paper's editor and explain, but Kagan urged me to keep quiet, quoting the Arab proverb that if you give a barking dog any attention, it would only make him bark all the more.

I did keep quiet; but a second, practical difficulty arose—the defamatory *Davar* article caused a rumor that I would sue the paper for slander. This made it harder for Ehud to find us a hall. What owner would be fool enough to get mixed up in a lawsuit?

Other papers then picked up the thread, and several other such articles appeared. I resolved not to read any, but it was hard—almost as hard as withstanding my recurring black dreams. It was as if a sinister force was determined to rob me of peace the moment I landed, any way it could. I could only hope that it would all end, once the play was performed.

The Kach youth did not let us rehearse in peace either. Yet over the next few days, slowly and imperceptibly, the opposing crowd of supporters seemed to grow larger and bolder. Its composition changed also, and it now consisted of nearly equal parts high school students and old and middle-aged folk. They came early every day, and stood outside the chocolate factory in the burning sun, some hatless, others with folded newspapers over their heads, nearly all with copies of the play in hand, listening to snatches of song, occasionally repeating the words in low unison. The Kach rowdies tried to drown out our voices, but the very calm presence of the supporters seemed to unsettle them, and presently their harassment stopped. Even so we still had to pass daily between these two crowds that were only a hairbreadth away from coming to blows.

What did not stop, however, were the dozens of acts of vandalism and violence directed toward anything and anyone connected with the play. The actor who played Yochanan got into a tussle in a pub at the old Tel Aviv harbor with a one-armed '73 veteran, who hollered drunkenly that it was a disgrace and dishonor for his fallen comrades to have any Jew act in such a dreck play. When our Yochanan said something idiotic in return, about the fallen having bequeathed theater to us with their spilled blood, the veteran smashed our Yochanan's teeth with his arm stub. The police refused to arrest him and equally refused to transport our actor to the hospital. He got there on his own, where he remained out of commission for three weeks, and Kagan had to choose a new Yochanan.

And other actors left us, some on their own, others because of mishaps. But as fast as actors left or were ambushed and hurt, others joined and learned their roles and plugged right into the rehearsals, eerily fast. It was as if the play had acquired a life of its own and was barreling forward despite all opposition, imbuing newly chosen actors with uncanny powers of recall, so it took newcomers only a few days to learn their roles. Indeed, the play was so easy to memorize that all the actors seemed to know everyone else's lines, and Kagan often had to stop actors from muttering one another's words during rehearsals, or humming one another's songs. It was unlike any play I or anyone else had ever attended.

If during the day the violence seemed contained, at night the chocolate factory suffered a spate of vandalisms, which cost us several rehearsal days. Ehud posted some chocolate workers as sentinels, but feces were being thrown in through the rehearsal hall windows, and furniture kept being broken. It was as if those who did this could walk through walls. Ehud was angry and exasperated. He had never produced a play, he said, that raised so much emotion. It often seemed as if it simply made people lose their senses.

Or maybe it was not just the play. With every passing day the elections came nearer, and the two main parties, Labor and Likkud, appeared unable to break their tie in the polls. The general frenzy intensified and even mild debates on street corners turned into fistfights. It often felt as though a sinister force, long dormant, had crawled out of its lair and was intent on pitting all against all. It was clearly only a question of time before we would have a melee in front of the chocolate factory as well.

"It's never been like this before. Never," Leibele assured me one afternoon in Café Cassit, after I had helped him break up a brawl among three ancient HaBimah actors, none younger than seventy. "But what do you want? Some people hear the name 'Begin,' they see the devil."

"And you?" I asked him. "Whom will you vote for? Begin, for a change?"

Leibele hoisted a thin shoulder. "I—I don't know—sometimes I think, maybe we should let Begin cleanse the land for a few years . . . After all, someone has to do this . . ."

"Do the necessary dreck." I was surprised at the bitterness I felt. What was I so bitter about? Someone had to do God's dirty work for Him, as Shafrir used to say, so the rest of the Jews could rejoice in their purity.

"Yes, that's it exactly," Leibele said. "Then we could bring Labor back, be clean again like before . . ."

I left him soon thereafter, mute with anger.

28

BUT THERE WERE MOMENTS of normalcy also, although I should have known that they couldn't last.

Friday evening, Ehud took the phone off the hook and Ruthy cooked a traditional Shabbat meal just like my mother—boiled chicken, soup with farfel, sweetened carrots, prune compote. My mother cooked in large pots because there were always charity guests at our kitchen table—poor actors and impoverished playwrights invited by my father, or Auschwitz widows with no kin and old rabbis whose congregations had gone with Hitler invited by my mother. In the small kitchen there was never enough room to sit, but always plenty to eat. But tonight there was plenty of room because the only charity guest was me. As Ruthy laid down the white table cloth, Ehud and I washed our hands meekly at the kitchen tap and dried them on a towel that Ruthy had given us, as if she were our mother; then we sat down, one on each side of Ruthy. She lit and blessed the Shabbat candles, covering her face with her palms briefly, as my mother did, and Ehud made the blessing on the wine, then, to my surprise, over the challah also, as my father used to. We ate and chatted peacefully. After we finished eating we sat barefoot, the three of us, on the living room carpet, and talked of nothing but the past: high school classmates who had fallen in '67 and '73; guys from the Unit, like my brother, who had gone on deep penetrations and never come back; books we had read ten years back, and old movies. We did not talk of the play, or the elections, or my father's murder, or the ruckus that all this seemed to generate.

Riva Yellin made an entrance a little after ten o'clock. I feared her anger would shatter the peace, as I knew she fiercely objected to Ruthy appearing in the play. Before I returned, Ruthy had agreed to abandon theater and dedicate herself to family life so that she did not end up like her mother, yet here she was, acting again. Or maybe Riva objected to the play because it brought Ruthy and me into daily proximity once more, though Riva made no mention of it now. She just nodded to me frostily and said she would take tea. Ehud she embraced sideways and let him kiss her on the cheek. Then she sat on the sofa and turned to me. "Someone wrote disgusting things on the fence downstairs. Better wash it off."

I grabbed a rag from under the sink and dashed downstairs in my bare feet and loose gym shorts. On the street side of the stone fence, someone had sprayed a message in large cursive Hebrew, in red:

"We shall get you too like we got him, *ya* Arab-loving *cholera*—!"

The paint was still wet and dripping, in slowly congealing drops. I rubbed at it in smoldering rage until the letters smeared.

These goddamn punks—calling *me* an Arab-lover!

I was so intent on my work that I did not hear the rustle behind me. But suddenly there came a whistling whoosh and a blue light exploded above my right temple. My head slammed against the stone fence and immediately something smashed against my right ribs, long and narrow and hard-edged.

Seven years melted away and training and instinct took over. Even as my head still gonged I let my legs crumple, and the second blow swished over my head. With my head

tucked under my arm I rolled left, and rose to face whoever
had hit me.

They were two stocky men wearing orange Kach shirts
clearly too small for their bulging shoulders. They danced
lightly right and left, boxer-style, swinging pieces of lumber
from their fingertips.

I stood still in the semidark. The streetlight had gone out.
Smashed, probably—I felt glass shards under my bare toes. No
one was about. Even the curtained Toyota seemed deserted. I
kept still, assessing, suppressing the dark Other inside me that
had been taught the necessary dreck, as the two shadows exchanged furtive glances. I had not uttered a sound when hit,
nor moved after my roll; just stood in a frozen wait. My im-
mobility seemed to throw them into unease; then, as if by silent agreement, they separated, preparing to attack from both
sides at once.

I heard a scrape behind me, but it was only Mr. Tzukerman, the Auschwitz survivor who lived on the second floor.
He shuffled by, carrying an embroidered prayer-shawl bag—
probably returning from the Jabotinsky synagogue. He flicked
a filmed glance at me and continued on his way up. As if by
tacit understanding my attackers waited. I bent my knees and
dug out a stone fragment from the fence, for ramming against
the soft bone at the temple. Then I rose slowly and waited,
scanning the advancing body parts—as I had been taught: solar
plexus, testicles, throat, eyes, nose bridge, temples . . . A car
door slammed. I ignored it and flexed my knees. Then a rough
voice rasped, "Stop. Where. You. Are. And. Don't. Move."

It was Amzaleg. What the hell was he doing here?

His scratched cruiser was parked parallel to the Toyota,
and he now stepped between the twin orange shirts and me,
a policeman's truncheon in his left hand. One shadow hissed,
"Get the hell out of here, *ya kaza* policeman." It was the

voice of the same yeshiva boy who had been outside Gelber's apartment.

Amzaleg paused.

Kaza is a derogatory term for Moroccan Jews. It refers to Casablanca, from where most arrived. Somehow it came to mean in Hebrew what "nigger" means in English.

I called at Amzaleg's back, "It's okay, Amnon, leave them to me."

He ignored me. I saw his right hand ram at his ample belly, slam on the belt buckle, twist, and tug. The belt slid out and the metal buckle was suddenly swinging, Unit style, in blurry figure eights.

Amzaleg?

The shadows paused, hesitated, then spread further and without a word plunged into the whirl, sticks swinging. There was a slash, and one shadow stumbled back, a dark welt on his cheek; another slash. The other held his neck. Amzaleg hissed something I could not hear. There was an uncertain interval. And then the two turned and ran off, and were gone.

Amzaleg said to me, "Drop the stone, you idiot. You want to be arrested?" He turned and thumped on the roof of the Toyota with his truncheon, hard. No one came out. I watched with surprise as Amzaleg swung his truncheon and smashed one of the Toyota's back lights, then hit the car's roof a second time. Nothing. He smashed one of the front lights, and again thumped on the roof, harder this time, denting it.

I could hear a sound inside the car. Amzaleg raised the truncheon. Now the door opened and a man came out—it was the driver of the taxi I had taken from the airport, when I arrived. Before he could speak Amzaleg said to him, "Give it to me."

"You fucking *kaza*—"

Amzaleg swung at the man's knee, slowly enough to let him jump back. I could not believe what I was seeing. What the hell was this?

The man moved his hand toward the small of his back.

"Yes," Amzaleg said in perfectly neutral voice. "Oh yes, do it."

The man's hand slowed; then very meticulously he pulled out a small Beretta, holding it by the barrel with thumb and forefinger. It was similar to the one Amzaleg had in Tveriah. Slowly he bent over and put it on the ground.

"Now the rest of it. Together with the film inside."

The man turned silently, leaned into the car, and pulled out a boxy Hasselblad camera, the kind used by our Intel patrols, with an infrared filter. I gawped at it.

"Now open it."

The man snarled deep in his throat, like a jackal, but obeyed. He pulled the back open and stripped out the film.

"Any more film inside?"

A shake of the head.

"If you lie—"

The man cursed at length, in military Hebrew.

"You finished?" Amzaleg said. "Now fuck off."

The man said in a voice of pure venom, "You are fucking crazy, you *kaza* policeman, you will pay for this—"

Amzaleg swung his belt in another figure eight, lazily, and the man sprang back and got into the car, started the engine, and drove off. I stood gaping at the Toyota as it drove away, then turned to stare at Amzaleg.

What the hell was that about?

Amzaleg bent over and picked up the gun, then opened the cruiser's door and crooked his finger at me. "Come inside."

Still dumbfounded, I got in beside him.

The cruiser's interior stank of stale cigarettes and cheap Nescafé—police-car smell. But on the dashboard was a sprig of white blossoms, of the kind that grows on every corner by stone fences. "Milk tears" we used to call them. He saw me looking and said, "Smells good. You have this in Canada, too?"

I shook my head. As Amzaleg adjusted his belt I said, "Were you in the Unit?" Because it was always possible he had taken a cold-killing course somewhere else.

"Yes, in fifty-one, the second course. The first Moroccan they took."

I felt myself redden at the express mention of this.

Amzaleg went on, "But your father said, doesn't matter, take him." He sniffed. "Now lift your feet."

"What?" I could not understand what he wanted, but Amzaleg grabbed my left foot and with his fingernails extracted some glass shards. "Now the other."

I turned in my seat in embarrassment and he grabbed the other foot and pulled more shards out of it. He rummaged in the glove compartment and from an assortment of police handcuffs, spare Beretta magazines, and plastic pens pulled an iodine bottle and proceeded to daub it on my cuts. Without raising his head he said, "Why did you accept the fight, you donkey?"

"They hit me, and—" I stopped. It sounded ridiculous, as if I were telling a teacher the other guys had started it.

He said, "You could have run off or shouted, something." He pointed with his chin to where the Toyota had been filming the provocation. "You wanted to spend the next thirty-three days in jail?"

The play's performance was due in thirty-three days. I said with wonder, "You *want* us to do the play!" I turned to face him, trying to understand.

Gershonovitz didn't want the play to be staged, and Amzaleg reported directly to him. Yet he had just come to my rescue. Nothing made sense here. "Why didn't they take you off the case?"

Amzaleg shook his head. "Not this one, not now." He stared at me with his puffy eyes, and suddenly I understood: they could not take Amzaleg off the case, but they could make him report to Gershonovitz, in an unsteady stalemate. I could almost glimpse the outline of two invisible bureaucratic forces poised, like two fists pushing against each other, unmoving, perfectly matched.

I said, "Because of the elections?"

Amzaleg shook his head.

"Because of the play, then?"

He said nothing.

I pointed to his belt. "They can sack you for this."

Amzaleg rocked his jaw from side to side. "In Casablanca," he said slowly, "my mother had four servants, my father was a lawyer. In 1932 he decided to bring us all here to Zion. I was four. You know how they treated us here, these Ashkenazi fuckers?" I could not see why he was telling me all this now. "Like niggers they treated us. Like Arabs!" He breathed through his mouth.

I recalled his daughter, now living with her mother and her Arab stepfather in Shfar'am, and held my breath, saying nothing.

Amzaleg stared ahead. "Forty-nine years old in July, and still only an inspector. Why?"

At last I said, "And my father—"

Amzaleg swiped at his eyes. "For him there was no difference. Arabs, Moroccans, Yemenites, Ashkenazi, it was all the same." He seemed unable to comprehend this. I couldn't either.

I said, "And that's why you—" I stopped.

What was I going to ask? Whether he'd be trying harder to find my father's killer, because my father treated him decently? And so imply that otherwise he wouldn't?

But Amzaleg nodded. "Yes, also."

"And also because of the play?"

"Yes. Also."

I weighed my words carefully. "So there are some who don't want the play produced, like Gershonovitz, but also some—others—who do?"

Amzaleg gave a squeak with his lips to indicate a maybe.

I said, "The *shoo-shoo* doesn't?" The secret services. "And who else?"

When he remained silent I changed tack. "Who does want it?"

I didn't think he'd reply, but he did. "Old *chevermanim*." Brave old fighters, from before '48. "Here and there, not in one place, not just the police, or—or anywhere special, just here and there." He paused. "Old, mostly." Then his mirthless grin reappeared, fierce and scary. "Bereaved parents."

I gazed outside the window at the dark sky, recalling Amzaleg's fallen son and brothers, and Zussman's, and my own brother, and the silent crowd outside the rehearsal hall. "But why now?" I asked at last. "What's with this play? It's just a play." And its essence could be read every now and then in *Ha'Olam HaZeh* editorials.

Amzaleg gave a double squeak of the lips. At last he said, "Go on up, finish your gefilte fish, or whatever." Then he added. "And be careful, *ya* donkey!" He thumped me on the shoulder, hard.

I wanted to tell him not to teach me my profession, but refrained. I nodded and stepped out of his cruiser, walking carefully on the sides of my soles. I was surprised no one had gone out to see what the fracas was about. But everyone probably thought it was just one more violent argument about the elections.

When I came back up I kept quiet about what had happened. Ruthy was tearing into Riva, fuming, talking about new beginnings, historic chances, the unstated wishes of the dead. Ehud, pale and blinking, was trying to pacify both; then Ruthy turned on him. I kept out of it.

At last Riva got up to leave. She gave me a brief nod, as if satisfied that there was indeed nothing between Ruthy and me; that whatever there once had been was finally over. Her nod filled me with unexplained joy, as if all the evil I had done to Ruthy was now absolved. I nodded to her civilly in return.

Later, when I told Ehud about the attack and how Amzaleg had intervened, he said sardonically, "Damsel in distress, eh?"

I knew exactly what he meant. The classic way to gain a patsy's confidence is to save him from a fake threat. Was this what Amzaleg had done here?

Ehud said, "And you shouldn't go naked anymore." He tilted the kitchen table until there was a click, and pulled the drawer out. At its back was a metal box with a combination lock, which he fingered open. Inside was an assortment of throwing knives, cobbler's knives like my father's, a standard-issue switchblade, and a Wiesbaden dagger with a rusty blood groove.

"I don't need a tool," I said irritably. What would I do, take someone down in mid Tel Aviv? I'd go straight to jail. "Give it to Ruthy, in case anyone comes after her."

"Who will come after me?" Ruthy called out drowsily from the bedroom.

"No one," Ehud said tightly. "Go to sleep. You, too, Dada."

I tilted my head toward the bedroom and asked Ehud in a low voice if he didn't want to pull out—meaning that this put Ruthy at risk, too.

He rattled his head tersely no and turned in.

His loyalty and Riva's absolution and Amzaleg's revelation that others might be rooting for the play filled me with such idiotic relief that despite the bruises and knowledge of the nightmares awaiting me, I went to sleep with an easy heart—

foolishly expecting that the blackness would soon turn into light.

A little after midnight I woke up, my head ringing with both songs and dead horrors. I went into the bathroom for a drink of water. Ruthy was waiting there for me, sitting on the edge of the tub, her face as white as her mother's.

Without saying a word she got up, closed the door, and silently and ferociously kissed me on the mouth. Still without speaking she stepped out of her pajama pants, rose on her toes to sit on the sink, and spread her legs wide. Then, silent still, she pulled down my gym shorts and pulled me to her.

We fucked fast and silently, mouths open, eyes an inch apart, saying nothing, listening to Ehud's snores coming from the bedroom. When it was over we stood wordlessly side by side, washing ourselves at the sink, looking neither at each other nor at the door.

The singing inside me had stopped and my head filled with pure blackness. I never knew it was possible to despise myself so much.

Ehud's snores stopped, then continued. Ruthy slipped out and was gone.

PART III

Al Dajjal

(The False One)

29

EARLY NEXT MORNING BEFORE Ehud and Ruthy awoke, I escaped from the apartment as if I had just finished a dreck job. The paint had dried on the low stone fence but the glass fragments were still strewn about. I ate a spicy-hot falafel at the Bazel *shuk*, then marched up Zhabotinsky Street to the Dizzengoff police station.

I strode in and said in a loud voice, "I'd like to report some thugs who attacked me last night—" but before I finished a door banged open and Amzaleg emerged from the corridor, unshaven and rumpled. His eyes glinted as he invited me into his office. I followed him in, touched my ear and pointed to the ceiling, twirled my finger, and raised my eyes. Amzaleg nodded briefly. Yes, it was possible.

I said in the same loud voice, "How's the coffee at the canteen here?"

"Shit," Amzaleg rumbled. He pulled a flat bottle of arak out of his drawer and stuck it in his back pocket. "Let's go to Berman's."

At Berman's kiosk Amzaleg led the way to the only table at the back, by a pile of Dubek cigarette cartons, Tempo bottles, and shelves crammed with Reznik chocolate bars. Old Mr. Berman beamed at me in recognition, but erased his smile as Amzaleg shook his head, and wordlessly brought up two glasses and withdrew. Amzaleg poured arak. "Inoculation against microbes," he said when he saw me squinting at the stained rims. It was a Unit expression.

We drank. Abruptly Amzaleg asked, "You carrying anything?"
I shook my head. "Naked."

He nodded with reluctant approval. I drank down my arak
and he poured me some more. I said, "If I file a complaint, can
you arrest them?"

"No," he said tersely. "You want a policeman to guard you
for a few days?"

"I only walk in crowds."

Amzaleg said, "They may try harder next time."

"And do what? They won't shoot me. This isn't Russia." I
sounded like Ehud.

Amzaleg said, "Not yet." He sounded like Ruthy.

I sipped.

"Listen, Amnon," I said. "What the hell do they have against
me? Is it this play?"

Amzaleg shook his head; his eyes refused to meet mine.

I waited. "You still think it's an Arab who did it?"

Again, no response.

"Because after last night . . . I kept thinking, maybe it's really
a Jew who did it? Because of something—before forty-eight?
And that's why Shimmel wants me out of here and doesn't
want you to catch him? . . . Maybe it was someone that my father knew, that he would open the door for?" It was a confused
question that would have gotten me an F in interrogations.

"Maybe," Amzaleg said.

He pulled out a pack of Gitanes, the kind Shafrir used to
smoke, and lit up. "These *bohema* people," he said into the blue
smoke. "Many were with him once in the Wrestling Club, no?
Maybe one of them came?"

This caught me by surprise. "And you think one of—them—
did it?"

Amzaleg gave a squeak with his lips, this one indicating
ignorance.

Berman served us two Turkish coffees with cardamom seeds, in glasses like those from which we had just drunk arak.

I drank the scalding bitter syrup.

"But why?" I persisted. "Why would any one of them do it—kill my father?"

"Jealousy, maybe."

There it was now, on the table, just what some of Paltiel's biographies had said, calling my father Paltiel's boyfriend as well as accusing him of stealing Paltiel's work. I grabbed the table's edge and leaned forward, but Amzaleg held up his hand. "Goddammit, Dada," he said levelly. "So your father wasn't one, but half the others were. Paltiel, Shein, Kagan, Tzipkin—"

I fairly shook. "Amnon, this was thirty years ago, all this shit. Thirty years!"

"I didn't say it was one of them. Maybe it was an Arab. They also had Arabs in the Wrestling Club before thirty-six, before they split, and some of them were also . . . you know, like Paltiel and Kagan . . ."

I wanted to tell Amzaleg that he and Shimmel could go screw themselves, but breathed deeply and said, "Did you ask any of those old wrestlers about the play?"

"Nah." Amzaleg evaded my eyes. "The play probably's got nothing do with it."

"Well, did you at least talk to Kagan about the play? Or to Riva?"

"I have better things to do than talk to old farts about prehistorical literature." He looked at his watch, suddenly eager to go.

"Suit yourself." I threw a ten-shekel note on the table, nodded to old Mr. Berman, and left.

Clearly it was not just the play, but any talk about the literary prehistory that filled everyone with unease. Why that was, I couldn't tell. But it was equally clear that if I wanted to find the answer to why my father had left me his play and why he had died, I had to seek it myself.

30

THE STREETS WERE ALREADY teeming with morning crowds when I walked up Dizzengoff to Riva Yellin's apartment, my tailers trailing behind.

Riva lived atop a decrepit old building on the corner of Dizzengoff and Bar Kochba. It was ten years since I had been here last. She opened the door a full minute after I had knocked, and glared at me. "Why did you come back from Canada?"

When I began to speak, she cut me off. "Because I don't need you, and she doesn't need you either. Go back to the diaspora. Don't ruin her life."

The previous night's absolution was apparently withdrawn.

I burbled that I had nothing to do with Ruthy, that I came to stay with Ehud, that it was Kagan who had picked Ruthy for the play. "And I didn't know she was living with Ehud—I wanted to leave after the shivah, but my father stipulated that I do this play—"

"I know." Wordlessly she moved aside and let me enter.

Her room was bare, with only four wooden chairs with woven seats, a plywood table with a telephone and an ashtray, a hanging gray blanket to separate the bed from the rest of the room, and a cheap Primus stove for heating food on a rickety table by the small fridge. It reeked of bohemian poverty even worse than Kagan's.

I sat down on one chair and she sat on another. I said I had been to see Mr. Glantz. "Just to get a few things from the room— he said you came to visit my father—"

Riva leaned back. "Oh ho ho, I heard you went with the policeman. But what did you need him for? In Cassit they say now you want to catch the killer yourself, this Arab burglar."

"It was not an Arab burglar. He was a Jew."

Riva's eyes turned opaque. "Yeah?"

"Yes. There had been a burglary at the Atta store a month before, so my father wouldn't have opened the door for just anyone—unless he knew him—" I took a deep breath. "Mr. Glantz said you came to visit my father every week—" I waited.

She stared at me, then gave a theatrical sigh. "Give me the cigarettes from my bag."

I handed her the crumpled packet of Dubeks; she lit one and inhaled. She said, "I had come to pick up my check, if you must know. From Paltiel's estate."

"Every week?"

Her eyes were black pinpoints. "Also I went to talk to your father, at the beginning, to tell him not to be an idiot—to go back to her—"

"To—my mother?"

Riva nodded diagonally, not denying, not confirming.

"But why did he leave her?"

"It's none of your business."

"She was sick already, when he left her . . . Why didn't she tell him?"

Riva let out a dry laugh. "She had her pride, too."

"But did they quarrel? Fight over something?"

Silence.

"He never fought with anybody," I said. "Not even with . . . with his murderer—" I waited, but she remained immobile, smoking in furious silence.

I went on. "Ruthy, she thinks it's somehow connected, to the thing from forty-eight, with Paltiel—because they did the same to him. The same beasts—"

At last I got a spark. "So what do you want me to do, Dada? Sit shivah once more?"

"Just help me catch him. When I catch him, I'll leave."

Riva lit another cigarette with the stub of her first.

I said, "I have a girlfriend in Canada."

For a long minute Riva stared at me, and all at once she seemed to have come to some conclusion. "In thirty-one, in Cassit, that's when I met him for the first time, your father. He just came to my table and told me I looked like his sister—"

"Her name was Hinda Malka. She went with Hitler." I felt my chin vibrate.

"I was sitting there," Riva went on, "talking Bialik and Shakespeare with Paltiel, when the lout suddenly left and your father sat down." She smiled bitterly. "I bet your father paid him to leave, so he could have a free hand with me . . . A Debba he could fight, this hero, but to talk to me, oh ho ho, for this he needed Paltiel's permission . . ." She stared at me with her made-up animal eyes. "But we were hardly ever alone. In one hour, five times he gave money to people. Paupers, actors, two waiters—"

"Yes."

"—and all the time he kept talking about this play he was writing—this shit in yogurt, the dreck about the Arabs, the poor beasts."

"And he wanted you to play in it, in this play?"

"Yeah," Riva said. "Me and him and Paltiel, and maybe Shein—but of course I said no. You know how many wrote plays for me? Bialik, and Tchernichovsky, and Cohen-Kadosh—" The famous names rolled off her tongue. "I didn't have time."

"So that's why you said no?"

She flushed. "You think maybe I was afraid to play in this dreck? That's what you think?" She raised her voice. "Well, I am telling you, I just didn't have time!"

There was a long pause. I asked, "Why did Paltiel give my father a half share in his work?"

Riva's face closed. "I don't know. Ask the lawyer."

"Gelber said it was in return for a favor—"

"He's an idiot. Asking to be paid for favors? Your father?"

I got up shakily to my feet and she grinned up at me. "So that's it? Nothing else you want to know? Maybe if I did it with him?"

I stopped. "Who killed him?"

Her smile did not waver. "Ask the police. They know."

For a moment we stared at each other. Riva's smile became fixed; then it twisted. "Three times, David, three times he asked me to take the role, three times I told him to put the play in the drawer, to forget about it, that it would only bring grief, to everyone, and to him—" Her neck swelled. "And it did . . . just like it did to Paltiel . . . and to her . . ."

My heart thumped. "So you also think that it . . . that my father was killed because of the play?"

Riva grabbed at my hand. "Dada, you leave Ruthy alone! You hear? She's just like Paltiel—this *shmendrik* just took anything and anyone he wanted, without thinking about the cost, to others, or to himself . . . She got it from him . . . and now you are here, with this play . . . How can she say no?" Riva's eyes blazed. "It caused so much grief already to so many, I don't want this dreck to bring grief to her also . . . and to you, too . . . Go back to Canada, leave . . ." Riva's knobby fingers clamped on my wrist with feral strength. "Leave!"

I had to twist my arm this way and that, before I could tear it away and escape.

31

FROM A MUCH DEFACED telephone booth at the Dizzengoff Center I called Professor Gershon Tzifroni of Tel Aviv University, who the week before had castigated the play in *Davar*. The Rubin expert whose book about Paltiel was no longer available.

"Oh, yes, Isser's son," he rasped. "What do you want? I have a lecture soon."

I saw no need to pussyfoot around. "So you think my father stole it?"

"I didn't say stole. I only said it was similar to Rubin's work—"

"So? They were friends!" I rattled off some famous cases of mixed artistic parentage. Cohen-Kadosh and Slonim, Bialik and Ravnitzki. "So why the hell couldn't my father and Paltiel Rubin also . . ."

Professor Tzifroni hung up in my mid-sentence.

32

I BREATHED THE BOOTH's fetid air, slowly, then called Uncle Mordechai in Tveriah.

"No," Uncle Mordechai said. "There's nothing to tell."

I said he had promised to tell me about the prehistory. About my father, and Paltiel, and the play.

"I said I'll tell you only before the Angel of Death comes for me, maybe. Until then, don't you mix me up in this! Understand?"

I wiped my face. Professor Tzifroni had hung up before I finished. And Uncle Mordechai did, too, after repeating what in one way or another every merchant on Herzl Street had said to me, what Mr. Gelber had told me the day I arrived, and what Gershonovitz had warned me against: getting mixed up in this.

But mixed up in what?

There was no other way. Swallowing my bile, I took bus number 1 to Abdallah's store in Yaffo.

It was twelve years since I'd been there last, when my father had taken me to buy the leather for my first combat boots.

Abdallah was sitting in the same old chair in his low-ceilinged basement, waving his arms and talking into a black telephone in rapid French. "But no, no!" he shouted, his silvery mustache quivering. "I told you, never on Friday! Never!"

I stood there, my heart pounding. The same faded theater photographs hung on the walls that his dead brother, the cinema owner and poet, had hung there many years before, the same stacks of yellowing Arab poetry magazines, the same smell of raw leather. I felt like a small boy all over again.

Abdallah slammed the receiver down. "Yes?" he snapped; then as he turned he saw me and grabbed at his aluminum canes. "Ach, ach, ach . . ." With the canes he herded me onto a hard grimy sofa near the wall, then clapped his palms over his head. "Mas'ouda! *Ya* Mas'ouda-a-a!"

A small crone appeared in a dark doorway.

"Coffee!" Abdallah shouted. "With *hel!*" Cardamom seeds.

He unfolded his thin legs sideways and sat beside me. "Ach, ach, ach."

I saw that he had tied a *sharit alhidad* on his thin right arm— the black armband of mourning; my nose tingled. From the wall, the large photograph of Abdallah's dead brother glared down at me.

The crone shuffled in with a copper tray carrying two tiny porcelain cups and a steaming copper *finjan.* She peered into my face as she poured.

"*Shukran,*" I said stiffly. Thank you.

Abdallah raised the cup toward the photo of his dead brother. "In the bosom of Allah shall he reside," he said in a ringing voice in literary Arabic, not making clear whether he meant this for his brother or my father, "with wings of angels above his head—"

We drank up in silence. Outside on the sidewalk, legs kept passing in the high narrow window. Legs in *abbayas*, legs in galabiehs, legs in blue pants.

I felt the same urge to flee that I had felt in Gelber's office, but suppressed it. I said bluntly to Abdallah, "I came to ask you, did my father write it? This play?"

Abdallah put his cup down. "Which play?"

"*The Debba.*" I explained my father's stipulation in the will, and what the newspapers were writing, hinting my father had stolen it, and how it prevented us from getting any hall. "I want to show it was he who wrote it, and not his friend, the poet."

"Baldiel," Abdallah said. Not as a question.

"Yes. You knew him?"

An undefinable expression crossed the narrow face. "His salesman, the liar, the skirt-chaser—" Two spots of dark had appeared in Abdallah's gray cheeks.

"Yes." But just to make sure, I added, "He who wrote *Golyatt, Ben HaTan*—" I stopped. To whom was I speaking of Hebrew poetry? An Arab?

But to my surprise Abdallah nodded. "And *Zonah Tamah*," he said, "and *Shimshon*, and *Flowers of Blood*—"

"Yes! You read this?"

An Arab, reading Hebrew poetry.

"Yes, of course. We published it in this—" He extended his curved fingers at the dusty heap of magazines, piled behind the mounds of leather. "I translated, and Haffi published—"

"Translated into Arabic?"

"Yes, yes." He stared at me, eyebrows raised. "Of course."

I tried to keep the incredulity out of my voice. "You published translated Hebrew poetry in an Arab magazine in forty-eight?"

My father had helped actors in the thirties; had staged an incendiary play in '46; his Arab ex-partner in the shoe business and his brother produced a poetry magazine with translated Hebrew poetry. How much more did I not know?

"No, not in forty-eight. In thirty-six." His voice changing, Abdallah began to recite an Arabic verse with an oddly familiar rhythm. I recognized the double-metered Syrian verse, and the floating stresses.

"And you did this translation?" I felt a tremor in my belly. *Golyatt* in Arabic.

Abdallah sipped the dregs of his coffee. "No, no. Haffi did, together with—with him, with Isrool."

"My father? He helped your brother translate?" I felt dazed.

"Yes, yes."

I made an effort to regroup my thoughts, to return to my first question. I said, "But did he also write other things, my father? Besides the Purim *shpiels*?" I had a hallucinatory odd feeling: talking with an Arab about Purim *shpiels*.

"Yes, yes. This play, that you said." His mouth pursed as if he shied away from mentioning the play's name.

"How do you know?"

"Because he showed it to me, to ask if he should translate it, so maybe we could publish it also, in the magazine."

Again I looked up at the wall, at the fiery black eyes of the man who had nearly published my father's play in Arabic after my father had failed to stage it for the Jews.

What else didn't I know?

Abdallah knocked on his canes with a yellow knuckle. "But Haffi died before we could do it." He paused. "In forty-eight."

"Yes" I said with an effort. "Could you—could you perhaps write all this down for me, as a testimony?" I didn't know why I needed this, or to whom I wanted to show it.

"Yes, of course." Without hesitation he hobbled up to his table, cleared a space amid a heap of bills, and scrawled for a minute, then handed me the note. It was written in flawless Hebrew. But the signature was in Arabic.

"*Shukran*," I said. Thank you.

I searched for something else to say but could find nothing. I got up to leave, and as I climbed the grimy stairs, I could see him looking at me from the bottom of the steps, framed in darkness, his face inscrutable.

I stopped. "Who did it?" I blurted. "D'you know? I mean, who could do such a thing?" And without letting him answer I went on, "Some young *shabbab* perhaps, someone strong— because he was strong—"

Abdallah's face closed like a fist. "Very strong."

I felt my eyes sting.

The old Arab stared up at me. "You want me to help you also, in this?"

I tried to speak, and couldn't. I nodded wordlessly.

Abdallah knocked on the stairs with a cane. "It's for you, or for the policeman?"

"For—for me."

"All right," Abdallah said at last, placidly. "I'll see."

He waited, unmoving, while I wrote down with trembling fingers the phone numbers at the apartment and the chocolate factory, then he turned and went back into the dark, his canes rattling on the floor, as I climbed back into the light.

I stood a moment in the fierce sunshine; but when I turned to go, I found my way blocked. On the cracked sidewalk stood a young Arab, arms folded, barring my way with his foot. His thin face was flushed.

"*Yallah,*" I said. "Move."

He barely reached my chin, and although his arms were finely muscled, he seemed more like a clerk than a street thug, in his faded white shirt with the buttoned low collar.

He tightened the fold of his arms and raised his leg higher against the wall. On his feet, I saw, were sandals just like mine, with biblical clasps.

"*Yallah! Imshi!*" I said in colloquial Arabic. Be quick about it!

The young man detached himself from the wall. "Stealing our land," he whispered, his voice quivering, "and our stories, too. You have no right." He tried to spit in my face, but no spit came.

I stared at him, waiting for him to back off. But he stood his ground. His large eyes, black with hatred and fear, held mine. I could see moistness welling up in their corners.

"Fauzi!" A raspy voice called from the basement. "*Ya* Fa'uz!"

The young Arab's eyes shut tight. "Soon," he hissed into my face. "Soon he'll come again, then he'll cut off all your *zayins*, and us he'll set free! Free from all—"

I pushed at him, blindly.

A voice came from downstairs.

"Fauzi! Where are you, you lazy cur?"

I could hear the canes knocking up the stairs.

"Coming, uncle," the young man whispered.

He picked himself up and disappeared down the stairs.

33

THIS WAS, FOR ME, the first sign that we would also encounter Arab opposition to our play. That we would encounter Jewish enmity was clear from the very start. Aside from my tailers, and Gershonovitz's warnings, and the attempt to frame me in a mock-brawl, we could not obtain a hall anywhere. The newspapers continued to write almost daily about our play in the most poisonous terms. And after the rehearsals' second week, the demonstrations before the chocolate factory grew larger every day.

The two crowds still just stared at each other, but a more violent confrontation seemed imminent. And then midway into the rehearsal period, someone broke into the factory and trashed our rehearsal room thoroughly, spraying on the walls slogans about doing unto traitors as they deserved, and nastier things still about my father.

I was enraged; but Amzaleg, whom I phoned, was coolly unsympathetic. "So put up more sentinels. We haven't got time for this small shit. You know what's going on outside?"

With the elections so near, in the last few days violent demonstrations were a daily routine in Tel Aviv, with the violence increasing as the prospects grew that Labor, the ruling party since the state was born, could be toppled for the first time ever.

"What sentinels?" I shouted. "It's a chocolate factory! Not an army camp—"

Amzaleg had hung up.

And I had thought he was for us; obviously I was wrong.

I told Ehud what Amzaleg had told me. Ehud nodded wordlessly and went to talk to the crew. That night, more of them—our gaffer, and the accountant's office crew—stayed behind after work and, armed with sticks, patrolled the plant's perimeter. Next morning, Ehud walked up to the crowd of supporters and spoke to a few, and that night some high school students joined in the plant's guard duty, as well as two older men, perhaps bereaved fathers; I didn't ask.

There were no more break-ins.

34

It was odd. The more the rehearsals progressed, the less Ruthy, Ehud, and I talked. Ruthy was mostly away, either at a poetry reading given by some rising poet, or at a drama class in which she had registered, to Kagan's irritation and to Ehud's, who had asked the actors, as a precaution, not go anywhere by themselves. Only late at night the three of us would sometimes meet in the kitchen and over glasses of tepid Nescafé spiked with 777, talk haltingly of things that did not matter at all. And later, after midnight, while Ehud snored fitfully in their bedroom, Ruthy would sneak out and wait for me in the bathroom, fulminating with angry silence, forcing me upon her the moment I came in; and both of us would ram against each other, breathing fast and shallowly like two hyenas in heat.

Every morning I vowed to myself to put a stop to it; every night I found myself at it anew. I didn't know how much longer I could stand it.

35

AFTER TWO MORE ACTORS were beaten up, our Yissachar quit.

"It isn't worth it," he shouted at Kagan, as the actors playing 'Ittay and Yochanan showed their bruises all around proudly, telling how they fought back. "It's just a play. I don't want to get killed over a fucking old story!"

Other actors also seemed to lose heart—our Yissachar was popular with them—so that same morning Kagan had Ehud convene all actors, stagehands, and the handful of high school students who had now become part of the crew, and Kagan gave yet another long emotional speech, speaking of duty and sacrifice, strangely resembling the speech I had gotten from the Israeli consul in Toronto. Later Ehud phoned around for a replacement; that afternoon we had him, and by evening our new Yissachar had learned most of his role by heart. He was not as good as the one who had left, but he would have to do.

The morning following the first technical rehearsal, the phone rang in Ehud's office at the chocolate factory.

"You want to come?" said Abdallah's voice. "Remember what you asked me to do, to check something for you? Last week?"

At first I couldn't remember, and then it hit me. "I'll be there in half an hour."

I splashed cold water on my face and ran out through the two opposing crowds to catch a taxi.

Abdallah was sitting as before in the middle of his dark basement, surrounded by rolls of brown suede. Behind him sat the
dark-eyed young man who had tried to bar my way last time.
Abdallah salaamed me and clapped his hands for coffee.

"From Lebanon," he said, pointing to the suede. "Came
today." He began to explain how the merchandise arrived in
unmarked cars from the tanneries in Lattakiya, how the police knew about this. "Also the border guard. But what do they
care? It's not guns. Everyone needs shoes."

The swarthy crone came in with the coffee. Fauzi shook his
head when she put a cup before him, but Abdallah barked an
order in Arabic, and Fauzi picked up the cup.

"Health." Abdallah raised his cup to the large photograph
behind him.

Fauzi performed the same salute, stiffly.

From the wall, Haffiz Seddiqi glowered down upon me,
and upon the dozens of theater actors all around him, in their
faded signed photographs.

"It wasn't Arabs who killed him, Isrool," Abdallah said abruptly.
"I already told Amzaleg that the old guys, they were not involved."

"Yes," I said. "He told me."

"So I asked Fauzi to check with the young guys, too," Abdallah went on. "And he just got the word from someone, that it
was not any of—them."

I made an effort to keep my eyes on the wall. What was I doing,
talking so chummily with Arabs who could get such answers?

". . . not PLO, not PFLP, not the Brotherhood . . ." Abdallah
rattled off names of organizations, of splinter groups.

I said, "Then maybe just young *shabbab*, some local hotheads—"

"No. Young ones would have boasted, told friends, put up
placards, something."

Fauzi thumped on the table. "No. It wasn't Arabs who did this. It was a Jew."

"Yes," Abdallah said. "It wasn't us."

And then, without any transition, Fauzi began to talk about his own family, and the '48 *Naqba*. The Catastrophe of '48. "They took our land, our brickyard, the fishing boats, the orchards, everything—" Breathing hard, he enumerated all that his family had lost. "And my father—" He jerked his chin towards the wall. "Him they killed like a dog—and now my uncle asks me to help you—"

Abdallah put a hand on Fauzi's knee. "Not as a Jew, to help him," he said in Arabic. "He is the son—he came as a guest—" He used the Bedouin word connoting an asylum seeker in the desert, one who may not be refused.

I felt my face burn.

"Guest? *Guest?*" Fauzi shouted. "They took our land, our honor, and killed your brother—and you want me to help—"

Abdallah motioned with his chin toward the wall. "Yes, they took our land, and the orchards—and they killed him—but I had always remained a merchant—you understand? And he, Isrool, was my partner—you understand?"

He had not spoken to me, but I nodded, my face flaming.

"Partner," Abdallah repeated.

Fauzi got up, kicked at the rolls of suede. "And our honor they took—the honor of the sons of Salach-ad-Din—"

Abdallah snapped, "Shit to all that . . . Making money, and poetry, is the only answer to . . . all this." He made a sweeping motion. "You understand?" I sat frozen.

"Poems!" Fauzi shouted. "Fucking poems! Look at this!" He kicked at the small rusty handpress at the corner. Several bound volumes fell off. "Money! Poems! What's the use of money or poems when honor is gone? Gone!"

I did not know what to say, how to escape.

Abdallah touched Fauzi's knee. "Politics, honor, *ya* Fa'uz, love, all melt away. Only money and poems last—"

"Fucking poems on your head, *ya* Seddiqi," Fauzi yelled. "This fucking poetry, it—it's become for us Arabs a refuge from action. Can't you see? Let us burn all our poetry books, then—then maybe we could act."

"Act how?"

"Act. Just act."

Abdallah said, "And then, once you burned all poetry books, how will you know what action to take, without them, if the time for action did come?"

"My heart will tell me. My heart."

"And until then? Will you leave all the poetry to the Jews?"

"Gladly! If it would make them choose dreams over action, as it did to us."

Abdallah said, "That it has, that it already has."

There was a long, congealed silence.

At last I said, "But why would the Jews kill him?"

This time it was Fauzi who spoke. "Because he did not hate us like they told him; because he did not hate us. That's why."

Their certainty felt like hot coal in my stomach; I needed some solitude, to think clearly. I took the bus back to Tel Aviv and headed toward the Yarkon River. When I reached the end of Ibn Gvirol Street I could smell the water. Half sliding down the grassy knoll, I descended to the tree-lined embankment and turned left, toward the sea. Walking in a dense thicket of wild mustards and reeds, Abdallah's words came to me.

"It wasn't us," he had said. "It wasn't Arabs."

And Fauzi had said, "It was a Jew."

But why would a Jew kill my father?

I stumbled among the gravelly pebbles. The heat, if anything, had turned more intense, more personal. I could feel it on my skin, inside my lungs. To my right flowed the river, half hidden by clumps of reeds. On my left were upturned rotting rowboats, perched on wooden sawhorses, with pots of dry paint lying about underneath, half buried in the earth, like the secrets I tried to uncover.

I heard a rustle behind me and looked back. But there was nothing. The trail had narrowed to one foot in width, hemmed in by *hadass* bushes, and I was as alone as if I were in the middle of the Amazon.

I cursed myself for having left the crowded streets, and quickened my pace. Without breaking stride I plucked a dry reed and slapped it rhythmically on the greenery right and left and walked on. I emerged into a narrow sunlit clearing, dropped into a crouch behind a *hadass* bush, and waited, still beating the reeds with my stick. The dusty, minty smell of the *hadass* wafted all around me.

Half a minute passed. A large man walked by, stepping silently on the outer edges of his Pataugas canvas shoes.

I let him pass, then rose and said to his back, "Why are you following me?"

He turned smoothly. He was the same height as my ephemeral attacker in Tveriah, but was ridiculously more muscle-bound. His torso was like layered slabs of concrete under his white nylon shirt, and his legs inside the tight blue sweatpants bulged with muscles like pythons wrapped around poles. More pythons writhed under the skin of his thick arms and neck, which carried a round head that was all jaw and cheekbones— and, to my surprise, also a small knitted skullcap of the National Religious Party followers, or Kach adherents.

I adopted a neutral stance and surveyed him further. He was perhaps three years younger than me, about thirty, and five centimeters shorter—just shy of two meters. But he must have weighed thirty kilograms more than me, none of them fat.

On both wrists, I saw, he had knitted bracelets of dark braided rope.

No, they were not knitted out of rope but hair. Braids of human hair . . . I felt my testicles constrict.

"Who sent you?" I rasped.

The knitted hair bracelets identified him as a Samson, an ex-bomb-loader. The air force had a small battalion of them, to lift quarter-ton bombs onto jet racks in times of war, instead of forklifts. The strongest, it was rumored, were assigned to the nuclear wing. When they finished their military service, many joined the Internal Security Service as professional bruisers. Now someone had sent one after me.

The muscleman did not answer, just turned sideways, his thick arms hanging in a neutral stance like mine, presenting a narrower target.

Not foolish, this one. I, on the other hand, had been stupid not to have accepted Ehud's knife. Stupid, stupid and conceited . . .

"What do you want?" I asked, to deflect his attention.

But he advanced carefully, his eyes on mine, saying nothing. I recalled Amzaleg's advice to avoid a fight, and so I glanced about me. The reeds hemmed me in the clearing; but the trail, I knew, led to the old exhibition grounds, and beyond, to the old Tel Aviv harbor and the sea.

I could still make a run for it . . .

But then the dark Other rose in me and spoke. *"Get out of my way you son-of-a-whore or I'll cut your dick off—if I can find it."*

The giant hissed, "Enough to stick it up your ass." His voice was high, almost feminine.

"An olive, I bet, is what you—"

All at once he kicked at my knee, swiftly and expertly. Yet somehow my right sandal lifted and blocked the kick with its sole. The impact sent a shockwave up my thigh but I ignored it, and before the giant's foot came down I slid forward and rammed my interlocked fists into his jaw, right and left, then brought the fists down on his nose, woodchopper style, using as many large muscles as possible—as I'd been taught. But when my fists mashed his nose they met soft cartilage only—his nose bone had been surgically removed.

The giant stumbled back, shook his head, then straightened and drove his fist into my forehead like a piston. I found myself lying among the reeds, blood in my mouth, my eyes unfocused, staring at the sky through a sheet of red pain. Half conscious, I stumbled on all fours and saw him advancing on me. I tried to tumble sideways but before I could move he kicked at my tailbone—there seemed to be steel at the tip of his Pataugas boot. An electric shock went though my spine and, head forward, I was sent flying through the reeds, my head splashing into the oily water.

I rolled about, spitting and retching. Rotting fronds seemed to be stuck in my throat, and some evil-smelling muck. I saw him standing not far off, arms hanging loosely, watching me. I thought of plunging into the river to swim to the other bank, but the dark Other would not let me, now. And so I kept rolling and retching even after my breath had returned.

The Samson waited, his knees bent judo-style—and then I knew. Without pausing I staggered up the slippery bank and before I could think, I threw an idiotic long right jab. I could almost hear the sergeant major shout, "Mistake!" as the Samson grinned and grabbed my wrist, pulled, twisted, and threw me over his shoulder like a sack of flour.

Although I knew it was coming, the power of the throw was a shock. I tried to twist in the air but my eyes seemed to point every which way. I landed hard and for a second lost my sight—yet somehow I was on my feet and facing the Samson's back just when he began to turn.

Now!

With my last reservoir of strength I slammed my cupped palms on the giant's ears—then again. There was a popping sound as he sat down with a thud, eyes bulging, shaking his head and flailing at me. I slapped his braided wrists away and slammed my cupped hands on his ears again and again, and he bent over. Before he could rise I clawed with my nails at a dried paint can and pried it out of the ground, and with both hands slammed it on the knitted skullcap.

He slumped sideways, his eyes rolled back in his head, and he lay still.

I stood for a long while, water oozing from my nose and blood dripping down my forehead. At last I bent over the prostrate giant and searched his sweatpants, my broken nails snagging on the cloth.

He had only a thin leather wallet with three hundred-shekel bills and a few fives, no driver's license, no ID card, no wage stub.

If I had doubts before, now I had none.

The Samson's eyes fluttered open as he tried to wriggle up, but he fell back, swaying. I knew his ears must be ringing fiercely and his balance gone. Ear thumps were far better than beatings, and they left no marks. The Intels did it to Arab infiltrators, to make them talk, and the Shin Bet did it, too. No matter how big and strong the man, when the ear's center of balance was destroyed, he became helpless.

"Who?" I hollered into his contorted face. "Who sent you?"

I cupped his ears again for good measure, then whacked him with the paint can on the temple. "Did they tell you why they wanted me out? *Did they?*" I could hear my own voice rising. Not only an F in interrogations, but in self-control, too. "What the hell do they want from my life?" I cupped his ears again, furiously.

He tried to roll away, but his balance was still all wrong. He lay on the ground, writhing, looking like the leather horse in our play.

A flicker of an idea went through my mind. I stuck my hand behind his back under the waistband.

Nothing.

I grabbed his left foot. He tried to kick at me but I hoisted the ankle high and peeled the pant leg toward the knee. Above the instep, inside a black plastic holster, was a slim black Beretta, the magazine clip fastened to the grip with adhesive tape.

No, not a Beretta. A Batya—the Israeli copy. It was flatter and lighter, its magazine containing fifteen rounds. The Shin Bet operative's weapon.

I stared at him. "*Shoo-shoo.*"

This muscleman was not just a bruiser—they did not carry guns. He was an operative. Most carried their guns at the small of their backs, but a few preferred calf holsters, because they were easier to hide, and easier to draw when crouched in wait.

This was not a mere Samson. It was one with brains—the rare kind. Why the hell did they send such a high-level operative after me?

I turned the little gun over on my palm, looking for the serial number. It didn't look as if it ever had one.

The Samson spat into my face. "Son of a whore—!"

In a fit of rage I cuffed him on the temple with the gun butt, then once more on the forehead, and he toppled back, arms and legs akimbo, like a dying donkey.

I dragged him under one of the rotting boats and left him there, with the little gun stuck down the front of his pants, then stumbled quickly back the way I had come, swiping at my eyes as I ran.

Fifteen minutes later I staggered into the Shekem supermarket on Ibn Gvirol Street. No one had followed me as far as I could see, when I fought my way through throngs of shoppers, to get to the public phone. I called Yaro Ben-Shlomo, my Unit buddy.

Luckily he was in his office.

"Could you check something out for me?" I said without preamble. "I think someone really, really doesn't like me, from the Shkettim." The silent ones.

There was a brief pause.

Yaro said, "You sure?"

"Yes." I squeaked with my lips to let him know I didn't want to talk about this over the phone.

There was another pause. "All right, come by."

Less than a half hour later, after another jog all the way down Ibn Gvirol and up King Saul Boulevard, I arrived at his office, which was in a ten-story building at the edge of the Qirya, the army and Defense Ministry HQ.

Yaro's office was a bare whitewashed room with yellow files piled along the walls. Below an agency certificate from HaSneh Insurance Company hung a few framed pictures of holy places: the Cave of the Machpela, the Tomb of Rachel, the Wailing Wall. The only furniture was a metal desk, two frumpy plastic chairs, and two metal filing cabinets. An empty Howitzer canister stood in the corner, with wild brambles inside, for decoration. No photos from the Unit, no mementos. Yaro was apparently trying to make an honest living selling insurance.

He himself had gone to seed in the last seven years. The thick arms had turned to flab, the chest had migrated downward and turned into a belly, and the curly red hair was nearly all gone. Only the eyes were the same as before, small and hard and pale blue, like prayer-shawl fringe knots. He wore faded khaki pants and shirt, like the kibbutznik he had once been, like his father.

He sat quietly as I told him of the Kach thugs' clumsy attack and Amzaleg's serendipitous appearance, of Gershonovitz's warnings, and of my recent tangle with the Samson. Of the ephemeral attacker in Tveriah I said nothing. Somehow that seemed too ridiculous to mention.

"Look here," Yaro said when I finished. "I am in insurance now, I know nothing anymore. So right after you called, I phoned someone, a friend of my dad. He told me to stay away from you, that you are not kosher. Why?"

"Someone from the *shoo-shoo*? They told you that?"

"No, no. Someone . . . higher up." He stared at me with his pale blue eyes. "You've been talking maybe to the PLO in Canada, or something? Playing politics?"

"Me? I am working in a bakery and screwing shiksas." I said shiksas, plural, to make it more convincing.

"So why?" He kept staring at me, his eyes unmoving, as if I were a prisoner he was interrogating.

I tried to suppress my anger. "I don't know. Maybe because I'm doing this play."

"What play?"

Apparently he read no newspapers. A typical ex-kibbutznik, reading only mushy leftist Hebrew novels and the Bible, and maybe poetry books that his kibbutz friends published through Shomron.

I repeated yet again the story about my father's will, and the play.

"That *he* wrote?" Yaro said "he" with the same inflection that everyone in the Anonymous Recon used, when speaking of my father. The Founder of the Mountain Jackals. The First Tracker. The Debba Slayer. More than once Yaro had clumsily weaseled an invitation to come home with me to visit during furloughs, just to see my father. Then he would sit mute and awestruck in our kitchen as my father poured us tea laced with 777 while my mother cooked chicken and farfel for dinner.

I hoisted a shoulder for a yes.

"What's it about?" He really read nothing.

I summarized the play for him while he fidgeted with a paper knife.

"About the Abu Jalood tall tale? So?"

"So that's it. Maybe it's the elections. Begin finally has a chance to kick Labor out, so they are jittery." It sounded idiotic in my own ears. "Or maybe they know who killed my father and they don't want me to find out." This sounded even more idiotic.

For a long moment Yaro stared at me with his protruding pale eyes. "Look," he said at last. "I'll talk to my dad."

Yaro's father, Asa'el Ben-Shlomo, had been one of my father's best friends in '48. Little Asa, they called him. He had commanded a unit operating Davidkas, the small noisy cannons, and nearly went to jail after refusing to fire on the *Altalena*, the Etzel ammunition ship that had arrived from Europe in '48, to supply the Jewish splinter forces in their rebellion. Finally they pulled him off and put in his place someone else who sunk the ship in front of Gordon Beach in Tel Aviv. A few dozen Jews were killed, but the State—so they said—was saved.

Asa retreated with his family into a kibbutz, but after a while came out and joined the *shoo-shoo*. I am told he had helped catch Eichmann. Some rumors said he and two others tracked down Josef Mengele in Brazil in '64 or '65, and killed him by themselves, slowly, against orders. I don't know if it's true. There are many other such stories about that generation of maniacs who had built the State. The Rishonim. The First Ones.

Today he is retired, back in the kibbutz. Not even kibbutz secretary. Just manager of the cowshed.

I said, "And I also need some help, something." Meaning beyond finding out what the hell was going on.

Yaro didn't say anything, just waited.

I said, "Maybe some Unit guys to watch my ass, until I finish with . . . the play."

I didn't say "*his* play" but it hung there, between us. At last Yaro repeated, "I'll talk to my dad. Come see me Thursday. Okay? No, I'll meet you somewhere."

"Where?"

"In Café Piltz? About twelve?"

"All right."

Nobody followed me home, as far as I could see.

36

DURING THE NEXT TWO days Amzaleg dropped in on the auditions in the mornings and sat at the back of the hall, listening and watching intently, his black eyes seemingly blank yet drilling into everyone, ignoring the rhythmic shouts outside.

The first time he came I accompanied him out. On the way to his car he stopped before the factory's gate and scrutinized the two opposing camps on the sidewalk, taking in both crowds, before driving off. Whether he had come because he wanted to keep an eye on them, or just because the play had struck a chord in him, I could not tell. The second day he stayed half an hour only; and this time, like the ex-Anon that he was, he left without anyone seeing him go.

I still hadn't told him of the Samson, nor did I tell Ehud; I no longer knew whom I could trust.

The next few days passed in a daze of pain and heat. The *khamsin* had soared and Tel Aviv lay smoldering under an anvil of boiling air. Also over the last few days the Arab garbagemen had gone on strike, and piles of rotting garbage, on which thousands of blackbirds had descended, had begun to accumulate on street corners. The chocolate factory had to detail two employees to transport the factory's refuse to the municipal dump in Chiriyeh. Since one of them was also our soundman, every rehearsal had to be delayed until his return.

"Shoot those *Arabushim*," snapped Amatzia Besser, our Debba, "then they'll learn."

"Then they'll stink, too," said Yaron Chamdi, one of our musical directors.

Ehud said nothing. Lately he had turned silent. Perhaps it was the play—he seemed consumed by it, like the plays he used to read obsessively at the Unit after operations. Every night now he pored over the script with a pencil, read and re-read Kagan's notes, and made notes of his own. The last few rehearsals, Kagan had indeed begun to defer to him, often accepting his suggestions and his whispered comments, as if he, Ehud, not I, were fulfilling my father's wish.

Did Ehud know that Ruthy and I were screwing behind his back? I doubt it. We took care to display only the rawest enmity in front of him. For Ruthy this may have been easy. But for me, this subterfuge proved the sheerest hell, as bad as my black dreams, which had intensified, barely kept in check by the play. It was as if with every passing day, my proximity to Ruthy brought back old-new memories of her and of this murderous place, my father's land; and so my love for both, which I thought I had managed to shed, now gripped me anew with a hundred talons of heat. It would be hell, I knew, when I must leave the land again, and her.

I tried not to think of it.

37

Thursday morning I skipped the rehearsal and went to meet with Yaro.

I got off the bus well in advance and walked down to Gordon Beach. An open space was best for shaking off a tail. So for half an hour I walked up and down the edge of the surf, my sandals slung over my shoulder, idly watching around me.

There was no one.

At five to twelve I put on my sandals and climbed the rickety stairs from the promenade to the glass-fronted café.

Yaro was sitting behind a thick stone column, reading *Ha'Olam HaZeh* magazine, oblivious to the view. There was a huge pair of bare *tzitzes* on the back cover.

"Shame on you, *ya* maniac," I said.

He put the magazine down. "You clean?"

I began to say I was, but suddenly I felt a prickling at the back of my neck. "Fuck! There's someone on our ass!"

I knew I hadn't been followed, so he must have been.

Yaro said, "I asked two guys from Detachment Bett if they could give us backup."

My nose stung. "From Bett? Who?"

Detachment Bett was my brother's old outfit in the Unit. One of their specialities was waiting hours without moving, to provide covering fire if needed. You had to be a bit phlegmatic to enjoy the wait, also a bit weird.

THE DEBBA   209

"You don't know them. Younger guys. Two kibbutzniks, came in after you left. They said they wouldn't mind. They've heard of you."

I threw a casual glance around the high-ceilinged room. Only old farts sipping their coffees, and a few tourists. Nobody young.

"Are they outside?"

"I don't even know."

I said desperately, "Yaro, I wouldn't ask for backup if it was only the Kahane maniacs—but these *shoo-shoo* fuckers sent a Samson—"

Yaro said abruptly, "It's not the *shoo-shoo*, or Kach. I talked to Dad. He said your name came up in the Mo'adon."

I felt a trickle of fear course down my spine.

The Mo'adon, the Club, was an informal committee of the current prime minister and all former prime ministers, whoever was still alive, usually not more than three or four. It gathered only infrequently, to decide on the most important matters of state that the prime minister didn't want to handle alone; for example, major peace overtures, or takedowns abroad.

I wiped my upper lip with a finger. It felt icy.

"You sure?" I said stupidly.

"Last week."

"But why?"

"My dad said he doesn't know. Or maybe he does and he didn't want to tell me."

"Yaya," I said desperately, "these *shoo-shoo* idiots flipped! I am telling you—"

"Yah."

The warm air suddenly felt cold. There was a long silence.

Yaro said, "Dad also told me you gave up your citizenship."

I said with an effort, "Yes." I looked away.

There was a pause.

"Because of—Um Marjam? Of what happened?"

"Also." I did not meet his eyes.

He nodded slowly. "So what? You are still a Jew."

My eyes stung again.

Yaro said in a matter-of-fact voice, "Gidi and Ami will stay on your ass, I don't care what they say about you. These *shoo-shoo* fuckers—" He paused, his nostrils white. "Don't you go killing anybody."

"Sure. They are Jews, too."

When we left I looked back. I couldn't see anybody, neither my regular tails nor the Detachment Bett guys. I should have felt better, but I didn't. As we were descending the stairs to the promenade, I said wildly, "I swear to you, Yaya, I never did anything against—" I stopped. What was I going to say? Against the State of Israel? Against the Jews? The Bible? Or what?

"Leave it," Yaro said. "We both came out of the same cunt."

As I walked home, I saw nothing and nobody. My name had come up in the Mo'adon. I couldn't quite grasp it.

I had seen the room where they met, in the Mossad complex near Glilot, on the hill beyond Ramat Aviv, where Ehud and I took a refresher course in jail endurance, before we went deep into Syria, to take down a captain in the Syrian *mukhabarat*. Five days of lying shackled in your own shit, being punched and kicked, with unshaven Moroccans shouting in your face in Arabic, pretending they are Arabs.

When it was all over, they gave us a tour of the premises.

I remembered the small room with the round table, and the six pink plastic chairs. Yellow flowers in a glass vase, and a platter with American oatmeal cookies for Golda. Her pad still had doodles on it: crooked flowers, a trio of small Stars of David, and two Arabic names crossed out with round angry swirls of ink.

I felt my teeth chatter.

38

I SPENT THE AFTERNOON on the beach, staring at the far horizon, gearing up for what I must do. Finally, as the sun set, I rose to my feet and made my way back to Ibn Gvirol. I could not see anyone, yet I spent an hour dashing into and out of yards until I was sure there was no one behind, and so it was after eight o'clock at night when I arrived at the back of the apartment house on Ibn Gvirol, hopped over the rear fence, and crawled through the low window into the basement bomb shelter, then climbed up the stairs.

Neither Ehud nor Ruthy were home when I came in. Still at the rehearsals, probably. I did not turn on the light. As I went through the kitchen, my stomach growled—I had not eaten since lunchtime, but I did not stop to eat. Making straight for the kitchen balcony, I headed to my mother's old Singer sewing machine and pulled out from underneath the first shoe box, then the other, and took them into the bathroom.

Sitting on the edge of the bathtub, with only the thin moonlight coming in through the narrow window, I stretched the black Nomex across my knee, and, as I had done a dozen times before, I sewed the tear in one legging, then looked for others. When I found none, I stripped naked, sprinkled talcum powder between my legs and under my armpits, over my chest, and at the small of my back, and pulled on the light-absorbing black coveralls. The leggings reached to the ends of my toes, the headpiece covered my head from eyebrows to chin with only a hole for the face, like a balaclava. It fitted so well, as if I had taken it off only yesterday.

I bent over a few times, then sideways, listening for crackles and creaks. Nothing.

Fishing around in the box, I began to fill the coveralls' myriad pockets with the peculiar collection of jimmies, lock picks, and rubber fingertips that I had once been issued hundreds of years ago, in my own prehistory. As I turned around, I felt a hard tube rolling under my heel, and picked it up. For a long while I stared at a yellow neoprene pencil that had tumbled out. I pulled off its plastic cover and squeezed the clasp, and the stiff tungsten filament sprang out, nearly invisible in its thinness. When pressed against a man's chest and sprung, it made death look just like a heart attack. For a long moment I looked at the hellishly thin blade, and at the other tools, remembering the times I had used them, and what they had done to others, and to me. Then I pressed the blade back into its yellow sheath against the mirror, threw it inside the shoe box, and finished filling my pockets.

Unscrewing Ruthy's electric shaver, I pulled out its two batteries, clicked them into my waistband, and, shielding the thumb-lights with a towel, flashed both on and off a couple of times. Both worked fine. I softly pulled the window shut, to cut off the thin moonlight, and checked myself in the mirror.

My body had disappeared; only my face and hands were still visible, hovering ghostlike in space. The Nomex did not even look black: it was more an absence of color, a sort of dark nothingness, a negation of presence, like my black dreams. I recalled all the other times I had watched myself vanish, in the past; when I called upon the Other in me to appear, to do the necessary dreck for the Jews . . .

Pushing the thoughts out of my mind, I jumped up and down a few times, listening for rattles. I padded a few pockets with puffs of Ruthy's cotton wool, one by one, until I could hear nothing.

Then I peeled the headpiece back, down to the collar. In the hall, in the semi-darkness, I pulled on my jeans, and one of Ehud's dark blue shirts, with the long sleeves. Finally I fished a tube of black polish from the shoe box and stuck it in my back pocket, laced on my old Pataugas canvas boots, and left.

When I returned, again entering through the bomb shelter's window before running up the unlit stairs, it was three-thirty in the morning. Ehud was seated at the kitchen table, filling a glass from a bottle of 777 and going over the script with one of my pencils. He watched me as I took off my jeans, and his dark blue shirt, saying nothing.

"How were the rehearsals?" I called to him.

"Good."

But as I began to remove my Nomex coveralls he put down his 777 glass, and the pencil. "Anything?" he said in a neutral voice.

I touched thumb to index finger, then went in to wash.

From the bedroom came a muffled call. "Is't Dada?"

Ehud said something in response. I couldn't make out what it was, and when I came out of the bathroom again, he had already turned in and closed the bedroom door behind him.

Next morning, after breakfast, I took the bus to the Dizzengoff police station.

Amzaleg was in the midst of a loud phone conversation when I entered his office.

"Yes! Yes!" he hollered. "Talk to all of them! I said to all of them! Everyone in the Wrestling Club! I want to know where—" He listened for a while. "Yes! The old members, too!" Then he saw me, shouted a booming "No!" into the receiver, and flung it into its cradle.

I sat down.

He snarled, "Someone burgled the Wrestling Club last night. Also Gelber's office."

"Who? Where?" I let my mouth sag. "What did they take?"

Amzaleg lumbered to his feet and closed the door. Then, so swiftly that I couldn't see him coming at me, he grabbed the front of my shirt with his beefy hand and twisted it, bringing my face down close to his.

I could smell the Gitanes nicotine on his breath, and the whiff of raw arak.

"Dada," he whispered, "if I catch you in any of these stunts in Tel Aviv—"

"Don't worry," I said. "You won't." I raised my eyebrows and pointed to the ceiling, then made spiral motion near my ear.

"It's okay now," he said, his eyes bloodshot.

Still staring into his reddened eyes, I pulled out of my pocket the folded letter I had taken from Mr. Gelber's desk the night before, when I had broken into his office.

"Gershonovitz wrote to him a week ago. It said there was a check enclosed . . ." I stopped, overcome with wrath.

Amzaleg threw the letter on the table. "We knew he was being paid. But he has an alibi."

I stared at him in surprise. "You knew?"

"Sure I knew! You think I was made by a finger? What do you think I am doing here all day? Scratching my dick?"

"So what else did you know?" I threw the other note on his desk, the one I had found in Judge Menuchin's drawer, with Gershonovitz's initials.

Amzaleg scanned it briefly, then looked up. "He has an alibi, too."

"Menuchin?" I blew out my lips. "He's seventy-eight years old and fat. My father would have eaten him without salt—"

"No. Shimmel." He stared at me stonily.

I stared back at him. "Gershonovitz? You checked *him* out?"

Amzaleg got up, opened the door, and looked into the corridor. The thin policeman who had sat at the front desk walked by, carrying a Tempo bottle.

Amzaleg called after him, "Nissim, go bring me a pack of Gitanes from Berman, without filter." The steps faded.

Amzaleg returned to his desk, sat down, and picked up a thick Globus pen and began to bend it, this way and that.

I said, "So who else did you check out?"

There was a loud crack as the pen snapped in two, one sliver flying into the wall like a bullet, like mine had done in Gelber's office, a hundred years back. "Everyone he knew, I checked. Everyone!"

I nodded at him slowly, and he slowly nodded back. For a full minute we stared at each other, no longer suspicious but not yet friends; something in-between.

We remained silent for a while; we heard steps approaching. Presently the door opened and the skinny policeman came in with the cigarettes.

"Go see in the back," Amzaleg said. "Ask them if they need a hand with the whores."

The policeman edged himself out, his eyes darting from Amzaleg's face to mine.

When the door closed, Amzaleg said in a low voice, "I checked them all out, everyone, what they did that night, where they were. Everybody." He looked into my eyes. The raspiness in his voice had disappeared, and it had now become soft, mellow. For some reason it gave me gooseflesh. "Nobody tells me how to do my work, you understand?" Suddenly he stood up and roared. "Nobody! But *nobody*!"

He sat down again. "Only Zussman, and his wife, and Riva's daughter. They don't have anything, no alibi."

I said, "Women could never do such—"

"Women can do anything," he said, "if they love or hate enough."

I didn't know where this came from. He was probably talking about his ex.

I waited, and presently he went on. "Also the old Arabs, the suppliers. Seddiqi, Mansour, Ayish—"

"Them?" I said, recalling the canes. "They are half dead already."

"So maybe they went with someone."

We were silent for a moment. I remembered Fauzi, and other Yaffo *shabbab*.

After a while Amzaleg said, "So you trust me all of a sudden?" A muscle twitched in his cheek, as in a wink. But the effect was not comic.

I looked away. "I . . . I was here, too, in your office . . . a few hours ago." For some reason I felt shame at this. "To check you out, to be sure."

I had seen the memos in his drawer, the ones from Gershonovitz, urging him not to make a fool of himself, to take care, especially now. Especially with this.

He nodded without surprise or rancor. "I figured." Then he stretched; first the palms, then the wrists, the shoulders, finally the mouth, the cheeks. Like a large gray cat. Again, the effect was far from comic.

"Come here," he said. "I'll show you some pictures. You think you can look?"

His thick fingers were already riffling through the inside flap of one of the files on his desk.

I tried to speak but no voice came. I nodded.

Without looking into my eyes he began to hand the photos

to me, one by one, speaking in a low monotone as he pointed with his thumb at details.

The photographs were of an astonishingly high quality and resolution, like those taken by a high-flying reconnaissance jet, or by an Intel patrolman with a miniature Hasselblad. Every detail showed crisp and sharp.

"That's how the boxes fell, see?" Amzaleg's beefy thumb swept the glossy surface. "From right to left, in one direction, then they stayed. See here? Looks like he pulled them down himself, trying to—to keep from falling, or something."

I nodded, dumbly.

The photograph showed a mound of shoe boxes, looking like some gun emplacement that had been leveled with a plastic charge. Two boxes had spilled their contents—children's rubber boots with felt lining. Another box had opened, empty. To the left of the picture a pale palm showed, the fingers curled—

The photograph was snatched away.

Something cold and rounded was pushed into my hand; a glass of water. I drank half of it and put it down. Amzaleg pulled the glass toward him and drank down the other half, then wiped his mouth in a short, violent motion.

He looked at me with mute inquiry.

I nodded.

Another glossy photograph materialized before my eyes. Amzaleg went on in the same low monotone. "See here? No sign of smear, or pulling, or anything, just a lot of—splatter, here." His thick thumb obscured the leftmost part of the photograph, pointing to a dark stain on the floor, in front of the inclined bench. I tried to push his thumb aside, and for a second saw a mottled wrist with the familiar Omega watch; then Amzaleg slid his thumb back.

"No," he said. "Believe me. No."

The photograph disappeared, and another flipped out of the deck.

"The cash register, nothing was taken as far as we could see."

"It was open, when you found it?"

"Yes . . . How much did he usually keep there?"

"I don't know . . . a few hundred shekels, three, four hundred, something like that." It was hazy in my mind. "Sometimes six hundred, maybe." I wiped my forehead.

Amzaleg said, "That was when? In 1970? When you left?"

I understood his drift. There had been some inflation since then.

Amzaleg said, "We found seven thousand shekels there." Then he added, "That's almost three thousand dollars."

"*How* much?" I stared at him. "And they didn't touch it?"

"No."

I said, "Where's it now?"

Amzaleg gave me a steely look. "In the safe—don't worry, you'll get it back."

"No, I want to see it now, smell it, what do I know?"

He eyed me narrowly. "All right." He got up, twirled the safe's combination, and pulled out a brown envelope. He slid a sheaf of bills out of it, in hundreds and fifties, clasped with a rubber band. "It sat just like this on the floor."

I sniffed at the bills. There was a faint smell of something, some odor I ought to have recognized.

"Anything?" Amzaleg looked at me aslant.

I shook my head. "I don't know."

I should know this smell. I really should . . .

Amzaleg waited, then pointed to the last photograph. "Anything you see missing?"

Automatically I scanned the photograph with my eye-corners stretched wide, as I had been taught. "I don't know."

The little heap of money lay on the floor in the midst of the usual assortment of junk my father kept in his cash box: rubber bands, a bottle of pills, the two black books of accounts—

I said, "Where is his inhaler, for his asthma?"

"It was in his pocket."

Another photograph flashed by, and for a brief second I glimpsed a pale face, the dead eyes staring upward with anguish so profound, so unearthly, that I felt a blunt fist slam at my heart.

Just as quickly the picture was gone.

"Sorry." Amzaleg's right palm hovered above my wrist, hesitated, and withdrew. A moment passed.

"I'm okay," I said.

After a while I asked, "Any fingerprints elsewhere? On the door? Anywhere?" I was surprised to hear my voice, so normal, so clear.

Amzaleg's face darkened with blood. "Shit in yogurt. The guy we sent to clear the floor? The donkey cleaned everything, with a loofah." He looked into my eyes with an effort. "The door, too."

I said nothing.

"It happens," Amzaleg said in a voice a trifle too loud.

"Yes." I wiped my neck. "Sure."

After a while the policeman said, "So what did you want this old actor for, this Ovadiah?" He inserted the photographs, one by one, into the flap in the back of the file.

"So he could tell me, maybe, what happened then." I didn't ask Amzaleg how he knew I was asking around. Maybe he had talked to Kagan.

Amzaleg squared the files on his desk. "In forty-six? In the show?"

I hesitated. It seemed silly somehow to suspect this bungling policeman of anything just because the man he had sent to clean the store had wiped off the fingerprints.

"Maybe," I said.

I could feel him tense up.

I said, "Also, from before, at the beginning, when they, Paltiel Rubin, and my father, when they were just starting." I waited, then added, "Before my father wrote his first skit, even, his first Purim *shpiel*."

Amzaleg lowered his gaze.

"You find him, let me know," he said, feigning disinterest.

"I'll tell you when I catch him."

And all at once my instinct told me I was on the right track, that this was where I should look.

39

WE LEFT THE NEXT day at seven in the morning to look for Ovadiah Tzadok, the old Yemenite actor, I driving, Ruthy sitting by my side. One of my father's smaller knives, still in its leather sheath, was in my back pocket. After the Samson's attack I made up my mind I was no longer going to play by Amzaleg's rules. It was Saturday, the Shabbat, and the traffic was still light. As far as I could see, no one followed us. But this of course meant little.

The day before, when I had asked Ruthy for her car to drive to some Yemenite villages in the Sharon valley, she said right away she would come along.

"What," she shouted at Ehud, "he'll look for this Yemenite to learn about Paltiel, and I'll stay home? I have the right to hear what this guy says about my father."

It was the first time she had called Paltiel "my father" in my hearing. I tried to dissuade her, but nothing helped.

We arrived at the Sharon by midmorning. At Moshav Elchanan, near Chadera, we found nothing, nor at Moshav Chanitt-LeMazmera, nor at Moshav Eliakim, nor at the next two *moshavim*. Only the land, its mood dusty and hot, kept flowing by the car window, making my nose tingle with a nameless emotion that I tried to suppress. Finally, at three in the afternoon, I called it quits. We drove back home in the baking Beetle, neither of us speaking. Just before Herzliya, on the outskirts of Tel Aviv, Ruthy said, "Turn here. At the beach, so we can at least talk."

I hesitated, remembering the Samson, then turned.

The Beetle hopped and rattled from one bump to the next, from one pothole to the other, the wheel shaking in my hands.

Ruthy rummaged in her raffia bag, unearthing suntan lotion, a crumpled Dubek cigarette pack, and, inexplicably, a dry yellow rose.

"From someone, I don't remember," she said, rubbing suntan lotion on her thighs. "No, not Ehud, someone."

"From when?" I didn't know why I cared all of a sudden.

"Six months ago, a year, I don't know. What do you want? You screw this shiksa in Canada, maybe her girlfriends, too."

"She doesn't have girlfriends."

"So her boyfriends," Ruthy said.

"I am not Paltiel."

Without warning she slapped my face. The car was still moving, but she had opened the door, and before I could find the brake, she had already jumped out, stumbled, and begun to run off into the dunes. "I hate you forever!" she shouted at me from some way off, her voice weak and wavering.

My cheek stung. After a little while I got out of the car and followed her up the dune.

I sat down beside her, on the hot sand, the sheathed knife awkward in my pocket. "I am sorry about—what I said."

She turned on her side, away from me. "I'm going with you to look for this Yemenite—why? I don't know why."

"To learn who killed—maybe also to help prove that the play—" I stopped.

"Prove what? That your father wrote it? Maybe that he wrote other things, too?"

"I already said I am sorry."

"So you said. *You* had a father." She stared at the yellow sky. There was a pause.

After a while Ruthy said, "I am sorry. I am a donkey."

I shook my head.

Ruthy said, as though continuing a previous line of conversation, "That's what my mother said, too, that your father had let him go, and now the Debba came back to kill him—"

"Stop talking nonsense."

Ruthy said, "Because even two people together—Mother said your father wasn't big, but he had the power of a giant . . . Once in Yaffo he wrestled a hyena in a cage, near the harbor. Did you hear about that?"

"Yes." I had read the stories.

"For a wager, because the Arabs taunted him. I would never do a thing like that, if I were a man. To save someone, maybe. But not for a boast."

"It wasn't a boast. It was for the honor of the Jews."

"'The honor of the Jews,'" Ruthy said. "Don't make me laugh. 'Honor of the Jews.'"

When we came home it was late and Ehud was already sleeping. Without saying a word Ruthy went into the bedroom and closed the door behind her.

I lay down on the sofa. Sleep took a long while to come, and when it did, it came with a dark force I had not felt for a while.

When I opened my eyes the apartment was in shadow. Ruthy, wearing her blue Atta shorts and a green T-shirt with the words "Peace Now" across the back, sat cross-legged on the living room floor, her chin on her cupped hands. The play's pages were spread before her in the white parallel moonbeams thrown by the shutter.

I shook my head groggily. Again I had dreamed that an animal, or perhaps the cold-killing instructor, had been shouting into my face.

I coughed thickly. "Where's Ehud?"

"Sleeping." She peered at me from under her rumpled hair, then rose to her feet and in one fluid motion lay down beside me. "This play, it really is a little like *Golyatt*—the meter, the words—"

"No, it isn't."

She let her thigh slide down mine and traced a line on my hip with her nails. "Maybe they wrote it together, what do I know—"

"It's my father's handwriting."

I got up and collected the pages from the floor.

Ruthy looked up at me, her eyes half open. Presently she got up, too, then swiftly removed her T-shirt and put on Ehud's checkered shirt.

"I think they grew," she said, and tied the shirt at the navel.

"I didn't look."

"*Nemosha*," said Ruthy.

40

I COULD RECOGNIZE MY father's handwriting anywhere, from his letters to me.

A mere week after my arrival in Canada, the first arrived. Then, every two or three weeks, I received another, explaining to me why it was important that I come back. Patiently, in detail, in words that sang and sometimes oddly rhymed.

At first I read them all, but afterward, when my black dreams returned and his words began to appear in them, I tore the envelopes up without opening them. Not once did I write back. Somehow I knew that if I recognized his claim on me, if I acknowledged it even once, I could never again cut myself loose and would end up going back: to his love; to his land, and to mine; back to Ruthy. Back to the dreck, and the blood.

My mother, too, wrote. Short letters, simple ones. You don't have to write, she said, if it's hard for you. Just tell Rina you are all right, and she'll write us. We love you, all of us. All of us, she repeated at the ends of her letters, as if she were a messenger for more than my father and herself, and my brother; a messenger for something else.

Ruthy, too, wrote, but her letters I never opened. Finally both she and my father stopped writing, and my mother's letters were reduced to a New Year's greeting card, until her death in 1974.

My brother, Avraham, had stopped talking to me even before I left. The moment I told him and my parents (he was home on furlough, about to return to base) that I'd be emigrating to Canada, he got up, spit on my Pataugas boots, and turned around to depart. But my mother grabbed his wrist. "Clean it, Avraham!"

"No!" He tried to wrench his hand free but she had used a correct *gimmel* grip, and pushed him to his knees. It was amazing, a slight woman like her, in her fifties.

My father said in Yiddish, "Leave him be."

"Isser, *hafef*," she said in colloquial Arabic. Butt out.

"Sonya," he whispered, "it's not your fault."

Her face went white and rigid. "Avraham, I said clean it!"

My brother struggled futilely. To unlatch a *gimmel* hold, he would've had to break her thumb. Tears of panic and rage rose in his calf-brown eyes. "I won't!"

"Then I will." She let go his wrist and went down on her knees, a towel in hand. I could smell her cyclamen eau de cologne, like a faint tingle in the throat.

"Sonya, no," my father said.

My mother said nothing; only her shoulders shook as she wiped my boots.

I stood frozen as Avraham tried to pull her up jerkily by the shoulders, but she would not rise. Finally he and I, not looking at each other, together pulled her to her feet.

My mother said, "He's your brother, no matter what."

I could not tell whom she was speaking to or about, and felt a nameless fear.

No matter?

I looked at my father but he said nothing.

My brother shouted, "No!" and clomped down the stairs. And from that moment on, he no longer recognized my presence. To my farewell party he did not even bother to come. Whether he stopped speaking to my mother, after I had left Israel, I don't know; but it might have been so. Men in my

family have a great capacity for grudges that never end. Maybe
it's something in the air, here. The Arabs have it, too, as did
everyone else who had lived here, before.

Later, in Canada, breathing the cold air of the north and
Jenny's love, more than once I thought of calling my brother,
to ask how he was and tell him I forgave him. He who, like me,
was sent by our father to learn the same evil trade that our
father once had. My brother who, when I deserted, only did
to me what I would have done to him, had he left me behind.
But I put off calling him and now he, too, was dead, without
even a proper grave; while I, the deserter, was here once again
in this goddamned land, playing a part in a play set in motion
by our dead father.

But what part? And for what end? And was my mother in on
it? How to find out?

There is a photograph of my mother in one of her childhood
albums. She is standing between two other girls in the shade
of the wild fig tree on Dizzengoff Street, right by her parents'
newspaper kiosk.

In the picture she is a slim girl of fifteen, her oval face shaded
by a floppy khaki hat—the emblem of the Haganah youth—
from under which a mass of wild curls tumble every which
way. The other two girls are hatless; but all three are wearing
the two-tone uniform of the Bnot Ya'akov Religious School
for Girls—mid-length dark skirts and long-sleeved white shirts,
with the school emblem on the right breast. All are leaning on
long sticks that reach up to their waists—they had probably
just returned from a *kappap* lesson—facc-to-face combat—
taught by some Haganah instructor, in the school backyard.
My mother had gone to school till she was sixteen, when she
had to drop out and work as a seamstress in Yaffo, to help her
parents.

She looks just like her photograph in *Vashti's Dream*, my father's Purim play in which she had played Queen Esther, many years later.

The scene is half in light, half in shadow, with my mother right on the dividing line, her left side lighter than the other. The photograph itself is brown at its edges, as if a dark fluid had seeped into it and begun to obliterate it, like time itself but not half as thorough, nor as pervasive as those who had kept lying to me ever since I arrived.

41

NEXT MORNING, BEFORE EITHER Ruthy or Ehud awoke, I took Ruthy's car keys, then squeezed myself into her Beetle and drove to Kibbutz Sha'ananim in the Sharon.

When I arrived an hour later, I made my way on foot down the main road, walking in the already sweltering heat through the orange groves, already blossoming, and the rows of dusty almond trees. Before me spread the wide fields of the kibbutz, and beyond them, the yellow-gray patches of thorns where the Arab village of Zachaleh used to be; and further away still, beige on gray-brown, rose the mountains of Efraim, ephemeral and craggy and blurred. Biting dry wind blew into my face, carrying ashlike dust in its wings, as if the door of a giant oven had been left open somewhere beyond the horizon. The smell of the orange blossoms and the mimosa was like a dainty foreign wetness upon the overarching heat and the desiccation.

As I marched between the two low stone columns that stood at the kibbutz's entrance, a balding kibbutznik passed by, a towel in hand, his head wet. I asked him where I could find Asa Ben-Shlomo.

He gave me a quick look, from head to foot. At last he seemed satisfied that I was not an Arab infiltrator. "And who are you?"

"Tell him Dada wants to talk to him."

"You have a full name?"

"Just tell him."

He left me in the dining room and went to fetch Asa. The room was the size of an average Tel Aviv cinema. Kibbutz Sha'ananim had more than three hundred members and they all ate at once, in this whitewashed concrete box with six wire-mesh windows, to guard against grenades, and two metal doors. The two windows behind me opened on a large swimming pool. Screams of laughter and the splashing of water came through. Beyond the pool I could see the pockmarked water tower. In '48 the Iraqi irregulars came within two hundred meters of the kibbutz. Until 1967, the kibbutzniks still had problems with infiltrators. I myself used to lie in ambushes, not far from here, during paratroopers' boot camp—

The door opened and Asa came in.

He was a small man with very large arms and a wild silvery beard that had streaks of red in it. He looked like an aging rabbi crossed with an orangutan walking upright in patched khaki trousers. He smelled of cow manure and his blue shirt was stained with water. He had probably washed up in a hurry, when he heard I was waiting.

"*Ahalan*, Dada," he said evenly. He didn't sit down.

"*Ahalan*, Asa."

There was a short wait.

"Do you want some coffee? Or something?"

"No, thank you."

He pushed by me and sat at the other side of the table, leaning forward on his thick arms. The family likeness with Yaro was striking. The hooked nose, the thick skin above the eyebrows, the tight manner.

"I was sorry to hear how he—how your father died."

"Yeah."

"I couldn't get away to come to the funeral—two cows were calving, one had twins—" He stopped.

I said nothing.

At last he said, "So?"

"Two *kackers* attacked me in Tel Aviv, last month. You heard about it?"

He performed a diagonal nod, then shook his head in sorrow, to indicate disapproval of such idiocy.

I said tightly, "Then the same people sent a Samson after me, last week."

A long silence while he stared at me, keeping his head fixed.

Finally he said, "So what do you want from me? Go to the police."

I said, "This donkey Samson? He had a Batya on his leg."

There was a pause.

"Shit in yogurt." Asa kept his eyes on mine, with an effort.

"Yeah," I said. "And three weeks ago, someone tried to steal my father's play. And right afterward, another someone tried to attack me in Tveriah . . ."

There was another pause.

"This I don't know anything about."

I said bluntly, "D'you know why the *shoo-shoo* is after me?"

A longer silence, this time. Asa passed his thick fingers in his beard. "Why do you come to me, about this?"

"Yaro told me you said my name came up, in the Mo'adon."

"So maybe I shouldn't have."

I said sourly, "Fuck off, *ya* Asa. You passed me a message. It was a message from them, that they had talked about me. What do they want from me?"

He straightened up. "Look, Dada. Why do you want to poke your nose into all this? Go back to Canada. This is not Toronto."

I was getting tired of this.

I spoke slowly. "Asa, if anyone wanted to take me down, they could have done it five times over. So why don't they? And why like this?"

He looked at me with eyebrows joined, his mouth clamped; then all at once he grabbed my palm with both of his. His callouses were as hard as pebbles. "Dada, do me a favor. Please. Go back to Canada. Today they are crazy. Crazy! If they think you are a risk, they'll send you back in a casket."

"A risk to what? To whom?"

"What do I know, to the State, to everything."

"But how?"

It was so idiotic! How could I be a risk?

Two young women came out of the kitchen and began to arrange plates on the tables for lunch.

Asa stared at them, unseeing. Without looking at me he said, "You diddling Ruthy again, I hear."

I fulminated in silence. What business was it of his?

"Dammit, *ya* Dada." He shook his head. "Isser would have belted you, for this."

"He screwed, too, when he was young. Actresses, soldier girls . . ."

"Not his friends' wives."

It was funny. The *shoo-shoo* guys fucked right and left. Everyone. To cheat on their wives was okay. But not their friends.

I said, "Can you tell me why they talked about me, in the Mo'adon?"

He shook his head. "I don't know."

"Yes, you do."

He sucked his lips in, hesitating.

"Is it the play?"

"Also," he said.

"And the murder?"

"Also."

He sounded like Amzaleg.

"And what else?"

He shook his head.

I said sarcastically, "Maybe the Debba? They're afraid he'll come back after the play, to save the Arabs?"

To my immense surprise, he nodded. "Yes, *hada hoo*." That's it.

I got up in disgust and, without looking back, made my way to the car.

Ruthy was home, but not Ehud. As I closed the door she came to me, and with a fierce and unexplained anger kissed me, as if punishing me for something. "Don't go away again without me."

Together we went to the kitchen.

I said, "It was the *shoo-shoo* that tried to filch the play."

"Sure," she said. "Who did you think? I knew all along."

"You did not," I said. "You said it was the police."

"The police, the *shoo-shoo*, what's the difference? They are all the same."

I could not understand her. I thought she would explode with rage, at least show shock, indignation, something. Not this calm acceptance.

"They don't want us to do this," she said. "Don't you understand? They never did, from the beginning."

I wanted to tell her that they were not all the same, that some were quietly on our side, like Zussman and perhaps Amzaleg, but with no pause she began to tell me about the rehearsals, how well the last songs were suddenly progressing, how the scenery buildup was nearly complete, the leather horse, and the costumes. Outside, the heat had intensified. Fumes and dust seeped in, as a bus roared by. Mad thoughts raced inside my head, round and round.

I said, "When it's over, if you want, you can come with me to Canada—"

Ruthy said, "No, you stay here—"

I shook my head. Rage, impotent rage, swelled inside me. What did they all want of me?

Ruthy got up and took off her shirt, then her skirt. "Come, Dada, come, before he returns."

Afterward, as I was dressing, she said abruptly that Jenny had called. "So I talked to her. You know what? She's nice—"

I said nothing; my heart was dark. I didn't care about Jenny anymore, or about Ehud.

Ruthy went on, as she put on her bra, "So I wrote down this poem she is sending you, I should look to see where I put it—"

"Doesn't matter," I said. Because now nothing really did. Nothing except Ruthy, and the play, and the beast that had killed my father.

42

EVERY DAY I VOWED anew not to read the newspapers besmirching my father's name, still alluding to the similarity between the play and Paltiel's work, yet I could not stop. I seriously considered suing some of the newspapers. But what good would that do?

"So write an article to *Ha'Olam HaZeh* magazine, with any evidence you have that he—wrote it," said Ben-Shoshan, the factory's accountant, after I had ranted about another poisonous editorial. "Let everyone read it; at least they'd hear the other side, too."

This struck a chord, and that afternoon I began to call around. But within a few hours it became clear I would have no such testimonies—none beside Abdallah's, that is; and I knew just how much good that would do, an Arab's word.

It dawned on me that the only one who actually saw my father write was Mr. Glantz. Yes, it was not the play he saw him write, but rather some poems, alongside Paltiel, but it was better than nothing. So by evening, after Ehud and Ruthy had gone to the last technical rehearsal, I called him.

"I need a testimony from you," I said bluntly, "that he wrote it."

If he interpreted this to mean that I would not mind if he stretched the truth, it was fine with me.

There was silence on the line, and I steeled myself for a morality speech about the importance of truth, like my father used to give me. I was not prepared for the animal sob. "There's a . . . something I . . . I didn't tell you . . . if you want to come—"

I grabbed Ruthy's car keys and ran downstairs.

Mr. Glantz opened the door, his old eyes puffy, and before I could speak he thrust two blue copybooks into my hands. "Please, Davidl . . . please forgive me—I didn't want to give them to you before . . . because I knew you'd take them . . . and he left them for me . . ."

I sat down and opened one copybook. It was filled with Arabic script. The other was in Hebrew.

"They're not in the will," Mr. Glantz wept, "but your father said I could have them . . ."

My eyes raced along the crabbed lines. "I'll bring them back. I promise." I devoured the words with my eyes. Then as their meaning sank in I looked up, dazed.

Mr. Glantz wiped his cheeks. "The other one I can't read, it's all in Arabic that they translated. You keep it—"

"Who translated?"

"Him, Isser, and his Arab friend, the cripple from Yaffo. He used to come sometimes Friday evenings, and they would sit on the terrace . . . maybe eat a watermelon, then translate this . . ."

I picked up the second copybook and opened it at random. The odd graphic pattern of Syrian double meter jumped at me.

I began to read:

For in the darkness of the cruelest night,
Amidst the hatred of a thousand kin,
'Tis you, O you, my love,
My friend, O beast,
O candle of my youthful blood—

I closed it quickly as if blinded by sudden sunlight. "This is what they did?"

"Yes," Mr. Glantz said. "Translating old poems of Rubin."

"Of Rubin." My knees were weak.

This was not a poem of Paltiel's. I knew them all by heart. This was a new poem. A new one. So much like Paltiel's as to defy comprehension. But new.

Mr. Glantz blubbered, "Your father said I could have them, after they finished translating . . . because I took him in again . . ."

"Yes." I was eating up the poems with my eyes, lapping at the lines, hearing their sound, like a voice singing—

Mr. Glantz babbled on about how Abdallah and my father used to work until midnight sometimes. "So you'll bring them back when you finish? You promise?"

"Yes," I said. "That I can promise you."

From a kiosk in Allenby I called Abdallah's store in Yaffo, but there was no answer. I got into the Beetle and raced to Tel Aviv University in Ramat Aviv.

As I barged into his office, Professor Tzifroni was standing near the window, leafing through a book.

"One question," I said to his back. "Can I ask you one question?"

He kept reading obstinately, refusing to turn, but I saw his shoulder quiver.

Using my military voice I quoted the first poem I had just read in my father's copybook, but stopped in the middle of the last line. "Did you ever hear this one?"

It was amazing how I already knew it by heart after only one reading. How easy it was to memorize.

He turned slowly. "Where did you get this?"

"Doesn't matter. Do you know it?"

He shook his head, his eyes on my lips, as if trying to extract from them the remainder of the last line.

I persisted. "Who wrote it? Can you tell?"

He licked his lips. "Rubin, for sure! It's his meter, but with an extra beat." He shuffled forward and clutched at my hand. "You found some more fragments somewhere? Where?"

Mr. Glantz had also thought these were Rubin's poems. But who wouldn't? The same floating meter, the same incomparable line reversion, the same heart-stopping mystery, the spurious simplicity—

I pulled one of the copybooks from my knapsack and put it on the cluttered desk. The professor licked his lips again, then opened the copybook with the tips of his fingers and began to read. Once or twice he looked up, his eyebrows knotted.

"*Nu?*" I said.

"Rubin, sure it's Rubin," he whispered. "But where did you copy this from? It's clean, not in fragments."

I said, "Look at the last three poems. See this ditty, about Rabin and Peres? And Carter?"

He read, licked his lips, then looked up.

"Same meter?" I asked sarcastically. "Prosody? Style?" There was a pause as I took the copybook out of his hand. "You still think they wrote it together? In seventy-six? That Paltiel's ghost came back, maybe? Like the Debba?"

The pause lengthened as Professor Tzifroni tried to speak; at last he whispered, "So he wrote them all? *Shimshon, Ben HaTan, Zonah Tamah—*"

"Yes," I said. "My father wrote them all."

"You fucking donkey," Ruthy screeched, her eyes white with wrath. "If you write this in the newspaper, I will do not do it. You hear me?" Her voice rose into a shriek. "I won't do it."

I stuttered that I'd only write about the play. "Not the poems, not the sonnets—just so that the newspapers won't drag my father's name in the sewer—"

"Well, I don't give a *zayin!*" Ruthy shrieked. "I am not going to stand there and sing, when everyone—nobody is going to say that my father stole—that he didn't—" She broke down.

I shouted at her, "But did you read what the papers are saying about my father—"

"So they are saying!"

She and I glared at each other; her father against mine.

Ehud whispered, "So maybe you'll write it only later—" He was pale, looking neither at me nor at Ruthy.

"When later?" I said. "A day after the show, who would care?"

"Well I am telling you," Ruthy hollered. "I am not going to act in it if—if David's going to say that he—that Paltiel stole—"

"But you have to," Ehud whispered, the pallor of his face darkening. "It's too late to get someone else—it's in one week. You have to do it!"

"Have to? I don't have to do anything if I don't want to!"

After a while Ehud said to me, "So maybe you—just postpone this article—what do I know—" He stared at me with eyes suddenly wet. "*He* also would have . . ."

I could not speak. "All right," I whispered at last.

To fufill my father's wish, it seems, I must let his name be dragged in the mud.

I stumbled blindly down the stairs.

43

Down in the street, buses roared by, billowing black smoke. All I could think of was my father relinquishing his work.

For what? Was it for money?

That my father gave money to actors, I knew. He had always given. But his work?

My father, who had never done a crooked thing in his life; my father, who noted down every shekel he had received, and paid tax on every penny. My father, who had refused to be reimbursed for his bus fare to his weekly meeting at the Wrestling Club, where he volunteered as a board member. My father, the honest Jew, who had never cheated, who had done only favors; except for his sons.

And for his wife?

I stood awhile in the hot sizzling sun, then, without premeditation, took bus number 63 to Pinsker Street, got off on the corner of Trumpeldor, and went to visit my mother's grave.

The old Trumpeldor cemetery had an aura of dereliction, as if it was a Muslim one about to be bulldozed. The trails were overgrown with *injill*, Arab weed, and scraggly dandelions and *hubeiza* poked between the stones. I made my way to the end row, looking around. It was seven years since I had been here last.

Grandpa Yoel and Grandma Leah were buried at the westerly end, and my mother just behind them, under plain mounds overlaid with rough slabs of rock. The *khamsin* had made the stones too hot to touch, so I sprinkled some sand on my mother's gravestone, and sat down gingerly on it.

All around me were graves, graves, with Stars of David on their faces, and square Hebrew letters half smothered with sand. Most were of rough sandstone and dark basalt, and just plain gray marble. Here was Nachman Shein's headstone, engraved with a large musical note, there Paltiel Rubin's, a pencil, or perhaps a quill, incised at its base. To the side, half fallen, were the headstones of Sirkis, and Gurevitch, and Shaposhnikov, the early dramatists, and three gravestones whose lettering had long ago been obliterated by the salty wind. Flies flitted everywhere, also a few sparrows.

Why was my mother not buried by my father's side? They, who were so loving in life; who often, after the Shabbat meal, sang together old songs from '48, and before, or recited Hebrew poetry in tandem, each quoting alternate stanzas, then alternate lines, then alternate words, faster and faster, until one stumbled and had to wash the dishes while suffering pinches . . .

What made them part?

The sun was warm on my neck but my heart felt cold.

I sat for an indeterminate while, looking around me, trying to imagine the old hatreds and the loves, the passions and the sorrows, all gone now; all but the one that had remained, the one hate that had come back to kill my father.

After lunch in Café Cassit, I sat drinking beer after beer. Presently Leibele came up and said someone was waiting for me outside.

As I emerged into the sunshine I saw Abdallah Seddiqi seated on an empty Tnuva milk crate at the edge of the sidewalk. Ten paces away, behind the wheel of a black Peugeot, sat his nephew, smoking.

When Abdallah saw me he rose creakily onto his thin legs, climbing up on one cane, then another. He said he had just been to the apartment in Ibn Gvirol but the lady said I had gone, probably to Cassit. "So I came to here," he said, in that odd Arabicized Hebrew of his. "I thought maybe I should tell you something." He gave me a gray stare.

I suggested we go inside, but he shook his head and pointed to the car. "There."

The nephew banged the car door open and Abdallah shuffled in. He patted the seat beside him. "Sit here, near me."

The air in the car was thick with the odor of sweat and acetone glue, so much like my father's, but also tangy with the smell of half-raw skins. Abdallah looked at me sideways, making a humming sound in his throat.

"No," the nephew said in Arabic. "He's with them."

Abdallah told him to be quiet. "He's not with anybody."

"He's with them, I am telling you. You are making a black mistake, *ya* Seddiqi—"

"Enough!" Abdallah turned to me, "I used to sell him leather, and also sandals, and sometimes glue—" He paused. "So Saturday afternoon, I came to see him, in the store."

"*That* Saturday?" My heart gave a jerk.

"A black mistake," said the nephew.

"Quiet, *ya* Fa'uz. Yes, Saturday, to talk about the shipment, also about—other things." He leaned forward. "Fauzi, turn on the radio."

Without speaking, Fauzi obeyed. To my surprise it was tuned to Galey Tzahal, the popular army music station. Voices of two women came on the air, singing of Jerusalem of Gold, Ne'omi Shemer's song from 1967, the unofficial paratroopers' hymn.

"Leave it, good."

There was a lengthy pause. I felt Abdallah carefully choosing his words; I couldn't even begin to guess what he had wanted of me.

"In thirty-six," he said, "we were partners in the store. You know of this?" He tapped with his aluminum cane on the floor, lightly.

"Yes. Before the First Events—"

"The Rebellion," Fauzi said over his shoulder. "The first Arab Rebellion."

A guitar began to strum harshly on the radio, accompanied by a flute.

Abdallah said, "*Ya Fa'uz*, don't stick your nose in. Let old men talk." He tapped his cane. "I had to sell him back my share in thirty-six. You know of this?"

I hoisted my shoulder and gave a diagonal nod.

"He didn't want me to, Isrool, but they forced him." Abdallah turned and looked at me. To my discomfort he put his hand on my knee. The hand was astonishingly hot, as if he were feverish.

I said lamely, "Glantz, his landlord—I saw the poems you were working on—" A muscle-bound waiter stuck his head in the window and spoke to Abdallah. "Where do you think you—" He saw me and stopped.

"We're talking," I said in English. "What's your problem?"

The waiter—one I hadn't seen before—disappeared.

Abdallah said, as if there had been no interruption, "As a favor. I helped him with some words."

"Words of a thief," said Fauzi. "Stole our land, then our stories—" He made a soft sound in his throat.

I felt myself redden. Abdallah's hand on my knee twitched. "We were friends once, so we met again, when he asked me to do this translation, of the poems." Another twitch of the hand. "Also we talked—discussed—like in thirty-three—"

"Discussed what, in thirty-three?" I felt myself suffocating in the heat, and the stink, and this talk of the prehistory.

"We had a committee, in thirty-three, Isrool and Baldiel, and I and my brother Haffiz, and the Nashashibis, from Jerusalem—" He stared at me hard, to see if I had grasped his meaning.

I shook my head. The Nashashibi family had once ruled Jerusalem, during the early days of the British Mandate, and were the main political opponents of the Grand Mufti, the Nazi sympathizer. Half the land around Jerusalem used to belong to them.

"We met, to see if we could make a compromise, between you and us—you see?"

I said, "What kind of compromise? Peace?"

I felt my face redden, saying such a foolish word.

"Not peace, just a compromise. So we can sell to each other, buy from each other, live together—"

"Live together." Fauzi's voice was thick. "Live? He who lies with the Viper—"

"Quiet, *ya* Fa'uz. Quiet." Again, Abdallah turned to me, "We came to an agreement, slow down Jewish immigration in some areas, purchases of land, a joint representation before the British authorities, a joint bank—" His voice droned on, like some radio announcer, clear and precise now, the Arabicized lilt gone.

I listened, dazed with beer and heat. At last he stopped. I said, "In thirty-three? All this?"

"Yes. Unofficial, it all was. Just some private people talking. Only merchants." He coughed, a caw of bitter laughter. "Just some Arab and Jewish merchants."

"But," I said, "in thirty-three he was already in the Haganah."

Abdallah gave another terse nod. "Yes, I knew. And my brother Haffiz, he was in . . . the Istiqlal. Isrool knew, too. So what? Talking—so what if we talked?" Then, without warning, he spat. "But nothing came of it. The hotheads on both sides—" He stopped.

I said, "And that's what you wanted to tell me?"

I couldn't see what was so secret about some committee of merchants forty-four years ago, trying to arrive at a half-assed private peace, so they could continue to sell shoes and do business with each other, and make money.

Abdallah went on, "Then, four years ago, in seventy-three, after the Yom Kippur War, he asked me if we could continue to talk." The hot bony palm massaged my knee tenderly, absently. "So I said, 'All right.'"

"Talk about what?" I tried removing my knee, but he had grabbed it with alarmingly powerful fingers.

"Some things . . . that people wanted to pass along . . . after seventy-three . . . first we talked about the things . . . before we let them know . . ." His eyes were unfocused, his words disjointed, as if some inner censor was wary of revealing too much.

"Let who know?" I suddenly began to pay attention. A gust of breeze came through the open window, carrying in it the smell of rotting garbage.

"Whoever asked us to pass it along. What we thought of it."

The understanding inside me was like a sudden radiance. "You acted as go-between? The two of you? That's what you came to tell me?"

A nod, slow and deliberate. *"Hada hoo."* That's it.

"Ach," said Fauzi, in pain and disgust, but whether at the stupidity of Abdallah and my father, or at Abdallah's foolishness for revealing it to me now, was left unclear.

"But—but why you? Why him?"

"Because he was no longer in—in any of this—" Abdallah paused. "And I—because I was never in any way—" A longer pause, now. "Our word was good."

"Merchants' words," Fauzi said in disgust.

"Merchants have honor," Abdallah said. "When we give our word, it's given."

Ten paces away, two new waiters conferred with each other.

Abdallah said, "In this place, many people want to tell something to the other side. It goes through embassies, through Americans; once the message gets over there, no one can say he believes it. Why? It came from the Jews. A message arrives here, same thing. No one wants to believe. Why? Because it's from Arabs."

"Because it's from Arabs," said Fauzi. "We are worms, only now the worms are growing teeth."

"But who?" I said, not looking at Fauzi. "Who wants to send messages?"

"Everyone," said Abdallah. "Fatah, someone in Egypt, maybe in Lebanon, Iraq—" At the Arab names, the very air in the car seemed to congeal into a different substance, heavy with danger and expectation.

I said, "You passed messages back and forth?"

"Yes. I to our people, Isrool to yours. But first we would talk, to decide if they were true—no, not true—but—" He searched for the word.

"Sincere," I said. I felt myself reddening again. Talking with an Arab about sincerity.

"*Hada hoo*. We gave our word, together with the message. That we believe it's sincere, what the message says."

"And if they lied to you?"

"Then next time we don't take messages, from those who lied."

I said, "You mean, you and—my father—you two they would believe, but not each other?"

He nodded with placidity. "Yes, yes. *Hada hoo*." He had extracted a chain of yellow worry beads out of his pocket, and was now rolling them between his fingers.

It was so absurd and yet so very like the Middle East that I knew it must be true. Those who would lie without remorse to a whole people would not lie to a man whose word of honor they respected.

There was a pause. Fauzi twirled the radio dial, then raised the volume. A commercial for Reznik chocolate came on the air. Something to do with sweet delight.

I said, "So that's why he was killed, you think?" I was surprised how normal my voice was. How ordinary.

The commercial ended with a jingle, and flowed into an
old song by the Nachal army band, about preferring guns to
socks.

Fauzi hissed, "They couldn't let it go on, all these generals.
I told him, the Seddiqi. You think anyone here wants to talk?
To Arabs?"

I felt my face darken. "And you, you want to talk?"

"Quiet," said Abdallah.

But I was in full flight now. "In forty-eight," I snarled, "you
could've made peace, then in fifty-six, we asked you again,
and in sixty-seven, after every fucking war we asked you, but
you—" I stopped. Who was "we"? I wasn't even a citizen here
anymore. Both he and Abdallah were. Arabs, but citizens.

Fauzi raised his hand, the fingers spread, and slapped it
against his neck. "Talk? Lying on the ground with your foot on
our throat and we'll talk? And honor? Where's honor?"

"Fauzi, start the car," said Abdallah.

I turned to him. "What did you talk to him about, when you
saw him—last?"

"Like the week before it . . . There was—something someone wanted to ask, of the Egyptians."

"Ask what?"

A shrug. I saw he was considering something, as before, as
if wondering if he should go on.

Fauzi let up on the clutch; there was a scratchy sound and
the car lurched ahead.

I said, "And he, my father, he gave you this message? To pass
along?"

"Yes."

"What kind of message?"

"Something, from someone old, he's no longer in the

government. A kibbutznik. Maybe someone in the government gave him the question, and asked him to ask it."

I waited, but obviously he wasn't going to tell me who it was. "Who was it for?" I asked at last.

Abdallah tapped his cane. "For Sadat."

The fingers left my knee, or maybe I had jerked my knee away. And all at once Abdallah began to talk. I listened in stunned silence as he spoke of messages, and suggestions of meetings, mutual visits, a grand gesture.

Fauzi said over his shoulder, "And leave us Palestinians rotting in the ditch."

Abdallah stopped talking and folded his hands on his chest, and once more had become just a dried up old Arab with a narrow unshaven face and a blue-black bow tie knotted crookedly at the throat of his *abbaya*.

No one spoke for a while. The almond trees of Har Nevo Street flashed pinkly by the window.

"A little honor, that's all we ask for," Fauzi said. "Someone to give us a little honor. Then we'll talk."

The Peugeot stopped before house number 142-Aleph on Ibn Gvirol.

I had a sudden urge to invite them both up; then sanity prevailed.

I said, "So you think—because of this—" I recalled Gershonovitz's warnings, and Asa's, the clumsy attacks, the attempts to stop our play by any means, the buzz on my phone, the merchants' fear.

"Vipers, all of them," whispered Fauzi. His eyes, fine and black with long curling lashes like a boy's, bore into mine. "Vipers defending their precious eggs, biting everyone who tries to—"

"And Fatah?" I interrupted him. The PLO. "What about them? Or the Ichwan?" The Muslim Brotherhood. "And all your other fucking murderers, who didn't want to be left in the ditch? Maybe they—"

"Don't worry! We won't be left in the ditch! If we are, we'll take all the world with us. Women, children, everybody."

We glared at each other with hate as naked and pleasurable as love.

There was a moment of vibrant silence.

"No," Abdallah said after a while. "It wasn't an Arab."

"But how do you know?" I couldn't believe it, asking him such a question, and expecting an answer.

"I believe them," he said. Then, absurdly like Amzaleg, he added, "Some of them, I believe."

Fauzi said through his teeth, "It wasn't us. I can tell you."

I stared at them, one after the other. It was clear that they were waiting for me to ask a question, or to open the car door and leave. Their message was over.

I stared hard at Abdallah, to make sure he understood I was asking him, not his nephew. "But why are you telling me—"

"We were partners, once." He rapped his cane on the seat, like a teacher making a point. "Partners, in everything."

I opened the door and got out. Cans overflowing with garbage were piled at the curb, and brown burlap bags stuffed with old newspapers. Across the street, a gray Toyota with a single headlight was parked, its windows curtained.

"Never cheated in anything," Abdallah said. "His word was always good."

Fauzi clicked the door lock. Without looking at me he said, "*Allah yerachmo.*" God will pity him. Then, as if to compensate for a gaffe, he spit, but dryly. "*Chalas,*" he said. Finished. "The Seddiqi will call you."

And all of a sudden it wasn't clear just who was in charge, Abdallah or he.

I began to climb the stairs, seeing nothing, when I heard Abdallah calling after me. *"Ya* Daoud!"

I turned, squinting. His head was a blur within the Peugeot's window.

He said, "You still need a hall, for this play?"

I tried to speak, and failed. At last I nodded.

Abdallah went on, "Maybe I can help you. You want?"

I nodded again. The sun's brilliance was so blinding I felt my eyes sting. *"Na'am,"* I said in Arabic. *"Na'am."* Yes, yes.

I did not know why I spoke Arabic to him all of a sudden.

He nodded to me in return; and then the Peugeot pulled away, with the Toyota close behind it, disdainfully close, not even trying to hide its intent.

Neither Ehud nor Ruthy had yet come back when I woke up at seven in the evening, my head aching as though I had been handling gelignite. Stumbling out of bed, I made for the kitchen terrace, pulled out my Nomex coveralls from under my mother's old sewing machine and, with my head hammering with mad thoughts and traces of the beer fumes, went into the bathroom.

I had been an idiot. It had been staring me in the face, this thing, and I had refused to look. Again I checked the waistband batteries, the thumb lights, the jimmies and the picks, then pulled on Ehud's dark blue shirt and my own jeans, cursing myself for being an unthinking fool, for not finishing the job last time. Deaf and dumb I had become in Canada. Deaf and blind and dumb. But no more.

When I returned to the apartment it was five-thirty in the morning. Neither Ruthy nor Ehud woke up as I washed and changed. I sat on the terrace, my feet dangling outside, smoking one of Ruthy's bitter Dubek cigarettes and looking over the city. Above the old Bazel *shuk*, glued to a tall wooden platform that someone had erected during the night, was a huge poster of Peres, leader of the Labor Party—it stared at me with puffed eyes over the expanse of white roofs, with a black-lettered slogan underneath.

"Vote for experience!"

Closer and farther down, in the street below, from along the entire length of the stone fences of houses to the left and to the right, a carpet of Begin placards, already there for a week, stared at me in a sea of thick glasses.

"Vote for change!"

I sat on the terrace, smoking and waiting for the sun to come up, then left at seven o'clock, without breakfast.

As I approached his kiosk, Zussman was loading Eshel crates into the back. At this early hour Herzl Street was still deserted. I followed him silently into the kiosk's interior, and stood by without saying a word, just watching him, as the color slowly drained from his cheeks.

He did not even ask me what I wanted.

"*Nu?*" I said, pointing to the wall.

His face fell to pieces.

"Swear to me, David, that you'll not tell. They'll take off my *zayin* if—if they knew I—that I told you—"

"That they were listening in on my father?"

His cheeks turned doughy. "D . . . David," he stammered, "swear to me! I—I beg of you—!"

I waited until his panting subsided.

"Why did they put a microphone in his store?"

"They d . . . didn't tell me—"

"Did they have a court order?"

He shook his head.

"So why did you let them?"

He whispered something.

"What?" I said.

"As a favor." His voice was nearly inaudible.

"To whom?"

He shook his head, saying nothing.

Probably to someone from his days in the Intelligence Service, in the prehistory.

I looked down at the gray plastic box in my hand. I had found it the night before, when I broke into the Tnuva kiosk. The diminutive Japanese tape deck had been hidden under a crate of Dubek cigarettes, the mike cord attached to the wall with gray military adhesive tape before disappearing into a tiny hole. Probably voice activated, like the ones we used to leave behind sometimes, in deep penetrations into Damascus or Cairo, to be retrieved later by Intel Recon patrolmen.

"How often did they change tapes?"

Zussman darted a quick glance at me. "I . . . I changed them, at night . . . They . . . they gave me a box of cassettes, and . . . every few hours I . . ." He began to speak faster. "David, they said Arabs sometimes came there, and talked among themselves . . . so it was important to listen . . ."

"What Arabs?"

"They said it was secret."

"And you believed them?"

He gave me a frightened stare, as if I had just gone mad. "Sure I did!"

A month ago I would have believed them, too.

"How often did they come for the tapes?"

"Every day."

"Who was it, who came?"

He shook his head.

"You knew him?"

Zussman hesitated, looked at my stony face, and finally nodded, diagonally.

"Who?"

He swallowed. "Someone. You don't know him."

There was a pause. His wife looked at us from the back, but came no closer than the furthermost table.

"You still have the last tape? Of the last day?"

I was surprised to hear how calm my voice was.

"No, they took it."

I turned to go.

"Swear to me, David!"

I said nothing, and left. Behind me I could sense his wife scuttling forward to talk to her husband. I did not turn around to look.

The eight-story building on King Saul Boulevard, two blocks away from Yaro's office, had just been built when I left Israel. There was a sculpture of a cube out front, and a little fountain.

They had the third floor all to themselves. A plaque on the wall said, unconvincingly, ZERACH FELDMAN, INSURANCE AGENCIES. I tried to open the door. There was a four-button combination lock on it. It stayed closed. I thumped on the door with both fists, then kicked at it.

"Fucking *shoo-shoo!*" I hollered.

A small TV camera buzzed as it turned in my direction. The Israeli consulate in Toronto had one just like that.

I could hear muffled voices behind the door.

I kicked at the door again. "I want to talk to you! If you don't open, I'll go holler in the street that you killed my father!"

The door hissed open, slowly. A small nondescript man stood inside, a row of pens in his nylon shirt pocket. "What do you want? You have an appointment?"

I pushed the door and barged in. Hard hands grabbed at me. I peeled one finger off and bent it back, then another. The other hand tightened its grip, and I raised my elbow for a down thrust.

Down in the street a Vespa engine died down, and I heard two crackling whistles. I delayed my elbow, and gave the same whistle back.

"Leave him, Yossi," said the nondescript man.

The hands slipped off me.

The man called Yossi was huge and hairy with a bristling mustache, and he reeked of sweat. It was the man who had broken into the Ibn Gvirol apartment and stolen my father's letter. "Who did you bring with you?" he snapped.

"Go jump on my dick."

He took a sliding step toward me.

"Yossi! Please!"

"Sit down," said the small man.

I said, "You bugged his store, you fuckers. You bugged my father's store. To listen in on him and Seddiqi talking. So the night he was killed, you heard everything, the killer, too. Who was it? Who killed him?"

They both looked at me in silence.

I said, "I can go to *Ha'Olam HaZeh*, tell them about it—"

"It didn't work that night," the small man said abruptly. "The tape."

"Balls! You know who killed him!"

He shook his head. "Someone screwed up, maybe when they changed the tape. The tape didn't work."

"Shit in yogurt. You know who it was, and you're protecting him."

I felt him relax, as though I had somehow committed a blunder.

"I think you should go."

I said to the large hirsute man, "Where is my father's letter that you took? What did he write to me?" I didn't want it to sound like a plea.

He looked at me silently, biting his lips. The small man stayed silent also. It was clear no one was going to speak.

I kicked at the table, trying to stifle the tickling inside my nose.

No one said anything as I left.

Back in the apartment, Ehud and Ruthy were gone. A hundred-shekel note was on the kitchen counter, and the Beetle's keys. I set to work. It took me half an hour to find the bug, using Ruthy's transistor radio with a fork for an omni antenna, twiddling the dial from side to side, listening for the faint echo from the hidden resonator.

Finally I found it, a standard *makshivan*. It had been glued to the back of the kitchen table, most probably at the time of the burglary, and was shaped like a beetle (the odd sense of humor of some *shoo-shoo* technician), the size of my fingernail, its thin antenna pasted to the table's underside with gray gaffer tape. Standard military issue.

I flushed the *makshivan* down the toilet and went to search for the other—they were usually left in pairs. I found it on top of the bathroom door, a standard echo chamber made to transmit voices not more than two hundred yards away, most likely to the Toyota parked on the street. At the U.S. Embassy in Moscow, one had been buried in the American eagle behind the ambassador's desk, for many years.

Barely able to contain my rage, I crushed it under my heel and threw its husk in the garbage pail.

If that's the way they wanted to play, it was fine with me.

44

NEXT MORNING EHUD AND I picked up Kagan and drove to the Waqf hall in Yaffo. But my seething dissipated when we arrived.

The old community center of the Muslim Religious Council stood not two hundred yards from the Yaffo beach, wavy lines of heat snaking above it in the *khamsin*. In the yard stood Abdallah, waiting for us.

"This?" Kagan yelped. "This *chirbe*?" This wreck.

"It's big," Abdallah said with equanimity, "and I can rent it to you. I am the treasurer of the Waqf."

We stood breathing the boiling air, staring at the hall.

"So what do you think?" I asked Ehud.

Ehud shrugged curtly. What was there to say? The devastation seemed complete and irremediable.

"But we own it," Abdallah said, a new note creeping into his voice, "the Waqf does, and I can rent it to you."

Ehud muttered, "We—we can't pay for this. We don't have much money left."

"So I will lend it to you, and get you some laborers to do what's necessary." He fixed me with his coal-gray eyes. "Don't worry, I'll make a profit."

When none of us answered he hobbled on his canes toward an opening in the hall's side, and entered, Ehud and I following, then Kagan.

It was a cavernous room crisscrossed with dusty light. Thirty years before it might have been a thing of beauty, with blue-white tiles set at eye level all around, but by now most of the tiles had fallen off, revealing the crumbling sandstone underneath.

Kagan said, "But—there's no stage, no seats, nothing—"

"We'll bring," Abdallah said fiercely. "Everything. We'll borrow from other halls. In Qalqilia, Jenin, Ramleh—" He rattled off a few more names from the West Bank. "Then we'll take it all back, so it'll cost only rental fees." He gave me a half grin. "*Billig,*" he said in guttural Yiddish. Cheap.

We went outside. "Here." Abdallah handed me a typewritten page. "I prepared the agreement."

I handed it to Ehud. He scanned it and looked up. "Five percent of the box office receipts? No cash up front?"

Abdallah looked at Ehud, then at me. "You want it?"

"Three percent," Ehud said. He seemed to have perked up a little.

"No, no," Abdallah said, his body filling up, too.

Finally they settled on four. Abdallah spit on the ground, for luck, and Ehud followed suit. I did the same, and we all mashed the spittle with the tips of our shoes and sandals. Then Ehud signed his name at the bottom of the page, and finally I did, too.

"You as witness," Abdallah said to Kagan.

Kagan signed, slowly.

"Now in Arabic, too," Abdallah said. "Everyone."

Leaving Abdallah behind, we went out, circled the building, and stood staring at the sea. The water glinted in the *khamsin* like a freshly polished mess tin, the horizon a shimmer of yellow.

Ehud said, "We don't have to kiss him or anything. We do the play, we pay him, then we're gone; we don't have to talk to him afterward."

"Sure," I said. "It's for the money that he does it, what d'you think."

Kagan remained silent.

We turned to go. But on our way to the Volvo, three young Arabs barred our path, their faces wrapped, two with red-and-white keffiyehs, the third's green and white. For a wild moment I thought there was going to be a brawl, but then the green-and-white keffiyeh was thrown back, and the young Arab touched fingers to his forehead. "*As-salaam alaikum*," he said gruffly.

"*Alaikum as-salaam*," I replied as evenly as I could.

It was Fauzi, Abdallah's nephew. The green, the Holy Color, meant he was a supporter of the Ichwan, the Muslim Brotherhood. The red meant the other two were PFLP supporters. Here, in plain daylight, declaring their support for murder and terror. My stomach began to sizzle.

"The Seddiqi said we should help," Fauzi whispered. "It's only because of him."

"All right," I said, keeping a lid on my temper.

"And he said also that you'll tell us what to do." I could hear the rage. "How to fix the place, and how to set it up—"

"Not me." I pointed at Ehud. "He will."

Ehud rasped, "Whatever I can." I could see it was costing him blood also.

The two other Arabs shifted in place, their eyes narrow with confused emotion.

Fauzi went on, "And after it's fixed, he said we should also guard it—" His eyes were hot and black, daring me.

I swallowed my bile. "I'll give you a hand there."

"*Shukran*," Fauzi hissed. Thank you. Yet the sarcasm didn't quite come off; and without further word, he and his two followers walked away.

Next day I awoke full of feverish excitement, and, alone in the apartment, hummed Yissachar's opening aria while I shaved. Then, shaven and cut and without breakfast, I took bus number 1 to Yaffo, and disembarked in front of the Waqf hall.

I could hardly recognize it.

Whereas the day before, the hall seemed like a large decrepit sheikh's grave, it was now more like a wrecking yard filled with noisy carpentry crews.

Cars sporting the green license plates of the West Bank were parked in the yard. Behind them, a group of fierce-looking boys were sprawled on a pile of lumber, hammering down nails with violent enthusiasm. Four other young men in burnooses passed, carting debris, then five others, lugging benches. A transistor radio yawled a song of Farid Al Atrash and all sang along with it. The scene had a wild comic air to it, but with a dark undertone, like an undefined act taking slow shape.

I looked behind. Two Toyotas were standing at the curb, their drivers smoking. In a rage I began to stride in their direction when Ehud limped out of the hall. "It'll never be ready in time!" He chortled. "Look at this! Not even a stage!"

"So we'll build a tent," I shouted, the *shoo-shoo* cars forgotten. "We'll build a Bedouin tent! *Arabushim* we already have."

Indeed, that we had. The yard was bursting with them, with gaggles of admiring Arab urchins looking on.

"Come inside!" Ehud hollered, and before I had a chance to reply he pulled me into the dusty light inside the hall, and, his cheeks shiny with happiness, kicked hard at a leg of someone lying under a wooden frame. The leg withdrew and our accountant appeared, his nose stained.

"Hi, Dada," he exulted. "We stole the lumber from a construction site in Lodd, me and Fauzi. Didn't cost a penny!"

Ehud began to holler again over and above the racket. Behind us, oblivious to the noise, a young Arab had knelt on a prayer mat and, with eyes closed, began to sing out the Fatiha, the opening verse of the daily prayer, his voice merging into the hammer blows:

'Alhamdu lillahi rab 'alalamin, malik yawm al-din,
iaka na'abudu wa'iaka nasta'in—

God be praised, ruler of all the worlds, King of Judgment Day,
Thee we worship, and thy help we seek—

My stomach churned; I recalled the times I lived among them, in Egypt or Amman, pretending to be one of them—hearing their own god's *Mein Kampf* sung over and over again, while keeping the Other in me in check, waiting to do the necessary . . . then I recalled the time on Um Marjam hill when I kept the Other in check, even as I heard the same detestable prayer, and so caused the death of friends . . .

I looked away.

A few Arab boys had begun to drag chairs in, standing them in rows against the wall, and I felt a dull astonishment at how fast the place had begun to resemble a real hall, with a stage, and benches, and a frame for a curtain—even rails for lighting were now being strung up at the ceiling's corner by a young chocolate-factory worker on a rickety ladder, with a young Arab shouting directions from below. Here and there some high school boys could be seen, dragging lumber, chairs, or rope bundles.

"*Salaam 'alaikum, ya* Daoud!" At the door, leaning on his canes, stood Abdallah, a cigarette in his curved mouth.

I mumbled back a shy *salaam*. I did not know what to say, how to praise the speed with which he had brought all these ragtag *shabbab* together.

But he was not waiting for praise. "A policeman came, before. He asked for our building permit, so I told him we don't need one. The hall belongs to us."

I stuttered, "I can call the lawyer, to—"

"No lawyer! The hall belongs to the Waqf! To us! We don't need any permit from anybody!" He thumped on the ground with his cane, for emphasis. "To us!"

"Yes," I said. "All right—"

As I went out, Fauzi came up to me and pointed with his chin. "See them? They have been here from the morning." He spit into his fist.

Beyond the fence stood five boys in orange shirts, and two burly men, all carrying Kach placards. The Toyotas were right behind them.

"Yes," I said. "I have seen them. Just keep your eyes open."

Fauzi said there were several *shabbab* staying in Abdallah's house. "I can go get them now, take these fuckers on, break their bones before they try anything—"

"Forget it. Do nothing unless they try to barge in. Understand?" He glowered at me.

I said, "You touch anyone now, you'll be arrested. You want to be arrested?"

"Them, the police don't arrest." He pointed to three burly men across the road.

"Because they are outside the fence." I pointed out five other men whom he had missed, three lounging in the shadows of an awning at the corner of Shazli Street, two at the back of a grimy house on Avoda Lane. "Keep a watch on them from here. And at night, stay hidden. And wear dark clothes. Understand?"

He said nothing, just kicked the gravel and left.

That afternoon I dropped by again, and, before leaving, organized a simple perimeter defense of the hall, in two layers. I placed Fauzi and five young Arabs from Qalqilia on the corners of Avoda Lane, two Arabs from Hebron on Shazli Street, and Ben-Shoshan and a young Druze on the corner of HaMeshorerim Street and Sefer Shir Avenue. A handful of high school boys (I could see no girls), pale with fear and excitement, were told to remain inside and keep watch through the windows. "If you see anything, whistle. Anyone coming from Shazli Street, whistle once. From Avoda, twice—"

It was a long, detailed instruction, and I made everyone repeat it until I was satisfied they had gotten it all. Then I gave Fauzi the pair of night-vision goggles that I had brought with me from Ibn Gvirol, and explained to him how to use them. "Everything will look green, but you'll see clearly, everything. Only don't look directly at bright lamps, or you'll burn the electronic retina."

He scrutinized the goggles in his hand, and tried them on. They were a bit loose, so I tightened the strap for him.

As he took them off he gave a clicking of the tongue, as though calling to an invisible horse, and nodded at me equably. For a moment I thought he was going to thank me, but he just nodded again, and walked off.

That same afternoon we had the first rehearsal in the Waqf hall, among the myriad benches, chairs, half-erected curtain frames, and heaps of partly sawn lumber. It went without a flaw. Afterward, as Ehud stayed behind to give the actors notes, I sat with Abdallah in Café Machfooz, in an odd one-sided companionship—he silent, I burbling desperately about how well it all went, telling him about Canada,

and Jenny, and my scribblings, avoiding even thinking about
Ruthy. Next morning was another rehearsal, just as flawless,
and immediately after, yet another. Or perhaps it was the
next afternoon. I no longer remember. The last days before
our performance have become an only partly remembered
memory—I was not entirely well. I had lost five kilograms
since my arrival, I hardly slept anymore, and I now smoked a
pack of harsh Lodd cigarettes and drank three or four beers a
day. Often, between rehearsals, I took notes and drew tables
and diagrams, like the ones I had seen Amzaleg do, to try
and fathom how and why my father was killed; but I could
no longer concentrate on it. All I could think of was the play,
and Ruthy. Every night at two in the morning she would be
waiting for me in the bathroom, silent and feverish and tense,
already seated on the sink, her legs spread. And later, as I
lay awake trying to think of nothing, groping for sleep, she
and the play and my father's other writings and the hope-
less investigation would merge in my feverish brain into one
opaque mystery whose purpose or ending I could not yet
fully see, or comprehend.

Mornings I would go to the Waqf hall, to view the rehearsals,
and to make sure the *shabbab* were at their posts; afternoons I
would interview yet another cabdriver, about passengers who
had either gotten in or disembarked near my father's store
that Saturday evening; or I would again talk to Abdallah, to see
whether he had come up with anything new among whatever
shadowy contacts he had in the Arab street. Amzaleg called
me from time to time, leaving messages for me at home, or
at Cassit, but I no longer bothered to respond. Ever since I
realized that he probably knew who the burglar was—since
the police and the Shin Bet often worked hand in hand—my
trust in him had evaporated. In a curious way, his betrayal had
touched me more than I cared to admit, perhaps because he

had served with my father, and loved him, yet found it expedient to betray him; while Abdallah, whose share in my father's store had been usurped, whose orchards had been confiscated, whose elder brother had been killed—perhaps even by someone in my father's unit—now risked his neck for me, helping me find the murderer, and incurring the wrath of the *shoo-shoo* by helping me stage the play, and probably losing money in the bargain. Did he do it for the sake of my father, his old partner and friend, or for mine?

So much gratitude I felt for him that it nearly eclipsed the gratitude I felt for Ehud, and the deep shame. Yes, the shame. I felt remorse for screwing Ehud's bride-to-be and for costing him money, but I was more ashamed of my gratitude toward Abdallah.

Gratitude to an Arab!

I had never imagined I could stoop as low as this.

45

THERE WERE ABOUT A dozen people in our small theater troupe, both actors and crew, yet it soon became clear it was Ehud who was the production's mainstay. With Kagan often hitting the bottle, and I away most of the time, it now fell on him to direct and handle the many annoyances that cropped up daily.

"It's only five days to the performance," Ehud said to me late one evening, when I told him he should sleep more. "After it and after the wedding I can sleep all I want."

The wedding had been planned for three weeks after the performance. Ehud had asked me once if I would stay for it; I said I could not, and he did not ask again.

Aside from such brief moments, I hardly saw him at all. He rose by five o'clock in the morning, and left long before either Ruthy or I awoke. He had lost weight, and had eerily taken on the lean look of my father in his early pictures.

"I hardly see him anymore either," Ruthy said as we lay entangled behind some *hadass* bushes on the Yarkon riverbank. "Except at the rehearsals. He can take a break from this, no? He doesn't have to do it all himself."

I said Ehud was doing a fine job. "He'll make you a star yet."

Ruthy flared up. "He make me a star? Do I need him to make me a star? I can do it on my own!" And then she said, as if the two topics were connected, "All I want from him is to be home sometime, to talk to me. I am going to be his wife in what? Three, four weeks?"

"Let's go," I said.

I didn't want to think of it, so ashamed I was.

When I came home (Ruthy stayed downstairs, so we wouldn't come in together), Ehud said Jenny had just called. She would be arriving in Tel Aviv in two days.

Whereas Jenny had briefly managed to hold my black dreams at bay, Ruthy made them worse. Every night the dreams returned, resurrecting all those lives I had extinguished, each more vivid than the last; but so did the inner chanting, where milky ghosts sang to each other on some inner stage, battling the dark. So vivid was it all that often it seemed as if my father's play were being rehearsed nightly inside me in front of a dark audience that refused to hear its words. Night after night, as the performance drew closer, the battle inside me grew more intense, more painful. I did not know how long I could stand it, and often imagined that even a real fight with flesh and blood opponents might be better than this ephemeral war within.

I didn't know how close I was to getting it.

46

"They took Fauzi," Abdallah's voice whispered over the phone. "The *mukhabarat*." The security services. "They came and they took him—"

I pressed the phone to my ear. "Did he do anything? Something?"

"No, no, he's a good boy, nothing, *ya* Daoud, nothing . . ."

Vibrating with rage, I dashed out, grabbing the Beetle keys.

At the Dizzengoff police station, I learned that Amzaleg was at Abu Kabbir, where the police took the most hard-baked criminals, and suspected terrorists, for "wet" investigations. We used to operate there, too.

I turned around and ran to the car.

The guard at the entrance of the gray detention center, behind the Abu Kabbir morgue, probably remembered me from years ago, because he didn't try to stop me. I barged past him, staring into cells right and left through the viewing ports. Unshaven men stared back at me, eyes puffy from beatings. A few were lying on the floor, vomiting.

Fauzi was in cell 5, seated on a metal chair. A deep gash ran along one side of his face and a trickle of blood flowed down his chin. Behind him stood Gershonovitz, and behind Gershonovitz, Amzaleg, holding the fat man's shoulder.

I slammed the door open. "Why did you take him in?"

Gershonovitz's small mouth pursed. "Ask him."

Amzaleg ignored me and said to Gershonovitz, "They cooked it, your guys. You know they cooked it, what they said they had found."

Gershonovitz tried to wrench his shoulder away, but Amzaleg's fingers stayed lodged in it. The fat man said, "You've been drinking coffee with them too much, Amnon. You're beginning to believe what they tell you."

"Fucking liars," Amzaleg said. "All of your guys."

Fauzi's eyes were black with venom and fear.

I turned to Amzaleg. "What happened to him?"

"He just fell, the *Arabush*," Gershonovitz said. "On his forehead. Tell him, *ya* Muchamad." With a slowness that was far more savage than any rage, he slapped Fauzi three times in swift succession.

Fauzi's head was thrown back, his chair nearly toppling. Without noticing it I was at his side and propped him up. "Enough, Shimmel. I said enough!"

Gershonovitz recoiled in mock horror. "Oh ho ho, Dada, you became a dainty soul again all of a sudden? Just like in Um Marjam?"

I felt myself go red and turned to Fauzi. "Fuck it, Fauzi. What did you do?"

He did not reply.

Gershonovitz said conversationally, "We caught him making a little bomb, with nails, and broken glass—we were watching him."

Fauzi shook his head violently, in obstinate denial.

"Where?" I said. "When?"

"In the back of the Waqf hall, backstage. We were watching him." Gershonovitz's face had acquired a sort of sheen, as though a lamp had been turned on inside it.

"Shit in yogurt," Amzaleg snapped. "We were watching him, too, and we saw nothing—"

"You did not want to see."

Amzaleg's cheeks stretched, the bones showing.

"Go, go drink some water," Gershonovitz said.

Amzaleg turned around abruptly and left the cell.

I turned to Fauzi. "Is it true? What he said?"

He spit at me. Gershonovitz stepped forward and raised his hand for a slap.

I caught the hand and bent it. "No."

Gershonovitz looked into my face, then calmly raised his other hand high in the air and snapped his fingers overhead. My eyes jerked up and at that very moment he slammed his commando boot down on my sandal, ground it twice, and, as I let go his hand, he smashed his fat fist into my groin.

I sat down on the concrete floor, on Fauzi's blood. Fauzi's eyes went from me to Gershonovitz, and back to me. I got to my feet. My instep was bleeding and my groin was throbbing as if an electrical current had passed through it. Gershonovitz had hit me so expertly, after his clever diversion, that I felt a grudging admiration. An old man like him, using Unit tricks. Without thinking, I took a floating half step in his direction, my hands at battle stance.

"Careful, now," he said, his hand at the small of his back. "You want to go into another cell?"

I stopped in mid step. "I am a Canadian now."

"So you are a Canadian! Let's rejoice! We have British here, Americans, two French whores, a Greek—"

Fauzi shouted suddenly in a high pitched voice, "Lies! I didn't do anything! Anything! It's because of the show that they took me—" His voice stuck.

"This piece of donkey shit," Gershonovitz said to me conversationally, "we also found his notes, they were planning to do something, the day of your performance—one day before the elections . . ."

"Lies!" Fauzi shouted. "Lies!"

The fat man went on, ". . . hang posters, that the Debba had been seen in the Galilee, or the Negev . . . then put bomb gifts in stores, in Allenby, in Dizzengoff, in the Shekkem store—maybe in a few kindergartens, too? Hey, *ya* Muchamad?" Another slap. Now the chair toppled. I righted it and helped Fauzi up.

Gershonovitz's flat eyes were on me, mocking. "Maybe you want to try again?" He extended his old arm, thick and suntanned and wrinkled. "Here, try again."

I said nothing.

"Or maybe you want to try with him? Like we taught you, before you forgot? Yes, why not, go ahead. Maybe you can get him to speak—"

The door banged open. Like a large gray cat, Amzaleg was back. "I just talked to Levitan. He said it's okay, that it's mine, this case."

Levitan was the chief of police.

Gershonovitz's face underwent a transformation, almost too terrible to watch. For a brief instant it looked like the face of an animal, or a wild dog.

"He said it's for me to decide," Amzaleg went on. "That it's my jurisdiction." He bent over Fauzi and began to untie his feet.

Gershonovitz hissed, "You are making the mistake of your life, Amnon."

Amzaleg helped Fauzi to his feet. Then, as Amzaleg was leading him out, he jerked Amzaleg's hand off, turned around, and shouted, "Yay, he hath returned, *ya* dogs. And may he soon come back to kill you all and cut off all your—"

Amzaleg pushed him out and banged the door shut with his heel.

Gershonovitz leaned on the wall. "Did you hear him? Did you hear what he said?"

From outside came a sharp honk. I turned to go.

Gershonovitz shouted into my back. "That's all they talk about, now, the *Arabushim* . . . about this fucking show . . . I am telling you, if we don't stop it, soon they'll start raising their heads—"

I left. Outside Amzaleg was getting into his patrol car. Fauzi was not there.

"I told him to take the bus," Amzaleg said.

We stared at each other. Finally I said, "Why?" Meaning why all this.

"This is not just a theater play," Amzaleg said. "Make no mistake." He slid into his cruiser and banged the door shut.

I stared after him numbly as he sped away, wondering once again what the hell he meant and whether I could trust him; whether I could really trust anyone in this goddamned place.

That same afternoon in the rehearsal Fauzi had taken his place as usual, at the back. The gash over his eye had been stitched shut, but every now and then it trickled blood.

Ehud did not even notice, so involved he was in the enfolding scene.

After the rehearsal was over, I told Ehud what had taken place. "They said he was preparing bombs—"

"Shit in yogurt," Ehud snarled. "Bombs!" I had never seen him so angry.

When I asked him if he wanted to ask Fauzi about this, just to let him have a chance to deny it, Ehud grabbed my arm tightly. "You leave him alone! You hear? He is helping us, you think he doesn't get shit from his own?"

"Yes," I said. "Probably."

"All right," Ehud said. "Goddammit. Second scene in ten minutes."

.   .   .

As Ehud prepared to go home with Ruthy, I said I'd stay behind. "In case these Kahane boys try something, what do I know?"

All during the day, outside, the rhythmic shouts of the Kach crowd had been rising in volume and in pitch.

He didn't offer any help; he just took Ruthy's car and left.

I was sleeping on the army cot behind the stage when Fauzi shook my shoulder. "You'd better come, *ya* Daoud," he whispered.

My phosphorous Omega watch said ten past midnight. "Where?"

"In Shazli Street, near the café. There are some new guys there."

I followed him to the yard. The street was dark, the café deserted. Four men in dark clothes were standing in the lee of a house, speaking in low voices. Another group was in Avoda Lane, leaning on an old Ford Cortina. I could see another Cortina at the end of Sefer Shir Lane, with a dipole antenna.

"Where are the sentinels?" I whispered.

"I'll take you."

Eight young Arabs were leaning against the hall in the darkness, smoking. I made them extinguish their cigarettes, and sent one to Abdallah's house. "Wake up the other *shab-bab*. Bring them to the café here, and wait. When you hear me whistle like that"—I whistled softly 'Um Kulsum's song "Ya Habibi"—"then you come."

I could see their teeth glint in the darkness. Then they dispersed, quiet as jackals.

In ten minutes they returned. More of our crew from the chocolate factory had also arrived, and together with other young Arabs, they crowded around Fauzi and me. Amid the silence I explained we might soon be attacked. "They'll probably swarm from several directions, try to wreck things. Don't waste time grappling with them. Don't shout, don't speak, don't scream. Be completely silent. Understand? Hit at their legs and at their balls. No shouting. Understand?"

Nods all around.

I distributed sticks. "And watch for guys with cans. You see someone with a gasoline can, or a lit match, everyone go for him. All together."

There was a tense murmur.

Our accountant said, "I called the police to tell Inspector Amzaleg, but a policeman said he was not—"

"Fuck the police!" Fauzi said. "This is ours. Ours!"

The little crowd gave a collective hiss, and then, wordlessly, everyone dispersed, each going to his predetermined station. Only Fauzi and I remained; and together, side by side, we stood in the shadows and waited for the attack to begin.

PART IV

Yawm Al Dinn

(Day of Judgment)

47

Next morning I walked into Amzaleg's office, dizzy with fatigue and dream residue.

"To drink the Jews' blood," Gershonovitz hollered at me. "That's what they scribble everywhere now, these *Arabushim*, on every wall! See what you did last night?"

Not an hour after our routing the Kach thugs, Arab graffiti had blossomed all over Tel Aviv, and in Yaffo. I could see it on the way home as I drove, on every fence. I had no idea how the news could have spread so fast.

"That's what you woke me up for?"

My ears were still ringing with the shouts of the night before. After the Kach youth were chased off, Fauzi and the Arab *shabbab* wrapped a keffiyeh around my head, and, ululating wildly, carried me on their shoulders around the Waqf hall. Only at five o'clock in the morning did I manage to escape to the apartment, where I plunged into a nearly dreamless sleep until Amzaleg's call woke me.

Amzaleg did not say a word now, as Gershonovitz kept bellowing that it was all because of the bedlam I had made in Yaffo last night. "Dammit, *ya* Dada! What are you doing to us? You want an Arab rebellion here, like in thirty-six? Just because of your father's fucking play?"

I said obstinately that the police did not want to come, so we had to defend ourselves.

"*We!*" Gershonovitz bellowed at me. "Who's *we?*"

Amzaleg growled into his desk, "I didn't get the call until three in the morning—"

"Tell it to your grandma," I said.

Gershonovitz kept up his tirade. He shook a sheaf of yellow onionskins at me and I recognized Shin Bet informers' reports. "Look what they've been writing on the walls of their hovels in the refugee camps—to get their souls ready for the rebellion— the military governors all recommend total curfew until after the elections—"

"So do it. Put on a curfew. What the hell do you want from my life?"

"We can't! Not now! Not a week before the elections! If this gets out of hand, Begin will get in for sure. That's what you want? Dada, you got to stop this play—"

I turned my back to him and left, in the middle of his wild-eyed tirade.

Ruthy was waiting for me in the apartment, Ehud standing five paces behind her, his face colorless.

"Look at this." Ruthy thrust a crumpled paper in my face. "Look what they say, these people—"

Dumbly I took it, and felt my neck crawl as the handwritten words registered. *The daughter of adultery hath continued her mother's ways—*

Ehud whispered, "I was not even going to show it to you—"

Ruthy said, "I found it in his Volvo, in the glove compartment. Someone had sent it to him."

Ehud whispered, "You know I don't believe any of this crap—you know this—"

"Shit in yogurt, 'don't believe.' So why didn't you show it to me?"

Ehud shuffled his feet as if he had been caught, not Ruthy.

"No, why?" Ruthy shouted, "You tell him, Dada! Tell him!"

I heard myself cussing the writer in Hebrew, Arabic, and Yiddish, denying it all, gesticulating with both hands. "It's someone in the *shoo-shoo*," I shouted, in panic and rage, "They don't want us to do this play. Can't you see?" In a long rush I told him what Gershonovitz had just told me, in the police station.

"Yes." Ehud kept his head low.

"Or maybe Gelber sent this," I went on, "after they paid him. It's possible."

"Maybe it's this policeman," Ruthy said. "This beast."

Ehud raised his eyes and looked at me, beseechingly, then at Ruthy. But she did not react, just snatched the letter from my hand and tore it to pieces. "I don't even want to talk about such shit."

None of us mentioned it again.

48

THE FOLLOWING DAY UNCLE Mordechai called and said he'd be arriving soon in Tel Aviv, and perhaps we could talk. My heart leaped; but that same afternoon Aunt Margalit called and said they had kept him in the Afoula hospital for an operation.

"It's in the throat," she said, her voice breaking.

I did not have to ask what was in the throat. With all his cigarettes, and the cognac.

Strangling on my words, I said I would go visit him right away.

Ruthy insisted on coming with me, and Ehud did not even try to dissuade her. Ever since the ghastly poison-letter episode, he was now ceaselessly trying to apologize to her, instead of wanting her apology, or denial.

Perhaps Ruthy did not give any reason because she rarely talked these days, and neither did Ehud or I. It was as if the three of us had slowly been disconnecting from one anther, coming together only in the rehearsals, or to fuck—Ruthy and Ehud in their bedroom at night; she and I by day, blindly dashing from Yaffo to Ibn Gvirol between rehearsals, to claw at each other on the roof, on a torn mattress in the peak of the day's heat, sweaty and dirty in the sun-broiled dust, like two scrawny Arab dogs. Or if the break was short, we did it in desolate parks or on the beach in Yaffo in semi-secluded spots, while Ehud remained behind, pale and silent, Kagan slumped at his feet. The silent Arab *shabbab* sat cross-legged all around on their prayer mats or stood along the walls, watching with the Jewish chocolate-factory workers, holding their breaths, absorbing my father's words and the singing battles between men and beasts.

We arrived in Afoula a little after two o'clock. Visiting hours had already ended, so Ruthy stayed in the car while I went to search for a way in.

Vigilant nurses seemed to be prowling the corridors, like military sentinels. Finally I found a back door, and sneaked into the oncological ward. I found Uncle Mordechai in a small cubicle all by himself, close by the back stairs. His face was half hidden amid the gray pillows, his stubble perhaps five weeks old. It seemed he had not yet shaved since my father's death.

He was not surprised to see me, nodded when he saw me walk in, and although he could barely speak, he answered my questions readily. "Because he let Paltiel put his name on *his* own poems," Uncle Mordechai rasped through his cancerous larynx. "I told Isser, it's yours! I told him . . . Why do you give this to him? . . . Your work, your writing . . . your name—why? Just to have a free hand with Riva?"

"So that's why he gave him the poems?"

"Why else? What other reason could there have been?"

I shook my head. It did not sound right. "So that's why you stopped talking to him? Just because of some fucking poems—"

"*Just poems?*" Uncle Mordechai's eyes caught fire, "It was *Shimshon*, and *Ben HaTan*, that he gave away to him, and *Golyatt—Golyatt!*—"

"But he kept half an interest," I said, stupidly.

Some floor-cleaning machine had started in the corridor, and Uncle Mordechai's voice was half swallowed in its racket. "—and not only the poems he gave to him, to this son of a whore Rubin, but his honor—his *honor*—!" The raspy voice grew stronger. ". . . because he let Abu Jalood go . . ."

My heart froze. So it was true . . . Or was it?

Uncle Mordechai whispered on, ". . . because he did not finish off this beast—this fucking lover-boy of Paltiel . . ."

I bent toward the splotchy face. "You—so you also think it came back—to kill him?" I could not recognize my own voice. "Because me, I don't believe this Debba shit—"

"No, it was no Debba that killed him—"

Uncle Mordechai's voice came out in raspy spurts. I tried to hold his hand, but he withdrew it under his sheet. I croaked, "You—you think *they* killed him, because they didn't want him to pass on these messages?"

I did not specify who "they" were; there was no need. When I told him what Abdallah had said, about my father and him acting as messengers, Uncle Mordechai did not seem surprised.

The gray lips barely moved. "I don't know."

The racket outside died down. Now a nurse's steps could be heard in the corridor, her flat heels thudding on the linoleum. I waited until the sound faded. "Abdallah, he said it's not the Arabs who did it . . . you believe this?"

The unshaven chin nodded, jerkily.

"So who? Who was it?"

Dust, blinding dust, was swirling in the air, in my ears, in my eyes.

"You know who killed him?"

He said nothing, his shallow breath coming in spurts.

"Tell me!"

He shook his head.

"Tell me! Goddammit! Tell!"

And then, as if on cue from some director, a nurse barged in and chased me out.

49

FROM THE BEGINNING WE knew that *The Debba* would be a contentious play. Yet none of us had any idea just how contentious it could be.

To the day of the performance, articles castigating the entire show appeared daily in the Hebrew papers, filled with so much venom that at times it seemed as if they had been written about something else, not about a mere piece of theater. No doubt some of the acrimony flowed from the fast-approaching elections. The Shovval Institute in Jerusalem had concluded one more opinion poll showing Labor and Likkud still running neck and neck, and yet another poll, by the left-leaning *HaAretz*, showed Likkud actually leading. For the first time since Israel's founding, the opposition party, Likkud, had a chance of taking over. Anything and everything was therefore construed to be political. Even a little thing like an old play. Even this.

The Arab newspapers, too, had at first turned against our play. *El Fajr* in Jerusalem led the chorus in condemning "those who shamelessly steal the people's legends for their own nefarious aims," as Fauzi had intimated; and *Al Bisr el Firaji* followed suit and said in all plainness that those whose land had been usurped would not sit idly by as their culture, too, was being kidnapped. "Rise and reclaim your legends, O Arabs!" one editorial thundered. "Grab back your patrimony, O sons of Salach-ad-Din."

But all this was before the night of the attack on the Waqf hall. The day after, it was as if a roadblock had fallen, and a long caravan of chortling and ululating Arab scribes had been unleashed, waving their pens. No Arab newspaper could praise the play highly enough—a play that, all reviewers agreed, had been written by an Arab, perhaps by Abu Jalood himself, then taken up by a compassionate Jew—some mentioning Paltiel Rubin, others my father—because, as an Arab play, it could of course not be performed.

Nightly they came to Yaffo to watch our rehearsals, from far and away—emaciated old *fellaheen* from the Gallil, and city Arabs from Nazareth and Nablus, and villagers from the Shomron—to stare at the Waqf hall from across Avoda Lane, and murmur among themselves. A few came up, shyly, absurdly kissing the wall, or the door. We couldn't get rid of them. Day after day they kept coming, in the early morning, to watch the actors, or, from time to time, they paid the boy from Café Machfooz to bring the actors a tray with coffees, and *baklawa* sweets. These watchers did not seem to eat or drink anything themselves, or even go away for a piss. Most just squatted in the dust across the road, their hands hanging between their knees, as though waiting for something or someone to appear. Even for prayers they stayed in place, rubbing their palms with sand, as permitted, instead of going off for ablutions.

After a while we just left them alone. Unlike the Kach thugs (of whom we saw no trace anymore), it was clear they intended us no harm.

By that time the stipulation in my father's will had also become known, which gave birth to an absurd and dramatic story of how Judge Menuchin (in one version he was accompanied by the minister of the interior) called on me at the apartment and beseeched me to stop the production.

"Do not make matters more difficult before the elections!" he was supposed to have said. He even offered me money (so went the story); but I held firm and resolute, vowing to fulfill my father's last wish.

Yet another story, which found its way to *Ha'Olam HaZeh*, was that my father himself had tried to resurrect his play, and was as a result killed by the evil forces of the security services. The play's only copy was then nearly stolen from my apartment, and were it not for my alertness—which I had learned at my father's knee—the play, and its message, would've been lost forever.

The police of course did nothing (according to the article). Not only did they not try to find the culprits, they were probably in cahoots with them.

And there were other such tales, more fanciful still, many to do with the hoped-for (in Arab newspapers) or dreaded (in Jewish newspapers) arrival of the real Debba at the play's end, to rescue the Arabs from their oppressors, as it had nearly managed to do in '46, before the show was interrupted.

The beneficial result was that tickets for the show had sold quickly, and were now fetching more than triple their original price on the black market of Lillienblum Street.

But there were other results, not all beneficial. The worst, for me, was that hardly anyone would talk to me, when I asked questions about my father or the past. Somehow a story had taken hold that the *shoo-shoo* was indeed involved in my father's death, and nothing was more certain to cause people to clam up.

The morning *Ha'Olam HaZeh* magazine appeared with the first of such stories, Amzaleg called me in cold anger. "What did you tell them this garbage for?"

It was the first I had heard from him in a week.

I explained I had said nothing. "I didn't even talk to them. They just invented everything—"

"No, tell me!" Amzaleg fumed. "You think I don't want to catch him? You think I don't? If you think this, come out and say it!"

As a matter of fact this is precisely what I had begun to think, but in the face of such vehement protestations, I told him I knew he was trying his best. But even this he must have taken as an insult, because he began to shout into the phone that Gershonovitz could go screw himself. "Your father was my friend also. What do you think? Ask Mordoch. He was my friend in the army, and before—"

"Sure," I said, taken aback by this eruption.

"—what do you think, that I don't want to catch this beast?"

Before I could ask him why he, too, now called my father's killer a beast, he hung up.

50

As the hot fetor swept Tel Aviv, with the Palestinian garbagemen on strike for the fifteenth day, the rumor about the Debba's second coming now included the conviction that it was he who had killed my father, as an advance warning of what he would do to all the Jews.

No one knew how this idiotic rumor developed, but somehow it stuck, and, for reasons no one could identify, it nearly emptied the streets. Or perhaps the empty streets were due to nothing more sinister than the *khamsin*, which would soon break all records. Or maybe it was due to fears that a new Arab terror group would take advantage of the crowds and demonstrations, before the elections, and stage some spectacular bombings in Tel Aviv.

Leibele, at Café Cassit, had another theory for the street's desolation. "It's their conscience bothering them," he said to me, pointing at a small group of actors who sat subdued in the corner, all engrossed in books, not a newspaper in sight. "For what they are about to do, vote for this beast Begin, so they don't show their faces."

"No, it's for what they've done to the Arabs," Ruthy snarled. (She now accompanied me to Cassit openly, no longer caring about the evil tongues.) "And now they're afraid this Debba will do the same to them, they'd even vote for this beast Begin so he'd do the necessary dreck, to defend them . . ."

"What do you want from him?" I hissed at her, when Leibele ducked his head and scurried to the kitchen. "He didn't do
anything to you." For some reason, her treatment of Leibele
pricked me more than any of her other antics.

"So what? I can say what I think, no? It's still a free country,
here."

At the sound of her raised voice, the actors got up one by
one and left, as if they, too, wanted nothing to do with her. As
though it were she, not the Debba, who was about to inflict on
them some sort of punishment, the one they were afraid of.

Often I felt this way myself.

51

THE PENULTIMATE REHEARSAL WAS progressing as if it were the last run before a military operation. Actors stepped into their precise marks on the floor cloth, on the dot of Ehud's hand claps, stared into each other's eyes, and sang with anguish all the more frightening because it was anticipated. Aside from the sound on the stage, and Ehud's sharp claps, the hall was silent. All construction had long been finished, but none of the Arab helpers had gone back to wherever they had come from. Half of them had stayed in the hall, at night sleeping on mats that they had brought with them from their villages; the other half went to stay at Abdallah's house. But now they all sat, silent and watchful, listening for the twentieth time to the songs they must have known by heart. Amzaleg had been absent; but in the middle of the Debba's final speech, he entered through the stage door, his police cap in hand. He sat down slowly on a bench by the wall, apart from the Arab crowd, and waited for the scene to end. Then, without speaking, he tapped me on the knee and I rose and followed him to the Waqf yard.

Before he had even opened his mouth, I knew.

"Mordoch," I said, feeling my stomach go all rubbery.

Amzaleg gave a short, military nod. "Yeah."

I could feel the oily sweat breaking on my chin. "Was it quick?"

"Two hours ago. They did an X-ray and decided to operate.

But when they opened him up, they saw they couldn't take it out. It was too big, the tumor—"

From within the hall I heard Ruthy wail, bemoaning her choice.

Uncle Mordechai with his stories, and his fried fish, and his cognac.

Amzaleg pulled out his cigarette pack, stared at it, then shoved it back in his pocket.

I said I'd better call Margalit.

"No. She'll call you later. She's resting now. The doctor gave her an injection—" Amzaleg gave a long cough, then said, "But I talked to him."

I wiped my eyes shamelessly. "To Mordoch? When?"

From within the hall came the metronomic yells of 'Ittay and Yochanan, the two Friends, beseeching Yissachar to consider his obligation to his people, and Ehud's metronomic hand claps.

"Just before they wheeled him in." Amzaleg squatted down on the floor like a Bedouin, staring at the wall. "He told me about this guy—in the first show—"

I squatted down slowly besides him, one Bedouin next to another. "About the Arab actor? In forty-six?"

"Yes."

Amzaleg coughed again, and suddenly grabbed my right arm above the elbow. "*Ya* donkey!" he snapped. "Why didn't you tell me?"

I hardened my bicep and with my left hand peeled off his fingers, one by one.

He said, "You're still thinking I am with them? No, tell me!"

I shrugged, then shook my head. "No."

"So why didn't you tell me?"

I wanted to say, "Because he's mine, whoever killed him," but no voice came. I tried to hoist a shoulder, but it didn't quite succeed either. I clamped my lips.

Amzaleg thumped on the hard gravel. "He was my friend, too," he roared. And then he began to weep, shamelessly and openly, the tears trickling slowly down the corrugated cheeks, like candle wax. It was the second time I had seen him show grief, after that time in Tveriah at my father's shivah.

Finally he said, sniffling, "Goddammit, this Mordoch."

I made my voice rough, as proper. "Was a good guy, the bastard."

And then we both got to our feet, looking away from each other, until, slowly, our eyes met. I said, "It was Haffiz Seddiqi, this actor, in forty-six. Not a Yemenite. I saw Haffiz's picture in Abdallah's basement, alongside the other actors' and actresses'."

Amzaleg gave a small angry sniffle.

"It was an Arab," I said, "that played the Debba."

Amzaleg nodded, a curt military bob of the head.

There was no need to say anything else. It was all so clear. It was Abu Jalood himself who had played the Debba's role in my father's play in forty-six. Two years before my father had "slain" him in the Castel. It was Haffiz Seddiqi who had been Abu Jalood. Fauzi's father. The bon vivant, the Arab man-about-town, the squire of countless actresses and café flies, in Tel Aviv as well as Yaffo. The theater lover by day, and the gangleader by night. The Debba.

Did he have matters with my mother, too? Did she sleep with him to get information, to help her people? In the service of the Haganah's intelligence service, the Shay?

I said, "Did you talk to Abdallah Seddiqi already? Did you ask him if it was his brother who played it?"

From within the hall came the rustle of the three attackers, rushing up to the Debba's lair.

Amzaleg's eyes had turned opaque again. A policeman's eyes. "He said yes."

52

LATE NEXT MORNING, A day before our performance, we had the final dress rehearsal—it took about an hour. Toward the end, as Ruthy was hitting the very highest notes, our accountant sidled up to me and told me I had a phone call.

I took it behind the stage door. It was Yaro.

"David, got to see you. Something came up." His voice was dispassionate, businesslike.

"Right now?"

For a week I'd been trying to call him, without success, and now this.

"Yes. Can you come here?"

I knew better than to say his name or ask what he wanted, over the phone.

I went back in.

"I got to go," I whispered to Ehud. "Can I take your car?"

"Wait five minutes," he whispered back. "I'll have someone go with you."

"No, no. I got to go."

There was a pause. "You sure?"

"Yes."

As I closed the door behind me, I could see Yissachar running to and fro, waving his arms at his two pursuers, shouting in anguish about the choice he must make.

· · ·

Yaro was alone in his office. He was seated upon his desk, his legs dangling in the air, eyes staring fixedly at the door.

"What is it?" I said, plopping into the chair before him.

Yaro said, "So you're doing the play in Yaffo?"

"Yes," I said. "We couldn't find a hall anywhere else."

I waited for him to tell me why he had summoned me, but he just sat on his desk, fat and flat-eyed, like a small version of Gershonovitz.

He spoke into his clasped palms, in which he was rolling a pencil. "You had some trouble there three days ago, I heard."

I fidgeted. "Yes, yes, the bastards of Kahane tried to burn us down—what is it, Yaro?"

Still he wouldn't look me in the eye. "So what happened?"

I couldn't see why he wanted to talk about this now, why this sudden interest. I stared at the droplets of sweat that rolled down the creases in his bald, sunburned scalp. "We chased them away, why do you—"

"Who's 'we'?"

"Me and the factory crew, and some *shabbab* from Hebron and Jenin, who came to help when the police—"

"So they are friends of yours suddenly?"

He raised his eyes and stared at me blandly, as we used to look at prisoners during interrogations, to indicate it was not personal. That we just happened to be enemies, that's all.

I tried to suppress my rage, but failed. "Fuck you, Yaya. Okay? Someone put out the word that we are not kosher, so we couldn't get even a toilet cubicle in Central Bus Station, to—"

"So you went running to *them*?"

I got to my feet, vibrating with fury. The shame came, too, in waves, but I suppressed it. "Damn you to hell! What did you want me to do, let these Kahane fuckers burn us down? These other guys came to help us for nothing! For the play! You want me to desert them when—"

"So you help the Arabs, now?"

I stared into his eyes; they had become hard and flat and distant; and all at once, I don't know how, I knew.

I kicked both knees sideways and let my body fall back, even as his body shot off the desk and his hand came up to grab my throat, the other hand jabbing forward, still gripping the pencil.

Once again the moves came back, as though I had just been thrown into water and half-forgotten swimming skills took over. Without thinking, I made quick cutting motions, right and left, and freed myself from his grip.

He landed on his feet—I saw he was barefoot, his sandals under the desk—and now he came at me again delicately, slowly circling the chair, the little pencil gripped in one fist, the other hand probing forward, occasionally swiping at his eyes.

I circled the chair at his exact speed, in the same direction, keeping the chair between him and me.

"Yaro," I croaked. "I don't know what these *shoo-shoo* liars told you about me, I—I did nothing to—"

I stopped.

It seemed so monstrous, so idiotic.

Just because of the elections? It did not make sense!

There was a flash and my legs were swept out from under me. Yaro had leaned with one hand on the back of the chair and kicked forward, then, when I fell facedown, he threw himself upon me, one hand around my throat, the other trying to turn me over on my back.

I arched my back and kicked upward with my foot, catching him in the groin. He grunted, but kept holding me like some obscene pederast trying to mount me from behind, trying to roll me on my back, the little pencil clutched in his fist.

No, not a pencil. A little yellow neoprene tube—

A silent grenade exploded inside my skull.

I didn't know what reason they had given to convince him that my death was necessary, or why the *shoo-shoo* had become convinced in the first place that I must die; but I knew Yaro had been told to do it cleanly, without leaving a trace. A heart attack. I had been working hard, and the tension got to me. I'd come to visit my good friend Yaro at his office, and suddenly it happened.

Twisting backward I knifed my elbows into Yaro's ribs, first to the right, then the left. His grip loosened for a brief second, and I threw him off.

He bounded off the desk's edge and came at me once again, immediately, his sparse hair falling crazily over one ear, the bull neck disappearing between the hoisted shoulders, his eyes dripping fat tears.

"Yaro," I said hoarsely. "Look at me—Yaya—"

But he would not look me in the face. His eyes were on my torso, somewhere under my solar plexus.

I didn't look at his hands, or at his feet, just kept my eyes on his, looking for the flicker of an eyelid.

On and on we circled.

It was still light outside when I emerged from the building. A white Toyota was parked behind Ehud's Volvo, and another, a gray one, with a single headlight, on the corner of Yud-Aleph Street. I sprinted across the boiling asphalt into a yard, rolled over the scraggly grass and kept on rolling, until I reached the garbage-can shed in the back, vaulted over the low wall, and rolled again. I kept running, my chest on fire, my brain and belly aflame. Blindly, seeing nothing, going by instinct, I kept going. Once, dimly, through a half-remembered memory, I gave a trilling crackle with my tongue as I ran, more a sob than a call. But there was no response this time. Only the wild hammering of my heart, and muted faraway shouts. I did not even bother to turn around and look. It was clear that whoever was guarding me before had now been withdrawn.

I reached Ibn Gvirol Street via back fences, dashing through bushy undergrowths in empty lots. I felt like a wild jackal, a Debba that had suddenly found itself in enemy territory, trying to find its way back to where it had come from, to the wild open country, to its lair. And as I ran, there was also the Other, now small and terror-stricken and yammering.

Why had Yaro agreed to kill me? Just because I had let Arabs help me defend our performance hall? Just because I was determined to stage my father's play? I had an insane urge to laugh at the comicality of it, the absurdity.

But if they had convinced Yaro, they could surely convince anyone, and other killers would soon come for me.

It all seemed like a monstrous joke, somehow. The entire *shoo-shoo* against one Anon, a burned-out drecker lured back to his birthplace to die for his father's old scribblings.

For *that*? For *that*?

53

THERE WAS NO ONE behind house number 142-Aleph, as I crept into the basement's window through the back, then rushed up the stairs. Ruthy was sitting in the kitchen when I burst in. An open script lay on the table before her. Apparently she had been practicing her lines again.

"Your shiksa called," she said tonelessly, "from Paris. She got stuck, she will come tomorrow, on Swiss Air—"

I stumbled to the sink and washed my face, then grabbed the 777 bottle from the cupboard above the fridge and took a long pull. I hardly felt it going down my throat.

Ruthy said, "I was right in the middle of the scene, I couldn't get the flight number—" She stopped, her face twisted; whether because of Jenny's arrival or because of the scene's demands, I could not tell.

"'A child I bear,'" Ruthy intoned, her face contorted, "'a child to the Debba, whom God in His wrath hath sent—'" She folded her hands on her belly, and began to weep.

I had no time for this now. For a long incoherent moment I babbled about the *shoo-shoo*, and my father, and Yaro. "He tried to take me down!" I shouted at her. "Yaro! Yaro Ben-Shlomo! He tried to—"

But Ruthy was not listening to me either. "Fuck it," she shouted back. "Do you hear what I'm telling you?" She peeled her T-shirt upward. Her breasts seemed swollen, inflated, the nipples dark and heavy with blood. She sobbed. "Look, Dada . . . look . . ."

But I did not want to look at her tits now. That was the last thing I needed. That, and love. I kept on raving about Yaro. "Is Ehud home? I need his help—"

Yes, Ehud. He would help me. He always had. He was my only hope now.

She shook her head. "I . . . no. Not yet."

She swayed on the chair, then rose to her feet and sobbed into my chest.

"Six years," Ruthy went on, "six years I've been fucking everybody, just about everybody . . . and nothing . . ."

"When is he coming back?" I asked. And then it hit me. "You sure?" I touched her taut belly, now hot and feverish, as though something were boiling inside.

"Yes." She almost fell. "Dada, hold me—"

It seemed she had not heard a word I said.

"It was me," she burbled, "who sent him the letter—I wanted you to tell him it was true—what the letter said—that we—that we—"

I asked her wildly how she knew it was mine. She wept with rage and said that since nothing had happened for six years, she was sure she could not have children. Once I returned, though, she became extra careful with Ehud because if anything did happen, she wanted it to be mine . . . and hers . . .

I stopped listening and steered her to the bedroom; there I made her lie down on my parents' bed, then lay down beside her, under the old HaBimah pictures, under the eyes of Paltiel Rubin, and my mother's gaze. Nothing else mattered anymore. Nothing.

"You will stay?" Ruthy wept. "You'll stay with me?"

"Yes," I said. "Yes, I will."

Somehow we fell asleep side by side, our legs enwrapped.

. . .

A line of blackened skeletons stretched before me all the way to the horizon. Their sunken eyes were fixed upon something I held in my hand, something vibrant and warm.

"Water! Water!"

I clasped the cup loosely to my chest—no, not a cup: a large white envelope fragrant with lemony musk. The envelope opened; yellow pages, written in my father's crabbed hand, rustled inside it. The yellow turned red and the envelope turned inside out, and suddenly I was inside it, a dove wriggling in my arms.

The skeletons yammered in my ears, their hands thrust out. From the muzzle of one hand came a long hot tongue of fire, wet and sweet.

The white dove rose, circling and screeching.

To my son, my eldest, my beloved—

I clasped the dove to my belly and its soft screeches were suddenly transformed into ululations. I opened my eyes. Ruthy was straddling me, her hands on my shoulders, and Ehud was standing by the door.

"She called me," he croaked. "She said I should come quickly—she had something to tell me—something important—"

Ruthy wriggled upon me, crying. "Tell him, Dada, tell him now!"

"Uddy," I croaked, "I—"

"Tell him!"

"Get out, David," Ehud said. "I don't want to see you—"

Ruthy slid off me, slime trickling down her thigh. "Tell him, Dada! Tell him that we— Tell him!"

I got up and groped for my underwear. There was a noise in my ears, like the sound of faraway mortars, crashing in waves. "The play—"

"Goddammit!" Ehud bellowed, in a voice like an animal's.

"We'll do the fucking play! We'll do it! Don't worry!" He grabbed Ruthy's arm. "Get washed," he said. "There's one more rehearsal tonight."

He didn't move a muscle as I squeezed past him, and for a second our bodies touched. Then he hit at my shoulder with a balled fist, hard.

"*Yallah, haffef,*" he said in Arabic. Get out.

Unseeing, I ran down the stairs, and mindlessly came out onto the sidewalk. There were two Toyotas parked in front of the house. As I emerged, the door of one of them opened, and a man got out, his hand at the back of his belt. I sprinted across Ibn Gvirol Street into a yard and cut through some *hadass* bushes, somersaulted over a garbage-can shed into a patch of dry grass, then streaked across into Bazel Street.

Behind me I could hear muffled calls in military Hebrew, and loping footsteps.

Sprinting in and out of yards, I bounded toward the Bazel market, then dove behind a heap of empty orange crates. There was a pile of rotting fruit behind it, and a mound of jute bags. Like a worm I squirreled my body underneath the rot, and froze.

No movement. No breath. No thought.

The footsteps passed by, then came back.

"Where did the *cholera* go?"

A car engine was gunned nearby; Ruthy's Beetle streaked past.

"The *sharmuta* picked him up! Go go go!"

A white Toyota raced up Bazel Street toward Ibn Gvirol, its radio crackling; then a police scooter, and right after it, a gray Lark, a fat man at the wheel.

Another Toyota passed, and another.

I kept to my spot; after a while there was silence.

Time passed.

.   .   .

There was a scraping sound somewhere—perhaps a cat dragging a piece of fish—and a clatter of garbage cans and the rumble of a bus; and farther away, the hot hum of the city, the city of my childhood, which had now, without reason or account, suddenly turned against me.

Time began to move again.

I listened for a full minute, for telltale breathing, the scrape of a shoe, the creak of an ankle. There was nothing. Then, without haste or premeditation, I began to move.

I remember very little of how I got to Yaffo.

As I crept under fences, slinking from one shadow to another, I could hear the laughter of passersby, glimpse the flash of white faces, the open mouths, the eyes of men and women: my people, my enemies.

Streets and lanes came and went. Avenues flashed by. Keren Kayemet Boulevard, where my brother and I used to play ball. Then Ben Yehuda Street, where I had once stood on one of my father's shoulders, to watch the tanks go by during the Independence Day parade, my brother standing on the other shoulder, my mother five paces away, looking not at the parade but at us.

Down another fence, and another, across HaYarkon Street, past the Israeli Aero Club, and Cinema Dan, where I had once seen with Ruthy two mushy movies in a row, both of us swearing eternal love—

Down the gravelly steps to Gordon Beach, where we used to lie at night, the two of us, in the pale dark starlight, and fumble with each other, talking laughingly of poems, and of us—

I sank to the sand and listened once more.

Nothing.

After an indeterminate while I got up, and, taking care to keep to the very edge of the surf so as not to leave footprints, I began to run toward the distant stained darkness that was Yaffo.

54

As the first shacks came in view I turned left and staggered up the embankment.

A hanging lantern swayed above a coffeehouse, in an invisible breeze, overlooking the dark beach. It threw greenish shadows on the jumble of fishing nets heaped between two boats that lay overturned upon the sand. Blurry faces of young men glistened from the circle of light. They were sitting around a little table, playing a card game of some sort.

Without pausing to think, I asked one of the men in Arabic for Seddiqi's house. My voice sounded strange in my ears; high pitched, like an animal yelp.

None looked up. "It's not far," one said.

"More are coming," said the first. "From everywhere."

Who? Who were coming?

Mindlessly I went on, stumbling on empty sardine cans, scraps of fishing nets, tangled nylon cords. Up, up the hilly mound, its smell a mixture of rotting fish and an undefinable raw tang of putrid open earth and ancient debris.

On and on I trudged, weeping in helpless rage. The stench, the debris underfoot, the imagined footsteps, all combined into a nightmarish sensation that mixed in my mind with Yaro, and Ehud, and Ruthy, the entire surreal sequence of events of the last day, now capped by Jenny's pending arrival. She, and Toronto, now seemed a million miles away.

Onward and onward. Before my pursuers caught up with me. Onward!

Then somehow I was not alone anymore. A doorway had opened in a two-story house, and a yellow light sprang to life. A tall man floated into view, his shadow detaching itself from the doorframe.

Weeping and cussing, I dropped into a semi-crouch, sending my hands snaking before me in *hikkon*.

Beware! Beware!

The man stumbled out, the light framing his *abbaya* in a yellow fuzz.

"Enter," he said. "My house is your house." His hand, bony and warm, grabbed my arm, the fingers wiry and strong. "Enter."

Helplessly, I let myself be dragged through the light.

The floor was composed of a great many mosaic tiles the size of my thumbnail.

"I . . . I—help—" I croaked.

Abdallah stood to the side. "Come in."

Light. Intense yellow light, and eyes. Pairs of black eyes staring at me, under the blaze of the fluorescent tube overhead.

As I straightened, I saw eleven young Arabs seated around a heavy dark table, mute and erect, all staring at me.

"*Hada hoo*," said one. This is he.

Incomprehensibly, the others around the table nodded slowly, making a collective sound of assent.

I nodded tremblingly in their direction, and then we were climbing up the stairs, Abdallah and I, he pulling himself up by the handrail, dragging his aluminum canes behind, I holding on to his coat, like a baby.

Midway on the stairs I stopped, yammering confusedly about danger, about pursuers, that I must take care, hide; but

he pulled me roughly after him, with a force I could not fore-
see. "First, to sleep, *ya 'ibni*. Then we shall see."

We passed through a small vestibule, then through another,
and finally came into a large bedroom. An old woman came
in after us, dressed in village black, the same woman who had
served me coffee, a hundred years before.

"Hanum," Abdallah said, "Daoud will stay here tonight."
Then, without any ceremony or further words, he closed and
shuttered all the windows, and left.

While Seddiqi Hanum spread a striped bedsheet on the high
bed, I looked about me, trying to suppress a wild panic: the
huge bed, the dusty photographs, the chichi chandelier with
its scruffy false crystals hanging over the low red table, all
seemed to be in direct enmity to something in me that would
not rest. Only with an effort could I stop myself from fleeing,
running downstairs, and running off.

Running off from what?

A glass vase full of cyclamens stood at the top of a tall com-
mode, as if surveying the room. Somehow even the sight of
the flowers rattled me.

I sat down on a narrow divan, as the old woman in black
occupied herself with the bed.

In the wall overlooking the street, two elongated windows
that began two feet above the tiled floor extended all the way to
the cracked ceiling. Between the windows, and flanking them,
hung a great many framed photographs, dozens and dozens of
them, all merging in the twilight murk. But as my eyes became
accustomed to the gloom, I began to discern tall mustachioed figures, and fezzes, and seated children. Arabs of all ages, men and
women, family pictures, and also an oddly jarring photograph of
a youthful trio: Abdallah, Paltiel, and my father on some beach,
embracing in a tight little circle, heads thrown back to look into

the camera. There is a shadow at their feet, the shadow of a large
man, probably the photographer, maybe even Haffiz—and here
was a large photograph of Haffiz himself (for I knew his face by
now) hanging above a radio cabinet the size of a small refrig-
erator, and to the left and right of it, tall bookcases with lead-
glass fronts, crammed with leather-bound volumes, and piles of
magazines tied with blue ribbons. Poetry magazines, probably
those Haffiz himself had begun printing for the Waqf, and which
Abdallah now continued. Before one of the magazine-crammed
cabinets stood a faded red armchair, like a stout sentinel, its
cracked leather overlaid with a dainty fleece of white lace.

I shivered.

There was a rustle and a whiff of dry roses behind me, as
Seddiqi Hanum whisked by in a wave of black folds.

"And now to sleep," she said to me in Hebrew. Her mouth, a
dark blur in the white gloom of her face, smiled at me queerly.
"You can talk with the others later."

I nodded and sat down on the bed, on which, I now saw, she
had spread striped green-and-white pajamas. Arab pajamas.

"Seddiqi Khan will take you tomorrow," she said.

I wanted to ask where he'd take me, but she had already left,
trailed by a faint perfume of roses.

As I slowly removed my sweaty clothes and put on the
scratchy striped pajamas, terror—abject, deathly terror—
gripped me.

It was odd. In all my operations inside enemy territory I had
never known a fear as deep as the one I felt now; fear not of
death, but of something worse, far worse.

What was it? What?

"Yes, you must go from here," Abdallah said.

"But why are they after me?" I shouted at him hoarsely, as if
he were responsible. "What have I done?"

"You must go away," he kept saying. "Away from here."

Through a thick haze I heard him say he could get me to the Gaza harbor, from where I could leave on a boat to Egypt, or to Cyprus. "Wherever you want. And from there, you can take an airplane back, to Canada—"

I said I had no money, nothing—but he silenced me with a wave of his thin hand.

"You'll give it back later."

Ehud's image flashed before me. The other man to whom I owed money, and my life. Another friend whom I hurt and betrayed, as I had betrayed before all who had loved me.

"Best is from Gaza—" Abdallah went on. "Not even they dare enter it now . . ."

"Gaza," I repeated, in a daze.

"They won't catch you, don't worry. People have gone out like this, by sea, all the time—"

What people?

Instead of answering, he began to tell me how, in '48, his cousins and uncles had all escaped this way, when Begin's forces had pounded Yaffo with their mortars. Only he, Abdallah, and his brother Haffiz had stayed behind. "But first you must go back to Canada," he finished. "Then we can talk."

Talk about what?

"I can't go," I said.

"You must, or they'll kill you—"

"I cannot." I looked away. "The play—I must—"

It sounded absurd in my own ears.

What did I care about the play, now? It was Ehud's, anyway. He had produced it, financed it, directed it, lost his woman over it—

Abdallah stared at me for a long moment. "You want to see her," he said at last. "Her."

I said nothing.

He got up, climbing on his canes. "Don't open the door to anyone. Anyone. I'll whistle, like this." He pursed his wrinkled lips as if for a kiss, and let out a few bars of 'Um Kulsum's "Ya Habibi." "Understand?"

Before I could answer he left, hobbling.

I woke in the afternoon, his hand shaking me. I jumped to my feet, rolled over the floor, and stood up in a wobbling *hik-kon* stance.

He did not smile. "I have tickets."

With his other hand he handed me an old blue *abbaya*. It was huge, and smelled of mothballs; probably it had belonged to his dead brother.

"So no one can recognize you," he said. "We all look the same to them, in *abbayas*." He handed me a keffiyeh also.

I put both on awkwardly, and stumbled after him downstairs.

The eleven young Arabs were still sitting around the table, like some mysterious sentinels. Fauzi was not among them. All looked up at me as I came down the stairs, and, as one, all touched their foreheads.

Abdallah paid them no heed.

"Cover your face," he said to me, "and let's go."

55

DURING THE PREVIOUS TWO days the *khamsin* indeed had shattered all records. Even at this hour, seven-thirty in the evening, the heat was suffocating—at least forty degrees Celsius. As I followed Abdallah down the cobblestoned lanes of old Yaffo, the buildings around me shimmered in the heat.

"Over here," Abdallah said.

I almost did not recognize the hall: it had been given a coat of green paint, the yard conspicuously cleaned of all refuse and broken furniture. The sycamores' trunks around it had been painted white and strung with yellow police tape to mark the border beyond which the crowd, standing silent and thick and patient, could not cross. A long line of shuffling men overflowed into Shazli Street, then cut through to Avoda Lane, and looped back to HaMeshorerim, from which it snaked back to the gate of the Waqf hall.

"Careful!" Abdallah hissed, grabbing my wrist. "Look down. Down."

Through a narrow opening that the police had left in the cordon, a policeman was now letting ticket holders through one by one, looking intently into their faces.

"Here." Abdallah's strong fingers pulled at me.

The thick line of men parted for us, enveloped us, and closed around us.

I stood still, absorbing the crowd's emanations.

All around me were Arabs: plump Israeli villagers from the

Gallil, narrow-shouldered sunbaked Bedouins in brown camel-hair galabiehs, suited city-dwellers in scuffed shoes. A long line of silent figures, watchful, dreamlike, patient. The smell of the *za'atar* and the *yachnoon* wrapped me in an embrace, the smell of the land—

Whose land?

"*Yallah!*" A policeman crooked his fingers at me.

Abdallah shuffled forward on his canes, showing our tickets to the scowling policeman.

"*Yallah! Imshi!*" Move! Be quick about it! He gave Abdallah a half kick.

One aluminum cane slipped, and the thin old man at my side stumbled. I felt my shoulders tense, my knees bending into a crouch.

"No, no!" Abdallah's whisper was like a whiplash.

My shoulders loosened. Head bent under my keffiyeh, I followed the old Arab through the gate. He leaned on my arm, saying nothing.

Someone made room for us in the dense line before the door.

"From Gaza, my nephew," Abdallah murmured.

"*Salaam,*" said someone, his face thoroughly cut up with meticulous shaving. He touched his fingers to his forehead, quickly.

Other muted *salaams* came from the dense line. Only men; no women.

I put the tips of my fingers to my own forehead, keeping my eyes lowered.

"*Yallah! Imshi!*"

More Arabs shuffled in. A young man with a pinched face slid toward me, bringing his lips close to my ear. "Blessed be the sons of the camps, *ya 'Azzati,*" O Gazan, "for they shed their blood for us all—"

I lowered my eyes in becoming modesty.

There were several murmurs of approval.

The Gaza refugee camp was apparently still under curfew, following the riots of the week before. It was an insanely brave act now, for a Gazan to come to Yaffo.

The crowd was growing thicker by the minute, yet still remained oddly silent, like a large snake, watchful, waiting.

Another line, thinner and noisier, stretched before the other door, to our right: actors from Cassit, and high school students, and a scattering of reporters, chattering in Hebrew.

"They are coming!" hissed someone beside me.

I ducked my head and bent my knees, and the crowd around me surged, protectively.

Behind us, three police patrol cars and two black vans had come to a stop, their radios crackling. One patrol car now spewed forth a thickset man in a rumpled dark uniform, cradling a walkie-talkie. Amzaleg.

"*Yechrebettam*," someone said in my ear. May their house fall down. "The *muchabaratt*." The security services.

Amzaleg, his eyes like lumps of pitch, stared at the Waqf hall's roof. I raised my eyes, too. At each of the two roof's corners stood two figures, heads wrapped in keffiyehs, arms folded. Two black-and-white keffiyehs, for the PLO; one red and white, for the PFLP; one green and white, for the Ichwan, the Muslim Brotherhood.

"They are together now," someone said to Abdallah. "No bickering anymore. Together!"

Several sighs came from all around, then a warning hiss. Steps approached, purposeful, large. Abdallah rapped on my back with his knuckles and I ducked my head under my keffiyeh.

Amzaleg went by, speaking into his walkie-talkie. For a second his eyes seemed to stare into mine, blind and unseeing.

"Send me five more, goddammit!" he growled into his radio. "I said five!" Then he disappeared behind the corner.

A short man and a tall red-haired woman came out of nowhere, he holding her arm, limping, she walking stooped. Ehud and Ruthy. They passed by, and for a brief instant I could smell her lemony musk, like an orange grove in bloom. Then the side door closed behind them.

Abdallah held on to my arm.

I said nothing.

The crowd gave a rustle, like a snake uncoiling. A gray official Lark had stopped on the corner of Yehoyada Street, disgorging a large fat man in blue pants and a white shirt who soon disappeared in the dark.

Another radio squawked somewhere, and a rough voice in Hebrew said, "Aleph one to aleph two, over." Then, absurdly, "Where is my cola?"

More squawks.

And suddenly the line began to move, quickly, purposefully, the policemen closing in on both sides, to hem its flow. "*Yallah, yallah!*"

Abdallah produced his two tickets, and we entered.

56

THEY SAT ON CHAIRS, they stood against walls, crammed themselves between the repainted crumbling columns, filled the cavernous hall with a hot, silent, humid presence—to the left the Arabs, to the right the Jews, the two peoples; and not a sound could be heard. Aside from the chirping of some walkie-talkies and the distant drone of cars outside, there hung over the audience an absolute deathly silence.

I watched them, my heart seizing; and as I sat there, sick with terror and longing, wrapping the keffiyeh around my face, I no longer knew whether it was my father's play I was longing for, to finally see performed as he had asked me, or whether I was merely waiting for it to end, so I could hold Ruthy just one more time, even though I might then be killed by my pursuers—

From behind the reddish curtain came muffled whispers. I rose slightly in my seat, devouring the sound. A hand tapped on my knee. "Lower your eyes!"

Two men in blue Atta jeans were passing in the row before us, looking into faces. A third walked behind, hand at the small of his back. In the first row, turning in his seat, Gershonovitz followed them with his Mongolian eyes.

The two *shoo-shoo* men approached slowly, stooping; I felt my body tense up—and at that same moment the lights dimmed and the curtain slowly folded back to reveal Yissachar in mourning, before a large leather lump, his dead horse. Behind him shone Mount Gilbo'a, dark and flat and primordial.

The two men retreated, muttering, to lean against a wall.

"O friend and companion," Yissachar sang on the shallow stage, "on whose back I rode in my ancestors' fields, who plowed with me the bosom of my motherland—"

From the audience came a low hum, like a beast raising itself up. Absurdly, a walkie-talkie crackled somewhere, as though it, too, were moved by the song. There was a creak, as the color wheel rotated, and a blue light was turned on; then, from behind a rock, rose Amatzia Besser in a striped blue *abbaya*, charmed out of his lair by Yissachar's song.

The hum in the audience intensified, like some unknown machinery beginning to rev up.

"You have charmed me, O son of man," Amatzia sang in a hard voice, "against my will you have turned me from all I know—"

In the first row, Gershonovitz, his face twisted, was staring at the stage as if seeing other people there, and other events unfolding. Amzaleg at his side, in a white shirt also, looked like a grown-up boy on a night out with his father. And then, as my eyes slowly got accustomed to the gloom, I saw behind them the shining pate of Mr. Gelber, and at his side, to my dull astonishment, Colonel Shafrir, and the bulk of Asa Ben-Shlomo—and by the wall, Ittamar the beggar, today in a clean, embroidered Russian *rubashka*, his hair combed . . .

"—against my will," sang Amatzia, "I shall help you cut the furrows of my cradle, this land—"

And the entire *bohema* was there, too, seated near the wall: Riva Yellin, Tzipkin, old Benvenisti, erect and tense in a white shirt—

Everyone had come to hear my father's words spoken, and sung. Everyone. They had fought the play, they had battled it at every turn, but they had all come.

Another walkie-talkie crackled; and then there was a collective hiss, an indrawn breath, as Ruthy emerged from behind the cardboard Gilbo'a, her hair dyed black, and stood staring with fulminating wonder into the Debba's eyes.

"Why have you this shiny pelt that asks to be caressed—"

One more crackle, and then a scream; and another.

Two frenzied boys in orange shirts had scrambled up the stairs and were now running to and fro on stage, their arms windmilling.

The Debba sang on, "O beautiful daughter of man, whose skin is thin yet hard as steel, whose eyes are soft as morning light—"

More shouts.

Ruthy cowered behind the rock, her hands laced on her stomach.

"Sit down, *ya 'ibni*! Sit!" Abdallah hissed at me.

On the stage, one boy swung a chair, and the Debba stumbled; then it rose to its feet, swung both arms, the fists locked. The boy went tumbling, yelping weakly.

Voices rose in the hall, angry and insistent.

Kagan, his hair wild, was on his feet, wobbling. "Jews!" he cried in Yiddish. "Jews! I beg of you! Do not—"

Then he was down. Three more orange shirts had careened past him down the aisle, holding long sticks. More screams in the crowd. "*Cholerot* of Kahane!"

"Sit down!" Abdallah tugged at my *abbaya*. "Sit!"

I tore away from him. A mass of bodies writhed around me; orange shirts, and a few *abbayas*. There was an unearthly howling in my ears.

Who was yowling like that?

On stage, Ehud was grappling with a large man in an orange T-shirt, stumbling this way and that. As I watched, Ehud suddenly snapped his fingers above the man's head, then, in an eyeblink, twisted sideways and hurled him into the first row. But almost instantly, he was pulled down by two others who had scrambled onto the stage, shouting to each other in military Hebrew.

"—and get the scenery! The scenery! Break it to pieces!"

"—no, no, go after the actors!"

I rose to my feet, the yowling rising again in my ears. A chair broke to my right, on someone's head. Another voice screamed. The audience seethed, boiled. Abdallah was pulling at my *abbaya*. "Let's go, *ya 'ibni*! Let's go from here!"

The yowling rose again.

"*Ta'al ho-o-on!*"

Who was howling?

"There he is!"

An orange shirt swam into view, and a hand holding a knife—there was a flash of silvery metal—I half twisted—not enough, not enough!—but then an embroidered Russian shirt and a halo of hair stumbled on the arm, deflecting it, and the knife slipped down my ribs, not deep; and then an aluminum cane swung down from the other side, in a long arc. The knife changed direction, flashed in and out.

Abdallah stumbled, a narrow red efflorescence blossoming upon his shirt.

"*Ya* Daoud! *Ya 'ibni*—"

He fell.

"You piece of Arab *cholera*." Teeth were bared before me. "And you too, *ya* Arab-loving—"

I tried to dive after him, but the crowd swept me away, in a doughy mass of flailing legs and yammering voices, all swimming for the exit. Someone grabbed my neck. I kicked back at a groin, twisted, kicked at another. Howling, I swam against the human tide, toward the stage. It, too, now was a thick stew of bodies, writhing, coalescing. I hopped on the shallow elevation, cupped one hand to my mouth, tore the keffiyeh from my head, and waved it in the air.

"Ta'al ho-on!"

There was a moment of slowness, as though a wave had passed through the writhing, twisting bodies. Two of the men I had seen leaning against the wall started in my direction. "Here he is!"

I stood on the leather mound and kept waving the keffiyeh, howling. *"Ta'al ho-o-o-oo-n!"*

All movement toward the exit stopped. Then, like the earth giving up the planted seed after rain, the bedlam began to disgorge men. Some in *abbayas*, some in baggy pants, walking slowly as though waking from a dream, toward the stage.

"Ta'al ho-o-o-n, ya shabbab!" Rise up and come, O brave ones!

The two tall *shoo-shoo* men swam against the crowd, their eyes fixed on me; to the side came the third, carrying something in his lowered hand.

And then, from the other side of the hall, came other men. Four, five, six. Thin, diffident, their legs moving in floating half steps, shoulders hunched, heads bent forward, half to the side. Anons. I hadn't even known they were here. Then at the far back came another, a bulky frog of a man with a shiny welt under one eye and a clot of blood under his lip. Yaro. Our eyes locked.

Gershonovitz, in his seat, made a motion toward me with his head.

As though from a great distance, I could see Yaro hesitate, then begin to march down the center aisle toward the stage.

"Backup!" I called to him; my voice came out a croak. "Yaro, I need backup!"

Yaro went on walking.

I went into a crouch. Behind me, incongruously, Kagan rose to his feet, swaying.

"Jews!" He wept. "Jews! I am begging of you! For *his* sake—!"

Then he toppled again.

In the aisle, Yaro stopped. He stared at the spot where Kagan had fallen; his face was stricken and hot. All around him the melee seethed and surged. Then, as though shaking himself loose, he continued to move, his eyes no longer on mine. A tall Moroccan spoke to him briefly. When Yaro did not answer, the man started to grab his shoulder; without even pausing Yaro hit him twice, swiftly, almost as an afterthought, once with the elbow in the ribs, the second time with the heel of the palm under the chin. The man crashed sideways into a trio of boys in orange shirts, then to the floor.

I raised my keffiyeh, waving it, waving.

Yaro jumped on the stage. Two thin young men hopped right behind him, their hands held akimbo at their sides.

Yaro stood beside me, his eyes refusing to meet mine.

"*Yallah*," I said. "Later."

Fauzi shouted at me, "We'll take the back of the stage, close the door!" His keffiyeh was askew, his face flaming with emotion. At his side was Ben-Shoshan, the accountant, his head streaming blood.

"No!" Yaro snapped at him. "Stay with Dada and Uddy!"

The two thin men at his side were dangling broken chair legs from the tips of their fingers, swinging them lightly. I recognized them vaguely—they were from my brother's old outfit. They nodded at me slightly, bashfully, while in the hall below the brawl seethed and boiled.

"*Ta'al ho-on!*"

I jumped down into the hall. It was a mass of bodies, congealing and separating, breaking and joining, in a seething dance of hate. Behind me I saw Ehud and Ben-Shoshan, broomsticks in hand, fanning left, then two of the Arab *shabbab*, holding chairs, fanning right.

Three more men in orange shirts stepped forward.

Ben Shoshan waved his stick in the air. "*Aleihum!*" At them!

Jews and Arabs, side by side.

"Ta'al ho-o-on!"

A heavy hand grabbed my elbow, hard, at the nerve joint. I swung sideways, once, twice, but couldn't shake it off. I twisted and brought him down, felt a large hand at my throat, and knifed with my knee. It was met with another knee. Another twist; this, too, was resisted. I brought my palm up, on the chin, and met another palm. It was like fighting a doppelganger who knew all my moves in advance. I peered into a dark face, the hooded eyes dark, the mouth gaping in a humorless grin. Amzaleg. His gun was out, a police-issue Parabellum.

"Enough," he said. "I'll take care of the rest."

He pointed the gun at the ceiling and fired once, then again. The sound rolled. There was a frozen silence.

Amzaleg reholstered the gun.

All motion stopped. Then, in the first row, Gershonovitz lumbered to his feet. "No one leaves until the ambulances arrive," he rasped. "This show is over." He pointed his finger at me. "And we want to talk to you."

The silence disintegrated. Policemen poured in through the open door, then men in white, with litters. Groans, and yelps of pain, were heard again.

I said to the fat man, "The show goes on." I pushed him into his seat, roughly.

"This show is finished!" He struggled up, his small mouth quivering with rage.

Amzaleg said, "Their permit says 'till midnight.'"

"Amnon," Gershonovitz hissed, "Amnon, Amnon, you don't know what you're doing—"

But Amzaleg had already left.

After the ambulances had come and gone (Abdallah, I saw from afar, was being taken out alongside a wounded policeman, side by side, on two litters), I saw we had no actors left.

The two principal ones had been taken to Hadassah Hospital, so we had no Yissachar and no Debba. Of the actors playing 'Ittay and Yochanan there was also no trace. Either wounded and taken to the hospital or escaped.

Ehud, miraculously, was safe. Ruthy, too, was unharmed. While everyone else was fighting, she had lain behind the stage, under the Debba's mound, hiding.

She now came out, her hands on her belly. "I—I couldn't," she said. "I had to protect it—"

Ehud stared at her, his eyes colorless.

"Yes," she said, her chin raised, as though ready to be hit. "I am. And not by you."

People came and went, collecting broken chairs and torn shirts.

I said to Ehud, "The two musical directors can do the Friends; they'll just have to sing it in a higher register—"

"I am telling you, Uddy," Ruthy went on, "at last, I am."

In the hall, the audience was sitting down, one by one.

I said to Ehud. "Can you take Yissachar's role? I'll take the Debba."

He looked at me, still saying nothing.

"Everything else, later," I said, gripped by panic. "First we finish the show—"

Ehud said, "But you got to promise me, first, something—"

"Everything later," I said.

"Now!" His face flowed in and out of shape. "You have to promise me now, or there's no show—"

"No!" Ruthy shouted. "No!"

"Promise"—Ehud stared at the floor—"that you'll leave her alone—don't worry about—but you must promise—"

"No!" Ruthy screamed. "Dada, no!"

"—on his grave—"

I looked over my shoulder at Ruthy, then at Ehud; Ben-Shoshan called out at me from behind the stage. I couldn't hear what it was. There was a hum in my ears.

Down at the hall, policemen were helping some men carry the last stretcher through the door. The audience was slowly sitting down; this time the Jews and Arabs sat mixed together wherever they found a chair or on the floor, looking up at the stage, at Ehud, at me. Waiting for my father's song to begin.

There was a long moment of absolutely no movement, no sound.

"*Yallah*," I said at last, through the sand in my larynx. "Let's get into roles."

Ignoring Ruthy's staccato shrieks, I walked away from her, toward the back of the stage, toward the dark.

Side by side we stood, behind the cardboard border, waiting for the call.

Snatches of a woman's wail came from backstage, and the sound of an Arab flute. A low wailing sound. Time stood still, like my enemy at my side. The enemy who had saved my life and had now chosen to take it back.

"One minute!"

A burst of applause came from the hall, where the woman had just finished singing of her love for the Debba.

"Five seconds!"

I turned to look at the man beside me. His greasepaint did not seem like a mask—it was more like a wooden part of his face in which his eyes were burning, burning. I wanted to touch him, to remove the mask from his face, to see what lay underneath; what he was really made of, this enemy of mine.

A hand thumped me on the shoulder. Ben-Shoshan.

"Go! *Yallah!* Go!"

The black tunnel loomed before me.

Where was I?

On all fours I searched for my hiding place, my secret lair.

There. There it was. Breathing fitfully I sat on the leather mound, safe at last, in the belly of my whale. Pale light shone from somewhere, from a small window high on the wall. The beam intensified. In a moment the submachine gun would open up with its song of death . . .

Down! Down!

I threw myself upon the rough floor, breathing hard and shallowly, listening.

A sound of hissing came in my ears, like the voices of a thousand hyenas, yelping.

Who was after me? Who?

Srik-srak. Srik-srak.

From where I crouched I glimpsed Ehud squatting at the foot of the stage, his head bent low.

Who was he? What was he doing?

Srik-srak.

Yissachar was sharpening his sword, making ready for battle. No, not a sword. A blade. A long knife he had made, a knife to kill his enemy with; his enemy, the Debba.

I crouched low, my knuckles on the land. A humid smell came in my nose, the smell of my motherland; a musky, lemony smell. I rose into it, my nostrils flared.

A woman's face floated before me, her eyes staring into mine. She sang at length, thanking God and cursing him at the same time.

Who was she?

Srik-srak. Srik-srak.

Two wiry monsters were crawling up the mound, hissing like khaki-clad lizards. Yissachar, my enemy, knife held between his blackened teeth, crawled before them, leading them to my lair.

Danger! Down! Down!

A wheel creaked somewhere; the light rose in intensity, and the woman's song turned into a shout of anguish and anger, mingling with the rhythmic whispering of the attackers.

"Now! Go!"

A single yellow Fresnel light had been turned on, and the three attackers rose to their feet. Knives in hand, hissing and shouting, they ran up the mound.

"Ta'al ho-o-n!"

Spreading my arms wide, I seized one attacker by the throat, prepared to fight for my lair, for my land, the cradle of my ancestors.

"Ta'al ho-o-o-on!"

Whose voice was it, yowling like that?

By the blinding light of the kliegs I saw the audience's faces frozen in terror, Gershonovitz, and Riva, and Gelber, and behind, improbably, Jenny, her eyes large and luminous, and behind them the entire lineup of old theater hacks and '48 fighters; and, as though from the top of a distant mountain, in a glutinous haze, I saw Ehud's face, distorted in a rage of fear and love, and his raised fist plunging, plunging, the knife sprouting from it like a flash of black silver.

And then the hand turned, and the balled fist slammed into my chest.

The world stopped. I tried to speak, to explain, but could not utter a sound. Only my sight remained.

And then, as I stood there, my sight began to expand. It blossomed and loomed, grew and widened, and suddenly it opened up to encompass the entire hall, the entire land, and at that very moment I saw it all; without the least effort on my part it all came together, and at long, long last, I finally understood.

I understood my father, and Ehud, and Gershonovitz; I understood Ruthy, and her infidelities; I understood myself, and my rage; and above all and beyond everything, I finally understood the Debba, his anguish, and his boundless wrath; why he did what he had done to my father; and how and why my father had died. And as the scales fell from my eyes, in that one bright instant I also understood, with an almost surreal lucidity, what my father had asked of me; and what, without any thought of refusal, I must finally do.

57

HE WAS WAITING FOR me, in the dressing room, slumped in his chair, Riva at his side. Even before he began to speak I knew what he was going to say.

"Yes," Gershonovitz said, "she was the one who sent me a note in forty-eight, your mother, warning me." The fan clicked and clucked and he gazed at it quickly, as if happy not to look at me. "About him, Paltiel."

I said, "That he was going to Yaffo, to warn the Arab?"

I could still breathe only with difficulty, after the horrible blow that Ehud had struck at my heart.

Gershonovitz gave a nod; I felt no surprise. Somehow I had expected it.

In the corner, Riva stirred. "But I wrote it . . . Sonya phoned Isser from Cassit, just before the Castel battle, to finally tell him who—who Abu Jalood was, and that he was going to be there . . ." Riva's eyes turned black and small. "This *shmendrik* Paltiel overheard her, so right away he ran off to Yaffo to warn this Arab boyfriend of his of the coming attack . . . Sonya saw him go and she guessed why, so she came running to me . . ."

I wanted to speak but could not.

Riva's voice was a rasp. "She was crying, Sonya . . . she asked me what to do—if she should go warn our boys, some-one, so they'd stop Paltiel before he warned the Arab—I was six months pregnant with Paltiel's child—and she asked *me*—"

Gershonovitz let out a whistling sigh, a slow exhalation, as Riva's black eyes turned toward me. "So I told her, Sonya, 'We must finish with this Arab, before he ruins us all—nothing else matters—'" Riva was looking at me directly, her eyes ageless. "I told her, 'Write a note, so they'll send someone to stop Paltiel—'"

Gershonovitz whispered, "You did right—I told you a hundred times already . . ."

Riva curved her mouth. "But Sonya, she couldn't write it . . . her fingers couldn't hold the pencil—you understand? . . . even after she'd already decided—she couldn't . . ."

"Yes," I said; or I think I did.

Riva said, "This *Arabush*—she knew him from before your father—you understand?—"

I nodded. The world was crystallizing into discrete objects, small and round and hard. Riva was saying, ". . . so I took the pen from her . . . and I wrote the note—and—then we—" Her chin vibrated. "We called someone we knew, who—he could get things to the Shay . . ."

"Who?" I was amazed to hear my voice, so normal, so clear.

"What does it matter?" Gershonovitz said. "Someone."

"Zussman," said Riva, "from the Tnuva kiosk on Herzl Street. I knew his wife—he had a bicycle—" She shut her eyes so tight they disappeared.

I said nothing. I think that Gershonovitz said something about everyone making a sacrifice, or something equally idiotic.

"Sacrifice!" Riva said with harsh contempt. "What do *you* know about it? You think *you* men sacrificed? You have any idea what *we* went through, in the prehistory . . . what we still . . ." She fluttered her palm in one of her famous dramatic gestures, the one of Leah'le from *The Dybbuk*, to signify it was useless to explain, then turned to me. "I told you to leave but you didn't listen! Now look what you've done to her." She got up, stead-ied herself, and, holding the rim of her embroidered galabieh, swept out.

I could hardly breathe; then little by little, life resumed.

"Who did you send, after Paltiel?" I asked Gershonovitz, not looking at him.

He tried to shrug. "Someone."

"From the Shay?"

"Someone, what does it matter?"

A wave of nausea washed over me. "My father?"

"No no no," the fat man fairly hissed. "Someone else."

Another wave rolled.

Gershonovitz was saying, "We had to do it . . . What do you think . . . Other times we had to do worse—"

"Yes," I said.

"For unity," said Gershonovitz, "what do you think? With-out unity there's nothing. Look at them, these *Arabushim*. Just look at them!"

"Yes," I said. "For sure."

"No, look at them!" The fat man was fairly hissing now. "You think I liked doing all this dreck? Doing all the necessary dirt so that one day we'll have all this—" He waved his hands about, then stopped. Ruthy and Ehud barged into the room. Ruthy was still glowing with the makeup and fulminating with the spirit of her role. Ehud held her hand, squeezing it.

"They want everyone on the stage," Ruthy said, her eyes, blindly glowing, looking through me.

Ehud rumbled, "This will go fifty performances for sure."

He looked at me. The flat stare had given place to another, harder still; like Gershonovitz's of the week before.

I said to Gershonovitz, "I have to go."

The clapping was turning rhythmic, insistent.

"They are waiting," Ehud said.

I got to my feet. Gershonovitz gave me one of his old looks, and then, for the briefest moment, I saw his eyes brighten with something akin to moisture.

"All right," I said, then added in Arabic, *"Illi fat matt."* The past is dead. Meaning we'll keep all this between us.

He tried to thump me on the back but his hand seemed to have lost its vigor. "It never is." He stroked my shoulder, almost gently. "Now go, go. They are all waiting for you."

"Bye, Shimmel," I said, and left. And this was the last I saw him.

There was a break in the line of actors on the stage; beyond it was a sea of hands clapping soundlessly under a white cloud of light. I moved into the break and gave one hand to Ehud, the other to Ruthy.

In the front row I saw the pinched face of Mr. Gelber (Jenny was no longer behind him), his eyes narrowed with an intense emotion I could not identify. And, beside him, Leibele, clapping with his soft hands; and Zussman and Amzaleg, side by side; and all the others, Arabs and Jews alike; my people, my two peoples; my father's folk for whom he had fought and killed, and for whom he had finally and helplessly died.

I left through the front door, openly and idiotically.

Ruthy's Beetle was parked at the end of the yard, its door unlocked. Or perhaps it was locked and I had kicked or wrenched it open. I no longer remember. My chest, the inside of my nose, the entire contents of my skull, were on fire. In the dark I rummaged under the steering wheel, for the ignition wires. I think I bared them with my teeth, before the engine caught.

As I sped along the dark empty streets, my clammy hands on the wheel, I kept glancing into the mirror overhead, half expecting the white Toyotas to converge on me; for the quiet men to alight, hands at the small of their backs, eyes hooded, ready for the kill. Yet like that far-off day, a thousand years back, in Toronto, when I had first heard of my father's death, I felt nothing inside; only tears, oily and fat, kept rolling down my cheeks, down the greasepaint, onto my *abbaya*, even as the inside of my nose ached with the remembered odor of the bills found beside my father's body, and with the knowledge of who had left them there, and why.

The driver-side mirror had been skewed when I had squeezed into the little car, and as I now drove, I could see my face in it, the face of an animal stricken with terror and grief and wrath, frozen in a death rictus under the blue-gray greasepaint. Once or twice I pulled out my handkerchief, to try to rub the paint off, but it resisted all my efforts. Finally I gave up.

On and on I drove, just as I was, a Debba in flight, now also pursuing.

The Hadassah Hospital yard was a yellowish gray desert in the wan moon. The building itself was dark, aside from three windows dimly lit at mid level, and the entrance where a lone bulb shone yellowly, surrounded by a halo of moths.

I parked the Beetle with a jerk, waited a second, then rolled out of the car, as I had been taught, and rose, my hands raised, spinning once, twice, to look around me.

There was nothing. No one behind me, nor in front. Aside from a police car and three curtained ambulances, the red Stars of David on their backdoors fuzzy and brown in the dim darkness, the hospital's yard was empty.

Forcing myself to move slowly, hands lowered, I walked into the dim light.

58

I SAT DOWN ON the edge of the bed. The thin corrugated face stared at me from the pillow.

"You killed him," I said. "After he had a heart attack."

Abdallah said nothing.

I said, "I saw the pill bottle, in the photograph. It was near his hand—"

Under the white bedsheet the narrow shoulders moved.

"Yes."

I said, "But—but you said, you gave your word to Amzaleg." I felt foolish, saying things like that.

The sleeping Amzaleg shifted slightly in his chair, near the window, his head thrown back. He had already been there when I arrived; somehow it did not surprise me.

Abdallah's mouth twisted in a crooked little smile. "Word of an Arab."

The lights outside dimmed, as if a switch had been pulled in the corridor. The room was utterly quiet. From the bed came a faint odor of disinfectant, mixed with the sour tang of tanning acid. Like the one I had smelled on the money taken from my father's store, a hundred years ago.

Abdallah said, "He is my friend, Amzaleg."

I didn't see what that had to do with my question, or with anything. I stuttered, "But why—why did you kill him now? After all these years."

Abdallah said, "I read in this book, that Sonya told Isrool about me, who I really was, before he left for the Castel—"

"What book?"

The skeletal outline under the sheet shifted. "About Baldiel's life—someone from the young *shabbab* gave it to me the week before . . . he got it someplace . . ."

"Paltiel's biography?" The scurrilous book that had to be withdrawn.

"Yes, about his life, Baldiel."

My ears began to buzz.

Abdallah said, "It said she knew who I was, all that time, but she never told Isrool—then when she did, Isrool sent someone to stop Baldiel, so Baldiel couldn't warn me—"

"No . . ." I croaked.

"Yes," Abdallah said. "I didn't believe this at first . . . then I realized it must be true . . . so when I came to the store . . . I told Isrool what I had just read . . . 'You had him killed,' I said, 'You' . . . 'No,' Isrool said, he had nothing to do with it, nothing . . . it was—others who sent the killer, not he . . . But I didn't believe him. 'No,' I said, 'it was you who sent them . . . Do not deny it . . .'"

"No," I croaked. "No. It wasn't like that . . ."

"Yes, it was so," Abdallah went on. "I told him, this I always knew, that the Jews had killed Baldiel, not us . . . They only cut his *zayin*, not his—not everything, like us . . . I knew it was the Jews, I said. But I didn't realize it was you—" A peculiar expression crossed his thin, ancient face. "You were jealous, I told Isrool. Jealous . . ."

The world turned upside down. "It wasn't him," I said.

"Jealous, I told him," Abdallah repeated, with soft malice, "because you couldn't write beautiful poetry like Baldiel."

I said helplessly, "It wasn't him."

I wanted to say that it was Gershonovitz who had sent the killer after Paltiel, and that Isser had nothing to do with it, that he had left my mother when he found it out, because he valued friendship even more than love . . . But I could not say it to this man who had loved my mother, too; nor could I tell him it was Isser who had written all the beautiful poetry, not Paltiel. Isser . . .

The invisible hand had once more wrapped itself around my throat with an unshakable grip; then it loosened. "And that's why you killed—"

"No, no," Abdallah said, "no . . . because he said he was going to tell you everything, Isrool. That he wanted you to know . . . so you'd come back . . ."

"What everything?" I asked. "That you—that you and my mother—"

Again, I couldn't continue.

Abdallah shrugged under the bedsheet. "It wasn't my fault," he said softly. And suddenly his emaciated figure filled, under the sheet, as he half sat up, his eyes black and flat, like Gershonovitz's. "She was very beautiful, it was the month of Tamuz"—he looked at me—"she got her orders—"

I wanted to say that it wasn't orders, and that even if it was, at the end she loved him . . . But the hand gripping my throat remained closed.

"The *mal'oona*," Abdallah said. The accursed woman. Slowly his head fell back to the pillow, as if this were some absurd TV drama. He spoke toward the ceiling. "In thirty-three, she worked in the house of my brother Haffiz, in Yaffo, that's when—when I first met her."

"In sewing," I said. "She was sewing, for people in their homes—"

"Yes, she made a lace dress for Haffi's second wife, for the wedding . . . Beautiful Jewish lace . . . We talked . . ." Abdallah raised his head and fixed me with a black stare. "Only talked . . . You understand? . . . Talked."

"Yes." I looked at him with mute inquiry.

He said, "I don't know what we talked about. The sun and the moon . . . books . . . newspapers . . . theater, poetry . . . She was also playing then in some play, I don't remember . . . in Tel Aviv . . ."

"*The Penny and the Moon.*"

"Yes. So she took me, to see it."

I said foolishly, "She took you? To Tel Aviv?"

"Yes," Abdallah said. "This was before thirty-six." He paused. "When everything split."

"The Wrestling Club? When the—when they expelled the Arabs?"

"Yes, also with—in business, with Isrool. When I had to sell my share to him."

There was a pause.

I said. "Did she know then that—that you and Isser were . . . friends?" I had wanted to say "my father," but it didn't come out.

"Yes, sure, I told her; also about—about me and Baldiel. But she never met Isrool. Only later."

"When?" I asked.

"Later, after it was finished between us, the first time— her father forced her; she then went to Isrool, to his store, the *mal'oona*. Her father sent her—" And suddenly he said, "I didn't—do anything to her, you understand? Nothing."

I stared at him with confusion.

He said, "We didn't, all that time. Not then. What do you want, she was a child."

I said, "Sixteen?"

"Yes, a child. Only later—"

I waited.

"Only later, in forty-six, when she said Isrool needed some- one, an actor—"

"Yes," I said. "In Haifa. For the show."

"Yes, in Haifa. To play the Debba. She was already married, a woman . . . I—" He stopped, staring in front of him, at the gray wall, his eyes unfocused.

I said, "Because Paltiel did not want to play it?"

He said nothing.

"No one wanted to play this role," I went on. For some reason I felt the need to display how much I had learned about those days. About the prehistory.

He kept staring at the wall, unseeing.

I went on, "It wasn't your brother Haffiz who played in the show. You were the 'Yemenite actor' Ovadiah Tzadok. You also played in Hebrew shows under that name, before." A strange volubility had seized me. "With Riva Yellin, too, and with Kagan, in my father's Purim *shpiels.*"

But he was not listening. "In Haifa," he said, "on the Carmel mountain, just before dawn—the moon, and the stars . . . You understand?"

There was a long pause.

"Yes," I said.

"The *mal'oona.*"

And all of a sudden I wanted to ask him if he loved her, really loved her; in spite of her belonging to another man, in spite of her treachery, in spite of her inability to leave her people to follow him. In spite of everything. But somehow it did not seem possible to ask.

I looked at the man who was my father, and said, "But why did you—kill him?"

In his chair under the window, his head thrown back, Amzaleg gave a convulsive snore.

There was a cough, almost a cackle, from the bed. Abdallah said, "He was going to tell you. To make you come back."

I stared. "Because he wanted to tell me about you, and—and my mother?"

"Yes, to get you to come back here . . . I had come to give him the money, like every month . . ."

I interrupted, foolishly, "That you gave him—to help pay—"

For me, for the son.

"Yes—he never made much, the *mal'oon*—" the accursed one. Abdallah's voice turned soft. "—always running around with actors, and theater people—was bankrupt once—if I hadn't given him—"

"Yes," I said through my parched throat.

Abdallah said, "After, he said to me, 'No more money, enough, he's gone . . .' He said: 'What good is money to me now, with one child dead and the other gone?' But I said to him, 'And what good is the money to me either? Here is more, take it, give it to actors—at least let theater live—'"

Abdallah's face darkened, perhaps in shame, perhaps in anger at himself, as though it was a shameful act he had just admitted to—helping the enemy in the service of a common cause.

I said nothing; my voice seemed stuck.

Abdallah uttered a peculiar cough. "After what I read in this book, I . . . I almost didn't come . . . but then I thought, Why should others suffer, so . . . I came to bring him the money . . . and talk, about the last message, that we had to pass on . . . to decide if it was sincere . . . then he showed me the letter he wrote to you—" There was another cough, now, a long one. "I told him, 'Leave him be, leave him. He's away from all this . . . You want him to come back to this? . . . To the necessity of killing friends? . . . To loss of honor?' . . . and Is-rool said, 'Maybe he can change things' . . . and I said, 'No one can change anything here . . . this place is rotten with books that fight each other through us . . . what are we against His books? . . . Let Daoud stay there,' I said . . . 'You had Baldiel killed already, you want Daoud killed too? . . . Leave him be.'

But he kept saying he wanted you to come back . . . 'What for?' I asked him. 'To do what? . . .'"

Abdallah spit weakly, sideways.

I said, "And that's why you—you killed him?" I felt a weak tremor in my thighs.

Abdallah said, "I told him, leave him be."

I waited.

After a while he said, "When he fell down, he asked me to hand him the pills—but I—I took the knife from where he sat—the long sawblade knife, and—and later, I made it look, like—like one of us." He stared at me, blindly, and for an instant I could see him staring at my father lying on the floor. "But I couldn't finish—"

I said, "You locked the door with your own key—you had one from the time you were still partners. He never made another key, but you had one."

Abdallah gave a jerk of his head.

I went on, "Then you slept in the garbage-can shed. In the backyard." I don't know why I had to show him how much I knew. "On the ground."

"Yes, like then. I used to roam all over Tel Aviv, go anywhere. Before."

"And in the morning you took the bus to Yaffo." Simply the bus.

There was a short silence. I tried to imagine the depth of the hurt he had supressed all these years, but could not.

"Go back to Canada now," Abdallah said in High Arabic. "Or they'll kill you, too."

I said nothing.

"Like they killed him, Baldiel."

I stared at him through a red curtain. I knew what was coming.

"The Debba's son. You understand?" He stared at me with a peculiar intensity.

I tried to shrug, but my shoulder quivered.

His voice grew stronger, more resonant. "You raise your hand, *ya* sharif, they'll all come. Like they came last night, in the show, to help you. You understand? All the *shabbab* will help you. All the Arabs. They'll shed their blood for you. Their souls they will give for you. Anything. You understand?"

I said something indistinct. My throat was frozen.

Not only had the *shabbab* answered my call the night before; Yaro, who had tried to kill me before, also did; and Ehud, whose woman I had taken; and my friends from the Unit, whom I had deserted, to keep my precious conscience pure. And the actors. And the Arabs, too. They had all come. Shoulder to shoulder they had fought against the rioters, to let the play go on. My father's play. Jews and Arabs together.

Abdallah said in colloquial Arabic, "Go away quickly, then wait before you come back. The Jews, they can't take the chance. They'll kill you."

The hand over my throat opened.

"What chance?"

"That you'll come to us—"

"And do what?"

"Whatever you say, we'll do." He curved his mouth into a frightful grimace. "*Ya Jalood.*" O Goliath.

Something hovered in the air, thick and watchful and dark. I closed my eyes. "And then, what then? More blood?"

"Whatever you tell us, *ya* Mahdi."

I shook my head, my eyes closed.

"You'll see," he said. "You cannot escape. You'll come back. The land will call you, your people will call you, your blood. And you will come back to us. To *us.*"

What land? Which people? Which *Mein Kampf*?

I opened my eyes, but he was not looking at me. "In forty-four, not only in thirty-six . . . we had another committee . . . six months we talked . . . we drew up a plan . . ."

My jaw shook. "In forty-four—"

"... the Mufti said no ... the Jewish Agency said no ... everyone wanted everything ..." His eyes flashed.

"And you did not?"

The man on the bed sat up, slowly. His eyes had turned into live coals. "I only wanted her. You understand? Only her." Just as slowly he let himself fall back.

"Yes," I said.

There was a long silence. Then I said, "And what of the messages, now? The ones you passed? What—"

"No more messages," he hissed. "No more. All along, he had lied to me. He had lied to me."

"No," I said. "No no."

But he wasn't listening. "Now it's our turn, *ya 'ibni*," he said, smiling tightly, almost amorously. "*Ya 'ibni el Jalood, el Mahdi al Mu'amineem.*"

O my son, the Goliath, savior of the faithful.

Amzaleg blinked several times, and blew his lips out. "Goddammit, I slept."

"Like a corpse," I said to him.

He looked at me, then at Abdallah. Something passed between them, sharp and swift.

Abdallah looked at me but spoke to Amzaleg, "Gershonovitz, he'll never let it come out." He seemed to have regained some strength. His voice was firmer now, with its previous rasp coming back.

"I don't give a *zayin* for Gershonovitz," Amzaleg said.

Abdallah went on, "What happened, happened. They'll never let all this dreck go to the newspapers, the radio—" Bubbles appeared at the corner of the thin mouth.

"No," said Amzaleg.

I stared at the man on the bed, the man who had killed my

father, the man who had first saved him from drowning, more than half a century before; who had helped him open his store; who had wrestled with him and loaned him money in his hour of need; who had helped him stage his one play; the man who was my father's friend by day, and his enemy by night; the man who had stolen his wife's heart and then slept with her—with my mother, yes, with my mother—only to discover that she was working for Gershonovitz, and the Shay, perhaps with the knowledge of my father.

No, not of my father. Of Isser.

Yes. Of my *father*. My *real* father.

I said, "Were you—him, Abu Jalood?" I didn't know why I needed to hear it again from his own lips.

"Come," said Amzaleg. "Let's go eat something. He won't run away."

I nearly asked him whether Abdallah had given him his word about that, too, but refrained.

"Yes, *ya 'ibni*," Abdallah said. "I was him."

There was a short silence.

"Come," Amzaleg said.

I said to Abdallah, "Why did he let you go, in forty-eight?"

"Come on," Amzaleg said.

Abdallah said in a flat voice of pure fury, "I said to him in the Castel, 'Yes, 'tis me, kill me.' But he wouldn't . . . He said, 'The father of my child I cannot kill . . .'" Abdallah looked at me with his olive-dark eyes, the pupils black on black, coal on coal, the eyebrows drawn together in ferocious puzzlement and wrath.

Amzaleg pulled at my hand, softly. "Come, *ya* Daoud."

Without much effort I disengaged his fingers.

Abdallah went on, "He said to me, 'Promise me you will lay down your arms forever, and I will not kill you . . .' His knife was at my throat—the long knife . . ." And suddenly Abdallah began to speak in flowery Arabic, in a singsong voice. "'No,' I said. 'Kill me now, for in a double shame I shall not live—' You understand?"

"Yes," I said. "Yes."

"So I said to him, 'It is not a favor that you wish to do unto me, to give me life. You have vanquished me, O enemy mine, do me the honor and slay me.' You understand? This favor I could not take."

I wanted to say he had done so many favors in his life, that he didn't know where to stop; but I could not speak.

I nodded.

Abdallah said, in the same odd singsong, "My child he took, and my woman, and my land, and now my honor—how much more? How much? 'Kill me, ya *mal'oon*,' I said, 'and be done with me. Be done.' But he would not. 'No,' he said, 'for kill thee I cannot. Swear to me that you shall lay your arms down, and I shall let thee go.' And as I looked up at the shining blade, the accursed '*Uzra'in*," the devil, "whispered in my ear, and made me say, 'If you will swear, so shall I.'"

There was a long silence. Outside in the corridor someone shrieked, at length.

"And he said, 'I shall give thee my word, *ya* noble Debba—'" Abdallah emitted a rough rattle, perhaps laughter, perhaps a cough. "'Thy arms for mine—'"

"*Yallah*," Amzaleg said, weakly.

"He hugged me . . . Bullets flying, men dying, we hugged—" Amzaleg cleared his throat, like a distant grenade.

"—then he said, 'Give me thy dagger, and thy rifle, and thy mustache—'" The face was so contorted now it looked nearly inhuman. "My *mustache!*"

Amzaleg gave an angry sniff, and smacked one palm against another.

"Goddammit," he said.

Abdallah hissed, "But the last laugh is on him. No David art thou, but Muhammad. That's the name I gave thee before he gave thee his. Not David ben Israel, but Muhammad bin Abdallah—"

A pale black-dyed redhead edged into the narrow room, followed by a short muscular man, his hand bandaged: Ruthy and Ehud. For a brief second they looked like strangers.

"I cut my hand," Ehud announced, "taking down those limelights—" He stood a moment by Ruthy's side, his eyes like stones, then went over to the bed. Ruthy went to sit on the windowsill, laced her hands over her belly, and looked at me from a long way off.

I looked away.

"I wanted to thank you for the hall," Ehud said to Abdallah in a tight voice, "also I saw you, with the cane, when this fucking *shoo-shoo* was going to stab David—"

He looked at Ruthy, his chin raised with pride at having congratulated an Arab. "It was very brave of him," he said to her.

I looked at him but he avoided my eyes.

Ruthy gave a chirp of laughter; it turned into a sob. She slid off the sill and put her arm around Ehud's shoulder, looking into my eyes all the while.

Amzaleg cleared his throat. There was a moment of silence.

Ruthy said to Abdallah, "Did you like the show?"

He said to the ceiling, "It was a good show. You were better than her." He didn't say whether he had meant my mother or Riva, and I didn't stay to ask. Amzaleg pulled me out; I no longer felt anything, or saw much. As I wiped at my face, my cheeks, smearing my blue *abbaya* with greasepaint, I heard Ehud and Ruthy walking behind, shuffling, as do two people whose gaits are different and who try to fit their strides to each other. I did not look back.

· · ·

Outside, in the hospital yard, in the predawn half-light, some remnants of the terror came back. I twirled around, once, my hands raised, watching for an attacker, but there was no one. The yard was deserted.

My heart slowly settling, I followed the policeman to his car.

At first, when I saw it, I thought he had gotten himself a new patrol car, but then I saw the car had merely received a new and crude coat of black paint; the Arabic cuss words were barely visible underneath. Tiny drops of dew lay on the window.

The heat had broken during the night and the air was surprisingly cool. It was going to be a fine day.

We didn't speak in the car; suddenly, halfway to Yaffo, Amzaleg said, "Goddammit, this Begin. If he gets in, I don't know what will happen."

I said, "Carter will bend his arm, something will happen, maybe peace, what do I know."

There was no escape for me, Abdallah had said. The land will call me back, and my people.

Which people?

"Yeah," said Amzaleg. He threw me a brief look through the corner of his eye, as if admitting that he, too, didn't know why we were talking about Begin and Carter.

I said, "Gershonovitz was your commander, once?"

"Yes," said Amzaleg, driving at great speed along the Herbert Samuel Promenade. The sun had risen and I glimpsed pigeons strutting above Café Piltz, just behind the Israeli Aero Club; then we whizzed past.

"When I was in the Shay in Tveriah, he was the regional commander of the entire Galilee, and when he moved to Tel Aviv, he asked me to come help," Amzaleg said to the windshield. "Then after forty-eight he moved to the *shoo-shoo*; I joined the police." His mouth twisted. At the time, the Internal Security Service didn't take in Eastern Jews.

I said, "So they knew all along who did it, from the tape."

Amzaleg didn't reply. What was there to say?

But I didn't let up. "They protected his killer. They didn't want this to come out—"

"They protected *you*," Amzaleg said to the windshield. "Only you had to barge ahead like a donkey—"

"It was for him," I said, meaning Isser.

"For him?" Amzaleg said, bitterly. "Do you think he'd have liked all this to come out?"

"Yes," I said.

When Amzaleg said nothing, I said, "So were you working for Gershonovitz?"

"For him, not for him, what do I know? We're all here in the same shit, working for the rabbinate . . . Look, look." Amzaleg pointed with a nicotine-stained finger at a line in front of Cinema Yaron. "See? They can't wait to vote, these corpses, to tell the fuckers what they think of them."

At first I couldn't understand. "Oh, it's today," I said. "Today are the elections." It had completely slipped my memory.

"Sure, today. Where have you been?"

I said, "So whom will you vote for?" I immediately regretted my words. It's the one thing one does not ask a policeman.

Amzaleg sucked on his teeth. The car accelerated, then sped on, past Manshiya, past the crumbling hovels of Adjemi. The tires screeched.

"I don't understand," I said. "Isser, letting him go like this, in forty-eight."

How virtuous can you get?

I felt dead inside, but tears, large and oily and thick, kept rolling down my cheeks, as they had when I first heard of my father's murder, a thousand years ago, in Toronto.

"Enough with all this," Amzaleg said gruffly. "Let's go eat." Without applying the brakes he threw the car into a screeching turn down a narrow alley behind the clock tower, the car nearly overturning. "Don't worry," he said, "in the army I once drove a tank." He guffawed at his own joke, without mirth.

We sat in the small dark back room of the same Arab café where I had once sat with Abdallah, and drank scalding coffee from cups of thick rough glass. It tasted just like the coffee Abdallah had served me, four weeks before, in the prehistory.

I wanted to ask Amzaleg what he was going to do now about Abdallah, and Gershonovitz; whether he was going to pursue this. But my tongue seemed to have dried up.

I said to him, "Did you like the show?"

I could still see Ruthy before me, her eyes made up garishly, her palms over her belly, swaying slightly in the yellow light; and Ehud's contorted mouth, and the knife in his hand; and behind them the hundreds of eyes, staring, looking on with nameless dread, their mouths open, Jews and Arabs alike, waiting for the Word.

"I saw only half," he said. And then he added, absurdly, "If they'll let him out of Hadassah today, even in a wheelchair, I'll take him to vote."

I stared at Amzaleg; he was drinking his coffee, his small finger sticking out. For the first time I noticed that its nail was longer than the others, like that of old Moroccan Jews. I had never noticed it before. Perhaps he had just started growing it.

"Well," he said tersely, "he's a citizen."

"Yes," I said.

We ate fried eggs and fresh white bread (the waiter apologized that there was no pita bread that day—the bakery had been sold last week to a new owner, a Jew), with sliced tomatoes on the side, red as open knife-wounds, soft and sweet like the ones Ruthy had served me after I arrived . . .

A giant hand squeezed my heart. I never knew it was possible to suffer like that—not only with yearning for Ruthy, but also with deep shame at what I had done to Ehud, who once again had rescued me by pushing himself into the line of fire, so I could be free . . .

Free to do what?

"It's just like a Tnuva kiosk, now," said Amzaleg. "Give them time, they'll be just like us."

I started to say that, after doing enough dreck, in time we'll be just like them, but refrained, minding Amzaleg's feelings.

When we finished, I didn't know whether to return to the apartment. I wanted to see Ruthy so badly I nearly cried, but I knew it would do me no good to go back now. So I asked Amzaleg to drop me at Café Cassit on his way to the Dizzengoff station.

I knew I was being foolish, showing myself so openly, but I no longer cared.

"Now?" Amzaleg asked. "It's only eight in the morning."

But Café Cassit was open, and volunteers from the voting station at the back sat and drank coffee, with strudel slices. Leibele came by as I sat down.

"Your girlfriend was here," he said, "looking for you."

A wild dark flash seared through me. "Who?"

"The blonde one, the Canadian," he said, adding shyly. "Very good-looking."

"Thank you," I said, not knowing whether I was thanking him for the information, or for the compliment about Jenny. And suddenly and idiotically I wanted very badly to find her, so she could console me for what I had lost, as she always had, to forgive all the evil I had done, as she always did . . .

I turned away, not wishing him to see me like this.

He loitered by delicately, averting his gaze, shuffling his sandals. "It was a very, very good show," he said at last. "I liked how you—how you—your role."

"Yes," I said. "Yes, thank you."

"Better than him, even, in forty-six, the Arab," said Leibele, and sat down beside me. He started talking, quietly and easily. "I didn't know how they could do it," he said. "Everyone knew he wasn't a Yemenite. It all started as a joke, when he—your father—when he brought him to the Purim party—"

"Yes," I said. Leibele put a coffee cup before me. I told myself I should not drink so much coffee, then drained half the cup.

"This friend of his, this *Arabush*," said Leibele. His face was composed, peaceful. "Isser thought it was a great joke, to bring him dressed as an Arab, and everyone thought he was someone from Petach Tiqva, or Kerem HaTeymanim. A Yemenite in disguise. But she—" He stopped.

"I know," I said. "My mother."

"Yes," said Leibele. "Sonya. This *sharmuta* Sonya." This whore. But he said it with affection, as though according a compliment.

I said nothing.

"We all loved her," he said. "What she did for us, we all loved her."

I nodded.

"Everyone loved her," Leibele said. "Everyone."

"Yes."

"But she only loved him. The Arab."

"You knew?"

"Everyone knew."

"No one ever told me."

"No."

There was a short silence.

Leibele looked at the empty street. "What will you do now? You going back to Canada?"

"Yes," I said. Then I added, "But I'll be back in June, to finish something, that my father asked me—"

I could not see how I could even think of it, now; how I was hoping to get out of here, let alone come back.

Leibele nodded slowly and got to his feet. "They only write lies, the newspapers," he said, "only lies—"

There was a little pause.

I said at last, "Why—why did he give Paltiel his poetry, my father?" My voice came out all rough, and I coughed, to clear it.

I had no idea why I was asking Leibele, but he answered, without hesitation or evasion. "Isser gave him everything, because no matter—no matter how he tried, this *kacker* Paltiel—after twenty-eight, he couldn't write any more poems for this *Arabush*—everything he wrote was for him—but he just couldn't write anymore—*challas*—" Finished, in Arabic.

There was a long pause as Leibele stared far away, perhaps at the other sidewalk, where a few stooped garbagemen were now collecting rotting bags into a wheelbarrow.

"Twice he tried to kill himself, Paltiel—twice—once in Yaffo, he tried to drown himself in the sewer, the other time—he cut his hands, in the store—each time Isser saved him—"

I tried to speak but no sound came.

"Finally Isser said to him, he said, 'Take my poems, give them to him, they are yours—'"

A gaggle of white pigeons flew past, in formation, their wings clacking. Leibele followed them with his eyes.

A sudden cheer erupted at the back, where some actors were listening to a transistor radio.

Leibele put down his coffee cup, and got up; only now did I notice he was not dressed in his waiter's clothes, but rather in blue Atta pants, and a white nylon shirt. But whether it was his day off, or he had put these clothes on to vote, I could not tell.

"They only tell lies," Leibele said, as though all he had just told was a mere continuation of what he had said before about the newspapers. "Lies, everybody. To themselves, too—only what they want to believe—"

Then he left.

59

WE STOOD ON THE empty viewing terrace at Ben Gurion Airport, Amzaleg and I, looking over the tarmac. The warm wind ruffled my hair, just as it did when I had landed, two thousand years ago.

I had left Jenny behind with the actors and crew and Kagan (his chin resplendent in a large bandage), all who had come to bid us good-bye, and gone out with Amzaleg for one last talk.

Amzaleg said, "Shimmel said he's sorry he couldn't come, but he had a meeting."

That morning the radio announced that Shim'on Gershonovitz had turned his political colors and accepted the post of interior minister in Begin's government.

I said now to Amzaleg, "What about you? Will they also kick you out of the police?"

Right after the play Amzaleg was suspended, for having disobeyed Gershonovitz's order to close us down. I still did not understand why Amzaleg had done it.

He shrugged, to show it was possible, then stuck his finger upward in the Arab gesture of *zayin* and spit fully, to emphasize he didn't care. I doubted it. A whole career down the drain like that—giving it all up on a moment's decision. And for what? Besides, it was not only he who would pay. His daughter could now lose her police-family scholarship, leave university, and have to go to work. And as a Moroccan girl, what could she do? Be a hairdresser, or a manicurist? Or live with her mother and Arab stepfather, and so become the only thing worse than a Moroccan?

But children always pay here.

There was a long pause as we both looked at the empty tarmac.

"It wasn't the Arabs," I said. "It was the *shoo-shoo* that did all these things to me."

"Only to scare you off."

"Shit in yogurt. Only scare. The Samson—that was to scare me? That was to put me in the hospital."

He looked away. "I had no say in it."

I should have left it at that but could not. "And later? When Yaro called me?"

Amzaleg said nothing.

I could see a small business jet taxiing on the runway, an Astra, braking every now and then, its nose dipping.

I said, "When he tried to take me down, to stop the play? All because of the elections?"

"Not because of the elections. No, no. By that time we didn't know if—if you were with us or with our foes." He used the biblical word, "haters," in its original construction.

And he had said "we."

I tried to look at his eyes but he kept staring into the distance as he spoke in a halting singsong. "We knew you were his—son, of Seddiqi . . . but we were sure you—that you didn't know . . . But then you went ahead with this play . . . and you didn't want to stop . . . All right, we said, he doesn't know, he wants to honor his—father . . . but then you began to organize the *shabbab* in Yaffo . . . and you helped them fight the Kach demonstrators . . ."

"Goddamn *Hitlerjugend*," I said, "that's what they are."

"And you taught them perimeter defense, night procedures . . . *gimmel* tricks . . . and then when Seddiqi told you about these messages—"

"You never liked what they did, did you?" I said. "That someone was trying to make peace behind your back. You had to listen in, to make sure nothing happened."

Amzaleg went on as if I had not spoken, "So Shimmel told Yaro to send the two Betniks away . . . so we could grab you, stash you someplace safe for the duration . . . but you went to live in that damn Waqf mosque." He turned to me, his bloodshot eyes beseeching me. "What'd you want us to think?"

I said, "Because Ehud kicked me out, that's why. I thought you knew. You had listened to every fart I made."

"But we didn't."

That's right; they couldn't. I had pulled the bugs out of the apartment.

"So some said, this is it, he went over . . . the Seddiqi had finally told him everything, and now that he knows . . . he has made his choice . . . the donkey is with them . . . *with them* . . . you understand? . . ."

Son of the Debba; descendant of the Prophet. The Jalood.

"Can you imagine? Every last *Arabush* here would rise up— you know how many *Arabushim* we have?" He sounded like Gershonovitz now.

"Half a million, what do I know?"

"A million and a half. Three hundred thousand in the Galilean Triangle alone . . . then in Haifa." His voice was strangled. "Yaffo, Acco, and Nazteret . . . another million in the Territories . . . If they all rise together . . ."

"Yes." Abdallah's words came back to me.

Amzaleg's fist hovered in the air, vibrating as if held captive by two opposing internal forces. "But I said, I argued, 'He's not with them.' I said, 'He likes poetry, Hebrew theater . . . he knows Rubin's poems by heart . . . he is the son of Isser . . . *his* son . . .''

I said tightly, "So what if I like poetry. They like poetry, too."

Amzaleg shook his grizzled head. "Not like this. They like the poems of what's her name, this *Arabusha* from Jenin, about eating Jews' livers raw, for the glory of Allah. Nothing about mercy, and pity, and love. Nothing like us."

I tried to peer into the swarthy face of this Moroccan policeman, an ex-assassin like me, who spoke now of mercy, and love, like Jenny; but he still refused to meet my eyes.

The small jet took off, leaving behind it a stink of burned petrol. A larger jet taxied up to the line, a 707.

". . . So I said to Shimmel, leave him alone for now, give him time . . . but Shimmel said, 'We can't take the chance,' he said . . . 'The Arabs know what he is . . . and they are already joining forces, because of *him* . . . just like then, in the Castel . . .' So we brought it to the PM and the PM took it again to the Mo'adon . . . and they all said . . . they said . . ." Amzaleg's dark face contorted and his lips disappeared as he pulled them in and bit on them, hard.

I said, "And that's when Yaro called me? To ask me to his office?"

Amzaleg's face screwed up like a prune, as if holding in something big and unmanageable that threatened to burst out.

I said, "And Yaro said okay? To this?"

I could not understand why I was so angry. I would have said okay, too. A direct order like that, with this sort of reasoning. Because what was the Unit for?

There was a long pause as, little by little, Amzaleg's face loosened. "At first Yaro said he didn't believe it . . . that you went over . . . so we let him see the video . . ."

"What video?"

"That we had filmed, how you helped the *shabbab* fight the guys in Yaffo . . . with perimeter defense, triple backup, *gimmel* tricks . . . how we could do nothing . . . nothing . . ." His face crunched.

I said, "And Yaro said okay?"

Amzaleg nodded quickly, not speaking of the obvious. Because it was clear that Gershonovitz had asked him first, since he was closest to me and had also once served in the Unit, but that he had refused. And that's why Yaro was called. But even if Amzaleg had refused, still he knew of it and acquiesced.

I took a deep breath and said, "Like in forty-eight."

There was a frozen silence.

I said, "It was you that Gershonovitz called then, in Yaffo, to go after Paltiel."

Amzaleg said nothing.

"In forty-eight," I said. "Before the Castel attack."

"Yes," Amzaleg said at last. "Shimmel called me."

I waited.

Amzaleg's voice was a raspy whisper. "They could never do it themselves, these dainty Ashkenazim in the Haganah. Not in a thousand years. So who could he call?"

"You . . . so you . . ." My own voice shook.

There was a pause, of a different, nearly religious quality.

"Yes, I killed him, Paltiel." Amzaleg sipped some water from the paper cup he was holding in his thick nicotine-stained fingers.

I could not speak.

Amzaleg began to speak again, conversationally now. "It had just begun, the attack on Yaffo, when I got Shimmel's note . . . He said, 'We need your help, please, Amnon, no one else can do it . . .' So I left Begin on the roof of Alliance school, with all his idiot advisers . . . and I went down to Zerach Brandt Street and waited . . . and after half an hour I saw Paltiel, walking . . . Glantz and Zussman and a few other Shay guys came out and called to him . . . begging him to come back, but he just kept on going . . . so I hid behind Shifrin's carpet store and I followed him in ... everyone was shooting like in the Wild West ... like in a movie ... mortar shells flying overhead ... but I recited psalms and followed, to see where he was going ... that maybe Shimmel had made a mistake ... but I saw where he went—three streets away he was already, from Seddiqi's house ... He was almost there ... So I called out to him in Yiddish, like I heard in rehearsals of Isser's plays ... 'Paltiel,' I said to him, 'come here a moment, I beg of you ...' So he came over and I let him have it." Amzaleg turned and looked at me, his eyes black and flat and empty, like Abdallah's. "With a *shubrieh* in the guts. Then I made it look like ... like it was Arabs ..."

"You ... cut—" I could not continue.

"Yes," Amzaleg said conversationally, sipping water. "I cut his *zayin* off, and—and did all the rest." He coughed and swiped at his lips with his knuckles. "Then after, I dragged him all the way back ..."

The roar of a jet engine intensified as a large Air Canada jumbo jet taxied by, faces peering from the windows.

Amzaleg was saying, "... was lucky, so lucky; if I were late maybe five minutes—five fucking minutes. Can you imagine what—" He gave his head a swift shake, then took another sip of water and spit it out.

I leaned on the low concrete rail and stared into the asphalted horizon, waiting for the tremor in my jaw to subside.

Amzaleg said, "Five minutes. Can you imagine? If the Castel had gone to them ... If *he* had gone on, to keep them together, like Ben-Gurion did for us—" Amzaleg poured the remaining water over the balcony and the wind took it away in a cloud of spray. "And this *feigele* poet, because he loved this cock-sucking Arab *cholera* ... for his sick love he would have given up all of this ... Everything ..." Amzaleg shook his head in wonder.

It was odd to hear this Moroccan policeman using so many Yiddish words; as if living among the Ashkenazim had rubbed off on him, just as living among the Arabs had rubbed off on the Anons; as it had rubbed off on all of us, here.

I said to him, "Did you read any of Paltiel's . . . stuff?" I had wanted to say poems but it didn't come out.

"Yes," Amzaleg said equably, "I read, I read." And suddenly, without warning, he mashed his large fist into the low concrete wall with a tremendous force. There was a sickening thud as the knuckles hit.

Amzaleg's thick nose rode up and down as he gave a loud sniff. "Was a good writer, goddamn him, a beautiful writer, with extra soul." He stared at me with his black Moroccan eyes, now filmed over with pain and moisture. I handed him my clean handkerchief to wipe his cheeks but he took it and wrapped it around his knuckles instead. They were red and raw and bleeding.

"Yes," I said. "Was a good poet, goddamn him."

I suddenly realized that Amzaleg, like everyone else (except for the discredited Professor Tzifroni), still thought it was Paltiel who wrote the poems, since Ruthy had made me keep quiet about it. It also dawned on me I would now probably continue to keep quiet, because my father would have liked it that way.

Another jet took off, trailing smoke that filled my eyes.

Amzaleg was saying something in a low guttural voice, but the noise of the jet swallowed up his words.

"What?" I said, leaning into him.

"'Thou art my enemy, O friend of mine,'" he said, "'my rival and my fate, thy giant shadow on my bride looms . . .'"

"Yes," I said. I recalled the words I had quoted to Mr. Gelber, the first time we met. "*Golyatt.*" My father's words. Isser's. *My father's.*

"Yes," Amzaleg said. "'In the midst of darkest night it blooms, thy hate; my love, my shadow, my one and only mate . . .'" He unwrapped the handkerchief and gave it back to me.

I finished the stanza for him, "'For till the end of days, and ever, until my heart, like slate, with stones and slings and arrows—'"

"*Yallah*, enough," Amzaleg said. "Let's take a piss before you go. I gotta be in Shfar'am by twelve."

As we stood side by side, shaking our dicks and bending our knees, the burly policeman said into my shoulder as though answering a question. "Goddammit. You want poetry, or you want a State." He did not say it as a question.

"Both," I said.

Amzaleg let go a huge fart, loud as one of Ittamar's fist trumpets. "Today you can have both." He zipped up, violently. "*Yallah*, go, or you'll miss your plane."

For a moment we stood outside in awkward silence, looking at the bustling terminal, the faded colors, the fluttering flags, anything but each other. I wanted to say I was sorry he had to be suspended, for my father's play to go on; that I understood his shame and anguish at losing his wife to someone he could not even hate; and that I forgave him for lying to me, and for acquiescing in the plan to kill me, because in this place people must kill not only their enemies, for the sake of old evil fictions, but also their kin; and if they didn't forgive each other, soon they would have no friends left. But there was no need to say anything, because whatever had gone before was now over. I was not one of theirs anymore, nor the others', since their fictions were no longer mine, and so there was no need for me to kill anymore, or to participate in killings. But their burdens were still mine to carry, and the burden my father had put on me, the one I could not escape, nor did I want to.

Presently a disembodied voice called for passengers to embark. Amzaleg extended his large hand and I took it awkwardly, minding the bruised knuckles. To my consternation he rose on tiptoe and laid both palms on my head, with the fingers spread in the gesture of Birkat Cohanim, the blessing of the priests. "God will bless you and guard you," he mumbled in guttural cantors' singsong; then he punched my shoulder with his bruised fist, gently (later I found blood stains on my shirt), and walked away in that lumbering gait of his, almost like an Arab.

Only later, on the plane, did I find in my pocket my father's letter, which he had slipped in when I wasn't looking.

Jenny was sitting where I had left her, at the coffee counter, among the throng of crew and actors and the few high school students who had come to see me go, yet apart from them, reading the Polish magazine *Mirror*, her fair hair (grown longer) reflecting the light. There was a picture of Gershonovitz on the front page, and some fat headlines.

The departure lounge around us was full. There was a large crowd of religious Jews, men in black, and women in brown and gray, shepherding dozens of twittering offspring; young ex-soldiers sitting on backpacks; and a large family of Arabs in colorful village clothes with half a dozen silent children. Arab and Jewish children eyed one another curiously while their parents pulled them back.

To the side stood Fauzi, his eyes hooded. On his arm was tied a black *sharit alhidad*. I got up and stood beside him, and for a while neither of us spoke.

"Goddammit," I said at last. "Was a good man, the Seddiqi—"

Fauzi said, "Another message arrived, just now, *ya Sa'eedi*."

He did not say who had delivered it, and I did not ask.

"They want you to take it to them, *ya Sa'eed*," he said in a voice like sandpaper.

I felt no surprise. Somehow it seemed logical. The only surprise was how fast the message had come.

"I'll be back in three weeks," I said.

Behind, the actors whooped it up, reading the latest reviews of the show.

I stared at the small group at the coffee counter, and the crowds behind. Neither Ehud nor Ruthy had arrived to see me off.

Fauzi said, "You think this *'ibn sharmuta* Begin will listen?"

He had said *'ibn sharmuta*, son of a whore, the way Leibele spoke about my mother; or Amzaleg about my father, calling him a bastard; a sign of grudging respect.

"He'd better," I said. "Or—" I stopped. Or what? Or I would come out? As what?

There was one last pause.

"*Salaam,*" Fauzi said; then, his face flaming, he repeated the word in Hebrew. Then he bent and kissed my shoulder, quickly, turned on his heels, and ran off.

I took one last look at the actors and crew, the faded corridor littered with old election posters, the children tentatively and shyly making faces at one another as the parents hissed at them to stop; then I went to join Jenny.

Her eyes were red and her face pinched, after all the crying she had done last night, following our talk. That is, she talked and I listened. I still could not see how she could possibly forgive me. How much forgiveness can one person have? How much?

But she seemed better now; I, too.

"They have magazines in Polish," she said to me in a low voice when I picked up her small bag, to carry alongside mine. "Look."

I tried to turn my face away—I knew there would be a picture of all the show's actors inside; Ruthy's, too—but Jenny would not let me. She grabbed my chin and turned my face gently to hers, looked into my eyes, then kissed me hard on the mouth and didn't let go until Ben-Shoshan gave a long wolf whistle.

Jenny smiled amiably at him and stuck her finger up in the Arab gesture she must have picked up from Amzaleg. Then she locked her fingers tightly into mine and together, hand in hand, we went out through the lighted gate.

Epilogue

In 1980, a year after the peace agreement with Egypt was signed in Camp David by Begin and Sadat, I came back for the Negev Theater's performance of *The Debba*, in Be'er Sheva. It was the fourth production of the play, not taking into account a number of high school stagings. A local actress played Sarah, and Moshe Geffen, the biggest Israeli rock star, played Yissachar. The Debba was played by Fauzi Seddiqi—he was the one who had written to me to Canada, to invite me to the performance. And although he is rather small, only one meter seventy, not at all what the role demands, he did rather well, I thought. In fact, he made the role his own. (The audience, which at first booed him, turned progressively quiet, until at the end he even got fairly loud applause, which I thought surprising. This, after all, was Be'er Sheva, where most residents are Eastern Jews who vote for Begin's right-wing Likkud and hate Arabs.) Yochanan and 'Ittay were played by two local boys. They got the biggest applause, winking and smiling at the public shamelessly. Ehud Reznik (who last year, following the bankruptcy of the chocolate factory, turned to directing and theater production full time), later told me he'd had the play translated into Arabic, and it had a very long run in refugee camps, touring several. (I had assigned to Ehud a half interest in the play, and full decision rights in all matters of production.) The Arab director asked for permission to change the ending, a request that Ehud refused. But the director bypassed the refusal and had the Debba, his *abbaya* flapping, rise silently from behind his rock as Yissachar sings his final aria. He was within his directorial prerogative, Ehud said, so there was nothing he could do.

An English translation has just been finished (I myself had helped Professor Gershon Tzifroni of Tel Aviv University do it), and one into French is in the offing. Half the revenues from all foreign productions are to go to the Re'uven Kagan Memorial Fund, which helps young actors with occasional loans and study stipends.

Kagan, who died last year of throat cancer, just like Uncle Mordechai, had been buried in the old Trumpeldor cemetery, just behind Paltiel Rubin's grave. It came out that Kagan had bought the plot years before. He would of course not have been able to afford it today. Not only apartments have gone up in price, following the peace agreement with Egypt; graveyard plots did, too.

Abdallah Seddiqi had been buried near the village of Tibrin, on the shoulder of a narrow hill overlooking Lake Kinneret. Uncle Mordechai was buried in the Jewish cemetery on the other side of the hill, near his son Arnon. It is convenient for me, I suppose, to be able to visit all the graves at the same time, when I come to visit.

Ruthy tried being a housewife for a while, raising her daughter (now almost three), but eventually returned to acting, in the Cameri Theater. She had not come to the performance in Be'er Sheva, and Jenny was disappointed. Lately they had begun to correspond. I have no idea what they say to each other.

Not long ago Jenny said she would not mind coming to live with me in Jerusalem for a time, while my own play, *The Moloch*, is being produced there by Lo Harbeh theater.

I said I would think about it.

Acknowledgments

Many helped me get this book published, either by teaching me how to write; by providing succor over the twice-*chai* years it has taken me to write this book; by helping me edit it—or by helping me edit me. The following are just a few:

Victoria Gould Pryor, Alice Rosengard, Sheryl Jaffe, Josephine Carson, Howard Junker, Jim N. Frey, Molly Giles, Ephraim Mandelman, Ayala Mandelman, Alona Pickovsky, Judah Rosenwald, members of my platoon in the Sinai, Chris Pryor, Ronnee Fried, Kathleen Schneider, Greg Michalson, Anna Lui, Judith Gurewich, Lorna Owen, Katie Henderson, my parents, Joe Garber, Marjorie Farkas, those whom I've omitted by necessity (you know who you are), and all others who have read the manuscript over the years and made useful comments. I could not have done it without you. My heartfelt thanks to you all: on my behalf, and (dare I hope?) on behalf of the readers.

AM

Vancouver—Toronto—Los Altos Hills—Toronto
1973–2009